Praise for Theresa Varela

"*Nights of Indigo Blue: A Daisy Muñiz Mystery* is a well-written, engaging mystery with nods to Agatha Christie, Santeria, romance, and spirituality. Varela's heroine, the young Latina sleuth Daisy Muñiz, is a fresh, relatable, and well-developed character. Daisy took me on a real mystery, with twists and turns I never saw coming. Varela has a real knack for writing great dialogue with keen attention to detail. A fun read." ~ Eleanor Sapia Parker
Author of *A Decent Woman* and *Tight Knots, Loose Threads*

"[*Coney Island Siren*] brings up questions of what life in this material realm means and what might be expected of those who exist in it. While every reader might not want to linger on the philosophical implications of the novel, this sort of thinker is exactly what I'm looking for in a book." ~ Sacred Chickens

"*Covering the Sun with My Hand* is a much-needed and insightful exploration of mental illness in a Puerto Rican family and how it impacts on the individual members. It gives voice to an issue too often hidden within our culture. I read this novel when it was first published in 2013, and it still lives with me these many years later. ~ Dahlma Llanos-Figueroa
Author of *Daughters of the Stone*, *A Woman of Endurance*, and *Indómita*

Works by Theresa Varela

Novels

Covering the Sun with My Hand
Nights of Indigo Blue: A Daisy Muñiz Mystery
Coney Island Siren

Poetry

Answered by Silence: A Collection of Poems

Oracle

Graciella la Gitana Oracle ©
El Oráculo de Graciella la Gitana

Murder in Red Hook

A Daisy Muñiz
Mystery

Theresa Varela

POLLEN PRESS PUBLISHING, LLC
NEW YORK

Pollen Press Publishing, LLC
New York

Murder in Red Hook: A Daisy Muñiz Mystery is a work of fiction. Names, characters, organizations, and events portrayed in this novel are either products of the author's imagination or are used fictitiously.

Theresa Varela
theresa@theresavarela.com
www.theresavarela.com

Distributed by IngramSpark

First printing, July 2022

Book Cover and Interior Designed by Jesse Sanchez

Library of Congress Control Number: 2022911810
Names: Varela, Theresa, author.
Title: *Murder in Red Hook: A Daisy Muñiz Mystery*
Description: New York, Pollen Publishing [2022]
Identifiers: Trade Paperback ISBN: 978-1-7327167-3-5
Subjects: LSCH—1. Women—Family Relationships—Fiction. 2. Mystery—Fiction. 3. Brooklyn—Fiction. 4. New York (N.Y.)—Fiction. I. Title

Dedication

To those whose thirst has parched their lives.

Acknowledgments

It would be unfair to my readers if I were not to give some insight into the background of my writing *Murder in Red Hook: A Daisy Muñiz Mystery*. The first book of this series, *Nights of Indigo Blue*, was originally published in 2016. My plan was to dive in and write the second novel right away, but life and Higher Power had different ideas. My dad was diagnosed with Alzheimer's disease, and my spouse and I took care of him until he crossed over in 2019. It took time to reintroduce me to myself, just in time to be catapulted into the era of Covid.

Throughout these events, I had many who helped me keep my sights on *Murder in Red Hook*. I must give thanks to Cindy Hochman, my first editor, whose opinions, along with her editing, strengthened my resolve to finish this book. I have much appreciation for my beta readers who gave me awesome input. Many thanks to Nydia Lassalle Davis, who helped me lift the novel with her painstaking editing. Many thanks to Jesse Sanchez and his impressive vision in this book's cover and design. My Author Whisperer and publicist, Vivian Monserrate Cotte, deserves special thanks for her expertise in publishing a book professionally with her knowledgeable and gentle personal touch. As always, I especially thank my spouse, Patricia Dornelles, who continues to support me and remind me that I can accomplish anything I set out to do! Lastly, I give thanks to you, my readers, who have patiently waited for this second installment of the Daisy Muñiz Mysteries. I love you and promise there is more to come!

Chapter 1

"Daisy, *yame!*" Sensei Red Norman yelled. "Stop!" He grabbed me by the collar of my *gi* and pulled me away from my pretend assailant.

"Yo, Daisy, it's me, Jake!" Jake Andrews cupped his own fist around his nose. His eyes squinted as tears sprung out.

Sensei ordered me into the corner of the dojo. "*Seiza*, Daisy. Think about your actions."

I knelt back in *seiza* with my legs folded underneath me, and my hands palms down on my thighs. Sensei was right. I was aghast at my behavior. I'd lost myself in that instant, which was supposed to be a practice punch to the nose. There wasn't supposed to be contact. The intensity that had crept into my body and that was discharged from my fist had shocked even me.

My adrenaline over the top, I had pushed my knuckles right into the bridge of Jake's nose and had felt the squish against his flesh. Dark warm blood had flowed onto my fist. The release of fluid matched the release of the old anger in my chest. I had rechambered my right arm and instantly readied to throw another punch when Sensei had stopped me.

The meditative pose allowed me to inhale deeply, and my feelings and thoughts merged before I exhaled. Both of my eyes were closed, but my third eye was wide open. In front of me stood Lou Galván. I pushed the vision of my ex away with a current of air that swept through the dojo. Time slowed to a standstill while I remained in position. I wasn't being punished, and I had to walk through my inner labyrinth before I could have healthy relationships in the real world. Jake just happened to be the unfortunate recipient of my mixed-up emotions, and it wasn't fair to him. The trick was to continue breathing. If I did that, everything would eventually settle.

When I opened my eyes, I was back in the dojo, the place of learning the art of Karate-Do: The Way of Empty Hand. I focused on the glowing oak floors beneath me and then on the bank of windows looking out onto Fifth Avenue. Outside, life milled about the storefront. The evening in Park Slope would be filled with couples and the lonely looking for drinks, food, anything to keep moving. In the dojo I had no choice but to concentrate on my new moves and motives.

"I've got to get up. My muscles are cramping," I finally said. My legs had numbed while my mind had traveled to a million places.

Sensei helped me up out of the torturous kneeling position. When I started the karate class a few months earlier, I realized that while others made it look so simple and elegant, I was nothing but a twisted bag of pretzels — easily ready to snap in two.

"You'll get used to it. Take a few minutes to stretch. You'll be a pro before you know it," he said.

Sensei's bear-like figure had shown me that size and shape didn't have much to do with capabilities. I guessed his name 'Red' came from his orangey-red curly hair that stuck out like a halo around his head. He would have made a great Santa, but he didn't seem like the cuddly type. Sensei was big, but he was rock solid.

I'd started taking karate classes at the Fifth Avenue dojo on a whim. Passing by on my way to meetings, I saw men and women practicing forms that I later learned were called *katas*. Sometimes they seemed totally absorbed, and at other times I saw them laughing on the mat as they did push-ups in pairs. Angela, my Alcoholics Anonymous sponsor, suggested that I open up my world a bit, and I enrolled in classes after observing a few of them.

"Daisy!" Sensei's voice broke through my bad habit of drifting off into never-space. "You with me?"

"Yes, sorry, Sensei." I rubbed my sore thigh muscles.

"When you get home, put some balm on that," he said. "Practice hitting your target more often. Stand in front of the mirror, and concentrate on your form. Let those negative thoughts go while you're in meditation."

"Yes, sir." I bowed to Sensei.

"One more thing," he said, tilting his head toward Jake, who sat to the side with an ice pack on his reddened nose.

"I'm sorry, Jake," I said. "I don't know what happened. There's really no excuse."

"It's all right. You know, Friday night is fright night. Next time, I'll block better." While his nose was slightly swollen, his eyes were twinkling. He was a looker. I hoped I hadn't ruined that for him.

"See you next week?" I asked.

"Yeah, I'll be here."

I nodded, certain that I would return. This time I noticed how deeply brown Jake's eyes were. Penetrating. He was probably trying to figure out how psycho I was. He'd earned a green belt and was about a half foot taller than me. The gnawing thought resurfaced that I needed more help than the program was able to provide. My anger was back. Angela kept bringing up the dirty word *therapy*. Maybe she was right. I'd already been to therapy when I first put down the bottle. I couldn't afford to be giving nosebleeds to someone who could take me out with one swift punch or kick to the solar plexus.

This wasn't the first time that someone had gotten hurt since I had started taking classes at the dojo. I was the first casualty. Ducking was a practice that I had never learned, neither while playing dodgeball nor during my relationship with Lou. If I hadn't learned that skill with him, I didn't think I ever would. I hoped that learning karate would help me to care for myself in a new way.

Class was over. The students each bowed on their way out, and we hurried to the locker room to change out of our *gis*, the traditional uniforms, and back into our regular clothes. I stopped in the bathroom first to wash the dried blood off my hands and then joined the others.

I snuck a look at the women. Some had orange belts, and there were a couple of green- and brown-belted women. There were two over in a corner taking off their black belts. That level seemed unattainable to me right now. I folded my white belt, placed it into my equipment bag, and got dressed.

I didn't feel comfortable butting into already buzzing conversations. I spotted my image in the locker room mirror. My wavy dark brown hair was pulled back into a ponytail and revealed how healthy my complexion had become. The shining brown eyes that were reflected were a far cry from the deadened ones that used to stare back at me. Even my upper body seemed a bit muscular. I couldn't help but smile. I liked my reflection.

I left after getting dressed, but not before calling out a universal good night. A couple of the women responded, and I took a deep breath of relief. Maybe I wasn't so invisible after all. I walked out into the cool early spring night to make my way home. After the busy avenue, the side street of the old brownstone I lived in was quiet. There were only a few people sauntering along the tree-lined streets. I spotted a few buds on the magnolias. This was one of my favorite times of the year in my neighborhood.

Tonight was the dark of the moon, which meant that whatever I wished for was sure to manifest. I'd read that somewhere and wasn't sure if my wildest dreams could come true, but there was no harm in sending a prayer out into the Universe on this exquisite night. I stood for a moment not knowing what to wish for, so I just gave thanks.

I made it to the four-story building and started the climb up the front stoop.

"Daisy, is that you? Why don't you stop by for a cup of tea, dear?"

I swiveled to see Marge Talbot, my landlady, standing at her first-floor entry. I would never miss one of her invites. She treated me like a granddaughter but never interfered in my personal business. I had the opportunity to fall in love with her after Rubio and Jose recommended me for the fourth-floor apartment.

"That sounds like an excellent idea, Marge. Perfect coincidence that you were picking up your mail just as I got here." We went inside.

"I'm so happy to have you here. Tell me about your classes." Marge set two steaming cups of tea in front of us on her burnished wood kitchen table. The smell of cinnamon tantalized my senses.

"They are great," I said. "But I have to admit that I feel left out. Everybody knows each other. It's probably just a feeling."

"Well, the beginning is the only place that we can truly start to learn."

"I guess I don't need Mr. Miyagi when you're around." I laughed. Just as I was about to dig into her cookie tin, my phone began buzzing. I fumbled for my ear pods, trying to answer before it was too late.

"Hello?" I waited, but the phone call had been disconnected.

"Did the call drop?" Marge asked.

"That was strange. I thought it might be Jose, but the call

came from an unknown number. Oh well. Whoever it was will call back." I stretched. "As soon as I go upstairs, I'm going to take a hot bath. My muscles are killing me."

We sat together eating homemade oatmeal raisin cookies and drinking our tea. Ruffian, Marge's blond golden retriever, sat alongside us. Eventually I was ready to turn in, and I walked gingerly around him so as not to disturb him as I left her apartment. Marge was blind, and Ruffian was her seeing-eye dog, always on alert for his owner.

Marge called out as I made it to the door. "Ice is what you need."

"What's that?" I poked my head back in.

"Ice will prevent the lactic acid buildup in your muscles. Hot water feels better, but ice works better."

"Really?" I had my doubts.

"Yes, really." Marge snickered as I made my way up the stairs.

When I reached the top floor, Ms. G, the black-and-white house kitty, stuck her paw out from between the balusters. I tried to grab her, but she shot across to the door of my apartment, determined that I let her inside. I had become her unofficial owner, but, the truth is, she owned me. I loved falling asleep with her on my otherwise empty queen-sized bed.

A few minutes later, I was relaxing in a tub filled with steaming hot water and soothing lavender salts. I woke to the sound of my name being called.

"Daisy?" Jose hollered through the apartment door. He followed up with a loud rap. "Are you in there?"

"Yeah, I'm here!" I yelled back. I stretched to get up, and my calf immediately cramped. Maybe Marge was right about the benefits of ice, but the heat was so luxurious.

"Hold on. I'll be right there." I pointed my toes outward, and the cramp softened. I climbed out of the tub, wrapped myself in my robe, and opened the door.

Jose walked in and plopped on the couch. His face was drawn. He pushed his hands through his curly dark brown hair.

"What's going on?" I asked. "Do you have the flu or something? Because if you do, don't come near me. I can't afford to get sick."

"I'm not sick." His eyes met mine. "It's Rubio. I just got a call that he's in the emergency room."

I reached out toward my best buddy. "What's going on?"

Rubio and Jose had been a couple since their first year in college. Jose was a whiz at finances, and Rubio was an artist. They complemented each other perfectly. While I loved them both, I had always felt closer to Jose especially since he'd Twelve-Stepped me into sobriety. My life had been a disaster until then, and I had had no clue as to the reason. It took me a while to understand that alcohol was making my life unmanageable, but I finally did. I'd do anything for Jose.

Jose sat in silence, helplessly.

"Are you okay?" I asked. "Do you want a glass of water or something?"

He shook his head. "No, it's just a lot to take in. Rubio was found shot at the gallery."

"Where is he? At Windsor?"

Windsor Medical Center was the local hospital where I worked as an assistant to the Administrator, Sophia Cornelius. It was only a few blocks away.

"No, they brought him to Sovereign Health Center. They needed to send him to a trauma unit where they would be able to handle his wounds. Can we leave now? We can talk on the way, okay?"

"Of course. I'm sorry. I'll be ready in a second."

I went into the bedroom and threw on the jeans and blue pullover that I had just taken off. I peeked into the kitchen before following him down the stairs. I knew there wasn't anything on the stove, but I couldn't help myself.

"Are you going to be warm enough?" Jose asked. He zipped up his leather bomber.

April was tricky. Warm days turned into cool nights. I found one of my fleece jackets and ran down the stairs after him. We made our way down to Fifth to hail a cab. Green cabs cruised the streets. I put my hand out to hail one, and it came to a stop immediately. A couple stepped in front of us and almost reached the cab's door before we did. The woman turned to the baby carriage that the man was pushing.

"Sorry." I grabbed the door handle. "We have an emergency. You have full rights to that one coming this way." There was a second cab crossing the intersection through a flashing yellow light.

With my other hand, I shoved Jose in. I looked back to see the couple hailing the other cab. I felt assertive after the few months of karate training, but the couple was probably chalking up the interaction to just another day in the Slope. We settled onto the soft leather seat.

"Sovereign Health Center, please," Jose instructed the driver.

"Would that be east or west?" The cabbie peered at us through the rearview mirror.

"The one in Flatbush," Jose clarified.

I immediately began a search on my smartphone for more information. "That would be east," I said.

The outer-borough cab cruised slowly on Prospect Park West toward Bartel-Pritchard Square. We traversed the neighborhoods going from Park Slope to Windsor Terrace. Farrell's Bar & Grill was at the next corner. I didn't have to set my eyes on it to know it was still in existence. Pete Hamill had written stories about the infamous landmark. Farrell's hadn't allowed women through its hallowed doors until the '90s. Shirley MacLaine had enjoyed drinks there. Probably with Pete. I'd also been in there, holding large beer-filled Styrofoam cups.

Now I'd be happy to never set foot in that bar again. We rode along Prospect Park Southwest until it rounded toward the Prospect Park Parade Ground.

"Daisy!" Jose seemed to be calling me from far away. We were here because Rubio had been hurt, and all I could think of was myself and beer.

I hoped he hadn't noticed how selfish I was being. "What do you know about the injury? Do you know how bad it is?"

"It's his right arm," Jose said. "They didn't give me any details."

"He can't afford that type of injury," I said. "He's an artist."

"Look, we don't know anything specific, okay?" he said. "Let's not speculate about the damage."

"You're right," I said. I was getting antsy. There was so much we didn't know.

"The police didn't have too much info when I talked to them. Of course, they're doing an investigation. It might have been a robbery. Chelsea, the receptionist, found them. It was her late day."

"Them?"

The light changed, and the cabbie slowed to a halt. The cab's digital screen showed an endless loop of a lady who had begun a business raising chickens in Red Hook. This had to be the fifth time it had played during the short ride.

Jose rubbed his eyes. "There's more."

I waited, although I wasn't sure I wanted to know.

"Do you remember Charley Sprague, the art curator? You met him at the opening night of Rubio's show."

"Sure. Charley is that funny little man with the white hair. He wears those red frames. They match his nose."

"Matched." Jose turned to look out the window. "He's dead."

"Dead?" I blanched. "Do you know that for sure?"

"Yes. When they called to tell me about Rubio, I asked. I knew they'd been working there together today."

"I'm so sorry." I moaned inwardly. This was more serious than I had originally thought.

We sat quietly for the remainder of the trip until we reached East Flatbush, where the hospital was located. Each neighborhood in Brooklyn had its own flavor. The Flatbush stores proudly displayed Caribbean food signs for roti, beef patties, and coconut bread. Other shops were dedicated to packing and shipping to the West Indian isles. The people who strolled the streets were diverse. I hoped that gentrification wouldn't mean the demise of yet another affordable neighborhood. I was astute enough to know that I was fortunate to live where I did.

The cabbie pulled to a stop. We had arrived at the massive health care complex. The area was a metropolis. Jose pulled a few bills out of his pocket and paid the driver. We climbed out onto a street that was filled with people as though it were still daytime. Red-and-white-illuminated billboards directed us to the emergency room entrance.

"Thank goodness for those signs," I said. "This place is huge."

My belly flipped when I saw that Jose was still standing at the corner. His eyes were closed. Jose wasn't the type to complain about what he was going through.

Just as I approached him and was figuring out what to say, he opened his eyes. "Ready?" he asked.

"Me? You're the one I'm worried about."

"Don't be. I'm all right," he said. "Let's do this."

We hooked our arms together and wove our way through the crowd. People moved haphazardly in all directions. The place was buzzing. My familiarity with hospitals meant nothing here. At my job at Windsor Medical Center, I could hold my own. Here, I had to admit that I was powerless.

The double doors to the hospital trauma center swung open. "I feel like we're on TV," I said.

"This is real, Daisy," he answered. "Come on."

The image of me running back home was even more real. That vision of me loping through Prospect Park back to the safety of my apartment made me realize three things—one, that I was still an anxious person no matter how much Step work I had done; two, that I was a narcissist and could only think of myself when my dearest friend was the one who was in distress; and, three, that I hadn't gotten over Lou's death. To think that I had practiced karate kicks earlier tonight, and now I was afraid to go into a hospital as a visitor although I was fine going to the hospital where I worked. Angela's suggestion that I might consider therapy was a good one.

Jose was grim. "Let's see if one of the security guards knows where Rubio is."

We didn't have to scout out the area too long. We spotted a guard walking in through the doors that had just swung wide open. I did a double take. He was no guard but an actual police officer. Close up, his weary expression surprised me.

"Excuse me, can you tell us how to find a patient who was brought into the emergency room today?"

He pointed. "See that desk over there? That's where you get information about patients."

"Thank you," I said. I turned to Jose. "Just look at this place."

The building was built like an old fortress. Some areas had been renovated with modern glass and steel, but it could easily have been a medieval castle. This hospital was no comparison to Windsor Medical Center; the two were starkly different. While I was proud of my job, being here showed me that I worked at Small Town, USA.

We approached the desk. "We're here to see Mauricio Rubio. He's in the emergency room," I said.

The officer merely nodded, uninterested in us. "Follow the signs to the ER. It's on your left."

As we walked along the corridor, it occurred to me that none of the security personnel were regular guards like the ones who were employed at Windsor. These were all bona fide New York City police officers. The blues were as unmistakable as the guns that were secured at their waists.

"Do you see this?" I whispered to Jose, who was still in a daze. We followed the signs until we reached the emergency room. As soon as we entered, I stopped the first nurse I saw. He escorted us personally to Rubio, and we avoided the gatherings of people who stood at their loved ones' bedsides. We got to Rubio's curtain-portioned cubicle, and I gasped when I saw him.

Chapter 2

Rubio's complexion was normally milky, but now it was ghostly pale. His abundant dark blond hair was tucked into a green paper cap. There were various monitors surrounding him, along with slowly infusing intravenous drips. I was jolted by the gravity of the situation. I swayed slightly for a moment but pulled myself together when I felt Jose grasp my arm tightly. This was a time that I needed to be strong and support him for a change.

The bulk of the cop's body sucked up whatever air was left in the windowless space. Jose's face was a weird shade of chartreuse.

"Can you tell me exactly what happened?" He directed his question to the policeman. "Did they arrest the person who did this?"

"There's a detective who's on his way," the officer responded. "He'll want to question you."

"Question me?" Jose sounded incredulous. "Excuse me, but shouldn't he be looking for whoever did this?"

I stopped him. "They probably think that you may have some leads."

"I can't think of anyone who would want to hurt him." A few minutes passed as Jose stood stiffly by the stretcher.

"Try talking to him," I suggested, giving him a gentle nudge.

"Rubio, we're here for you," Jose said softly. "Daisy's with me. Don't talk if it's too much for you."

I interrupted Jose. "But if you can, please talk to us. Let us know what you need."

Rubio's eyes fluttered, and his lids opened slowly a second before he winced.

"Call my mother." Then Rubio's eyes closed, and he passed out.

"Excuse me. We're about to wheel him into surgery." A young woman wearing green scrubs tapped me on the arm. She took the bags of intravenous fluids off the poles and placed them on the pillow next to Rubio's head.

"Can you tell us how long he'll be in there?" I asked.

The nurse's eyes narrowed. "Are you Mr. Rubio's wife?"

Without even looking, I knew that Jose would be exasperated. He turned to her. "I'm Rubio's domestic partner, Jose Castillo."

"And I'm Rubio's friend," I added.

"Daisy, please, can you let me handle this?" Jose turned back to the nurse. "We'd like to talk to the doctor."

"Excuse me, but I am a nurse." She stopped what she was doing and looked right at us. "Mandy Jennings. You can ask me what you'd like to know."

Jose's complexion flushed a dark rose. "Sorry, of course. Is he injured very badly? I thought it was just his arm. He seems so out of it."

"Well, he is, but it's because I gave him his pre-op meds a few minutes before you got here. We've got to get that bullet out. It's lodged in his shoulder. We saw the bullet on the emergency MRI that was done as soon as he arrived. Hopefully, there won't be any nerve damage. Is he right-handed?"

Jose touched Rubio's face tenderly. "Yes, he's a painter. An artist. Did it look like he'd have nerve damage? I didn't even think of that."

"We'll know after the surgery." Mandy's tone was firm. "You only have a minute to talk with him. Let him know if you'll be here waiting for him after the surgery."

Jose sighed. "Yes, sure. I'll be here."

I watched as he whispered into Rubio's ear. I could barely take the gentle wave of love that emanated from Jose to Rubio. It was almost painful to absorb such sweet intimacy.

Mandy spoke again. "Can you confirm that he doesn't have any allergies?"

"He never mentioned any." A couple of emotions quickly crossed Jose's face.

"As soon as the procedure is over, the surgeon will come out and speak with you," she said. "Stay close by so that she will be able to find you."

"Can you tell us the surgeon's name?" I piped in.

They both looked at me as if they'd forgotten I was there.

"Dr. Gilroy," Mandy said. Then she offered what I took to be a note of solace. "She's the finest trauma surgeon here, and that's saying a lot. This is the best place for anyone who has the type of injury that Mr. Rubio has."

A few minutes later, Rubio was swept out of the area by Mandy and an orderly who came to assist.

"Should we get some coffee?" I asked. "It's getting late, and we need to stay up."

Jose stared through me as if he were in a different world. Something clicked, though, and his eyes took on a fiery cast. "We've got to talk to the detective."

"Let's go to the cafeteria," I suggested. "I'm sure they'll come find us. They must be used to this sort of thing."

"These Styrofoam cups are awful. They taste terrible," I said, as we waited like hostages for word that Rubio was out of surgery.

My phone buzzed in my pocket, and I took a quick glance at it. It was Letty, another of our closest friends.

"I'm going to take this outside," I said to Jose, who barely acknowledged me. "There's too much noise in here."

I went out into the corridor. "Hey, Letty, I guess you heard."

"Yes, Mike told me what happened," she said. "Did anyone get there yet to ask questions?"

Letty was married to Detective Mike Ramos, and he must have immediately contacted her. Brooklyn news traveled fast.

"No, we just got here," I said.

I hoped it would be Detective David Rodriguez, but by the end of the conversation, I knew it wouldn't be. Rod was still in Chicago taking care of personal business that I had no clue about. When we started dating, I'd decided not to be pushy when it came to his privacy. I also had things I wanted to keep to myself. How that would help in terms of our building a relationship I wasn't sure. We both needed to be more honest, open, and willing. Whatever that meant. Letty had to go, and we ended our phone call. I returned to the cafeteria to find Jose pacing.

"Come on, let's sit down," I suggested. "Your being so nervous is not going to help."

"What am I supposed to do?" Jose asked. "You tell me. It's not a stranger in there; it's Rubio."

"I know who's in there." I tried to keep my voice level. "I also know how it feels, just in case you forgot. Which you seem to have done."

"Whoa, wait a minute," he said. "I really don't want to compare, okay?"

I found myself getting heated. "Why? Because you love Rubio? It wasn't my intention to compare. I'm just saying that however it ended, I did love Lou at one time."

Jose covered his eyes with his hands. "I'm sorry. I know all that. I just don't know what to do with myself. I'm racking my brain as to why he got shot. Was the bullet really meant for him? If not, how did he get caught in the crossfire? And mainly what I'm thinking is that he's alive. I'm thinking how lucky we are that he didn't get killed out there."

I reached out and patted his forearm. "I was being overly sensitive. Rubio's been working really hard as far as I know. I can't think of why anyone would try to shoot him. It had to be a botched burglary."

"He's become a workaholic since he put the show up at the gallery. I told him that he needed to pull back a little. But a heart attack is not a gunshot wound."

"Definitely not," I agreed. "I'm curious to hear the details. I hope the detective gets here soon."

"Remember, Daisy, the detective is going to want us to give details, not the other way around."

"Mr. Castillo?"

We both turned to see a towering large-framed man addressing Jose. A stereotypical gumshoe. His herringbone coat topped off his baggy-styled cuffed pants. Despite the somber circumstances, he looked like an old-fashioned forties dick. Not many people knew how much I loved watching old black-and-white movies. They helped me stay out of my head, especially when I went down a negative alley.

"Detective Sam Harris." He shook Jose's hand. "The officer described you to me."

"This is our friend, Daisy Muñiz."

I felt a chill. This was too déjà vu for me. But there was something about him that made me relax.

As he took my hand, he said, "Would you mind waiting in the lobby while I ask Mr. Castillo a few questions? I'd like to speak with you right afterward."

"No problem," I said. I walked into the lobby, glad that I had my smartphone to keep me busy. I could download a book to read if I ended up waiting too long. Maybe even a crime novel that I could devour. No, on second thought, that might not be such a good idea. One death today was one too many. Poor Charley Sprague.

I picked up my phone and called my sponsor. "Hi, Angela. I know it's late. My friend, Rubio, was shot tonight. I'm in the hospital with Jose right now. I'm so glad Rubio is alive. I don't know how I would have handled it if he had been killed."

I rolled my eyes as she reminded me that the *poor me's* were my default ways of dealing with stressors. She had encouraged me to call her whenever there was a problem, but now I was sorry that I had bothered. The conversation was not going where I wanted it to go.

Detective Harris came toward me. He took his handkerchief out just as he sneezed. He blew and stuffed the hanky back into his pocket.

"Angela, I have to hang up. I'll call you later." I was just shutting off my phone when the detective reached me.

"Miss Muñiz, why don't we go sit over there on that bench?" he said. "I won't take up too much of your time."

I knew the drill. It wasn't the first time I'd been questioned, although last time it had been conducted by Detective Rodriguez, or, should I say, the Divine Detective Rodriguez. We walked over to a glass wall that looked out onto a barren courtyard. Leafless bushes lined the brick wall of the building that shared the area.

"Rosebushes." Detective Harris gazed in my direction. "In just a few days I'll have hope again. It'll soon be time to prune my roses, and, once I do that, spring can't change its mind."

"You grow roses?" I asked. Maybe that was our connection. I was developing a green thumb in Marge's yard. We'd decided that this year we would plant a few rosebushes in the backyard to take advantage of the impact of the full sun.

"First Saturday in April is the only time to prune those

babies. My neighbors usually go wild thinking that I'm ruining them. I start pruning just as the new shoots come in. After a few weeks, everyone has forgotten my dastardly deed."

"That sounds like something I would do," I admitted. "If I were your neighbor, I might have left a nasty note in your mailbox. I had no idea."

"My father, God rest his soul, was a master gardener. Roses. We had an apple orchard at one time, but that was when we were still living down south."

"I lived down south once too," I said. "South Brooklyn."

"South Brooklyn?" he asked.

"It was a joke," I said. "I'm kidding."

"Los Sures."

"Yes. How do you know about Los Sures?"

"Oh, I've been around a really long time, Miss Muñiz." He took his handkerchief out and blew his nose. "So, tell me what you think."

"What I think? About roses?"

"No, not about roses. What do you think happened to your friend in there? Mr. Rubio."

"You've got me," I said. "I have no idea." This old cat was good. He'd pulled me into his confidence with roses, and the next thing I knew I'd be spilling my guts. Except I had no information about Rubio.

"How often do you see your friend?"

"Well, we sort of live together." I smiled at his befuddled expression. "What I mean is, they live on the third floor, and I live on the fourth floor of the building. I meet Rubio on the stairways sometimes. I see Jose more often."

"Is there a particular reason for that?" he asked.

"We have different living habits. I'm at work by nine. My boss has a fit when I'm late. Rubio has a more laid-back schedule. He used to work in his studio all night long most of the time. But I don't think he's doing much of that lately. You know, he's been concentrating on his show."

"Have you been to the gallery?" His smile was as chilled as the early spring night. I wasn't as comfortable as I'd been just a moment earlier.

"Of course. He's my friend," I said. "I don't really buy art, but it's nice to look at. My budget. The apartment has an old-fashioned setup. I can fit one canvas over the fireplace mantel, but every other space is taken up by a gas light fixture or a window."

"You must live in a brownstone." His matter-of-fact statement was tinged with skepticism.

"Yes, but I guess that isn't important, is it? You want to know about Rubio's habits, not my housing situation."

"Well, it is kind of surprising that you live in an exclusive neighborhood, and Rubio has an art show. I just take you for —"

"What?" I asked. "Because we're Latinos, Detective?"

Harris sighed deeply. "Take a good look at me, Miss Muñiz. No. The reason I'm surprised is that you're a young group of kids."

"I take offense to that," I said. "We aren't children. In fact, we're far from it. We all work hard to make a decent living."

Harris suddenly laughed. "Okay, you got me there. My age is talking, and you just put me in my place. I'd like to offer you an apology and a cup of coffee if that's okay with you."

My tongue was still singed from the last cup I tried to swallow. "If you're talking about that machine over there, forget it. That coffee isn't something you'd like to offer to anyone. But as for your apology, no need. I'm a bit on edge with what's going on here."

"Did Mr. Rubio ever speak of anyone who was harassing or threatening him?"

"Not that I know of," I said. "I can't think of anyone who would want to hurt him. Not a soul. He's a good guy. He has an art show installed at the gallery on Atlantic Avenue. The neighborhood has really changed. It's the place to be seen in Brooklyn if you're an artist. It's near the transit hub. He worked day and night to get that show ready. He rolled his sleeves up; that much I can say."

"I'm guessing there's a lot of competition for the art space on Atlantic Avenue. What about the leasing?"

I squirmed. "I don't know anything about that. Rubio is an artist."

"By the way, do you know the owners of the gallery?"

"Of course. I met them at the opening. Selena and Papo Montoya. I don't know Papo's real name, but that's what everyone calls him."

"The Montoyas? Well, thank you very much. You've been helpful." He stood up. "I may want to ask you some more questions, but this is good for now."

"Thank you." While I shook his hand, it occurred to me that I had no idea why I was thanking him.

As soon as he left, I dove into my bag for hand sanitizer. I was not about to catch his cold.

Chapter 3

"Really? Because he asked?" Jose fumed. "Why would you tell him about the Montoyas? What's wrong with you, Daisy?"

Steam practically poured out of Jose's ears. I couldn't remember the last time he was so livid. His dial was usually turned to neutral.

I flinched. "I thought I was helping."

"You could have said nothing," he said. "Or you could have told a little white lie."

"I thought you couldn't lie," I said. "At least that's what you've told me before. Wasn't that in your *Ita*?"

"I know what was in *my* reading," Jose said. "It didn't say I couldn't lie if what I had to share could be incriminating evidence to a detective while he's writing it all down in a little black book. For sure, it didn't say that *Daisy* couldn't lie if my boyfriend got shot and had surgery to remove a bullet from his right shoulder."

"That's harsh," I said. "But, still, how can anything we say be incriminating? It was a robbery."

The moments it took him to answer were too long.

"Rubio wasn't in any trouble, was he?" I asked. "He was living a decent life, wasn't he?"

No one could ever tell Rubio what to do, and no one ever tried. Maybe he was a bit more guarded than I thought he needed to be. But, on the other hand, he was always ready with a smile, agreeable, and willing to help anyone in need.

"I didn't really mean him," Jose admitted. "I was thinking about Selena and Papo. The dragon lives on with those two. I've heard they can be vicious, and I don't want anyone to think we implicated them in any way."

"Dragon?" I thought for a minute. "You mean they're still using heroin? But what does that have to do with Rubio?"

"I'm not sure. I do know that they don't have a squeaky-clean business ethic."

The image of Selena wearing a drop-dead gorgeous evening gown with a choker of fine emeralds popped into my mind. In a visualization I'd had of her, she'd been surrounded by a bevy of men who had poured her champagne, lit her cigarettes, and hung on to her every word. That was the essence of Selena Montoya. I'd experienced that imagery at the time that Rubio was considering signing the lease. I thought that he had signed that lease, and, according to Jose, he had. He told me so during my first-year-sober anniversary celebration.

"Do you remember that snippet meditation I had right before we caught Dr. Campbell's murderer?" It was all coming back, even though there wasn't that much to chew over.

"Yeah." Jose nodded. "Last autumn when Rubio was planning to sign the lease."

"Did he or didn't he? I thought you told me that he had."

"I thought he had." Jose didn't seem so happy when he said this. "It wasn't until much later that he admitted that he hadn't, and that he'd just signed a contract for a show."

"It was a crazy time, huh?" I laughed, trying to keep things light. "You had just been initiated in *Lucumí* and were still a *iyawó*. Dressed in your whites. The security guards thought you were a doctor. You really pulled it off. Hmmm, you just did the same thing now that you had done then."

"What are you talking about?" he asked.

"You didn't tell the security guard you weren't a doctor. You just kept quiet. And this time you didn't tell Detective Harris the name of the company that owns the gallery. You don't commit a lie that someone can catch you on. You just omit giving information."

"I don't really see things that way." He seemed irritated and changed the subject. "How long do you think he'll be in surgery? I can't take it. The waiting is killing me."

"It can't be more than an hour that we've been waiting. You need to chill. You don't want this rushed. You want the surgeon to take her time."

Jose scoffed. "Of course." After a pause, he asked, "Do you think I should have said something to the detective?"

"I think that doing anything that might help Rubio is what you should do."

He shook his head. "Those Montoyas. I think they hide their true interests in their legit business."

"Do you think that the gallery is a cover? That never occurred to me. Even if it is true, how does Rubio factor in?"

Jose sounded annoyed. "He doesn't. Not even a little bit."

"I don't know if I could be that trusting," I said. "I'm sorry."

"The detective asked me why we call him by his last name," Jose said. "He said, 'His first name is Maurice, isn't it?' Why was that important? I responded that his name is Mauricio but that he's always gone by Rubio. His parents are the only ones who call him by his first name."

Jose groaned. "Oh, God, I have to call Colombia and contact his mother."

"I can help you do that," I said.

"No, I have to do it."

I watched Jose as he made the phone call. My gut told me that it was possible that Rubio could be involved in an unsavory activity. I finally owned my feelings, and, even though I loved Rubio and Jose, I wasn't going to deny that Rubio might have

known what was possibly going on in the dry goods section
of the gallery. But, no, that couldn't be true. I was caught
between being a *bodeguera y una borrachona*, stuck between
being a business person and a drunk. The program's *Think* sign
was hung upside down for a reason. It reminded me that my
thinking was often awry. But while my thinking might be off,
the feeling that I had was something else. I had to listen to my
feelings and give space for whatever they were. Even if they
were unwelcome.

"Forget about what I was thinking about Rubio, and I'll try
to do the same," I said.

"I don't know what you were thinking, Daisy." Jose gave
me one of his too-bright smiles. "But, yeah, peace to you too."

We settled on one of the hard plastic benches in the waiting
area. It occurred to me that Rubio wouldn't be returning to the
emergency room but would most likely be sent to the recovery
room after the surgery. I was about to mention that to Jose when
I saw that his eyes were closed and his breath even. Nervous as
he was, he'd somehow managed to fall asleep.

"Mr. Castillo." A woman's soft voice woke us up. "Sorry to
disturb you, but Mr. Rubio is in recovery."

My eyelids opened. We were still in the waiting room.
According to my watch, it was one in the morning. There were
only a couple of people there, and one was snoring with his
mouth wide open, drool spilling onto his collar.

Jose stood up. "Does that mean he's okay?"

The woman extended her hand to Jose. "I'm Dr. Gilroy. I just
finished his surgery." The doctor's deep hazel eyes contrasted
nicely with her green scrubs. "He's going to be under the effects
of anesthesia for a while. Why don't you go home and come
back after you've gotten a decent night's sleep; these benches
aren't the most comfortable. We were able to remove the bullet.
There was quite a bit of muscle and nerve damage to his right
shoulder area."

"What exactly does that mean?" Jose interrupted. "How much damage? He's an artist and it would be devastating for him to lose the use of his arm."

"We won't really know until the swelling goes down. He's receiving anti-inflammatory medication. Hopefully, he'll have an uneventful recovery, and we'll be better able to assess the damage at that point."

Jose was crestfallen. "I thought we would know right away. When he wakes up, what do we say?"

"He'll need physical therapy and possibly occupational therapy, but let's just take this one day at a time." She was speaking our language.

I chimed in and said, "That's an idea. We should try to *easy does it* while we're at it." The program slogans sounded trite to some ears, but they were great in mapping out a direction when things were tough, and this was one of those times.

"I'm sorry," the doctor said. "I didn't realize you two were together. Of course, you are." She smiled at me. "I'm Dr. Gilroy."

I nodded, since there wasn't much to say. She probably thought I was an idiot, spouting off AA slogans.

"What if he wakes up in the middle of the night, and I'm not here?" Jose asked.

"I think it's important for you to get a good night's sleep," the doctor said. "Mr. Rubio will be all right. When he's awake and stable, he'll be moved into a room on one of the floors. We'll also be starting him on a course of antibiotics. He had a foreign object in his body, and we want to prevent an infection."

"In other words, we'll still be waiting even if we stay."

"Yes, Mr. Castillo," she said. "Don't rush things. He'll need time to recuperate."

"Okay, I get it," Jose said. "Will we speak again when I get back here later?"

"I'm the surgeon on call. He'll have another doctor, one that will be assigned in the morning to handle his case. You'll be able to get all the information you need when you return."

We thanked her and picked up our things to leave. As we made our way to the exit to hail a cab, I could see Jose's jaw pulsating.

There was a line of taxis outside. We ducked into one, and Jose gave him our address. We settled back into the seat.

"You want to tell me what's going on?" I asked.

He glared at me. "My partner, who happens to be an artist, was shot and may not be able to use his right arm anymore. Need any more details?"

"We already know that, and you know that I wouldn't ask you something stupid like that. There's an undercurrent of something going on that you're not addressing."

Jose rubbed his eyes. "I'm not sure what you're talking about. Just let it go, okay? I already spoke to the detective, and I don't need any more questions from you."

"Yeah, sure," I said. "No problem. But if you change your mind, I'm around to talk."

I took his hand and squeezed it briefly, and then I let it go, just as he asked. He was acting like a grouch, but even if I didn't know the reason, I'd have to let him be.

The taxi traveled through the Flatbush neighborhood. It was early morning, and there were a few people walking through the streets. The scene reminded me of the many times I had walked home late after partying the night away before I got sober. One thing I knew for sure was that I wouldn't be doing that anymore. That was a closed chapter in my book.

The taxi pulled up in front of our house, and we said our good nights at the foyer on the second floor. We could chat later in the day. It was very possible that Rubio had been a victim of a random robbery, and the culprit was still out there.

I climbed the stairs to my apartment. The door was open. I'd left it that way purposely because I loved going inside to find

Ms. G, the black-and-white fur ball, waiting for me. She was a great welcome home party. Her purrs let me know that she wanted my company too, and this made me feel less lonely. I hurried to get to bed. My shower could wait until the morning.

As I felt my eyes closing, I thought about Charley Sprague. Was he also the innocent victim of a miscalculated crime?

I woke up to find the kitty kneading my pink damask duvet cover. Gently moving her aside, I reached over to my nightstand for a glass of water. It wasn't there. I must have fallen asleep quickly and forgotten to fill my nightly tumbler. I looked at the clock. It was three in the morning.

I took a quick look through the window. There was a fingernail-width crescent moon high in the sky. Sometimes I felt as though the moon was calling to me. These were my private moments, and they helped me make sense of things. I filled the glass and walked into the living room to sit at the bay window. If I imagined hard enough, I could hear the howl of wolves sing through the night. There was another brownstone across the street, and its windows were dark. Right next to it was a playground. There was a man sitting on a bench almost directly in front of our house. It was odd for him to be out there. He might have been homeless, but Park Slope wasn't known for its acceptance of drifters. I saw him look up toward my window, and I backed away. I knew him and didn't want him to know that I'd seen him.

I returned to bed, where little Ms. G waited for me. I pushed the thoughts of the man away and forced myself to think about Rodriguez, who loved that I called him Rod, and his lack of communication. There had been a shift in our relationship, and I wasn't quite sure what had happened. I wasn't going to burden either him or me by hanging on to someone that had so much mystery attached. I didn't deserve that. If he really did care, he'd better start talking and soon.

Chapter 4

The sunlight shone directly into my eyes and woke me. I wasn't deliberately trying to be a neighborhood native by not having curtains on my window; I'd just never gotten around to hanging them. The wooden shutters worked, but I never thought to close them. The light-filled room was a welcome gift. I felt under the comforter for Ms. G, who must have scooted off for an early breakfast with Marge. I suddenly remembered the man who had stood across from the brownstone the previous evening. I jumped out of bed and snuck into the living room for a quick glance out the window. No one was there.

After a shower and a peek at the television, I determined that there was no coverage about the shooting. It was still too early to call Jose; he needed his sleep. Time was valuable and I wanted to use it to check on the items I needed to receive my *Guerreros*, the spiritual ceremony that I had planned with Hector. White skirt? Check. White blouse? Check. White underwear and bra? Check. White shoes? Check. I had everything on my list except for my white headscarf. All the other items were in place on my bed. I dropped to my knees and looked under the bed skirt. There it was. I heard a *mew* and turned to see Ms. G staring at me.

"Did you steal my kerchief, you little thief?" I picked up the gauzy white material and placed it next to the rest of my outfit, and then I picked up the black-and-white puffball of a cat. She scratched my arm as she tried to scramble away. I placed her back on the floor before she jumped onto my pristine clothing. I fingered the *collares*, spiritual beads, that I'd hung around my neck. Receiving them had been a turning point in my spiritual life. In a few days, I'd progress in the Orisha tradition, and Hector, my *Padrino*, my godfather, would present me with the *Guerreros*, Warriors.

Ellegua. Ochosi. Oggun. I would receive the three Orishas that comprised the Warriors. The book that Hector recommended I read was on the nightstand. He was tickled when I asked him at a *misa*, spiritual séance, whether it was okay to learn about the Orishas by reading. I'd turned beet red when one of the elders shook her gray curls at me and told me that I needed to learn by practice. Hector had said, "The more you know, the better it will be, and don't sweat what others think about you."

As I folded my clothes, readying to put them in my large duffel bag, the phone rang. I answered it.

"Hi, Letty. I'm surprised to hear from you already. We don't have any more updates on Rubio, other than that he did okay in surgery. He'll probably be transferred to a regular floor today."

"Daisy," Letty interrupted. "I'm calling about Hector. I don't know how to tell you this, but he's been in a car accident."

I sat down on my bed. "Oh, no, when did that happen? Will he be able to fly back?"

"Really, Daisy, what you should be asking is whether Hector is okay and how bad are his injuries."

I flopped over on my belly. "That's what I meant to say. I'm sorry. I'm just shocked. What happened?"

"Hector was on his way back from the *ebbo*, the offering, for Lionel." Letty's voice was nasal. She was crying. "He never made it to the plane."

"He's still in Florida?" I fingered the hem of my shirt.

"Daisy, he's badly hurt."

"How about I come over to your place," I suggested. "I can't imagine what it must be like to get this news about your brother." Letty and I had been friends since high school, and Hector was Jose's godfather, and mine too.

"It's not good timing. Mike and I are looking at airfares. We want to take the kids with us, but we're not sure if we can swing that. The tickets are expensive. We'll be staying with my sister and her husband."

"Who would you leave Nati and Jorgito with if you don't take them with you?"

"We could always leave them with Mike's sister, Eva. I'll tell you once we figure it out. Mike is on the phone right now trying to make flight plans."

The sense of relief was overpowering and embarrassing. "I'm glad that you have her," I said.

My heart beat wildly. There was no way that I could take care of them. Jorgito was my godson, but Angela had suggested I first try taking care of a plant before a human. That's all I could manage at this point. I hadn't told her that I'd planted bulbs in Marge's garden, and the daffodils and tulips were starting to bloom. Ms. G slunk in, and I patted the bed for her to jump on. I rubbed her fur as Letty and I continued our conversation.

"Can you take off from work without notice?" I asked.

"Daisy, I work at a jeweler's," she said. "It's not like they can't do without me for a few days."

"So what exactly happened?" I asked.

"A woman in an SUV went through a STOP sign." She paused. "It happened last night about ten. Hector was on his way to the airport. The driver is badly injured too. She might not make it. Lionel called us. He was in the car with him."

Something wasn't right about this. First Rubio, and now Hector. I was a newbie when it came to spiritual matters, but two events like these within the last twenty-four hours added up to something going on. But it was all too intangible for me to really know what.

"How injured is Hector?" I asked.

"His spleen might be damaged," Letty said. "He's bleeding internally, and they had to give him a transfusion. He's still having tests done. Daisy, Mike is motioning to me. I've got to go. Do me a favor, and let Jose know. Please."

"Sure, just try to take it easy." I hung up.

I threw on a shawl and went down to Jose and Rubio's apartment. I knocked and waited. No one answered the door. I returned to my apartment. I'd try again later in the day.

I spent the rest of the morning and early afternoon lounging on my couch. *Strangers on a Train* droned on in the background. Half-asleep, I wasn't sure what was going on between the two men in the Pullman car. It was an old black-and-white flick, and that was good enough for me. When I'd finally woken up enough to feel a bit more clearer, I freshened up and crept down the stairs. Jose might be in. He, just as I, had probably needed to get more sleep. There'd been no messages on my phone.

All seemed still in the hallway. I knocked, but there was no answer. I tried again to no avail. Just as I was about to turn back upstairs, I heard the door creak open.

Rubio stood there. His snarled hair was pulled back into a ponytail. Skin pale, eyes deeply shadowed. An immobilizer encased his arm.

"What are you doing here?" I asked. "Are you okay?"

"What's up?" He seemed to gaze right through me.

"I'm surprised they discharged you so soon," I said. "Aren't you going to let me in?"

Rubio stepped aside, and I entered the living room. Their apartment was usually so neat that it could be on a segment of television's *NYC Finest Living* on a moment's notice. Today wouldn't be that moment. I pushed a load of documents over on the couch and sat down. There were a couple of tumblers half filled with fizzless soda and a mug of cold coffee on the table's surface.

"It's so dark in here. Did I wake you up or something?" The curtains were closed, which was odd for the usually well-lit living room. Rubio remained quiet. I tried again. "When did you get released from the hospital?"

"This morning."

"Already? We just left you there!"

"I'm all right. There really wasn't any reason for me to stick around," he said. "I have a lot of things to do."

"Did they discharge you, or did you leave on your own, Rubio?"

"I signed out against medical advice. Please, if you have an opinion on this, keep it to yourself. I had to listen to Jose's and the doctor's already. I don't need another."

"I'm not going to say anything, but really." I sighed. "The reason I came here was that, well, I have news."

Rubio's face was impassive. He picked up a couple of the documents and held them as he sat in a comfy club chair.

"It's Hector," I said. "He's been in a car accident."

"And you want *me* to tell Jose?"

"Why are you making things so difficult?" I asked.

"Hel-lo, Daisy," he said with a smirk. "I just got shot. Now you want me to tell Jose that Hector's been in a car accident?"

I was officially annoyed now. "A minute ago you told me how well you were, and now it's too much for you? Everybody's in a bad mood. I hope you get over it fast. You know, be grateful you survived. If, by chance, you do see Jose before I do, please let him know that Letty and Mike are flying down to Florida as soon as they can."

Rubio quietly folded up some papers and sat back in his chair. His eyes were closed. I'd never experienced him like this before.

"I couldn't stay still in that stupid hospital," he said. "I worked with Charley. I can't believe that he's dead. It wasn't his fault."

"What do you mean, it wasn't his fault? I don't get it."

Rubio's chin drooped. I'd never seen him in a slow nod either. "Nothing. Never mind," he said. "I'm just thinking out loud."

"If you need help or something," I said, "I'd be happy to do anything for you."

"I don't need a thing," he said.

"All right, then, I'm leaving," I said. "Do you have any idea when Jose will be back?"

Rubio barely opened one eye. "You know how Jose is. He has that new job. He's practically never at home anymore."

"He did say he has to prove himself as a new associate at his company. Being a financial planner is a big responsibility."

"Thanks for standing up for him, Daisy," Rubio said. "He'll appreciate that."

"I'll see you, Rubio. Feel better. Don't bother coming to the door. I'll let myself out."

I stood in the hallway. Music wafted upstairs from Marge's parlor. She was back at the piano. While the general tone of the house seemed in order, something was energetically wrong in the Castillo-Rubio apartment. Jose would have to tell me what was going on, but first I'd have to find him.

Back in my apartment, I sat on the living room window seat. The park across the street was empty except for the maintenance man, who puttered around as he engaged in the annual spring cleanup. There were several boxes of lawn and leaf trash bags off to the side. I checked my phone for what seemed like the four-hundredth time. Jose hadn't returned my numerous calls. Letty hadn't left any new messages. Rod hadn't tried calling me either. Nobody was around. That is, nobody who meant anything to me was around. I decided to go down and speak to Marge. She, at least, was dependable.

I peeked into Marge's parlor and saw her perched on the bench in front of the baby grand piano. "Marge," I called. "Mind if I sit here and listen for a while?"

She swiveled around on the bench. "Of course not, dear. But I can tell by your voice that you're not here to listen to me play."

I slumped into one of the plump upholstered chairs. "We got some bad news late last night. We didn't want to bother you. It's Rubio. He was shot, but don't worry. He's okay. He's actually home already. Against medical advice, but he's upstairs."

"Oh my." Marge clasped her hands together. "What happened?"

"We think there was a robbery attempt at the gallery yesterday. The curator was killed."

Marge shook her head. "How terrible! I'll go check on Rubio." She prepared to get up.

"I don't think you need to right now," I said. "I just left his apartment. He's as closed as a tomb."

"He probably just needs a little time," Marge said. "We should give him that."

"And Hector's been in a car accident," I cried.

"Daisy, I'm so sorry to hear all of this. Is he badly injured?" Marge's genuine concern soothed my soul.

"He's not doing so great. But he's still alive. Thank God for that."

We sat quietly for a few moments listening to the roar of the strong wind outside the window. Sunlight patterns changed in the room as the large sycamore branches swayed.

"Rubio is a mess, and so is their apartment."

"Is that important right now?" Marge asked. "You just told me that Rubio was shot. Cleaning the apartment is probably the last thing on either of their minds."

"I've never seen their apartment look like that before. It's so unlike them. I mean, that didn't just happen. There was probably a few days' worth of mugs around that living room. And Jose is a neatnik."

"I think that you should mind your beeswax." Marge's voice was as soft as honey. "Leave them alone."

"That is not what I ever expected you to say," I admitted. "I care about them."

"Let them work things out on their own." Marge got up and sat next to me in a matching chair. "You're their friend. Friends support but don't get involved in the minutiae. In fact, you sound like a mother hen. Stop worrying so much about them, and take care of yourself."

"But Rubio was shot."

"Yes, we know that, dear," Marge said. "But there really isn't all that much you can do except to be here if they call on you."

"You mean that, don't you?" I said.

"Yes," she said softly. "Not everything has to be fixed. So what? Their apartment could use a cleaning. They're grown-ups."

"And Hector?"

"You tell me, Daisy." Marge's love came through her words. She was right. There was only so much worrying that I could do.

"I can pray for him, can't I?" I said. "You know, you're right. I'll do that, and then maybe I'll go to a meeting. I think there's a four-thirty over at St. Augustine's. A beginner's. It'll keep my mind off all this."

"Enjoy, dear," Marge said, as she cautiously made her way back over to the piano bench. I needed a meeting, and I let my smart feet walk me there.

It was nearing eight in the evening as I strolled down the sycamore- and magnolia-lined sidewalk. Attending the beginner's meeting had evolved into my helping several other members make an inventory of needed literature. We walked over to Dizzy's for burgers and hung out together, relishing a sober evening.

As I got back to the brownstone, my stomach lurched. A man's silhouette was visible in front of the second-story landing that I use to enter my apartment. It had to be the man who'd stood across from the house the night before. I slowed down but continued to move closer. Not sure what to do, I stopped as I reached the gate.

The man moved out of the shadow, and I almost fainted in relief. Detective Rodriguez stepped into the full light of the streetlamp. I climbed up the stairs, and we stood across from each other in the doorway. I was struck by an onslaught of emotions.

"What are you trying to do, scare me?" I asked. The thrill of seeing Rod gave me a delicious sensation in my lower belly.

"I caught an early flight," he explained. "I couldn't wait to see you."

"Why didn't you call me to let me know you were coming instead of standing here in the dark?"

Rod smiled at me, showing his beautiful straight white teeth. He was tall and *trigueño* and knew exactly how to wear a suit. I liked to think of myself as Lauren Bacall to his Humphrey Bogart.

"I had a hunch that it might not be a good idea to wait for you like this. I was about to call you." He opened his palm to show me his cell phone.

"I'm glad to see you," I said. "Things have been freaky around here."

"You mean like the dude who's sitting in front of the playground watching us?"

I resisted turning around. "That, and Rubio was shot in the shoulder. He had surgery."

"Did you just come from the hospital?" he asked. "I'm sure he appreciated that."

"Would you believe he's home already? I went down to talk to Jose about Hector. But instead of Jose answering the door, Rubio did. There's another thing. Hector was in a car accident in Florida. I have a feeling something's not right, but I'm not sure what it is."

"That is a lot," he said.

I dug deep in my bag for my keys. "Coming inside?" I beckoned.

"You mean I'm invited?" It might have been the reflection of the streetlamp, but I was sure I could detect a twinkle in his eye.

"Yes, you're invited."

I opened the door, and we walked into the second-floor foyer of the brownstone. There was a pile of mail on the floor, and I riffled through it, picking up a few letters and bills. I placed the guys' mail on the table attached to the floor-length mirror that took up the side of the wall.

"This is what I meant when I told Marge how messy they've been lately. Most of this mail belongs to Rubio and Jose. They've been so unavailable. It's so unlike them."

"Can you forget about those two for a minute?"

My whole body seemed to turn into molten gold. I allowed him to embrace me for a moment. It was good to be held this way, but I had to preserve some self-respect.

"Sure, I can forget about them, as you put it, but I'm still not ready for this." I willed myself to pull away.

"Still mad?" he asked. "I thought you might be."

"Not really mad. More like, what the hell happened here? Why'd you go to Chicago without saying anything to me?"

Rod looked sincerely apologetic but offered no explanation that adequately matched his expression.

"How about I ask again. Or maybe you don't think that you owe me an explanation for picking up and leaving without communicating something? If I were leaving New York, I'd let you know. In fact, I'd be excited to let you know. I'd want to share every detail."

Rod grabbed my hands and kissed them. "I was wrong. I know that. I have lots to explain, but I'm just not ready. I'm sorry."

"Well, then I'm not ready either." I pulled my hands back and moved away from him even though his heat practically seared through me.

We each waited for the other to say something.

"If you have any skeletons in your closet, I wish you'd just tell me," I blurted out. His blank expression told me everything I needed to know. "Maybe it's not time for any closet cleaning yet."

I led the way upstairs to my apartment. "Do you want something to drink?" I asked. "I can make you a cup of tea." I was turning into Marge fifty years too early.

"That would be great," he said. "I'm starving."

"I said tea. I didn't say tea and crumpets." I stretched to get the tin of oatmeal cookies that Marge made a few days earlier.

"You're a soft touch." I didn't like what his words implied, but his tone and expression made me instantly forgiving.

"I'm not really," I said, dropping tea bags into a couple of mugs.

"Have you spoken to anyone at the precinct about the shooting?"

"Detective Harris," I said. "He came to the hospital when Rubio was in the operating room."

"Sam?" Rod nodded. "He's one of our best."

"He was pretty nice, I guess, for a person questioning me," I said. "Definitely more easygoing than Munroe. Or you, for that matter."

"I thought you and Munroe had made your peace."

"Sure, sorry. I'm getting as testy as everybody else. Forget I said anything, please."

I'd met Detective Rodriguez and his partner, Liz Munroe, when a surgeon at Windsor Medical Center was found dead. The truth is that I was jealous, but when I saw how well they worked together, I finally understood what partnership was about. I needed to cool it on that account.

"Didn't you buy a camera recently?" Rod was on to the next topic. "Is it handy? I'd like to see if I can get a close-up of that guy who's camped out across the street. He's dressed too nicely to be homeless."

"Are you sure we should do that?" I asked.

"Don't you want me to ID him?" Rod looked at me quizzically.

"Yes, of course."

I went into my bedroom and rummaged through my bags for the camera. I'd bought it on sale and wished I hadn't charged it. Buying unnecessary items with my credit card had become a bad habit. I found the camera and brought it out to Rod.

"Here it is." I handed the unopened box to him.

"Thanks." He didn't say a word about it still being in the box. "We'll have to charge the battery."

"No, we won't," I said. "The camera comes with one."

"I don't mean you have to buy one. I meant we need to give it some juice."

I flushed. "I misunderstood you. I don't know what I was thinking."

Rod took the instructions out and, following them, began charging the camera while I peeked out the window.

"He's gone," I said.

"Really? I wonder if it's because he saw us come upstairs together. Maybe he didn't expect you to have a man up here. That leads me to think that he's up to no good."

"He was out there last night. I'm sure he's harmless." I

sounded inane to myself.

"Well, let's get the camera ready anyway. I want to show you a few things in case you need to use it tonight."

"You're thinking I may not be safe here."

"I'm sure you are," Rod said. "Marge is downstairs as well as Rubio, you said."

"An eighty-something-year-old and a guy who can't use his arm? I'm not sure how helpful they'll be if there is trouble."

"I'll stick around awhile, at least until we know that Jose is home. Why don't you text him, and let him know what's happening?"

While I texted Jose, I wondered how things had changed so much in the last twenty-four hours.

An hour later there was still no word from Jose, and the battery hadn't completed charging.

"You should go home," I said. "You look bushed. I know I'll be all right. The guy is no longer out there. How about I call you if anything changes. This is our house. We'll be safe here."

His sheepish look told me how exhausted he really was. "You don't mind?"

"Of course not," I said. "You traveled from midway across the country to walk into the crazy. Everything will be fine; you'll see. Now go!"

"Wait a minute. The green light is on. The battery is ready."

Rod set the camera up on the tripod I'd bought along with it. He positioned it next to the window. As he left, his lips were warm on mine. I was glad that I had already opened the door; otherwise, I might have asked him to stay.

"Daisy!" I was jolted out of my sleep. I was alone, just as I had been when I'd finally turned in. Three o'clock in the morning. I walked into the living room. The stalker was at his post. I stood there in the shadows for a few minutes and then backed away from him and the camera.

Chapter 5

"I refuse to wait for any one of those creatures to call me back!" I aimed my phone toward the nightstand, but, instead, I threw it on my bed. I'd texted Rod and Jose, and neither one had answered. Annoying. I did some stretches and went to the living room.

The morning sunlight filtered in through the window. The magnolia across the street had begun blooming. In front of the house, the sycamore showed tiny leaves that were of the palest green. Both promised that full spring would soon arrive. No one was outside.

I took a quick shower and pulled on a pair of loose rose-colored sweats and a matching top. My *gi* was ready in its bag by the front door. The surest way to get in a workout was to be prepared. I smiled to myself. Sensei Red Norman had asked me to come in to help with the little white-belts. To progress in the martial art, I was expected to teach in the dojo. The kids were adorable. The best part was that I could leave them after an hour. I thought of Nati and Jorgito. Letty was another one who hadn't called me back. I wondered how Hector was doing.

As soon as I arrived at the dojo, I changed into my uniform. When I bowed into the room, I saw that Sensei was speaking to Jake. It was a small class for a Sunday morning. There were seven little ones in the room doing their warm-up exercises. A couple of girls had their hair pulled back into ponytails. One kept sweeping her bangs back as she concentrated on her front kicks. The boys were intent on showing Sensei how serious they were by focusing on their stretches.

"Jake, take Daisy over to the *barre* and help her with her side kicks," Sensei instructed. "I'm going to concentrate on the kids. See what they're made of."

"*Ichi, ni, san, shi.*" Jake counted in Japanese as I kicked. One, two, three, four. I had studied the instruction sheets that Sensei had given me the first night of class.

Twenty minutes into my lessons, perspiration rolled down my back. Fortunately, I wore an undershirt that kept the wetness from sticking to me too much. I held on to the bar as I began the roundhouse kicks that came after the side ones. I was exhausted but refused to let Sensei or, worse yet, Jake know that I was.

"I'd like to take you out for coffee after class," he whispered, as he lifted my leg to show me how high it could really go.

"I thought you were mad at me." I sputtered. "For popping you in the nose."

"Let it go," he encouraged.

"Daisy, drop down, and give me ten!" Sensei yelled in my direction.

My body automatically dropped to the floor into push-up position. I was getting stronger. My puny biceps were filling out, and I completed the ten and jumped up to a standing position.

"Do you know why I gave you those?" My instructor's nose was almost flat against mine.

"Because I was talking, sir?"

Sensei stepped in closer but whispered loudly so Jake and the children could hear him.

"No, Daisy, it's because you answered. Anyone can try to get your attention, but it's up to you not to engage. Get it?"

"Yes, sir," I said. "Don't engage. I get it."

Sensei nodded. "Learn the meaning of *pause*."

Warmed up, I began helping with the children. The rest of the class involved doing lunges. The trick was sliding my feet across the wooden floor. My bare soles were burning. I was eager for the calluses that no doubt would develop. The children didn't seem to notice the pain. They probably ran around barefoot at home all the time. When class was over, I bowed out and hurried to shower and change.

I couldn't get dressed fast enough. Since it was the children's class, I found myself stepping over little girls and trying to avoid mothers who were trying to get them ready for jam-packed weekends.

On my way out, I saw a group of men and women gathered to take the Orisha dance class. Sensei rented out the studio for activities other than karate. I had a yearning to take the Afro-Caribbean-style dance class. The women were fluffing out white skirts from their backpacks and totes. This was a class I so wanted to attend but didn't have the courage. My two left feet walked me out of the dojo.

"Daisy!" Sensei called, just as I was about to walk out the door.

I turned back to him.

"You're ready to test for your yellow belt," he said. "We'll have testing within the next couple of weeks. I'm telling you early so you'll be prepared. Know your *kata*."

"Sure thing." I loved practicing my *kata*. The moving form was, for me, a special way of meditating, fluidly and physically.

"We'll do a little *kumite* too."

"Sparring, sir?"

"Yes. The testing is a formality. You've been here pretty steadily and are ready to progress." He turned to speak to one of the mothers.

I bowed to his back and left the dojo, bumping into Jake, who was standing right outside.

"Would you like to get something to eat instead of just a coffee?" he asked.

"Sure, why not?"

Jake was good looking, with his swag of curly black hair swinging low over his eyes. He was in excellent shape too. I'd watched his reflection in the mirror as the class did exercises together. I learned from their diligence, and I was sure they learned from my imperfections.

We went to the low-key Fifth Avenue Diner, and, for the first time, sat across from each other in a booth. Other than a few early 1900s black-and-white photographs, there was not much décor. A few couples filled the other booths.

"What interested you in martial arts?" Jake asked as we waited for the server.

"I liked what I saw whenever I passed the dojo," I said. "I hope I get stronger soon. I hate when my legs tremble. I was never an athlete."

"You're doing great," he assured me. "You'll strengthen soon enough. It's about building stamina. Those stances are difficult to settle into in the beginning."

"Not to mention the kicks." I laughed. "But I do love it. What about you? What made you start as an adult."

"I actually started as a kid. I was on the tournament track, and my dad would take me on the rounds to the different competitions before I was ten. Then my dad was killed in a construction accident, and it was years before I had the nerve to return to martial arts."

"That's rough on a kid."

"It was like I couldn't do something that I really loved when my dad died. I couldn't allow myself. I'm getting better at that now."

"I'm sure he's glad that you're back. You're his champ, I bet."

"I think that too." Jake sighed deeply. "At least that's what I'd like to believe."

"Then do it," I said. "I believe. Without belief, there's not much is there?"

The moment had turned much more intimate than I had planned.

"Look, I'm really sorry. I'm not being fair to you," I apologized. "I should never have said yes to eating out with you. I'm sort of seeing someone."

"This is just a meal," he said. "Not sure if you're going to believe what I'm saying, but I thought it would be nice to have a burger with a dojo chum."

"Friends?" I laughed. "You mean, just hang out?"

"Yeah," he said with his toothy grin.

"I guess I don't get out much," I admitted. "Most times a guy asks me out, it's for a date. My radar was way off. Should I be embarrassed?"

"We could go Dutch if you prefer," he suggested. "I did mean to pay for your meal, though. Just this time."

I sniffed the air. "Those burgers do smell delish."

"Sounds good to me." Jake waved at the waitress, who brought over a couple of laminated menus.

"I already know what I want." I ordered a burger with fries, and Jake did the same.

After we finished our meals, we paid our respective checks and got ready to leave. No sex involved. That simple. Most of my relationships with men had been about sex, drugs, and violence, and not always in that order. I left feeling accomplished and relieved.

We parted, and I headed up Fifth Avenue toward St. John's Place. I took my time and window shopped. I browsed through a few stores. Trendy shops, vintage clothing, and organic food joints filled the avenue. I passed one baby shop that had all the items a well-bred Park Slope tot could need or desire.

I took my time as I passed by the bars that had beckoned me once too often when I first got sober. The colorful liquid-filled bottles in the Spirits and Soul store window had seemed to blink and wink at me. Those times were over.

As I made my way closer to home, I saw a familiar figure up ahead. It couldn't be. I had to be mistaken. I hurried to catch up.

"Rubio?" I asked. "What are you doing here?" I put my hand on his good arm.

"Daisy?"

One look in his vacant eyes, and I knew something was wrong.

"I've got to get going," he said. "I've got someone waiting for me."

"Who? I don't think you're ready to be out of the house." I practically clucked my tongue like an old mother hen.

"I'm a big boy, Daisy." He softened his voice. "Lighten up, okay?"

"I know I can't tell you what to do, but—"

"Do us both a favor," he interrupted me. "Go spend some time with Jose. He's been having a hard time, and I don't want to make things worse."

"Talk to me. What's going on?"

"Now's not the time. Like I said, I have something to take care of, and I'd better be on my way. You'll have to excuse me."

Rubio brushed me aside when I made a last attempt to keep him there in front of me. All I could do was watch him walk off into the distance. I noticed that his gait was a bit off-balance, most likely due to the arm immobilizer he was wearing. Slung over his other shoulder was a large bag. He seemed as awkward as the situation. Things would work out, I told myself.

My thoughts as I walked home were completely taken up with Rubio. I got to the house and strode through the gate.

My heart lurched. Marge was sitting on the lowest step of the stoop. She wore a thin short-sleeve dress with her apron over it. Ruffian was nowhere near her.

"Marge, what are you doing out here? Where's your jacket?"

"Daisy?" she asked through chattering teeth. "I'm so glad to hear your voice! I came outside to throw out a bag of garbage, and, the next thing I knew, someone was asking for Rubio."

"Come inside." I helped her up and held her around her waist. "You can tell me the rest once we're in the house."

We settled into the kitchen, and I picked up a flask of brandy she kept on a shelf. I poured a bit into a mug and handed it to her. Ruffian ambled over to her and settled at her feet.

Marge drank it down quickly and inhaled sharply. "Imagine! He came right in through the gate. My heart sank, so I closed the door behind me. It was so odd. It's almost as though he was waiting for me."

"As long as you're all right, Marge," I said. "That's all that counts."

"I forgot my key. I usually keep it in my pocket. So silly of me. Downright dangerous. I was so afraid that he'd come inside the house."

"You did the right thing. You're safe." I paused. "Did he say anything?"

"Well, yes, he did," she said. "He told me to tell Rubio that he needed to give him what belonged to him and to keep out of his business."

"Mind his own business? I wonder what he meant by that." The peril that Marge might have been in suddenly took root. "He didn't touch you, did he?"

"No, dear, he didn't do anything to hurt me," Marge said. "But he didn't say that Rubio should mind his own business. What he said was that he should keep out of his business. Those are two very different statements."

I took a sweater off a wall hook. "Here, put this on. The last thing you need is to catch pneumonia."

"It wasn't that cold." Marge protested but willingly put on the sweater.

"What time did this happen? How long were you out there?"

Marge thought for a minute. "I had just finished watching *The People's Court,* so it had to be four o'clock."

I glanced at my watch. "It's four-thirty now. That means you were out there for a half hour! That's awful. Do you want some soup to warm you up?"

"No, the brandy did me just fine," Marge answered.

"The police," I said. "We need to call them."

"Oh, don't do that!" she answered vehemently. "Nothing really happened that needs to be reported. They'll chalk it up to an old lady who's going dotty."

"I don't agree, Marge."

"Of course, all the man did was ask for Rubio. He didn't touch a hair on my head. I'm the one who shut the door on myself. In fact, the police would probably suggest I get a different type of lock. One that won't automatically shut. They would be right, you know."

Aside from today's near fiasco, she was right. Marge was getting older, and sometimes I couldn't help but worry about some catastrophe happening. A little over a year ago, she had taken a spill on the stairs and fractured her hip. All I could do was hope for the best and not be in the wreckage of the future.

"Did you know his voice? If you heard it again, do you think you'd recognize it?"

"Plain. American. No accent. It all happened too quickly. I'll put my mind on rewind and see if I can come up with any more details, dear."

"If anyone can do it, you can, Marge," I said. "If you don't mind, I will at least call Rod. He needs to know."

"Oh, is he back from his trip?" she asked. "That's good news, isn't it, dear?"

"Yes, it is."

"I'm really okay, Daisy. Please go on upstairs. I'm planning to lock this door and not leave again for the rest of the evening. If *you* need anything, don't hesitate to come back downstairs."

I got up to leave, smiling inwardly. Marge was a trooper. She'd been the one in trouble, and here she was offering to help me. My decision not to tell her about the man who'd been standing outside for the last couple of evenings was solidified. I refused to frighten her any more with unnecessary information. I should contact Detective Harris. After all, it was for a situation such as this that I carried his card in my wallet. Instead, I called Rod and left a voice mail for him to return my call.

My apartment was dark, and I could practically hear the echoes of my footsteps across the parquet floor. I turned on the television in the kitchen and watched as Bette Davis malevolently teased Joan Crawford in *What Ever Happened to Baby Jane?* This movie would require a super-big bowl of popcorn. A commercial came on, and then the trailer showed that Audrey Hepburn in *Wait Until Dark* was next in the queue.

I nixed the popcorn. Instead, I pulled my basketful of tarot decks off the shelf. I closed my eyes and picked the *Rider-Waite* deck. It was easy and dependable for me.

I centered myself while Bette cackled in the background, and then I shuffled the cards. I fanned them out in front of me and chose the one that practically shouted, *Pick me, pick me.* I placed it face up on the desk.

The five of pentacles in reverse. The image was of two figures who were the epitome of poor. They were stooped and appeared cold and worn where they stood in front of a well-lit church. It reminded me of my childhood image of the *Little Match Girl.* While it could mean negativity, it probably meant that I was dealing with something that needed tending to in a different type of way. I couldn't help but think of Jose and Rubio. They were not in a good way. They seemed to be literally out in the cold. Marge had been left outside freezing because of Rubio. I realized that I hadn't set an intention. Maybe it was my parents that the card referred to. I had no idea. I was usually better at reading cards than this. Rubio being shot and Marge's ordeal were affecting me more than I realized.

Turning the card over in my hand, it occurred to me that I wasn't meditating as often as I had planned. After the last *misa*, spiritual séance, I'd meditated daily for about a week and then promptly lost my focus. For some reason, television called to me when I returned home after work or a meeting. I couldn't count the few minutes in *seiza*, posed in the kneeling position with my eyes closed, at the dojo as a true meditation. I replaced the card. If I wanted to have a well-lit spiritual life and not wish for one as I stood on the outside of my personal temple, I needed to meditate. *Me*. The card's message was for me. No one else.

I turned off Blanche Hudson twirling around in her wheelchair and Baby Jane's maniacal laughter. The box of candles were on the shelf with the basket of tarot decks. The box was almost full, although I'd bought the candles months earlier. I placed one of the candles in a holder and lit it. I knelt in *seiza* and allowed myself to become immersed in the stillness of the room.

I opened my eyes slightly and gazed at the flame atop the candle. The purple center drew me in and invited my third eye to open. Images started flickering like an old movie reel. The image of a man bending to tend to a small child quickly changed to a woman who looked into my eyes and began to sway and dance. Her skirt was made of a patchwork fabric. While I didn't know who the man or child was, I was almost certain that the woman was the gypsy spirit guide whom Hector had described to me. Everything was hazy, but I was able to discern her as a woman older than me. I felt she had a great deal to teach me.

The images stopped as I began thinking about Hector and the car accident. I stood up and touched my forefinger and thumb to my lips and wet them slightly. I pressed my fingers against the flame and heard the hiss as the fire went out. The room was completely dark. Time seemed to have run away from me. I knew that I should meditate more often. I had to think of it as defragmenting my personal computer — my brain. I said a short prayer and prepared for bed.

Chapter 6

Sophia Cornelius peered at me over her reading glasses. The black silk sheath she wore set off her necklace of double strands of hematite with a large garnet set in the middle. *Zaftig* was how my nurse friend, Allie, described her.

"Were you able to send those reports up to Mr. Donaldson?" she asked. "You know how nervous he gets if he has to wait for anything, Daisy."

"Yes, Sophia, I sent them to him last Wednesday," I said. Working with Sophia was a job that I was beyond grateful for, but her constant follow-up, as she liked to call it, was annoying. Being assistant to the Administrator was a treasured job, and I didn't want to lose it by showing her how I sometimes felt.

"Yes, of course, you did," Sophia said. "Don't mind me. He gets nervous, and then I get nervous."

My cell phone vibrated from my half-opened desk drawer. *Rod.* Finally getting back to me, a day too late. I ducked close to the desk to answer. Sophia was adamant about keeping one's business and personal lives separate during work hours. I understood that to a certain point. I was the common denominator in both areas, and sometimes it wasn't so easy to accomplish the division.

"Hey, I can't really talk now." I launched into the phone. "I thought I'd have already heard from you by now."

"Daisy, hold on," he said. "Are you sitting? I've got some hard news to tell you."

I was chilled by his tone. "Yes, I'm sitting." I suddenly didn't care that Sophia didn't want me to take personal phone calls.

"I'd rather be telling you this in person, but I need your help."

"Sure, just tell me," I said. "Go ahead."

"Okay." His calm was unnerving. "Rubio's body was found early this morning. He's dead."

I pushed my chair abruptly against the wall. There was silence at the other end of the line. Then I heard Rod's voice. It had a hollow ring to it. "Did you hear me?"

I nodded.

"Daisy, talk to me." His voice was plaintive. "Are you okay?"

"Yes." A sob caught in my throat. "Oh my God. I don't know what to say."

"Drink some water. Then tell your boss you have to leave, and I'll meet you in front of the emergency room."

"The ER?"

"I want you to go to the Medical Examiner's office. Jose will need your support. He's on his way there with Sam Harris."

I sobbed again.

"Can you do that? Are you up to it?"

"Yes."

"I'm outside waiting for you," he said.

"Okay." I hung up, picked up my handbag and tote, and went into Sophia's adjoining office.

"Sit down, Daisy," Sophia ordered. "You don't look well."

I sat as she had instructed me to do. I was treading water and about to sink. Fast.

Sophia stood up and poured me a glass of water from the carafe I'd filled for her earlier in the morning. "Here, drink this." She sat back down and waited as I gulped down the cool water.

"Are you ready to tell me what's going on?" Sophia put her reading glasses on but kept her eyes on me.

I nodded, ready to tell her the news, but my throat closed.

"Take a couple of deep breaths," she suggested.

Again, I followed her instructions, and this time I could feel a release in my throat muscles. I took one more deep breath and then began talking.

"It's Rubio," I blurted out. "He was found dead."

The only clue that Sophia had heard the news was the tightening of her lips. Eventually, she asked, "How did you find out about this? That phone call?"

"Yes," I said.

"You must be on your way to see Jose, I presume?"

"Rod was the one who called. He's picking me up so I can meet Jose at the Medical Examiner's office."

Sophia nodded and stood up again. She led me to the door. "If you need to take a day or two, I have no problem with that. Just call me to let me know."

"I will." I nodded.

As rule oriented as Sophia portrayed herself to be, she had been sympathetic to me in the past, and she was again today. She opened her arms to give me a hug. We parted, and I left.

Rod stood outside next to a silver sedan and opened the door on the passenger side for me. I slipped into the car and leaned back against the upholstered seat. He closed the door and walked around the car and sat next to me.

"Are you sure that you can handle this?" he asked. "I'm sorry to put you on the spot, but if there's anyone Jose would want to see, it's you."

My unanswered calls to Jose flooded my thoughts. "I'm not too sure about that. He's been avoiding me. I left him a couple of messages. Oh, Rod, things have been strained with all of us. I don't know if they were even talking."

Rod interrupted me. "Do you want details?"

"You mean, how he was murdered?"

"Well, *that* we don't know for sure yet," Rod said. "An autopsy will have to be done."

Somehow, I felt like I knew this already. "Was it the same person who killed Charley Sprague?"

He shook his head. "We don't have those answers yet. He was found in Red Hook."

"Red Hook? What was he doing there? When? Who found him?" The more questions I asked, the more tumbled into my head.

"He was found early this morning by a security guard."

"But where was he?" I asked.

"His body was found on the wharf, at the waterfront. The foreperson from the clock factory a couple of doors down opens about four each morning. Apparently, a streetlamp was out, and she felt something wasn't right. She contacted Security, and they found him near the railing overlooking the water."

"You're going to have to walk me through this before I see Jose," I said. "A streetlight being out can happen, so why would she suspect anything was wrong? It doesn't make much sense to me."

"I had the same thought. There's a lot to be clarified. According to this person, the community board had approved a proposal to get old-fashioned streetlamps. You know, the fancy black ones. It seems that they recently got rid of the standard city lights."

"That would make it easier to bust a light bulb, wouldn't it?" I asked. "They're lower to the ground, aren't they?"

"True. The other detail is that there were no surveillance cameras operating at the time. The electricians had just finished one job and hadn't completed the whole scope of the project. The cameras were disconnected."

"Oh no!" My insides were crumbling. "Are you serious?"

"I know." Rod was gentle. "It's a freak thing. Random."

"Random?" I was taken aback. "That's the last word I'd use to describe what happened here."

"We're looking at everything," Rod said. "Harris and Munroe are officially on it. I can't be since it would be a conflict of interest. Just know that I'm going to do whatever I can, albeit unofficially. This is top priority."

"Does Jose know everything you just told me?"

"Yes. We told him everything we could when we broke the news to him earlier," he said. "Let's go. Jose might be there already."

I thought of my cab ride with Jose just a couple of evenings earlier. The Medical Examiner's office was at that same huge metropolis of a hospital, Sovereign. That would be hard for Jose. One of the last times we were all together was at that hospital. I stifled a sob that turned into a series of hiccups. I tried holding my breath to stop them but couldn't.

"Did you drink any water?" he asked. "Do you want something to help stop those hiccups?"

I stifled another one. "I saw him yesterday. I called you to tell you that Marge was outside. Freezing. But you didn't call me back."

"Whoa, hold on there," he said. "What are you talking about?"

Rod checked his phone and nodded. "I didn't get a chance to listen to this. I'm sorry. I was meeting with Liz, and I let the call go to voicemail. By the time I remembered, it was after midnight. I didn't want to wake you up."

I turned to the window. I felt the tears coming but didn't want him to see me cry.

"It's all right." My words sounded robotic, even to my ears. "Mercury is in retrograde."

"I wanted to call you back," he said. "So much has happened since then that I forgot—until now."

"Let's just forget it, okay?" I said. "We have to think about Jose. How did they know it was Rubio? He wasn't in the water, was he?"

"No, he was on the wharf, not in the water," Rod said. "He had his wallet in his pocket. ID. A couple of dollars."

"It couldn't have been another robbery attempt, could it?" I asked. "What about his phone?"

"That was near him, but it was smashed," Rod said "You say that you saw him yesterday? When?"

"Sometime during the late afternoon. He'd left the hospital early, against medical advice. I'm sure Jose will tell you that, if he hasn't already. I saw him on Fifth. I was window shopping. He basically told me to leave him alone. Not to worry. That I should focus on Jose instead."

Rod sighed deeply. "Can you remember whether he was carrying anything? A bag or something?"

"Not really. He was wearing the arm immobilizer. I think he might have been carrying something else. I'm not sure. It was all so awkward. He didn't want to talk with me. He said he had a meeting. I got the vibe that he wanted me to stay out of his business. And then, that thing happened with Marge. That took priority at the time."

"I need to take some of this down, Daisy. I'm not questioning you, but you were probably one of the last people to see him. Now tell me what happened to Marge."

"When I got home from the dojo, after speaking to Rubio, I found Marge outside sitting on the stoop. She was trembling, Rod."

"Had she been assaulted?"

"No," I said. "She'd gone outside to throw out the garbage and some guy scared her. Marge said she slammed the door behind her so he wouldn't get into the house. Ruffian was inside. There I was sauntering home. If I'd stayed out any later, who knows what might have happened to her."

"I wonder if it was that guy who was sitting in front of the house."

"That hadn't occurred to me, since he asked for Rubio," I said.

"Hey, did you get any photos of him?"

"No." I swallowed hard. "He hadn't come back."

"We need a statement from Marge." Rod wore an expression of concern. "It's no coincidence that Rubio is killed, and some guy accosts Marge. You all live at the same address."

"What do I tell Jose?" I asked. "Should he know about this?"

"Just sit tight and be his friend. That's all he needs at this point."

Rod swung out into traffic, and I sat tight just as he suggested.

We walked away from the mortuary. Jose had just identified Rubio from a photo that had been taken of him. It was ghastly, but maybe it had spared Jose some torment.

"A picture," Jose said quietly.

"I know." There wasn't much else to say.

"I want to see him." Jose was dressed in his whites. He had such faith in the religion's traditions.

"You'll see him at the funeral parlor," I volunteered.

"I have to call his mother. God, I got all caught up with being angry with him when he checked out of the hospital. What a waste."

"Don't be so hard on yourself," I said. "That was a normal reaction. It wasn't the best idea for him to leave. He probably didn't even finish the antibiotics that the doctor said she was going to order."

Jose's jaw throbbed. "I'll never forgive myself. I acted like an ass. He said he could take care of himself, but I kept at him. Worst of all, at the end of his life, I wasn't even talking to him."

"You were right, though," I said. "He couldn't take care of himself, could he?"

Jose inclined his head slightly and walked up a little ahead of me. He turned back. "I'm going to walk home. I need to be alone."

"I'm sorry," I said. "I shouldn't have said that."

"It's true." He shrugged. "He couldn't, could he? I'll see you later, okay?"

I nodded and lagged back. I'd get a cab home.

Despite my best thinking, at three that afternoon I was sitting in the front row at the Teaching with Clarity meeting of alcoholics. These meetings had been originally set up by a core group of neighborhood teachers who'd been off the sauce. They had found that spending their days with young children had resulted in their craving a liter of wine at the end of the school day. The meetings now included other professionals and business owners who took their lunch at a later hour so as not to miss a meeting. The stress of tending to their customers during the busy lunch hour was tempered by an hour of quiet, sober camaraderie.

I could barely pay attention to the speaker, who owned a paper shop. The feasibility of owning a store that sold a multitude of paper products seemed unbelievable. The speaker said she owed her success to the clarity she now faced life with after losing almost everything to margaritas. I knew her face from other meetings and focused on it. Familiar, yet not heavy with relationship. Rubio's features seemed to merge with hers. I couldn't get him out of my mind.

The speaker chose to make her qualification a drunk-a-log.

That was fine. I couldn't pay much attention anyway. I had done the same when I first came into the program. Tasting my parents' wine coolers had eventually led to a taste for daily vodka. My freezer had been stocked with Mason jars filled with the icy drink. It had become a major component of the blood in my veins. Even Lou had made wisecracks, asking when the last time was that I defrosted a chicken or hamburger meat instead of my favorite beverage.

I found myself raising my hand. The speaker never called on me, although I was sitting right in front of her. Instead, she seemed to choose every other individual in the room. At the end of the meeting she suggested that those she hadn't called on could speak to her or someone else after the meeting. I quickly left when the circle of people disbanded.

"Daisy!" I turned to see Ryan, a guy who was fairly new to the program. He seemed uncertain and had his hands jammed into his pockets.

"Hey, Ryan," I said. "I'm on my way. Sorry I can't—"

He interrupted me. "No worries. I get it. I'm just wondering about Rubio. I haven't heard from him. I know you guys are friends."

I stood there wondering how much to tell him. I wasn't ready to start sharing the news about him in the rooms.

Ryan started up again. "I guess I can tell you. He's my sponsor."

My belly flipped.

"I probably shouldn't say anything," he said. "But you know how they tell you that you're as sick as your secrets?"

I nodded and waited for him to go on. The more he talked, the less I had to say.

"I'm just gonna say this because I don't want to go out and get drunk on this. I heard that he relapsed."

That piece of news was more shocking than the fact that he'd been murdered. It was way too much for me to absorb right now.

"I'm sure you can find someone else to talk to," I said. "Make sure you do." I hurried past him out into the late afternoon sunlight.

I'd just broken the cardinal purpose of the program. The objective was to stay sober and help another alcoholic to achieve sobriety. Ryan might be headed for a scotch and soda. I might be headed for a vodka on ice.

Instead, I followed my feet and returned home. I climbed the stairs and crept underneath my comforter. I kept the apartment door open in hopes that Ms. G would follow suit. I hated being alone.

Chapter 7

It was twilight. I'd slept most of the afternoon away. Ms. G must have done the same. I watched as her rump leapt off the bed, most likely in search of her dinner. The events of the day came flooding back. I'd often heard people say that they'd never left a meeting feeling worse than when they entered. That had not been my experience today.

After I freshened up, I knocked on Jose's door. He opened it immediately and stepped aside for me to enter. Rod was sitting on the couch with Detective Harris. The papers and debris had been cleaned up. The living room looked closer to the way the boys usually maintained it.

I kissed Jose on the cheek. "I see you had time to clean up," I observed.

"Clean up?" Jose scoffed. "Are you kidding? When?"

I ignored his comment and especially his tone. He was obviously still peeved at me.

Rod stood up. "Daisy, you've already met Detective Harris, haven't you?"

Detective Harris answered before I had a chance to open my mouth. "Yes, at the hospital a couple of days ago. I'm glad you're here, Ms. Muñiz. May I ask you a few questions?"

"Sure," I said. "But I've already told Rod everything I know."

"I wasn't there, though, and I'm the detective on this case."

"Gotcha." I sighed. They'd make me repeat everything. It was tiresome, but I'd do anything to find out who murdered my friend.

"When was the last time you saw Rubio?" Detective Harris asked.

"Yesterday. Wow, that seems so long ago." I shook my head.

"I spoke with Rubio on Fifth." I continued. "He really didn't say much. He told me to take care of Jose."

The room suddenly seemed to darken. It appeared tinged with blue, and, although I didn't see the color, I felt it. It was as though Rubio were standing there with us. He was. I was sure of it.

"Can you feel him?" I asked.

Jose covered his face with his hands for a moment and nodded.

"He says that he's going to help us find the murderer." The words slipped from my lips.

Rod looked a bit flustered, and Sam Harris squirmed in his seat. Neither said anything.

Jose rubbed his eyes. "Make no mistake. We will find whoever did this. This is not going to go unresolved. I promise."

The ceiling light in the adjacent kitchen began to flicker. "Would someone get me a piece of paper?" I asked.

Harris pulled his notepad and pen out of his jacket pocket and handed it to me.

I was compelled to draw. An illustration began to emerge on the small sheet. A map of some sort. The land was surrounded by the ocean.

Jose wept. I drew an anchor in the body of water. A shaky sketch of a fortress-like building. Lastly, I penned a car. The light in the kitchen went out, and I put the pen down.

"That's it," I said. "Maybe more will come later. For now, this is enough." I was certain of this.

Detective Harris cleared his throat. "Land and water."

"That must be the wharf," Jose said. "He's showing us where he was murdered."

"We could compare this to a map of the area," Rod said. "Otherwise, we can't really be sure that this is what he meant. If that's really what happened here."

"You're such a Doubting Thomas, Rod." I was so disappointed. "Of course Rubio would speak to us through pictures. But, sure, we can do that. We can check whatever maps you'd like."

A moment later, everyone was startled when the light in the kitchen brightened again.

Rod spoke. "There's been a man lurking near the park across the street, and I think he may be the one who accosted Marge yesterday."

Detective Harris's ears seemed to perk up. "That I didn't know."

"He warned her that Rubio needed to stay out of the business. This may have to do with the Montoyas."

Harris took a deep breath. "Could be. But it's possible that it doesn't. That statement could pertain to a lot of things that we're not aware of yet."

"There's a lot of that, isn't there?" I turned to Jose. "Isn't that *Irosun*? You told me about that. *No one knows what's at the bottom of the sea.*"

"Come on, Daisy, this isn't all about magic and spirits." Rod grimaced. "There's a time and a place for everything, and this isn't it."

"That's unfair," I said. "I know some things. Everything has meaning to it."

Jose finally chimed in. "She's right. That saying means a lot to me. It's something that I heed. And whether you believe in it or not, this is how I operate. Rubio didn't follow the tradition as closely as I do, but I believe that his spirit was just here and that the drawing is important. Daisy, thank you."

"Daisy," Detective Harris began. "Do you know what Mr. Rubio, I mean, Rubio, was carrying with him that last time you saw him?"

"Not really. I think he was carrying some kind of bag. It's hard to remember. He didn't hang around for very long."

"Jose, have you noticed anything missing?" Harris asked.

"No, I don't think so." Jose gazed around the apartment.

"How is it so clean?" I tried a different way to broach the topic. "No offense, but when I was here the other day, it was a mess."

"Rubio must have cleaned it," Jose said.

I was getting frustrated. "Jose, he just had surgery. He was in that immobilizer. I doubt he could tidy the place up."

"Well, I don't know."

"How could you not be sure?" I asked. "This is major."

Jose flushed. "I wasn't here."

"What are you talking about?"

"We were arguing. I had lots of work to do, and I didn't want to continue fighting. I was angry at him for leaving the hospital against medical advice, but I didn't want to keep at it. I went to work."

I remembered being surprised that Rubio had answered the door. I had expected Jose to be around and tried calling him. Come to think of it, he hadn't answered any of my calls.

"That's how it is in relationships sometimes," I said.

"Would you mind coming down to the station tomorrow so we can get a formal statement from you, Daisy?" Detective Harris asked. "I'd like you to look at some photos and see if you can identify the guy who may be stalking the house."

"Sure. I'll be there first thing in the morning." I wanted the evening to end.

Rod left with Harris. He didn't give me any special goodbye. There was no reason to expect that anyway. We still had lots of talking to do.

I sat next to Jose. "Can I ask you something without your getting mad at me?"

"Go ahead," he said, "but I can't promise I'll answer the question."

"Had Rubio relapsed?"

"Is that really important at this point, Daisy?" Jose asked. "My boyfriend is dead, and all you can think about is whether he was using?"

"I went to a meeting earlier, and some guy walked up to me. He said his name was Ryan and that he was Rubio's sponsee."

"And?" Jose's eyebrow began to twitch.

"He said that he was concerned about Rubio because he hadn't been calling him back, and then he said that he was worried that Rubio had relapsed."

"What ever happened to, *What you hear here, please leave it here*? So much for anonymity." Jose stood up.

"Oh sit down," I ordered. "Ryan cared about Rubio. That's why he asked me. There was no other reason."

"I don't feel like sitting. Let's talk about this another time, okay?" Jose said. "It's been a long day. Are you going to work tomorrow?"

"Yes, but I have to get down to the station first and do what Harris asked."

"I have to go call Rubio's family. I'll see you tomorrow." Jose swung open the door. As I left the apartment, he said, "I'm not mad."

"I know." I gave him a quick hug and returned to my apartment. It was the perfect time to immerse myself in an old movie. *Splendor in the Grass* had just started. Natalie Wood had just jumped out of the tub. Her naked torso and mother's shame reminded me of my own mother's brand of crazy. I could watch that movie repeatedly and had. As I sat in front of the TV, I couldn't hold back my tears.

This wasn't the first time sleep had done nothing to refresh me. The clock said nine, and my body rebelled at getting up. I stumbled out of bed and made a fresh pot of coffee. I hurried to get ready. The interrogation at the precinct would probably be a repeat performance of the previous night.

I had my hand up, ready to knock on Jose's door, when he opened it. Again, dressed in his whites. I looked down. I was in gray pants and a deep claret sweater. I wanted to be as neutral as I possibly could today.

"Where are you off to?" I asked.

"I have to settle some things at work."

"I think they'd understand if you stayed home today." Again, I was walking on eggshells.

"I want to close up a project. Then I can have some peace of mind as I plan whatever it is that needs to be done."

"Were you able to get Rubio's parents last night?"

"Yes. His mom," he said. "They want him buried in Colombia."

Inwardly, I fumed. "What? But he lived here with you for years. You're his next of kin."

"I'm his partner," he said. "She's his mother. They want him to be buried in the family plot."

"In Colombia? How are you going to visit him?"

"Earth to Daisy. Would you please stop with this whole thing? I won't be visiting him. I'd be leaving flowers on the ground once a year if he were buried up here."

"Did you talk to them about it, though?"

"The phone call was hard enough. His mother was screaming so loudly that I thought she'd have a heart attack.

Luckily, his sister was there, and she managed to calm her down. They know that an autopsy has to be performed before they release Rubio's body."

"What did his father say?"

Jose shrugged. "Nothing. He wasn't there. The sister said he's in California."

I sighed. "I'm sorry."

Jose looked at me with his sad eyes. I needed to stop asking so many pointless questions.

"Hey," I said. "Do you want to walk over to a meeting this morning? I think there's a ten o'clock at St. John's."

"No, I can't. I really do have to close up shop. You go."

"I can hold off getting to the precinct." I paused. "I'll go afterwards."

"Do me a favor and make a meeting, Daisy, okay?" he said. "I can't have you relapsing."

"That's not going to happen." I was more concerned that Jose would relapse with all the stress he was under. Maybe I needed an Al-Anon meeting.

"That's exactly what Rubio said when I saw he wasn't getting to the *Midday* meeting anymore. He always had some excuse."

"Are you ready to talk about that?" I asked. Ms. G crept up the stairs toward us and purred loudly against my leg.

"A classic story of boy doesn't go to meetings, boy forgets he can't drink, and boy takes a drink."

"Alcohol, huh? I wondered about that."

"Well, the truth is that he had that drink. More than one. Wine. Champagne. They drink at those art events. You've been to one, haven't you?"

I turned beet red. I'd acted like an ass at Rubio's first gallery showing on Atlantic Avenue a couple of years earlier. I had swayed to the background music as if I were at a calypso show in the Caribbean. Letty had begged me to put down the glass, and I refused. I ended up in bed that night with Skyler from work. I wished I'd never gone to that opening. A blackout would have spared me the memory.

I nodded, at a loss for words.

"Alcohol, and, the next thing I knew, Rubio was snorting again. He always said he wasn't a drunk, but obviously alcohol was the precursor to the drugs." Jose's eyes filled with tears. "He made it back, though, and I'm glad he was sober at the end. He even had sponsees. I'm proud of him."

"Me too," I said.

"I've got to go. I'll call you when I get back. Maybe you can be with me when I call Hector. He has to set up the ceremony for Rubio."

"You might want to sit down, Jose," I said. "I spoke to Letty about Hector."

"Is he still out of town?"

"I'm sorry. I couldn't reach you," I said. "Hector was in a really bad car accident. Letty flew down with Mike and the kids, as far as I know."

Jose sat on the staircase. Stunned. "Hector? What the hell? Why didn't anyone tell me? Is he all right?"

"He has some pretty extensive injuries. He's going to have surgery for a bleeding spleen. I think it's going to be a while before he's well enough to travel back up here."

Jose was downcast. "I don't know what to do. Rubio needs him up here. I need him."

"Talk to Ana. She'll do something. I know it."

"Ana? She's a woman. I need an *oriaté*. A male priest who can officiate."

The only reason that Ana wasn't an *oriaté*, a high priest, was because she was a woman. Men monopolized the religion. Still, she'd know where Jose could turn for help.

"I'll try to connect with her this afternoon," I said, "and work something out."

"Okay. See you later."

I walked down the two flights, and he followed behind me. We separated in front of the house. Things would go so much better with us if we were heading in the same direction.

Chapter 8

The precinct waiting area was bustling. I tried to be patient and forced my legs to stop bobbing up and down as I sat on the uncomfortable wooden bench. The woman at the desk finally signaled for me to go into the detectives' office.

I sat in front of Detective Liz Munroe, who looked close to perfection as always. Her sleek blond hair was pulled back in a chignon, and her ruby red lipstick shone as if she had just applied it. As usual, her suit was sophisticated and stylish. This one was marine blue, which matched her eyes.

"Daisy?" Liz asked. "Did you hear me?"

"Yes, of course," I lied. "Wasn't Detective Harris going to be here this morning? I thought he was going to ask questions and show me some photos."

"He'll be in later." Liz's left eyebrow lifted sharply. "Why would you be looking at photos?"

"There's a guy who's been hanging out on a bench across the street at the playground. Rod and Detective Harris think that maybe he is the one who killed Rubio especially after what he did to Marge yesterday."

"Marge? How is she involved?"

I paused. I had repeated the story one too many times. "Didn't Rod say anything to you about it?"

The detective tapped her desk with a sharpened No. 2 pencil. Its staccato rhythm reverberated across the surface to me.

"That man is either stalking one of us or the house. He sits there without doing anything but looking up at us."

"What would you expect him to be doing?" If a pencil could tap out the word E-X-A-S-P-E-R-A-T-E-D, that one did.

"Let's face it. Most people are buying drugs, hustling, looking for a comfortable bench to stretch out on, but this guy just sits. Doesn't even look at his phone or read a book. I felt a strange vibe from him, so I stopped standing in front of my window."

"Vibe, huh?" Liz's reaction was hard to gauge.

"Yes, vibe," I echoed. "You know that Park Slope citizens don't put the welcome mat out for loiterers. You might as well forget about the homeless. That shelter on Eighth Avenue—not popular, believe me."

"That may be true, but there will always be unfamiliar people sitting at playgrounds by themselves. It may be unfortunate, but there really isn't anything we can do about that."

"This is exactly why I didn't want to say anything and why Marge didn't want to report the guy when he walked right up to her while she was throwing out the trash."

"Did he say anything to Mrs. Talbot?"

"Ms. Talbot," I corrected. "The message was basically a warning to Rubio to keep his nose out of his business."

Liz considered this before speaking. "He didn't happen to mention what type of business he was referring to, did he?"

"I think there are two businesses going on. One is the art gallery Rubio might have been in the process of leasing. The other is the Montoya family business. Crime, drugs, take your pick."

"Did you call an ambulance for her, Daisy?"

"No, I didn't," I admitted. "She'd already said she didn't want the police to be involved. I didn't press her. You know how independent she is."

"Yes, I do."

Instead of tapping, Liz began drumming her nails against the wooden desk. There were ink doodles on the paper calendar that was perched on it. She might have been nervous too. Like me.

"I'm sorry about your loss," Liz said. "I know you two were good friends."

"Thank you," I said.

That statement came totally out of the blue. I waited for a barrage of questions, but they didn't come. She sat there quietly this time with her hands folded on her lap.

"Go ahead," I said. "I'm ready."

"I've been thinking about this," she said. "You two knew each other for years."

"We've all been friends since high school."

"I also know that you often *know* things. You were helpful during the Campbell case. A little unorthodox but still helpful."

I couldn't believe my ears. Acknowledgment from the grand detective herself.

"Think, Daisy, or do whatever it is that you do. I want to know what some of the connections are from your perspective. You led us right to Dr. Campbell's murderer."

"Last night we were going over the events, and I got an incredible urge to draw a map of land that was surrounded by a body of water. I'm not sure about the locality of the water, but of course I'm thinking of Red Hook, the Gowanus."

Liz gazed into the distance before responding. "Did you bring the map with you?"

I had dropped it into my bag before leaving the house. I fished it out and handed it to her. She gingerly unfolded it and placed it face up on the desk.

"You think it's dumb, don't you?" I uttered before I could stop myself.

Liz ignored me while she logged in to her computer and

pulled up a website that offered maps. "Come around the desk. Look at these."

"This is exactly where Rubio's body was found," she said. "These box-like structures are buildings. They're built like fortresses. Here's the clock factory, the stained glass showroom, and the bakery. This one here is a welding company, mostly decorative."

"Great." I couldn't help but feel disappointed. I returned to my seat. "Last night I had the hunch that what I supposedly channeled was fantastic news for the case."

"As far as I know, you haven't been there before, have you?"

"Well, Rod did describe some of the businesses in the area to me before this. So, yes, I knew."

"You had the information, but you weren't there. By all rights, you shouldn't really have been able to draw a picture of the site."

"Small consolation," I said. "But what about the car? That doesn't fit the river motif."

"True." Liz nodded.

I turned my attention away from her and looked through the glass partition to the next room. Rod was inside talking to someone who was seated at a large corporate desk.

"He's talking to the captain," Liz volunteered.

"I didn't realize he was here," I said.

"Can we get back to Rubio?"

"Sure," I said. "I went to visit him the day before he was found. The house was in disarray. That's another thing. When I went there last night, it was the complete opposite. It was neat again, the way it usually is."

"What do you think about that?" Liz scribbled on the desk calendar.

"I don't know that it means anything, but how does a person who has his arm in an immobilizer clean the house? There were papers all around."

"What type of papers? Newspapers?"

"No, pages. Documents of some sort. Maybe blueprints," I said. "But that's not unusual if he was in the process of leasing the gallery. Or buying. It's confusing."

Liz's eyebrow lifted. "Buy on Atlantic Avenue?"

Sadness enveloped me. "I guess that he's not buying or leasing anything at this point. I'm just speculating. I don't really know anything about it at all."

"Can you tell me anything else you may have observed about the apartment when you were there?"

I paused. "It was dark. They have heavy curtains, drapes, but they're always open. I think it's more for the décor than for privacy or lighting."

"The drapes were drawn?"

I nodded. The drapes were drawn was a phrase I'd never think to use. It sounded like something I'd hear someone say on a daytime soap opera.

"Did he mention anything to you about what he was doing? Regarding business with anyone? Did he talk about the leasing?"

"No. He couldn't wait for me to leave."

"What were you doing there? Had he or Jose invited you down?"

"I'd received a call from our friend, Letty. She called to tell me that her brother had been in a car accident in Florida. She wanted me to connect with them. It was all emotional, you know."

"I take it that this was a close friend," she said.

"Jose's godfather. Hector. Hector is usually the support system, but now I don't even know how he's doing."

I rubbed my eyes. Things were going way too fast and slow, simultaneously. I was supposed to call Ana. Or was it Jose who was going to call Ana?

"Look, do you mind if I text Jose? I don't remember if he asked me to do a favor for him."

"Sure, but would you mind taking it outside?" she asked. "In fact, we should finish this up later."

"But wait, I was supposed to look at some photos to see if I could identify the stalker," I said. "I don't know if someone in particular has to help me do that. Can you?"

"I'm sorry, Daisy, I don't mean to put you off," she said. "I know you came down here for that, but Sam isn't here yet. I'll let him know you were here when he comes in later."

Liz's eyes were riveted on the other room. She stood up and walked toward the partition. She must have been summoned.

I walked outside and texted Jose. I waited a few minutes. His new habit of ignoring me, along with Liz's brush-off, were worse than annoying; it felt unsafe. I was about to call Letty but decided against it. She was busy. I looked at my watch. Eleven o'clock. I had enough time to get to the Midday Two-for-One meeting. I wanted a drink but needed a meeting. It would take me almost an hour to get there. I headed in that direction.

"Hey, hold up! What's the rush?" I turned around to see Greg, one of the meeting regulars. This *was* Park Slope. Program meetings outnumbered the pubs. Everywhere you turned, another sober person showed up.

"*Midday*," I said. "You?"

"Nah, not today." There was a bit of a blush under his cinnamon-hued complexion.

"Oh." I stopped short. "Where you off to?"

"Lunch. Want to come?"

I looked at my watch again. "It's not even noon."

"But your belly! What does your belly say?" Greg's close-cropped 'fro was seventies conservative, but his hazel eyes were mischievous. I'd heard his qualification in the rooms.

Haitian-born, Greg had come to New York with his parents when he was three years old. The cultural differences between his home and the real world as he shared it at meetings were drastic. His dad was alcoholic, and Greg had vowed never to drink like him. He came into the program when he realized he had become his father.

"My belly says, hmm, I don't know."

"Just ask it, and it will talk. Listen." His broad grin was the brightest thing I had experienced in the last forty-eight hours.

"My belly says I'm starving."

Greg looped his arm through mine. "My treat. Let's go over to that Turkish place. What do you say?"

The glee in his demeanor was infectious. "I say yes!"

"Did you know that I live right around the corner on Twentieth?"

"Why don't you show me your place?" I said.

"Sure thing!" Greg pulled me closer to him as we turned the corner.

Two hours later I turned over to see Greg sleeping with his arm over his eyes to block out the light. I sat up and quietly moved to get out of bed.

"Wait," he said. "I promised I'd treat you to lunch."

"Lunch?"

"You are hungry, aren't you? We can still get lunch. Think of this as an appetizer."

I laughed, despite my mixed emotions. "If this is the appetizer, I can imagine what the meal will be."

Greg pulled me back toward him and kissed my neck lightly. "We can have tapas now. If you think about it, we missed lunch."

I gathered the blanket to me. "I hadn't planned this at all."

"And?" he asked. *"We will not regret the past nor wish to shut the door on it."*

There was suddenly a sour pit filling my otherwise empty belly. Using the AA Promises for something like this just didn't feel right. I changed the subject. "Who's your decorator? You've got some great art here."

"What I will tell you is that some of this art is mine, and some I've picked up from home."

"Where, in Haiti?" I asked. "I don't really know anything about Haiti."

"Port-au-Prince," he said. "But that was a long time ago. Too much strife. You know."

His tone had become serious. I often thought my life was about strife during my early years, but it probably couldn't compare. The perils of comparing and despairing came to mind.

"Which is yours?"

"My what?" he asked.

"Your art? Didn't you just tell me that some of this art around here is yours? Which?"

The walls were laden with ceremonial and ancestral masks. On one wall there was a shelf holding carved wooden statues. Each piece had to be a one-of-a-kind creation.

"Art is a personal enterprise." This time his laughter was annoying. Rubio's art had been something he shared with everyone.

"And sometimes it's not," I interrupted. "I have to go."

"Already? You just got here. I have food in the fridge. If you don't want tapas, I'll make you a real lunch with real food."

I looked down at my body hidden under the blanket. *What had I been thinking?*

His eyes followed mine, and he laughed again. "You girls make everything so complicated."

Greg pretended to push me out of bed. "You can take a shower. I'll wait here. Just in case you're shy."

"Thanks." I wrapped the blanket around me more closely and jumped up for a quick shower. "Where's the bathroom?"

Greg walked over to his closet and pulled out a fluffy towel. He handed it to me. I held it to my nose, and it smelled fresh. I wondered why I felt such relief about that. He pointed me in the direction of the bathroom.

A few minutes later I was out of the unfamiliar bathroom with the towel covering my torso tightly.

"My turn," he said. "I'll be right out."

I gathered my clothes and dressed as quickly as possible. I checked my cell phone. No one had called. I took a deep breath. *Just concentrate on lunch, Daisy*, I told myself.

Our eyes met over chicken wraps. These were not my favorites, but I was famished. The menu choices were different than the usual fare, like the rest of the afternoon had been. I pulled the red peppers out of the wrap and stacked them on my plate.

Greg eyed the pile. "That is not attractive."

"Neither am I after eating a load of peppers," I said. "Belly bloat."

"No more details, okay?" He laughed jovially.

"I think this was a mistake," I said.

"I do too." He nodded. "You can order tuna or something like that."

"I don't mean that," I said. "I mean, you know."

"Nah, there are no mistakes in life," he said. "We do things because we want to. I don't believe in explaining an action away just because it's hard to face your motives."

My cheeks stung with that statement.

He laughed again, but kindly this time. "Relax, girl. Nobody's going to know what happened unless you tell them. Me? I'm copacetic. Life is good. I've got a place to live. A job.

I'm sober for today. I spent some time with a beautiful woman. I'm not into creating complications where none exist. Got me?"

Greg's voice had turned soft.

"I'd like to think like that too."

"The *Big Book* talks about, 'Trudging the path of happy destiny.' Why trudge, Daisy? Why not hop and skip? It's a choice."

My phone started to vibrate. My hand went automatically toward it, but I hesitated before turning it over.

"Go ahead, I'm good." Greg turned slightly to look out the restaurant window.

I flipped the phone over. Rod. I turned it back over.

"I can take this later," I said. "They can leave a message."

We settled in to eat our wraps. What was my true motive? Was I still angry at Rod for not telling me the reason he had gone to Chicago?

George took a swig from his ginger beer. "Don't be so hard on yourself. You missed a meeting. So what? What would you have shared if you'd gone?"

"Oh, I never play this game," I said.

"It's not a game. It's about one alcoholic helping another. I'm here to help." When he smiled, it reached his eyes.

"Okay. My friend was just killed. I think he relapsed and got into some kind of criminal activity. My best friend is not talking to me. Granted, it was his partner who was murdered. Some man might be stalking me. Not to mention that my godfather was in a terrible accident." I decided against mentioning the part where I spent the afternoon in bed with an almost total stranger and that the man I wanted to think of as my boyfriend had just left a message on my phone.

"Girl, sounds like you need a witch doctor to give you a good cleansing."

"Funny, but remember that if this is a real meeting, no crosstalk or advice should be given on shares, Greg."

"You're right," he said. "I forgot that this is a real meeting.

Sorry about that."

Greg called the waitperson over for the dessert menu. I watched his hands as he mulled over the sweet options. He'd never told me which of the pieces of art at his apartment were his.

"What do you do?" I asked. "It's funny how I know some pretty detailed pieces of your life but have no idea what you do for a living."

Greg laughed easily. Before this afternoon, I'd had no idea that he had a knack for laughter. At some point I realized that I had a knack for smirking, but this time I couldn't help but laugh too.

"Well, what?" I asked again. "Sculpt. You must sculpt with those hands."

"Sculpt?" He shook his head. "Nah, guess again."

"I don't know. Maybe you're a pianist."

"Closer, but no. I play the sax. I teach part-time afternoons and some evenings. This way I can get to sets late at night."

"I get it. That's why you're home now. At three in the afternoon." This time I exploded with laughter. "I thought you were unemployed, and that's why you go to the *Midday* meeting."

"Oh, that hurts," he said.

"I didn't see your sax back in the apartment," I said. "Where was it?"

"It was there. You were just concentrating on other things," he said. "How about some baklava?"

"No, thanks," I said. "I should be heading back home. Somebody might be trying to reach me."

He looked pointedly at my phone. "Sure, whatever you say."

Greg ultimately insisted on paying the check, and we stopped for a moment on the avenue. Seventh Avenue was always a busy shopping location. I stood there a bit uneasy.

"Mind if I break this uncomfortable silence?" he asked. "Can I call you?"

"Uh, yeah, that would be good," I said. We hadn't exchanged phone numbers during any of the meetings we'd both attended. The saying, "men stick with the men and women with the women" was meant to avoid what had just happened.

Greg pulled a card out of the pocket of his jacket and gave it to me. He almost dropped it but caught it immediately.

"Don't let this be the thing that gets away," he said. "I like you, Daisy."

I nodded and took the card. We separated at the corner. My phone vibrated again. I held the card in my hand with the phone. A gust of wind almost swept the card out of my hand. *Oya. The winds of change*, I thought, as I hurried away from my afternoon.

Chapter 9

The tiny television on the kitchen counter droned on in the background. I sat at the old-fashioned Formica table near the window. The day was overcast, and the nearby tree branches moved with the breeze. I still hadn't listened to Rod's messages. My hand moved toward the phone, but I caught myself and, instead, took the silver spoon and stirred the tea. The fragrant lemon aroma was comforting.

After a couple of sips, I pressed the voicemail icon and listened. "Hi, Daisy. We need to talk about a few things. I owe you an apology and a truthful explanation about what the Chicago trip was about. I'd like to see you but, in the meantime, be careful around the house. We might know the identity of the guy who's been hanging out there. Give me a call when you get this message."

I didn't want to talk to him just yet. Not after what I'd done this afternoon. I got up and turned the television off. I put a heavy cable-knit sweater on with my jacket over it and went back out. There was something that needed to be done.

The Uber left me at the corner of Lorraine and Clinton. I walked the rest of the way. By walking this route, it was possible I would discover something about Rubio's last moments. Maybe he would show me something. The air was chilled and matched the way I was feeling about myself.

I walked past the projects and people hurrying by with strollers and shopping carts as they tended to the business of their lives. As I walked farther, I noted there were less populated areas filled with factories. Several empty industrial buildings had "For Sale or Lease" signs plastered on them. I kept walking farther toward the river. The gray of the clouds and water matched the atmosphere of Red Hook. I was getting closer to the place where Rubio had been found.

Rubio was a child of Oshún. I shuddered to think that he was murdered at the river. Oshún was the Orisha of the river, of charity, love, and compassion. I hoped he'd found those things in his death. Rubio had seemed terribly isolated in his work and maybe in his drug use. While I didn't know this for sure, my instincts told me that he'd been on a slippery slope for a while, and now I was on one too.

There it was. The spot. Yellow and black cautionary tape had been pulled from the railing and flapped in the wind. One seven-day votive with its wick long blown out stood in the corner. That sight made me sadder than if a shrine of candles and pictures and notes were there. Those would at least have shown how many people loved Rubio. I hadn't thought to bring a candle or anything else myself. I tried to think of a prayer, and none came to me.

"Hey." I jumped and swiveled around. A young woman in horned-rimmed frames was standing there. Her short braids jutted out all over her head. A navy-blue security guard's uniform fit snugly against her ample frame.

"I found the body, you know," she murmured.

"You?" I searched her eyes.

The woman pointed to the headphones covering her ears. "Wait a second, I can't hear you. Bob Marley. Classic. Sorry!" She removed them and placed them around her neck.

"What did you say?" she asked.

"I just asked you whether you were the one who found him.

Didn't you just say that?"

"Yeah, I'm a security guard. The lady from the clock factory alerted me. At first I thought it was some homeless person. Sleeping, you know? Then I saw that it was a body."

"Are you just, like, talking to everybody who comes by?" I asked. "Telling them about *the body*. That body belonged to a human being! That body was my friend."

"Wow, Miss, I am so sorry to hear that," she said. "Who was he? I mean, I found him, I learned his name, but who was this guy?"

"Wait a second," I said. "If you found him before dawn, how is it that you're here so late in the afternoon? Shouldn't you be home by now?"

"Yeah, usually, but I've started doing long shifts," she said. "Was he married? Did he have any kids?"

"Yes and no. He was practically married." I thought of Jose.

"So, you two were friends? That's why you came down? There's almost nobody come down here."

I looked at the lone candle mournfully. "It does seem kind of isolated around here."

"Well, there's mostly factories. Look around. All you see are these warehouse-type buildings. Some people have made a go of these businesses. Otherwise, especially in this type of weather, you don't see practically anybody down here. Unless they come to drop off packages at night. You know, in cars. The winter is worse."

I did as she suggested and eyeballed the dock. The whole area was secluded. Squat brick buildings with ornate arched doors. A fortress—just like Liz Munroe had said.

"I'd seen him down here before, you know."

The wind seemed to blow the words away from me. I couldn't believe I heard what she'd just said.

"My name is Nikki Peebles. I know what you're going to ask. Am I named after the famous Nikki Peebles? No, I'll answer that before you ask. Her name is Nia Peeples. No relation. The 'n' and 'i' make the names seem the same, and the 'p' and 'b' make it different."

After she made her little speech, she put her fist out to bump mine. That fist bump was a first for me.

"And you?" she asked.

"Sorry. My name is Daisy Muñiz."

"The cook? I mean, the chef." Nikki looked apologetic.

"No. Muñiz. You're thinking of Martinez."

We stood there facing the buildings and at the same time turned toward the battleship-gray water. The waves were strong, and foam appeared at each splash against the rocks.

"When did you see him?" I asked. "Do the police know that he was here before the night this happened?"

"I told them. I'm not saying I ever talked to your friend or anything. I noticed him. He seemed different than the usual people who come down here."

"What kind of people come down here?" I asked.

"Usually people who have something to do. Workers. Mr. Rubio must have had business, though. He carried a case. A big one. Like he was a businessman, except he had that long hair and usually wore jeans."

I nodded. That was Rubio. "Do you remember the last time you saw him? I guess what I'd like to know is, who did he visit?"

"I thought he lived down here."

"Why would you think that?" I asked. "Did you see him going into one of these buildings?

"That I don't remember. I do remember the time he took the water taxi. I was sitting down there in front of that restaurant." She pointed at a building that suddenly became a restaurant before my eyes. It had looked like another warehouse to me just a moment before.

"He took the water taxi?"

"Yeah. The reason I noticed it was that he hooked his bike

right up there to the railing. I figured he was just taking a chance that nobody would steal it or take one of the tires off. But he had that way that some people have."

"What do you mean?" I asked. "What way?"

"You know, the kind of white guy, sorry I don't mean nothing by it, that can just leave their bike there because they know that no one is going to mess with it. Now, me, I'm different. I live down here too, but I don't leave my bike anywhere. If I rode one, that is."

"I get it." I gave her a thin smile. I had often thought the same thing about Rubio. Part of his aloneness was his aloofness. He wasn't the warmest guy in the world. He did his own thing and let people do theirs. It wasn't about a sense of entitlement; he was a bohemian.

"Where does the water taxi go?" I asked.

"Look over there. There's a schedule on the fence. One should be coming anytime soon. It goes over to Manhattan."

"Manhattan?" I looked up to see a water taxi approach the dock. A few people had come out of the restaurant and were standing at the landing. It was close to evening and the waters were becoming choppier as the temperature dropped steadily. Spring in New York.

"I think I'll take a ride," I said. "See what's over on the other side."

"The city." Nikki was matter of fact.

"Yes, I'm sure that's all I'll see, but I want to be in touch with Rubio, if that's at all possible."

"You mean his spirit," Nikki said. "They say that people who die suddenly stay on Earth until they get used to the idea that they got to be moving on. Kind of like in that movie with Whoopi Goldberg."

"I've heard that too," I said. "Can I have your phone number just in case I think of another question or two." I took a piece of paper out of my handbag, tore off an edge, and wrote my number on it. "Here's mine."

"Sure, but I don't really know much," she said. "I found him; that's all."

"You've been helpful to me," I said. "Or maybe I'll call just to connect. I appreciate everything you've done." I took my phone out and put her number in as she recited it to me. Nikki, not Nia, Peebles, not Peeples.

"Miss, how will you know where he got off?" Nikki asked, just as I began rummaging through my bag for my wallet. I stopped in my tracks.

"Doesn't this go straight to Manhattan?" I asked. I hadn't thought to pick up the schedule that was in a pocket on the fence.

"Yes, but first it stops at Atlantic Avenue and then DUMBO before it gets to Manhattan."

I rushed to look at the schedule. She was right. Two stops before Manhattan.

"He must have been going into the city," I said. "Otherwise, he would just have biked the rest of the way. But, knowing him, he could have ridden his bike to there too."

I was one of the last to board the water taxi. I sat down and watched the security guard's figure diminish as the water taxi pulled farther away from the dock. I wished I'd brought my hat or at least my scarf. My fingertips and nose began tingling with the cold.

The waves were gray and choppy. The river was a city of freightliners and tugboats engaged in business. Since I lived my life on land, I had never really thought about the busy waters. I allowed my thoughts to turn inward as the taxi sped through the river. I didn't know what I'd find when I reached Manhattan.

As we neared port, my phone began vibrating. I hadn't received any calls on the ferry, or so I thought, but, in fact, there were three calls. Greg. Jake. Letty. I was in no shape to talk to any of them. I was in the city with not a clue as to my next destination.

My fingers automatically went to my cell phone. Maybe it wouldn't tell me which call to return first. Maybe it wouldn't hold a message that it was all a mistake and that Rubio was still alive. But it did direct me to search the Intergroup website. I needed a meeting. I needed to stay sober.

Exchange Views, the nearest meeting, was a few blocks away from the pier. I got there in time to hear the chairperson finish reading How It Works. I settled back into my seat as the speaker began her qualification. I identified with her story. The slow descent from having aspirations to becoming a person I barely recognized, full of despair and loneliness. It didn't matter that the speaker had almost lost her condo on Park Avenue and was divorced by the love of her life, a celebrity she left unnamed. That didn't happen to me, but I identified with believing that a drink was the only thing that was holding my life together. It had become the friend who welcomed me into long nights of oblivion. Her story resonated with me deeply. I found myself raising my hand to share when she was had finished. She quickly called on me to share.

"My name is Daisy, and I'm an alcoholic. Thank you for coming here today to share your experience, strength, and hope. I'm here because I don't want to drink. I'm doing other things that I did before I got sober, and I know it's a slippery slide. I don't want to pick up, but somehow feel like I already did. I'm not emotionally sober. My excuse is that one of my close friends was murdered. I can't drink over that. I needed to hear what you had to say today. Thank you."

Others in the room nodded when I spoke. I couldn't save my face and my butt at the same time. The speaker went on to choose another member who raised his hand to share.

As the meeting ended, we were asked to put our chairs up in the back of the room. I picked my chair up and found myself face to face with Ryan, Rubio's sponsee. Dread filled my stomach. I had no desire to talk to him.

"Daisy, I'm surprised to see you here." He took the chair out of my hands and placed it on the bracket for me.

"Thanks. Ryan, isn't it?"

"Yes, that's right. You have a great memory for names. We spoke so briefly at that Brooklyn meeting. I just found out about Rubio."

I nodded. Another man jostled me as he tried to put his own chair up.

"Let's step outside," Ryan suggested. This time I followed him.

We stood to the side of the building's entrance. The area was bustling with pedestrians. New York City was always moving no matter what time of day or night.

"I have to get my bike." Ryan guided me to the curb. "Rubio was really good to me when I was counting days, you know. I owe my sobriety to him. I mean, he helped me to stay in the program."

I winced inwardly, remembering how I didn't want to speak with Ryan at the Brooklyn meeting when he'd reached out to me. Emotional sobriety was not for the weak.

"I'm glad to see you," I managed. "Do you work around here?"

Ryan pointed to the large bag that was anchored across his body. "I'm a messenger. So, yeah, I do work around here. All around here."

"Well, I don't want to keep you."

"I'm done for the day but, yeah, I have to be on my way." He was thoughtful. "This is one of the harder meetings to come to. This is where I met Rubio. He gave me his number on my first day. I was green around the gills. Hungover and weaving through this downtown traffic. Not too smart."

"Why would he come out here for meetings when Park

Slope is Brooklyn's meeting mecca?" I wondered aloud.

"I don't know we ever talked about that," Ryan said.

"Well, it was good to see you again."

"Are you going to see his paintings?" he asked.

"You mean at the Atlantic Avenue Gallery?" I asked. "It's off limits."

"There are a couple of galleries in SoHo he did business with." His eyes searched mine. "You didn't know that, did you?"

"No, I didn't," I admitted. "I guess there was a lot that I didn't know about him."

Ryan gave a short laugh. "Yeah, Rubio was a private guy. He has paintings at two shops down there."

"Really? I'm surprised that he would keep that to himself. That's odd."

"Anonymity was important to him."

"Which galleries?" I prodded. "Do you know?"

"The White Buffalo Art Gallery and Miguel's Moratorium," he said. "I've got to be heading out. I hope to see you again, Daisy."

"Thanks, Ryan. Me too."

Ryan swung his leg over the seat and began pushing off. I stopped him.

"Listen, hold up," I heard myself say. "I want to apologize for not being there for you that day at the church in Brooklyn. I don't know what's wrong with me sometimes."

"Hey, no worries," he said. "I get it. We're similar that way."

With that, Ryan wove his way back into the traffic. I stood watching after him. His was probably the most unsung job in America. I'd never really thought of messengers and the danger that was inherent in their work. Surrounded by the tall buildings, I had no idea where I was going now that the meeting was over. I could go to scout out Rubio's paintings. The other option was to tell on myself.

Chapter 10

For the last couple of years I'd kept a box of tissues hidden at the side of the couch. This particular box had only a few left. After speaking with Angela, I'd need to buy a new one. The tears just wouldn't stop coming.

Angela's voice was level. "You're only as sick as your secrets, Daisy."

"How do I know that you're not going to hold this against me somehow?" My sniffles came through, despite my best efforts to suppress them.

"I'm not judging you. You can use this little episode to feel sorry for yourself or you can learn something from it. There's no harm in wanting a little softness in your life when things are rough. You didn't drink, Daisy. That's the important thing."

"I kind of felt like I wanted a drink," I said. "I didn't feel like I wanted to get laid." I flipped over on my belly. Moonlight soaked the room. The bluish tint had become a blanket of ocean.

"Have you been getting to meetings?" she asked.

"Yes, I have. How is it that I can go to meetings and still end up in bed with Greg? I barely know him. It's like the old me is still there."

"You know what they say. The disease is doing push-ups the longer we stay sober. The disease doesn't go away. You still feel. You feel loss. Rubio. It sounds like Jose is pushing you away. Your beau disappeared for days. These are losses, Daisy. Loss can feel terribly lonely."

"I don't know if I told you that my godfather was in a car accident. Letty went to Florida and is supposed to let me know how he is, and I haven't heard from her yet."

"I'm sure she'll call you," Angela said.

"Oh wait. She did," I said. "I had forgotten to listen to her message. Here I am complaining! She called me, and I never called her back." This realization primed me for a fresh set of tears.

"Take it easy, kiddo." My sponsor was the only person who called me that, and I liked it. It reminded me of a neighbor when I was growing up who used to wear a head full of lavender curlers. She used to tell me, *Go slow, kiddo. Don't grow up too fast.* I had no idea what she was talking about then. Now I did. She probably saw the words "Future Alcoholic" etched into my forehead.

I counted to ten as I tried to hold my breath. My sobs finally subsided.

"Are you still there?" she asked.

I exhaled. "Yes, I'm here. So, it's more meetings I guess?"

"Daisy, I think it's time for you to tackle Step Four. Do that, and before you know it, you'll be feeling better again. At least better than when you started."

My phone beeped. Another call was coming through. Rod. "I have to go, Angela. Thanks for listening. You're the best. I'll call you soon. I promise." I barely gave her time to respond before I clicked to hear his voice.

"Hello, Miss Unavailable." That melting sensation threatened to overtake me. It wasn't the healthiest thing for my mood to swing so wide due to a voice. But, that voice!

"I'm here now," I assured him. "I'm glad you called. I'm sorry I didn't get back to you. I'm all over the place. But I did get to the precinct, and Liz told me that she couldn't show me any photos. I saw you. Did she tell you I was there?"

"Yes, she told me," Rod said. "It's late now, but can we meet tomorrow? Maybe an early breakfast? I don't mean professionally."

"Sure. Why don't you come here," I said. "I'll make you breakfast before going to the precinct. We can talk. Clear the air."

"Sounds good. Seven too early?"

"Perfect. I'll see you then." I hung up and immediately pulled on a pair of jeans and threw on my jacket. I'd have to go out and pick up food. I couldn't make breakfast with an empty cupboard. It was ten o'clock. They were probably just taking fresh bagels out of the oven at the Fifth Avenue Deli. That would make it a great breakfast.

The bagels warmed the brown paper bag and felt good against my hand. I couldn't resist and began chewing on a cinnamon raisin as I walked slowly back home. Up ahead I spotted a figure. *Rubio.* I shook my head. It was dark, but I swear that I could make out his blondish hair cascading down his back. He seemed to turn. I knew instinctively that I should follow him.

I walked behind him along the side street. There were only a few people out. I began to daydream about the season of renewal and hope. A feeling of safety enveloped me. I hadn't felt this peaceful in a long time. I didn't want to catch up to him because I was afraid that I would break this almost magical spell I'd longed for.

The streetlights suddenly flickered and turned up to what seemed to be a high voltage. Across the street, sitting on the park bench, was the familiar figure.

"Daisy!" he called. "Ain't you gonna talk to me? Too good now?"

I ignored him and hurried trying to catch up to Rubio, but he was gone. I was in front of the house and ran up the stoop to the second floor, where I quickly unlocked the door. I slipped inside and rushed to lock the door again behind me. Rubio had guided me home safely. I was certain of it.

The next morning, I sat across from Rod at the kitchen table that fit neatly into the tiny nook. The assortment of bagels was piled on a plate next to a tub of cream cheese. Smoke emanated from our coffee mugs.

"Jelly?" My knee bobbed up and down.

"No, thanks. I'm good." He picked up an "everything" bagel and began spreading cream cheese on it. "Why so nervous?"

"Me? I'm not sure why you'd think that." I grabbed at a poppy seed bagel and wished I'd thought to buy scallion cream cheese.

"Look at you," he said. "So far we've been able to avoid talking about ourselves, but we can't keep doing that. The way things have been going, I'm not sure if there is ever going to be a right time for this conversation."

I nodded. "You're right. There's so much up in the air. I don't know if anything is going to be resolved. At least not anytime soon."

"I'm not sure that after this conversation there can be resolution," he said. "Things are complicated, Daisy. I hope you're ready to hear this."

I interrupted him. "Do you guys have any leads on who did this to Rubio?"

"Can we talk about that later? I came here for another reason. If you don't want to talk after all, just let me know."

He put a piece of the bagel into his mouth and chewed, quickly following it with a swig of coffee. I watched as he ate.

"I'm sorry," I said. "Go ahead."

Rod breathed deeply. "And can I ask you not to interrupt? Please. Even if you don't like what you're hearing. Okay?"

"Promise." I picked up the mug of coffee, trying to keep my mouth and hands occupied.

"The reason I went to Chicago. I need to talk about that. But first I need to tell you why I transferred here to New York." He breathed audibly again. "I had to leave. It wasn't safe. I was on an important case. I don't want to get into the details of who did what, but someone took it upon themselves to target me. And my family."

"Your mom?"

"Please. You promised not to interrupt. No, not my mom."

"So you mean that story you told me about her being a nurse was true? And your dad too?"

"Daisy, can you please just let me talk?" His voice rose. "Yes, all of that is true. I didn't make anything up. But there's more that I didn't tell you. I was targeted."

I bit into a bagel in order not to mention that he'd already said that.

"I have a wife."

I went to place my mug on the table and missed the surface. The mug smashed against the table's edge, and hot coffee spilled across the table and streamed onto the kitchen floor. Rod jumped up for paper towels and dabbed at the brown liquid. I was motionless. My legs became immobile, although my insides were jumping.

"I know I shouldn't have led you on, Daisy. It's not like you think."

The piece of bagel swelled in my mouth. I choked. Rod smacked me a few times between my shoulder blades.

"Stop!" I spluttered. "Just stop." I kept my back to him, infuriated by the tears that had formed in my eyes.

"Let me finish," he said. "I need to tell you what happened."

"I don't think I want to know." To make matters worse, as I stood near the window I saw that the stalker was sitting out there again. "Can't you do something about that man? Aren't you supposed to be a detective?"

Rod came near me and eased me away from the window.

"Sit down," he said. "The guy's not really doing anything. Benches are meant for people to sit on. Unless we spot him engaged in criminal activity, he's allowed to sit there."

"You're married?" I asked. "Why so secretive? I remember you saying you didn't want to go into your past. Now I know why. Your past is your present, that's why."

"Not exactly." He paused. "There's more."

"I already said that I didn't want to hear any more."

We sat across the shiny table with our arms folded, studying each other. The Kit-Cat Klock on the wall clicked rhythmically. Its mechanical eyes shifted from side to side. A car horn blared in the street.

I finally broke the silence. "The coffee's getting cold."

He took my hand in his. "Daisy, I have a daughter."

I retrieved my hand and stood up. "You have to leave."

"Please," he implored.

With what seemed clearly against my will, I sat down. "Talk."

"I'm married, but we're separated. My wife is undercover. She's been living like that for a while. I was too. I had to get out. It had gotten too dangerous. She's still in that life."

"Where is she?" I asked. "And your daughter?"

"My daughter is with my parents. My mom thought she could care for her better than either of us could. I've been a wreck. I went to see her."

"What's her name?" I asked softly.

"Christy."

"Your wife's name is Christy?"

"No, I misunderstood. That's my daughter's name."

"Why would your wife put herself and her baby in danger like that? Is your daughter a baby? How old is she?"

"Christy is three," he said. "The higher-ups warned Larissa about going into this situation with a baby. In the beginning, my wife thought the case would be over quickly. It dragged out. I can't describe it. It's as if Larissa got subsumed into that world. I don't even know what's going on with her. She's basically off the face of the earth, the way I see it."

"Because she's undercover, you consider yourself separated?" I asked. "I need clarification, Rod."

"We're separated," he said. "It didn't start out that way, but that's how it turned out."

I nodded and stood up. I poured us both another cup of coffee. I sat down again, feeling leaden inside.

He closed his eyes. "I was so afraid you'd be angry at me."

"Angry? No. I'm not sure what I'm feeling, but anger isn't it," I said as I shook my head.

"I think I get why you didn't tell me about her earlier," I added. "But why now? What changed?"

"The reason I went to Chicago is that my mother called me to say she can't take care of Christy anymore, and we needed to talk about it, make a plan. Mom's retired. I thought it would be easier once she was retired. Christy's about to start longer hours in school, but my mother said she can't continue to do the juggling. She's feeling her age. Plus, she has diabetes. The fact is that my mom has always been a caregiver. For her to say she can't do it anymore is a big admission on her part."

"She's her granddaughter," I said.

"I think she wants me to raise my own child," he said. "And I think she's right."

Rod got up and stood in front of me. He reached down and pulled me up close to him.

"Daisy, I'm sorry," he said. "I should have been more open about my life."

"But wait a minute," I said. "How is it that you're working here? Just out of the blue you were transferred to New York. I'm really at a loss here."

"I had to leave. The chief had a connection here. He owed him a favor."

"Rod, I can't listen to anymore, I need some time." I pushed him away.

"I thought you weren't mad."

"I'm not," I acknowledged. "But I have to take care of me too. Just like your mother. I have to figure out what I want."

Rod appeared dejected. "Maybe I got my signals crossed."

"I'm not sure what signals you got because I don't think I sent you any. I just told you that I need to know, for me, what I can and can't do. It's not so easy. You come here and tell me this story. You knew it all along, but I didn't. I'm already in a place of not knowing."

The thought of my recent afternoon with Greg popped into my head. I could never tell Rod about that. How easy it had been for me to slip into my old habits. The shame in me was so familiar. And maddening. I was tired of it.

"I need a break," I said. "There's a lot going on. Do you get that?"

"Yeah. I'm sorry for the timing."

"Saying *sorry* once should be enough. Can we talk about something else? I really can't do this right now."

"I was wondering if Jose gave you any details on the viewing?" he asked.

"Jose? Viewing? That came out of left field. I don't think there's going to be one. There has to be a religious ceremony. But a burial? I think his mother is going to send for him for a burial in Colombia. I don't even know if they got the results from the autopsy yet. But you would know that, wouldn't you?"

"You've got to talk to Jose," he said. "I'm sorry."

"Thanks. You've been a big help today."

"Please, Daisy."

"You have to go now." I marched over to the front door and opened it widely.

"Can I at least call you?" He turned back as he reached the stairs.

I nodded. He was almost at the second floor when I called after him. "When is she coming to New York?"

"Soon. Maybe a couple of weeks," he said.

"A couple of weeks?"

"Yes. I have to make arrangements for childcare or a day care. I'm not sure which."

I walked back into the apartment and closed the door. I couldn't solve his problems. I needed to solve my own first.

I sat on the sofa until the buzzing phone roused me out of my stupor. I had to get moving. It was Letty.

"I'm so glad to hear your voice," I said. "You can't even imagine what's happening up here."

"Really? Then call me back next time I call you. I only have a few minutes. We're about to go in to see Hector. I just wanted to let you know that he has major injuries to his abdomen. Luckily there was no head trauma, so he can still communicate. He's in a lot of pain, though. They removed his spleen, and they had to fix his bowel. It was perforated. That's not going to be pretty, but at least he's alive. The doctor wasn't sure whether he'd survive. But they say as long as he doesn't get an infection, he should probably make a full recovery."

"I'm glad to hear that," I said. "It's been really chaotic at home."

"I've got to go," Letty said. "I'll try calling you again soon. Mike has to return to New York, but I think I'm going to stay down here a while with my sister."

"Your sister?" I asked. "Things must really be tough."

"My God, Daisy, family is family. We may not always agree, but she is my sister. I've got to hang up. Please call Ana and let her know that we're pretty sure that Hector is going to pull through."

"Yeah, sure. Will do. Take it easy, Letty. Kiss the kids for me."

I looked at the phone in my hand in surprise. Letty staying with her ultraconservative religious sister was something I could never have foreseen. Everything was upside down these days. Everything.

Chapter 11

Later that morning I sat at Ana's kitchen table listening to Los Panchos playing from the old-fashioned stereo in the living room. She handed me a cup of aromatic hot *café con leche,* and I drank it as though it would fill my soul. A cream-and-yellow canary jumped around in its cage, and a bell tingled. I had come home.

"*¿Quieres un poquito de flan?*" Ana bent low to peer into her refrigerator.

"Flan? Sure. I haven't eaten flan in a long time." It seemed a lifetime ago that Rod and I had dinner at a Mexican restaurant and shared the delicious dessert.

Ana chuckled. "Eating flan is like eating a piece of the past. We suddenly find ourselves sitting at our *abuela*'s kitchen table. While we eat, we can feel our little brothers pulling at our pigtails and our mothers reminding us of our manners."

I took the plate she handed me. "So much is wrong, Ana. Things aren't fair."

"What *is* fair, *mi amor*?"

"It's not my fault. I tried." I swallowed a spoonful of the pale-yellow custard.

"I'm not sure what you're talking about, *hija*, but we all own a little piece."

"Maybe." I barely agreed. "This is delicious, but should I have expected anything less?"

Ana laughed again. Her laughter was so hypnotic. When I was in her presence, I felt calm and safe.

"How long have you had that bird?" The canary's chirp made the kitchen a sunnier place to be.

"My ex-brother-in-law gave me *Chuito* when I closed the botanica. It's been a couple of years now. I used to tell him that I'd take the bird off his hands, but I couldn't because of all the hours I needed to put into the shop to keep it going. The minute I closed, he came here with the bird, the cage, and all the supplies. I had no more excuses."

"*Chuito*, that's cute." I closed my eyes. I wished I could sit with Ana forever. The music reminded me of my parents; that is, one of the better memories I had of them. Angela kept telling me that once I made amends to them things would get better. But that was several steps away and wasn't something I looked forward to doing.

"Letty wanted me to see you and to tell you about Hector."

"Hector?"

"And Rubio. Do you know about Rubio? Did Jose call you?" I was on uncharted territory.

"Jose left a message for me, and when I tried to call him back, he didn't answer. I left a message for him." Ana was most likely in her seventies, and she was one of the sturdiest-looking persons I'd ever come across. She could handle the news about Hector, who was one of her closest friends, and about Rubio.

"Hector was in a car accident in Florida," I said. "He's had surgery to repair some injuries, but Letty said they think he'll be all right. She's there too."

"*Ay Dios.*" Ana had been standing at the kitchen door but went into the living room and slumped down in her upholstered rocking chair.

"Are you okay?" I placed my spoon next to the remainder

of the flan and went into the living room.

"This is terrible news. He was just about to fly back, wasn't he? He had ceremonies planned for the next few weeks. We spoke before he left."

"I was one of those ceremonies."

"You have on your beads, don't you?" Her eyes searched me. My hand instinctively went to my neck. I rarely wore my beads.

"Right now? No. You two were planning to give me the Warriors. Now that's on hold."

Ana nodded. "I hear the disappointment in your voice, *hija*."

"Is it terrible to feel disappointed? I mean, I know that it was an accident, and I should be grateful that he's okay, but still."

"Still, nothing. You don't have time to feel sorry for yourself. Things happen because they are meant to. Receiving Warriors isn't like shopping at a store. The Orishas know when it is your time, and if you are meant to receive them, you will. On their time, not yours."

I was stunned by her response, but I knew that I shouldn't be. I'd sat with her before and had experienced her startling clarity and pragmatism.

"Who has your head, Daisy?" Ana asked.

"My head?" I was confused. Ana was my *ayubona*, second in command to my godfather. She should know.

"Obatalá, isn't it?" Ana answered her own question.

I nodded.

"Obatalá should bring calmness and an overall understanding as to what is happening to you. Listen, and you will hear."

"Easy for you to say," I said with immediate regret. "I didn't mean that."

"Of course you did," she cackled. "Just because you have an idea about your path, it doesn't mean that things are going to go exactly according to your timetable. The Santos know more than all of us. They will show the way."

"You sound pretty decisive about that." I wasn't so convinced. "How about Rubio?"

"What about him? You were going to say something."

Suddenly my narcissism was crystal clear. "He's dead, Ana." I sobbed. "It's been a couple of days. They found him at Gowanus; you know, Red Hook."

"*Es una guerra*," she said. "It's a war."

Ana stood up and walked into an adjoining room. I'd been here before and knew that her altar was in there. "I'm going to light a candle for his spirit."

I sat quietly until she returned.

"What is Jose's plan?" she asked. "Do you know yet?"

"No," I said. "Jose and I spoke about you figuring out who could do the ceremony since Hector is unable to do it. That's why Jose called you. He needed to be guided in finding out who would be the best person to do the ceremony. I forgot what it's called."

"*Itutu*. I know of someone. He's an *oriate* in the Bronx. He can officiate if he's available. He's very busy, very popular in the community."

"Hopefully that will work out," I said. "I haven't heard much from Jose either. He's sort of turned in to himself. Away from me. Quiet."

"He's hurting," she said. "*Tenga paciencia*."

"I know I should be patient," I said. "I'm doing my best. It's hard because I loved Rubio too. I was the last of us to see him alive. I'm not sure exactly where he was going, but he didn't want to talk to me."

"He had something important to take care of, no?"

"Yes, except that he wasn't found until the next morning. All alone. At the river on the waterfront."

"Oshún wanted him back."

"Do you really believe that?" I asked. "He was murdered. Does that make sense?"

"I have to believe that. Otherwise, nothing in my life makes any sense at all."

"I think Rubio relapsed. Maybe heroin. He'd gotten shot a couple of days before he was murdered. At the art gallery. We thought that it was a robbery that went sour. Now I don't know. The art curator was killed there that day. Rubio had surgery to repair the gunshot wound, and he left the hospital before he was discharged. He signed out against medical advice. Jose admitted that Rubio had relapsed before. It's possible that the pain medication opened a door for his addiction again."

"That's your fear talking, Daisy." Ana seemed so sure of herself. I wanted to believe her.

"I hope that his addiction wasn't the thing that took him out. I keep imagining that he went to buy drugs and was caught up in some kind of deal that went awry. That his murder wasn't a chance happening. I know he's dead, but he deserved the dignity of an honest death."

"Come here."

Ana reached out her arms to hug me. I cried until I felt completely emptied.

"I love you, Ana. Thank you for being here for me. I didn't realize that I needed to cry like this."

"There's more. What's going on with that boyfriend of yours? There's something there, isn't there?"

Ana's perceptiveness was uncanny. She had a strong reputation as a Spiritist. I had the feeling that she knew things even before the spirits did.

"It's not him. Well, yeah, it is him, but it's really me. I've been intimate with someone else."

"There's a break in your bond, isn't there?"

"Yes, but I'm confused as to how strong that bond really was. Rod told me that he's married, and he has a little girl."

"*Cálmate*, Daisy. Give it time. When the waters are rushing and colliding and the waves relentless, that is the time for you to be *tranquila*."

"I'll try. I don't want to be reckless again. I'm making things worse for myself."

"Until your *letra* is pulled, your head belongs to Obatalá. You won't know more until we ask specifically who your guardian angel is, and you're not ready for that. That said, you have a strong connection to Yemayá. That was clear when you had the reading from Hector. Pray. Meditate. You will have the clarity you desire."

"Will I?"

"Yes. There's always a solution." Ana smiled in her timeless way. No connection to a beginning or an ending. How I longed for her serenity.

"I guess I should be heading out. Work awaits. Sophia said that I shouldn't worry about it, but there's a lot for me to do. On the plus side, it will keep my mind busy while I wait for word on Rubio's arrangements."

"They're doing an autopsy, aren't they?" Ana asked.

"Yes, since his death was a crime. I wonder how long that will take to get done." I gathered my jacket and my bag. "I'll be going. *Bendición*."

"Santo," she said and embraced me. Ana pushed my hair out of my eyes and straightened the strap of my handbag over my shoulder. Suddenly I'd become a small child she was readying for school or maybe the cruel world. I wasn't sure which.

On the way out the door, I remembered the *oriate*. "What is the name of the person who can do the ceremony for Rubio?"

Ana had been walking into her apartment but turned back to me. "I'll write his name and phone number down for you. Remember that he's busy. Keep trying until you reach him."

Just as I had promised myself, I went directly to work. My desk was as I'd left it. Piled up with reports, contract folders, and charts. The usual. There was also an additional couple of stacks of paper that had collected in my absence.

Sophia looked forward to a hot cup of coffee the first thing each morning. When I reached the carafe, I saw that it was half filled with lukewarm liquid.

"Daisy. You're here." Sophia stood in the doorway of her adjoining office.

"I couldn't stay home. I thought I'd come in and get some work done."

"As long as you're certain you can handle it. I'm not about to complain about you working. I do depend on you."

Sophia and I made a solid team. Her role as Administrator at Windsor Medical Center was pivotal, and her trust and confidence in me was astounding. I didn't want to jeopardize that.

"I'll just look through the mail and then maybe we can meet to discuss the priorities. Is that okay with you, Sophia?"

"Of course," she said. "If you're going to pick up lunch, please think of me if you pass the donut shop."

I smiled inside. The thought that I'd just arrived, hours late, and that it was okay didn't elude me. I busied myself shuffling through the mail and outstanding reports on my desk. As I stopped to call the Seventh Avenue Donut Shop for an outgoing order, I flashed back to the times I'd leave for a coffee and not return for hours. A beer at the local pub usually took the edge off after a night of partying.

When the food order arrived, we ate our way through corn muffins, oozing with butter and jelly, accompanied by a fresh pot of brew. I felt a sense of calm returning to my work. The afternoon gave me a chance to regroup and reenergize myself. The pain of Rubio's death hadn't gone away, and I was still able to have a moment of peace. Even Mr. Donaldson, the CEO, couldn't shake my mood when he paid an unannounced visit to the office.

"Hi, Daisy. You're looking great this morning." He leaned against the desk and leered at me.

I was used to his barely concealed flirtations, and I ignored him, picking up my phone to let Sophia know he was there. I could practically hear her sigh through the closed door. As I told him that he could go right in, I remembered the junk mail I'd set on my desk and began riffling through it. There were circulars for local pharmacies, a new gym opening in the area, and an advertisement for Red Norman's Karate-Do class. I'd completely forgotten about the class and the scheduled promotion testing. I was shredding some of the credit card offers when I came across a plain white envelope with my name typed on a label. There was no return address. I was distracted by Sophia calling me into her office, and I placed it on my keyboard.

I squeezed past Mr. Donaldson as I entered her office. The faint smell of liquor permeated the air around him. He'd probably just come back from a three-cocktail lunch. I knew the signs. I'd had plenty of them myself. I sat down.

I waited for Sophia to start off with her usual, "Daisy, we need your help." Sophia and Mr. Donaldson were known for coming up with special projects and then handing the details to me. I'd need to get numbers. Maybe look up some hotels. Surf the net for similar projects.

"Daisy! Are you listening?" Sophia's irritation was apparent.

"Yes, sorry," I said. "I'm listening."

"I'll just come out with it," she said. "We've discussed the fact we think you need to take some time off."

"What? No! I mean, I'm sorry that I took yesterday and this morning off. I'm here now. There's so much for me to do. I thought you were glad that I came in today."

"I am, but Rubio was a family member to you," Sophia said. "Granted, not by blood, but he was like a brother to you. You need to take the time off. Two, maybe three weeks."

Mr. Donaldson nodded his head in agreement. "Yes, Daisy. Sophia gave a good argument. It's almost time for the Spring Gala, and we need you fresh, well, as a daisy, for that."

What would I do with my time off? I knew myself. I wasn't good at loose ends. I'd get into some sort of trouble. In fact, I hadn't taken a vacation since I got sober. The closest thing to it was my business trip to Puerto Rico with Sophia and Todd Roberts from the Research and Education Department at work. That trip had fortified me, but I had come too close to a drink. The image of Todd placing a tumbler of scotch under my nose was as strong as the smell that accompanied him wherever he went.

I faltered. "Can I think about it? I don't know what I'd do with myself."

"Well, this is a first, little lady!" Mr. Donaldson snorted. "You heard her, Sophia. If she doesn't want a vacation, who are we to force her?"

"Oh, Ralph, please." Sophia put on her half-moon eyeglasses and peered at the papers on the desk. "Daisy, you're due. I strongly suggest you take some time. Even if you decide on a staycation. You know, one of those planned stays at home."

I slumped in my chair. Defeated. This was a command. An awfully nice one but still a command.

"Okay," I whispered. "I'll take a vacation."

I tucked my tail between my legs and slunk back into my office. The difference I'd made since coming in just a short time ago was obvious. My obsessive sorting had eradicated the piles of papers. I picked up the envelope that I had placed on my keyboard and opened it. I unfolded the white sheet of paper, preparing to read the letter's contents. The words jumped out at me. Blue marker.

I'm watching you.

I gathered the letter and envelope and shoved them into my desk drawer. I returned to Sophia's office. I closed the door behind me.

"Daisy, you're as white as a sheet, and you're trembling! What's happened, dear?"

I thought quickly. I hated to do this but was compelled. There were things no one would ever understand.

Before Mr. Donaldson made a hasty retreat, he said, "I've got a conference call to get to, girls. I'm sorry, I must leave. Sophia, you'll handle this, won't you?"

Sophia gaped at me as I disclosed my discussion with Rod about his wife and child. I ended by telling her that the little girl would be in New York within the next couple of weeks.

"My goodness, now that is a turn of events." Sophia gazed out her window. After a couple of minutes, she said, "Go slow with this, Daisy. I think it's going to be all right. Try not to rush things. That wouldn't be the best way to go about it."

I agreed. "You're right. There isn't much for me to do anyway."

A text came through on my phone. It was Greg. *Let's go to a movie. Call me.* I shoved the phone back into my pocket. My life was a tornado.

"Okay," I said. "You're right. I may be better off taking some of my vacation time. I'll tidy up here and make a list of the most important things that have to get done."

"Call the personnel pool for a temp," she said. "There's no way I can do my work and yours."

"For two weeks?" I asked. "Would that be okay?"

"If you have that amount of time accumulated, of course." Sophia was generous under certain parameters.

"I do," I said. "I have plenty of unused vacation time."

Another Twelve Step promise come true. I wasn't sure which, but it had to be one of them. When I was still drinking, I never accumulated vacation or personal time. I used those days up like sponges soaking up a lake.

"Let's meet about four o'clock so we can settle things out," I said.

"Yes, dear." Sophia's tone told me she was already on to the next thing.

I was about to shut her door when she called out after me. "Don't forget to order a temp!"

Chapter 12

It was five o'clock, and Sophia and I had just pushed our chairs back from the desk. My phone buzzed. I automatically answered it. "Hello?"

"Daisy, it's me, Jose."

"I'm relieved to hear from you," I said. "Do you want to meet up? I just finished for the day. Actually, for the next two weeks."

"Yes, that's why I called you," he said. "Would you meet me down at the precinct? The ME sent the preliminary report, and I don't want to hear the news alone."

I breathed deeply. He sounded like his old self again. "I'll take a cab down there. Give me fifteen minutes."

"Daisy, before we meet, I want to apologize."

"Apologize?"

"I did my best to shut you out. Everybody out. This hurts. Real bad."

"No worries, my friend," I said. "I'll see you in a few."

It wasn't long before we walked back up toward Sixth Avenue. The brownstone was in the near distance.

"Up until Detective Harris read that report to us, I could make myself believe that maybe he'd died of natural causes."

Jose's eyes glistened with tears. His nose watered, and I automatically searched in my jacket pocket for a clean tissue.

"Here." I handed him a crinkled one. "I think it's clean," I stammered. "I'm sorry."

Jose took the tissue and flattened it out in his palm to be certain it was unused before he blew.

The blooms on the magnolia trees would open soon. They complemented the old sycamores that lined the streets. The cool winds had helped me forget that we were in spring. I wasn't even sure how long it had been since Rubio had been found at the waterfront. The days were cramming into each other.

Jose spoke. "During the last couple of days, I've pretended that Rubio was away on a business trip. That report made it all too real. I still have to get that ceremony done."

"I got the name of someone who could do it from Ana. She thinks highly of him." I fished the piece of paper out of my bag. "Here."

"Thanks, Daisy," he said. "I know I kind of disappeared there. It's my ineffective way of dealing with my grief."

"I understand," I said. "Would it be possible for me to go to the ceremony? Sort of make it a final good-bye?"

"Only people who are initiated can go," he said. "Another rule."

I sighed. "Okay." I battled my selfishness.

As though he could read my mind, Jose said, "Not Warriors. A person would have had to receive *Ocha*.

"Oh. Crowned. I get it." Outwardly I managed to maintain my composure, but inside I was annoyed.

"Have you heard from Letty?"

"Yes. Hector had major surgery to remove his spleen. His intestines were also severely damaged."

"Too bad they couldn't have found Rubio quickly enough to repair his injuries. That bullet to his chest was probably meant to make it certain that he wouldn't be found alive. That no repair would be possible, even if someone had found him right away."

The reality was dismal, I thought. I shuddered. "Do you think it was a professional."

"Someone hired to take his life?" Jose's expression showed his surprise. "Who would do that, though? He was an artist. He didn't have ties to anyone who would do that."

"Of course he did," I said. "The Montoyas."

"They were in business with him, not against him."

"Well, I hope they pick them up and start questioning them."

"They will," Jose assured me. "These aren't the Keystone Cops we're working with. On the plus side, Rod knows us well. Or, at least you. He has to care."

I kept my mouth shut. It never occurred to me that my relationship with Rod would have any effect on how closely the detectives would work the case. We neared the brownstone.

"Look, Jose. The house is completely dark," I said. "That's unusual. The hall and door lights are always left on in the evening."

We entered the gate, and Jose rang the bell. There was no answer, and he knocked on Marge's front door. The electricity in the old house had been iffy, and we'd convinced her to have the wiring updated. The brownstone was one of the few in the entire neighborhood that hadn't undergone millions of dollars' worth of renovations. The house still had most of the original fixtures from when it was built in 1899. The date had been inscribed into the cornerstone by the builders over one hundred years ago.

"Didn't the electrician come out?" I asked. "Wasn't the wiring replaced?"

Jose knocked harder. There was still no answer. "Marge!" he called out. "Are you home?"

All we heard were the tree branches brushing against the window.

"Let's just go in through the second floor," I said. "I'm worried!"

I spun around to glance at the playground. The stalker wasn't there.

Jose's senses finally kicked in. "I have a key!" He opened the door. We entered, and I flicked the light switch up. The dim hallway bulb turned on. Ruffian was asleep in his doggie bed.

"Jose, something's wrong," I said. "Marge doesn't usually keep Ruffian's bed out here."

There was a banging sound coming from the back of the house.

"Hurry!" I commanded. "Something's going on!"

We rushed to the back of the first floor, through the kitchen, and arrived at the mudroom. The door was swinging back and forth in the wind. The garden was also unlit.

"Something's happened to Marge!" I wailed. "Where is she?"

"Stop, Daisy." Jose grabbed my wrist. "She might be upstairs. Don't go bananas here, okay?"

My insides quivered. "What if the stalker did something to her?" I ran back into the hallway, where Ruffian was snoring deeply.

"Jose, Ruffian's totally out. That doesn't make sense. He never leaves her side."

"I'll check upstairs." Jose took the steps two at a time and then I heard him open and close the doors on the parlor floor as he checked each room.

I went into the kitchen and found a note on the counter.

I've decided to visit my niece in Poughkeepsie. Please take the trash out on Thursday. I'll be back soon.

"Look, this was on the counter." I showed Jose the note when he returned from his search. "Blue marker."

Jose grabbed it and read it. "Now, I'm freaked out. We have to call the police."

I grabbed my cell phone, and, instead of calling 911, I made a direct call to Rod, who answered on the first ring. I explained the situation to him. I ended the call and turned back to Jose.

"He's on his way," I said. "He said that we shouldn't move or touch anything." I paced the kitchen while we waited. Jose stood near the entry with his eyes on Ruffian, who was still zonked out in doggie dreamland.

A few minutes later, the siren alerted us that the police had arrived. I opened the door and stepped aside to let Rod, Liz, and Detective Harris enter Marge's living space. It was an enormous house, but with the five of us in the hallway and a sleeping Ruffian, the entryway seemed to have shrunk in size.

Liz nudged the dog. "Is this beauty usually such a heavy sleeper?" she asked.

I shook my head. "The opposite. His job is to guard Marge. This isn't good."

Rod scanned the stairs. "Have you been up there yet?"

Jose nodded. "I went through the rooms on the second floor. She wasn't there."

Harris asked, "Did you go up to the third or fourth floors?" He put his hand out to his waist, and I caught a glimpse of the gun that was nestled in its holder.

"I didn't think of that," I said. "I only thought of Marge's apartment."

"Come on." Rod tilted his head to the stairs. "Let's go."

Liz was right at his heels. I'd seen them together in action before. If anyone were upstairs, this pair would find them. I watched as they quietly climbed the stairs. I hoped there wasn't anyone in my apartment.

Detective Harris headed toward the back of the house. We hadn't closed the door to the mudroom, and it continued to swing in the wind. Harris went into the garden and took his phone out of his pocket. He used it as a flashlight to examine the area. The light reflected on the old shed in the corner of the yard.

"She hasn't used that shed for years," I said aloud. "It's probably locked."

Jose stood next to me. "I was in there a few days before the robbery. Marge wanted to surprise you. Since you started gardening, she wanted to have the shed cleaned up and ready for your planting supplies. She thought the mudroom was too small."

"I had no idea!" I cried.

Harris walked to the back of the shed, but, instead of his phone, he had his gun in his hand. He circled the area around the shed surreptitiously and called out, "Police!"

He tried the doorknob, and it turned easily in his hand. He opened the door and went inside. A moment later, he called out, "She's in here. I just called for assist. Be ready to open the door for them!"

"Oh, Jose, do you think she's . . . dead?"

Chapter 13

Jose and I stood immobilized in the kitchen. Rod entered the room, with Liz following closely behind.

"It's clear upstairs," he said. "There's no one up there."

"Detective Harris just called for an ambulance," I said. "Marge is in the shed."

Liz held up her radio. They already knew. The two moved as one and left the house through the mudroom. Jose and I looked at each other. Before either of us could speak, we heard sirens blaring and then the sound abruptly cut off. The EMTs had arrived.

I ran to the front of the house and held the door open. They unloaded their emergency equipment from the vehicle and made their way through the house to the shed. It seemed like hours had passed before the EMTs returned through the kitchen with Marge on a stretcher. The three detectives followed closely.

"Stop." I placed my hand on Rod's arm. "Is Marge going to be all right?"

"She was tied up and gagged in the shed," he said. "I'm sorry to say that she took a few blows."

"Is she alive?" I whispered.

"She's semiconscious," he said. "It's good that you got here when you did."

"Oh, Rod, what if we hadn't come home right away?"

"Why would anyone try to attack such a frail woman?" Jose sighed.

"That's something we plan to find out," Rod assured us.

Jose took a step toward Rod. "When? When are you going to find who did this? Let's face it, Rubio's dead. Marge was assaulted. Who's next? Me? Daisy?"

"Please, Jose," I pleaded. "I know you're upset, but they're doing their best."

Rod moved out of reach. "We're going to the hospital. Please stay here. Keep an eye on the dog. I don't doubt that Ruffian's sedated. Otherwise, with all this commotion, he'd have gotten up. We'll let you know how Marge is doing."

"Please, don't forget to call," I said. "We'll be waiting."

As they left the brownstone, Rod looked over his shoulder. "Lock up tight. I'll see about getting a patrol car to the area. If you see that guy who sits out there, call us right away."

Reluctantly, I closed the door and turned to Jose. "Can I stay with you tonight?" I asked. "I don't want to be alone in my apartment."

"Yeah, but I think it would be better if we stayed up at your place. I really don't want to face the mess in my apartment."

"Great, I'll feel a lot safer," I said. "We can check on Ruffian in an hour or so. Give him time to sleep it off. Come to think of it, I haven't seen Ms. G. She's probably hiding in a closet. I'm sure she's okay."

We locked up the first and second floor entries and walked up to the third floor.

"Let me pick up something that I can sleep in," he said. "Wait in the living room. I don't want to be separated from you, not even for a minute."

I sat on the couch while he went into the bedroom. Something wasn't right, but I couldn't put my finger on it.

Suddenly, what Jose had said a few minutes ago became clear. "You're right!" I called out. "It is messier in here than it was the other day. I mean, it's really messy."

"You're actually criticizing the apartment?"

"I don't mean it like that," I said. "When I was here the other day with Rubio, there were heaps of papers around. I'm sorry, but the place was a pigsty. But he wasn't in a communicative mood, so I left. Then when I was here the other night, it was immaculate. You remember that, don't you?"

Jose came out of his bedroom and gazed around the room. "I guess. I mean, I don't know. I haven't really been paying attention. But, yeah, you're probably right."

"Did you clean up at all?" I asked. "Or did you add to the clutter at any point?"

"No. I've hardly been around."

"Okay, so who tidied up the apartment the other day?" I asked. "And whose been in here? It looks like a hurricane went through it!"

"Someone has definitely been here. I can feel it. Rod and Harris wouldn't know that because they were here only once. Liz might have noticed something because she's like that. Astute. But she wasn't here that night; the men were."

"Are you going to call them back?"

"We have to," I said. "They might not come back, but they need to know."

"I'm a hundred percent sure that the door was locked, though."

"How can you be so sure with everything that's been going on?" I asked. "You might have forgotten to lock up. There aren't any strangers in this building. It's just us."

"It's the type of lock on the door. Look at it. It automatically locks without a key when I shut the door. I don't have to worry about locking it when I leave the apartment."

"Is that safe?" I asked.

"I wasn't worried about safety," he said. "Until now."

"We should leave," I suggested. "We can stay at a hotel or something. Someone might have your key. They might have gotten it from Rubio that night. I'm totally creeped out, and I don't want to stay here any longer."

"We can't go, Daisy." Jose returned to his bedroom, and I could hear drawers being pulled open and banged shut again.

"Why not?" I called into the bedroom, while shifting from foot to foot.

"First of all, Ruffian," Jose yelled back. "We can't just leave him here. We might have to take him to a vet if he doesn't wake up soon. We have no idea what they gave him. Second, we're here now. No one has been here since we've been back. They waited until we were out. Third, they'd have to be stupid to return tonight. Sirens and flashing lights usually scare the bad guys away."

I shuddered. "I hope you're right because I'm not feeling it. I would rather be somewhere far from here."

Jose emerged from his room carrying a stuffed leather duffel bag. "I get that, but I'm not running away. Whoever did this may be Rubio's murderer. I want to find out who and why!"

"Hurry, though, please," I said.

We climbed the steps to the fourth floor. My apartment door was open. "Did Rod and Liz say they were up here already? I don't remember."

"Yes," Jose said. "Don't get in a panic. That's the last thing we need."

We entered my apartment. Everything seemed to be in its place.

"I'm going to the bathroom," I said. "Don't leave."

The minute I went into the bathroom, I knew someone had been in my apartment too. My eyes canvassed the room. A couple of bath oil jars and the body powder case were out of place.

"Jose," I hollered. "Please come in here."

I showed him the toiletries. "Some of my things have been moved."

"Come on," he said. "Why would these bottles be moved? Who would do that? Anyway, how do you know they've been moved? They look fine to me. Nothing's been opened."

"Because I know," I said. "You'll have to take my word for it."

Now wasn't the time for me to go into my obsessive-compulsive tendencies. I wasn't certifiable, but after living with Lou, who thought it was fun to annoy me by going through my personal things, I knew exactly, intuitively, when my things were touched. Not having anyone intrude upon me was the best thing about living alone. I didn't miss trying to prove that he, or even my mother before him, had nosed into my items.

"Okay," Jose said. "Just don't touch anything. Maybe the police can get fingerprints. What are they looking for? I can't figure it out."

"You've been sober way too long, my friend," I said. "Dry goods. Didn't you ever hide anything when you were still using?"

"I guess, but not in the bath salts."

"We've missed a whole generation of getting high with bath salts," I said. "Just think, they've been inside and know everything about us. I hate that. I used to feel so safe in this house."

"Me too," he said. "I'll give Rod a call."

"Do you think it's okay for me to go to the bathroom, or will they need to get prints off the toilet too?"

"Do you think they used the toilet? Come on, Daisy, really."

"I don't know if they did," I said. "But one thing I'm certain of is that we're not safe in our building anymore."

A couple of hours later, I was stretched out on the couch. Ruffian was asleep on the floor next to me, snoring lightly. "I thought they'd never finish dusting for prints. Are you going to work tomorrow?"

"I don't know what I'm doing," Jose admitted. "I still haven't made arrangements for Rubio's ceremony."

"Did you try calling the person who Ana said would do it?"

"No. I still have to do that," he said.

"I'll be up here waiting for you when you do get it going," I assured him. "You know that, don't you? I wish I could be there to honor him."

"I'm sure he knows that." Jose smiled. "You've done so much already. I'll call the *oriate* in the morning. Have you heard from Hector yet?"

"No. I wasn't expecting him to call. According to Letty, it will be a while before he's able to do that."

Jose paced the living room. "I wish I believed that everything is going to be all right."

"I wonder if they got any good prints." I wondered aloud. "They might be able to identify Marge's assailant."

"The only good things going on here are that Ruffian is all right and that Marge is conscious," Jose said. "We need to connect them. They need each other."

"I'm on vacation," I said. "I'll be happy to bring Ruffian over to Marge, and I'll call a locksmith to change the locks."

"My parents had a good old-fashioned police lock." Jose gave a slight laugh. "It was an iron stick that bolted the door. Maybe we should get one of those."

I smiled at Jose. "We had one too. I had totally forgotten about that. But we don't need police locks; we just need to find the people who did this."

My belly grumbled. "I just realized that I'm starving! How about you? I can whip something up. Eggs. Maybe some toast. Gosh, this is the day that never ends."

I dug into the refrigerator and pulled out eggs and milk. There was bread in the box. Together they would become French toast. That would be the cure for our hunger. I cracked open the eggs and whisked them lightly.

Jose casually glanced over at the window. "Daisy, that guy is outside looking up at the apartment."

"Get away from there," I said. "I'll turn the light off, and we'll look out together."

An instant later, in the darkened room, we both peered at the figure who was sitting on the bench across from the brownstone.

"That proves it," I said. "He couldn't have had anything to do with this. He wouldn't be here if he had."

Jose gave a low whistle. "Rod is going to hate us. How many times are we going to call them tonight?"

"He said he was going to request a police car to stay out there, but I don't see anyone."

I began counting backward from five hundred. I needed to keep my bearings. As I counted, I continued to peer through the wooden slats of the shutters.

"Daisy, don't you think you should buy some curtains?" Jose asked as he went for his phone.

"Never mind calling, they're out there," I announced. A dark sedan had pulled up in front of the lurker. Two undercover policemen emerged from the car and began talking to him.

"I can see them," he said.

"What's with the tone?" I asked. "So now I'm getting on *your* nerves?"

"Sorry, forget it." His voice sounded completely detached.

"I don't want to bicker back and forth. Give me a break, okay?"

"I already said forget it," Jose countered. "Look, he's getting into the car with them."

Both of us were unnerved and powerless. "I know it's tough for you, but it's tough for me too. We're captive in this stupid apartment on top of everything else."

"I need a meeting," Jose said. "It's been a while."

"Go to the early-morning one at St. A.'s. That's always a good one. Maybe I'll go with you."

"Or maybe we can make a meeting here," he suggested. "I have a copy of the *Big Book* on my phone."

"There's one on the shelf right over there," I said. "Pick out a story, and we'll share on it. Two people are all we need. Ruffian can be at our meeting, even though he's still sedated. But whatever he took was against his will, so he doesn't have to count days."

We downed our French toast with cups of decaf. Jose washed the dishes, and we opened the *Big Book*. When we finished reading and sharing on How It Works, we ventured to peek through the window. The street was still empty, and I was grateful. It had been a long day, and we were ready to turn in.

Chapter 14

The incessant peal of the alarm pulled me out of a deep dream. My memory of the dream was cloudy. I had stood in the middle of an empty garage. There wasn't a car or a mechanic in sight. Rust battled oil stains that were scattered on the concrete floor. The cavernous room was dark. I had been alone but was unafraid. I gazed around my room and was glad to be in my bed with the sun breaking the spell of the dark. I opened my dream journal and began to write. When I had finished retrieving my dream and documenting it, I reached with my feet for my slippers and hit against something furry. *Ruffian.*

He was asleep on the throw rug next to my bed. Behind me, Ms. G was kneading my comforter. I gently pulled her to me and rubbed her little head. I'd become mommy to Marge's loves, and I wasn't unhappy about that.

I heard the shower being turned on and remembered the fourth member of our quartet. I stayed in bed for a while and then got up to pull a tarot card. It would give me much needed guidance for the day.

After rubbing the sand out of my eyes, I pulled a card from the deck. The Two of Swords. I pondered the image of the woman dressed in a simple white gown who sat blindfolded against the sea with two swords pointed upward. A chill went through me. Marge was blind. The white dress appeared almost as a hospital gown. That had to be a picture of her. No, that wasn't it. The woman in the cards was *me*. I was blinded. Stuck at the fork in the road. I had decisions to make and didn't want to continue in this uncomfortable spot. The air appeared cool and the swords heavy. The yellow shoes reminded me of love and compassion. Although the woman sat in front of the ocean, I understood the image to be Oshún, the Orisha of the rivers. Oshún signified beauty, kindness, and motherhood in their purest sense.

I gasped, realizing that the woman in the card could also be Rod's wife. Her burden of choosing between her work and being a mother came at a cost. According to Rod, she'd virtually become invisible in their lives. Her responsibility had been as heavy as a sword. She'd lost her husband, motherhood, and her life as she'd known it for however long it had been. That was a terrible cross to bear. I hadn't thought about his wife's plight, only my own.

There was a soft knock at my bedroom door, and I opened it to find Jose fully dressed in a business suit.

"Are you going to work?" I said, wiping my eyes with my fingertips.

"Are you crying?" he asked. "I thought you were still asleep. I didn't want to wake you too early."

"It's nine-thirty," I said. "It's not that early. I thought you were staying home."

"My boss called me in." Jose smiled gently. "I told him that I could only stay for a while this morning, that I had personal business to take care of this afternoon."

"Are you saying that he doesn't know about what happened to Rubio?" I was aghast. "Wait a second. Did he know about Rubio? Or that you were a couple?"

"It's a new job, Daisy. I didn't want to disclose too much to start out with. I planned to tell him, but you know how it is. Then again, you don't really."

"You're right, I don't," I snapped. "I'm not going to apologize for that either."

We stared at each other for a moment. I took a deep breath and let my ego deflate with my lungs.

"I'm going to walk and feed Ruffian. He needs his real mama. She must be devastated without him."

"Possibly not." Jose was flustered. "I spoke to Rod this morning. It seems that Marge took a bigger hit than we thought."

The room started to weave around me. I sat down. "Oh no!"

Jose quickly explained. "No, it's not what you're thinking. They found a hairline fracture in her arm. Someone manhandled her."

"That's horrifying! Poor Marge. We have to bring Ruffian to her. I don't want her getting depressed without him."

"It is overwhelming," he said. "She's just healed up from that tumble down the stairs, and I'm not sure how much more her body can take."

"But we can't stay here watching her all the time. We both have jobs. Maybe she could have someone come in a few hours a day to help her out. She'd probably hate that, though."

Jose commiserated with me. "I'm not sure that she'd agree to having a stranger come in to help her. In the meantime, I've got to eat. Let's get breakfast."

"Didn't we just have breakfast? I'll make a pot of coffee. I need to figure out what I'm doing today. I make plans and then another thing happens, and another, and I totally lose track of what I'm doing. But you, I remember, were planning to call the *oriate* to schedule the ceremony for Rubio."

"I did already," Jose confirmed. "He'll be over by the time I get home from work."

"It's going to feel strange." I got up and walked into the kitchen. The coffee had just finished brewing. "You must really have gotten up early. The coffee's ready."

"Why strange?" Jose poured a cup for himself.

"Think about it," I said. "We spent the night together because of possible danger last night, and suddenly it's safe? You're going to work and then having the ceremony. I don't think it's safe yet."

"You'll be fine. You can stay up here. The ceremony's not going to take all night. I'll come up when it's over."

"I don't really want to be alone here is what I'm saying."

Jose nodded. "Don't worry; maybe you can stay in the bedroom or something. We'll figure it out."

"I just want to know who's behind all of this," I said. "That's all I want."

"Look, I'll take Ruffian out for his walk while you get ready for the day. It'll only take a few minutes.'

"Thank you, Jose. I appreciate you."

I opened the front door to the living room as Jose leashed Ruffian. Once they were gone, I immediately peered through the window. There was no one there. Granted, it was broad daylight and the police had picked him up, but I did have the heebie-jeebies. I went into the bathroom for a quick shower. I opted for a comfortable pair of linen pants with a matching ecru colored shirt. When I returned to the kitchen, Jose was leaning against the window. Ruffian was licking the remains of his bowl and Ms. G her paws.

"Did you ever think that something like this could have happened?" Jose's mood was somber. "I thought that Rubio and I were going to be together forever—at least until we were gray. We used to joke about which one of us would have the walker first. I never prepared for this."

I walked over to my friend and hugged him. While it hurt me to see the tears rolling down his face, I was glad that he was unloading some of his feelings. Avoidance and isolation were never going to help him heal from the reality of Rubio's death.

Jose's phone vibrated on the kitchen table. I snuck a peek and saw Rod's name.

"You might want to get that." I disentangled myself and stood a distance away from him.

I drank some of my coffee while waiting for Jose to finish his conversation with Rod. There wasn't much talk on our side of the phone. The wait was longer than I expected, so I pulled two banana crumb muffins out of the fridge. They'd been in there for a while but weren't stale yet. I popped them into the toaster oven while I waited. The alarm signaled they were done just as Jose finished his call with Rod. He looked perturbed.

"Are you okay?" I pushed one of the muffins toward Jose. "Eat. You have to have something."

He picked it up and complied. "This is the oddest. The stalker. He didn't leave with the police last night."

"What are you talking about? We saw him get into that car with the detectives."

"No. We thought he did. Those weren't detectives. We left the window when the car pulled up and they came out of the car. It seems that when the police got here, they didn't see the stalker at all. I guess we were having our makeshift meeting when that happened. We don't know who that guy is. We're just assuming that he has something to do with Marge and the break-in."

I flushed and veered the focus of the conversation. "Rod said that they're going to question the Montoyas. They're planning to pick the couple up and bring them down to the precinct. And I'm not surprised. We all know that there's something fishy going on with that pair."

Jose picked at the muffin. "I can't help but think of that vision you had several months ago of them toasting. Well, that celebration turned into a funeral."

I waited. It was obvious that he had more to say.

"Do you want to know something? I hope they're not in on this," he said. "The Montoyas were supposed to help him get a space for his artwork. That was it. Rubio went to them in good faith. He trusted them. None of this should have happened."

My head told me that Rubio had been too trusting. That he'd relapsed at some point while working with them. *Hospitals, institutions, and death.* Those were the places that we were sure we'd end up in if we picked up alcohol or drugs again. I needed to make Rubio's death my lesson. He relapsed so that I didn't have to. I had to trust in something too. If I didn't, I'd go down the same road. I shuddered.

"Okay, I hear you," I said. "Let's not make any judgments until after the questioning."

If the stalker were watching us, he would have thought we didn't have a care in the world as we buttered our muffins. Ms. G gazed out the window at the birds that teased by alighting onto the sill. Today would be another long day. I had to take time out for a quick visit to see Marge. Then I had to do something that I dreaded. I had to call Letty. It was time she knew about Rubio's death; despite the fact she was already overwhelmed with anxiety about Hector.

I sat on the couch with my feet tucked under me. I was certain that Letty would need a moment to let the news and its ramifications sink in. I needed a little time as well. Meanwhile, Jose was downstairs with the *oriate*.

Letty sounded exhausted when she began speaking again. "I had no idea. I wish I could have been there for you guys. And the police have no idea who murdered him? If we were up there, I'm sure Mike would have been on it right away."

"I don't think he could have," I said. "Rod can't be on the case because he knew Rubio, so I doubt if Mike could either. Detective Harris is in charge, and he's been working with Liz Munroe. But Rod has pitched in and has basically done everything he can."

"I thought he was here for a special case from Chicago."

"You know about that?" I asked. "How do you know about Chicago?"

"I don't, really," she said. "Mike said something about it one night, but I was half asleep. I'm sure I don't know anything more than you do. I think it was when you came to dinner. The very first time you met Rod at my place. Oh my God. I wish I were back at my place! It's been such a struggle here. Hector is doing better. Staying here at my sister's house, I'm reminded of how conservatively religious she is."

"You're religious too, though." I decided to drop the Rod thing. I didn't want to go into detail on that. At least not yet. I needed to focus on Letty.

"No, I'm not." She sighed. "The only things I'm religious about are taking care of the kids and keeping my marriage together. Mike is ready to fly back up. Neither of us can stay here any longer. We both have to work."

"So soon? I'm surprised. I thought you'd be there for a while. You flew down with the kids. It must have cost a pretty penny."

Letty's voice level dropped to a whisper. "Marisol expects me to go to her services. I don't really want to do that. I don't go to services anymore. The kids like going, though. They like the church songs."

"That's not so bad, is it?" I sensed I was treading on dangerous waters, but I couldn't help but ask the question anyway.

"Being down here has me thinking and acting like I'm the little sister again. Not in a good way. Did you know that my sister's husband has his own church? He's a pastor."

"No, you never told me that. Look, everyone has family issues, but you're not a little girl. You have your own kids now."

"I know that." Letty hissed into the phone. "Let's change the subject, okay?"

"Sure," I said.

But she continued on the same vein. "Did I tell you that Marisol said that Hector was probably hurt because he engages in devil worship? Not only him. But me too."

"She said that?" I was used to family ways, but these words were reminders of how blatantly hurtful loved ones could be in the name of love.

"Maybe I'm wrong for being in this religion," Letty said. "I'm beginning to doubt myself."

"Of course not." I was getting angry. I had no balance anymore and didn't know how to find it. This wasn't about me, but the situation reminded me of my mother, who left a lot to be desired in the mothering department.

"What I mean to say is, don't doubt yourself," I said. "You don't have to be your family. You can be you and still be a vital part of your family."

"I'm not so sure about that."

"Maybe you should come back up," I suggested. "It'll be better for the kids to be home."

"I don't know how Hector will do if he stays down here alone without me."

There was only so much ruminating I could do with her. I tried changing the topic for my own sanity this time.

"I went to see Marge this afternoon," I said. "She has a fractured arm and will be there for a while, and then to a rehab. I brought Ruffian to her. I think that really helped."

My phone buzzed. Another call was coming through. It was Sensei. He'd never called me before.

"Letty, I have to go. Tell *Padrino* he's in my prayers."

I switched calls and heard Sensei's booming voice. "Daisy, we've missed you! Is everything all right?"

"I've had some family stuff to deal with, but I'm okay."

"We're testing for promotions this coming Sunday."

There was a sinking sensation in the pit of my stomach.

"I'm not sure I'll be ready," I admitted. "I haven't really been doing my *katas*."

"Come to class. Saturday afternoon. Let's see what you can do."

"Yes, Sensei." The testing was going to be a disaster; I could feel it in my gut. I was no good at this or anything. I could almost hear Lou's jarring laughter as I hung up the phone.

It was late in the evening and I'd spent the last couple of hours practicing my *katas*. I was doing the most basic forms. *Gekisai Dai Ichi.* Sensei told me that if I did these regularly, I'd never have to go to the gym. Just as I was about to jump into the shower, my phone rang again.

"Hey," I said.

"Are you mad?" Rod asked.

"Please, do we have to go through this again?" I asked. "I'm tired."

"I haven't had a minute to call before now. Can I come over?"

I quickly looked at my watch. "It's ten thirty."

"I know," he said. "It's important, though."

"Is it about the Montoyas? Did they do it?" I interrupted him, suddenly alert to the fact that Rubio's killer might already have been apprehended.

"No, this is about us," he said. "That's just as important, Daisy."

I held my breath. "Just talk?"

"Yeah." Rod's voice quavered. "Just talk."

"Give me about fifteen minutes; I've got to shower."

Exactly a quarter of an hour later, the bell rang. I hadn't heard from Jose yet. I was curious about the ceremony. I ran down to open the door dressed in a pair of navy sweats with a white top piped in gold.

"Thanks for saying yes." Rod kissed me lightly on the cheek.

I walked ahead of him up the stairs. Ms. G looked down at us through the balusters.

We sat next to each other on the living room couch. I felt a break in our energy connection. I'd heard that when someone is sexually intimate with another, their energy remains in the other person for a full year. I wondered if my time with Greg counted and hoped it didn't. *Why did mistakes count?*

"Do you want something to eat or drink?" I asked.

"Daisy." Rod seemed to be fumbling for words. "We had, or have, something good going on. I know there are serious hurdles. Is there any way you could see yourself through with me? I mean, through the obstacles?"

I took his hand and closed my eyes, and my feelings overwhelmed me.

"You sure have come right to the point," I said. "I'm mixed up about this. I can't help but wonder what others would think if we were to go forward together. What would your parents say?"

"They'd say that they were glad I was ready to open to life again and not stay stuck in my sadness."

"I'm surprised to hear you say that."

"Why? Because I don't show my feelings so easily? Because when you met me you had no clue as to what was going on?"

"No," I gently interjected. "I get the part of not sharing your innermost feelings when you meet someone. I do remember thinking that you had an air of mystery about you. I actually thought that you had to leave Chicago because of some crime protection program or something."

Rod laughed. "You're not that far off the mark. Not that close either, but close."

I laughed with him, but then he laughed again, this time with a deeper timbre.

"What?" I asked. "What just happened here?"

"Not anything to get into right now."

"Oh. So I was right! There is more, isn't there?" I shook my head. "You're just like a chocolate cake. You have so many layers to you."

"There was a catalyst to my leaving Chicago," he said. "I thought we went into that already."

"You've got to be frank with me. There's no way I can commit to anything, if that's what you're asking me, if I don't know what I'm walking into."

"I'll tell you what I can."

"Wait a minute," I said. "*Are* you asking for a commitment?"

"I guess I am. I'd like for us to date just each other. No other parties involved."

I flushed a deep crimson. "Have you been dating anyone else?"

"No, Daisy," he said. "But that wasn't really the point. I want it to be just us."

I remained quiet. It was probably better not to get into the specifics of who was dating whom. We were back at square one. I needed a meeting.

"There was an issue with a district there," he said.

"A district?" I echoed. "What does that mean?"

"A district, or rather, a territory. Let's just say similar to what my wife was dealing with—maybe still is. I had to get out. My primary concern was for my wife and daughter. But then she got sucked in. Deeply."

Rod at least had the decency to wince when he said that his main concern was for his wife. I understood that. That's the way things should have been.

"Things were hot out there," he said. "It was suggested that I take a breather and come out here. I never expected to meet you."

I thought of our meeting when he questioned me about the Campbell murder, and then later at Letty's house. I'd never expected to meet him there either. I also didn't expect to care so much.

"What else do you need to know?" he asked. "What more can I tell you?"

I sighed. "I'm not really sure. I'm at a loss. Literally and figuratively. If all this hadn't happened with Rubio, I might be clearer, but I'm not."

"What does that mean? Do you need time to think about this? I can give you time. All the time you need."

I gathered my hair into a topknot as I quickly thought that statement through. I did need time, but not the kind he meant; it was a different kind of time.

"Rod, when we met, I told you that I was in my first year of sobriety. I'd been warned that the first year isn't the best time to make long-range decisions. Now I'm in my second year. I'm still a baby when it comes to being sober. I can't even consider being around a toddler. So, yes, I do need time. I need more sober time!"

I gulped down a sob. I wanted him so badly, but I knew the timing was way off.

I took his hands in mine again. "Listen to me. I care about you. I really do. But right now I need to keep the focus on myself. I need to be in a relationship with myself before I can be in a relationship with anyone else. I hope I'm being clear and that you're not taking this personally."

Rod removed his hands from mine. "You may not mean it to be, but, boy, does it feel personal."

We sat next to each other in the gloom of the dimly lit room for a while. The quiet embraced us like we couldn't, or maybe wouldn't, embrace each other. A feeling of remorse crept over me.

"I don't want to feel guilty about my decision," I said.

"Me neither," he said. "Let's just be cliché and say that we're in the wrong place at the wrong time."

I moved to kiss him, and he shifted. "No, Daisy. It's either yes or no. I hear you saying no, and I want to respect that."

"Let's be friends," I suggested. "We can do that."

"That's so lame, Daisy, and it would be awkward. Let's just give each other some space. Deep down, that's what you want. And it may be exactly what I need too."

His words hung in the air for a while before he slowly got up and walked to the door. As he left, he promised to continue to assist with Rubio's case in any way he could.

I opened the door for him. He didn't look back. I closed it gently.

Hours later, Jose paced the length of the living room. "You've got to be kidding! We've got people watching our every move, and you tell the only detective in Brooklyn who's in love with you to back off? That you need space?"

"I have to maintain some self-respect," I said. "Haven't you ever done anything like that before? You tell me that you're sober, and yet you don't understand my creating some boundaries!"

"I can't right now, Daisy." Jose's voice was anguished. "This is deeper than protection, I understand that, but I just finished a ceremony for the man I love who is dead, for God's sake. I can't even begin to try and figure you out."

I flopped down on the couch. "I still need to take care of myself. Just because this is going on doesn't mean that I should be a parent to a three-year-old. A kid who, by the way, already has a mother."

"I thought you said she had disappeared."

"Because of that, am I supposed to commit myself to a going-nowhere relationship? Rod is married. MARRIED!"

The energy in the room seemed to change, and the severity of the situation was suddenly clear.

"Why is all this happening, Jose?" I asked. "Rubio's gone. Hector was in that awful accident, and now Rod and I have broken up. It's like someone cast a major curse on us."

"I don't know about that, but my sense of loss is tremendous. I told the *oriate* that I'd arrange to meet with him at some point for a reading."

"Do you want to talk about tonight?" I asked. "I mean, what it was like for you?"

"Not really. I'm bushed." He combed his fingers through his hair. "I've got to get some sleep. I don't have another ounce of energy."

"Here, let's pull out the sofa bed. It looks like we're going to be living like this for a while."

"Yeah, okay." We piled the sofa cushions off to the side and pulled out the bed.

A few minutes later I was in my bed with Ms. G curled up next to me. Her soft fur was a comfort. I fell asleep to her purring but was awakened by the sound of a text coming through. I'd forgotten to silence my phone. I looked at the name. *Greg.* I decided to ignore the text. This night was for endings, not beginnings.

Chapter 15

The house was quiet. I stretched my arms and legs out as far as I could and grazed the soft downy pillows and sheets. Ms. G wasn't around. I was alone, but now I was glad for it. It was almost noon. I couldn't remember the last time I'd slept this late. If I could, I'd stay in bed forever, but the adult Daisy wanted coffee and to watch the news. I picked up the remote and turned on the TV set over the fireplace. The midday hour was about to start.

A few commercials ran together, and finally the newscaster began to report the headlines. I wasn't interested in knowing the Dow-Jones Index, but my curiosity was piqued when they showed footage of a suspicious fire at the Bergen Street station. That was my neighborhood subway line. A satchel had been about to go up in smoke, but a quick-thinking attendant put the fire out with an extinguisher he had in his booth. They arrested a homeless man for the incident. I was about to turn the set off when the announcer said that the satchel was somehow related to a recent murder in the Gowanus Canal. The slogan, "If you see something, say something," had become real.

The segment was over before any more information was divulged. I changed the channel, hoping I'd hear more about the incident. While I skimmed through the channel list, the phone rang.

"Did you hear the news today?" Jose asked.

"Just now," I said. "What does it mean?"

"I haven't heard from Sam or Rod, but according to the news, the bag they found belonged to Rubio. They said there were papers inside, and the detectives were keeping them as evidence. Those bag questions were important after all. Or at least someone thought the bag was important."

"I'm still not sure," I admitted. "I thought he might have had a bag, but with the arm immobilizer on—I don't remember. I was too busy worrying about him."

"I'm hanging up now," he said. "I'm at work. We'll talk tonight."

"I told you that he had papers all over the living room the last day I saw him in your apartment. I don't know how you didn't notice it."

"Daisy, I've got to go."

We hung up simultaneously. I guessed that he didn't want to speculate, and neither did I. I snuggled down under the covers. I felt Ms. G jump on the bed and knead the coverlet. I wouldn't come out again until Jose came home. This was supposed to be my vacation, but my work life had ruined those lazy all-day bed marathons for me. I got up a couple of hours later and made my way to the shower. The water felt like icy hot spikes hitting my skin. I reveled in it; that is, until I heard the bathroom door creep open, which startled me.

"Jose?" I yelled out. "I'm in the shower. Close the door; I don't want to get sick. I'll be right out."

I climbed out of the shower. The bathroom door was still open and the apartment was empty.

"Ms. G!" I called. "Be patient, I know you're hungry. I'll be right out, little one."

When I emerged from the bathroom in my robe, I spotted Ms. G at my front door. It was unlocked but closed. I must have forgotten to lock it. *So careless.* I must have been hearing things. The last thing I wanted was to invite danger in, so I secured the door as it should have been and fed the cat.

That evening, we sat drinking lemonade in the backyard at the bistro set we'd picked up for Marge. The crocuses and daffodils we'd planted the previous autumn dotted the garden spot brightly under the festive lights we'd strung on the fence that surrounded the yard.

"What have the police told you about the bag?" I asked. "I've been on pins and needles all day."

"I haven't heard from the detectives yet. I'm trying to stay chill. I've got to believe that if they had any new or important information, they'd let me know."

"I'm like you," I said. "I believe and then I don't believe in them. I go back and forth. It must be my paranoia. Would you believe that today I actually thought that someone had come into my apartment while I was showering?"

"It's your nerves," Jose said. "No one would come here in the middle of the afternoon."

"Well, that lowlife did come in the afternoon and totally terrified Marge," I said. "I miss her. I thought that when the weather was warm enough, we'd be sitting out here with her. And Ruffian."

"Yeah, well, she'll be back home after a few days in rehab." Jose was dejected. "Rubio is never going to be out here with us."

"You're right." I took a deep breath to stop myself from saying something that I would regret later. I didn't want to annoy Jose, but in my heart I knew that Rubio wouldn't be sitting out here with us, even if he were alive. Rubio had been a loner. He was either in his studio or at the gallery. He had become a shadow among us.

"Come to think of it," Jose said, "I'm not sure Rubio would have joined our little group out here."

I was taken aback. Had I spoken out loud? "What do you mean?"

"You know how Rubio was. Always by himself. We'd gotten closer again during the last few months, but it was tenuous, Daisy. I loved him, and I don't doubt that he loved me, but he was so secretive. I'm not looking forward to going through his things. I'm kind of afraid of what I might find."

I poured more lemonade into his glass. "Would you like one of these pastries? I picked them up at Cousin John's this afternoon. They're fresh."

"Food. Always there to soothe the savage breast."

"You mean music."

"I'm not following you," Jose admitted.

"Food doesn't soothe the savage breast. It's music that can do that. Music soothes the savage breast." I cut him a piece of a sweet cinnamon apple turnover. "Here, eat. I'm sure it'll do what it can to make you feel better."

"Are you changing the subject? Does it make you uncomfortable when I talk about Rubio like this? I loved him, but he wasn't such an easy guy. He looked as carefree as could be, but he wasn't. Rubio was always battling those demons. That much I know."

"I hope he finds his peace now," I said. "I think that sometimes people can't make their peace until after they leave the Earth."

"You're philosophical, aren't you," Jose said. "And I'm feeling just a little bitter. I worked hard to make our relationship work."

"I'm sure that he did too." I took a sip of the cool drink. "You guys were so happy during my first-year anniversary party. We were all so happy."

My recollection of Jose and Rubio holding hands and looking as though they were totally in love also brought back the memory of my growing love and desire for Rod that day.

"Maybe this isn't the best thing to be doing right now."

"What do you mean?" he asked.

"Thinking of that horrible thing that happened to you two. I know that it's not the same thing, but Rod and I aren't together either."

"That's something you can work on, though, if you both want it enough," he said. "For us, I really think that it was the drug that got between us. What drug, I'm not sure. It could have been the actual drug, or maybe the drug of success."

"I can identify with that. Although right now I don't know what my success would be. Let's face it, all I'm doing is going to work and coming home. And meetings."

"Notice how you just made this about you?"

"You think?" I did have that tendency. "I can't forget that the two major things keeping Rod and me apart are his wife and baby."

"It may not be as terrible as it looks to you right now."

We both leaned back in our chairs and gazed at the weakening sunlight that filtered through the pale green leaves of the trees. We weren't in our best states, and the ease of the early evening helped us to at least relax.

"Do you think we're both in a kind of grief?" I asked. "Like I said, what I'm going through may not be anywhere as bad as what you are, but I'm in a sort of mourning too. Not only about Rubio, but Rod too. Of what might have been."

"You two could still have a strong relationship. Just not in the way you had envisioned it."

"Do you think I'm shallow?" I didn't wait for him to answer. "It's just too complicated for me. I can barely feed the pets. How am I supposed to feed a kid?"

"That makes no sense. You two have been seeing each other for a few months. I don't think that he's asking you to raise his child. There's so much you don't know about each other. A relationship takes time to grow."

"Well, I don't have that much time."

"What are you talking about?"

"I spent too much time partying," I said.

"Remember that *we will not forget the past nor wish to shut the door on it*," Jose reminded me. "You are definitely more accountable for your actions."

"Thanks, I appreciate that," I said. "You are great for spouting AA slogans today, my friend. When did you last get to a meeting?"

"That's one of the Promises, not a slogan." He yawned. "It's been a while."

"Can I ask you something?"

"Okay, although I reserve the right not to answer." Our eyes met. His seemed veiled.

"What's your plan with Rubio's body now that the ceremony is over?"

"Whoa. I wasn't ready for that. How can you say *body* so easily? I'm basically waiting for forensics to say they've completed the autopsy."

"You're right," I said. "I'm sorry."

"I can answer that question anyway. His body, as you put it, is going to be shipped back to Colombia. The motherland."

"How's that going to be for you?" I asked. "I can't imagine not being able to put flowers on his grave, or going to the cemetery a couple of times a year."

"When I said *motherland*, I meant it. It's his mother. She's insisting he come home. That's what she said. He should come *home*. As though *this* isn't his home. As though he hasn't lived here all of his adult life and—"

I interrupted him. "You were practically married."

"That doesn't fit into his family paradigm. According to them, Rubio should have been married, yes, but to a woman. There was Rita. She would have been the perfect wife for him. I was a bad influence, you see."

"How come I never heard about Rita before?"

"Well, the topic of Rita only came up when his mother was visiting or when we got into an argument. And that usually happened when she came up to visit. Rarely, but it happened."

The sun had set and twilight was upon us. I shivered a bit. "Who is Rita?"

"Rita was born the same year that Rubio was. Both sets of parents were close and very old-fashioned. Traditional. They got it into their heads that the two would make a good couple. Both families were moneyed and made of good stock."

"It all turned out to be moot, though, didn't it?" I asked.

"Yes," he said. "His parents never respected our time together."

"What about your family?" I probed. "Did you tell them? Do they know?"

"It's getting chilly out here. We should probably go inside."

"What just happened here? They know about you two, don't they?"

"Of course." He smiled and shook his head. "My parents know. The rest of the family, probably not. We were roommates to them. You'd think we were living in the fifties. Both Rubio and I had to play that for years. You know that." Jose paused and became wistful. "I don't really want to talk about it tonight."

I stood up. "Are you staying in my apartment?"

"I'm not sure." He took a deep breath. "Daisy, part of me wants to go away. I don't really want to be here right now."

"I need you, though," I admitted. "I don't feel safe here alone. Please."

Jose was thoughtful for a moment. "I'll stay, but I need some space."

"Sure. Me too," I said. "I think."

We reentered the house, making sure that the back door was securely locked. We walked upstairs. I went into the dark of my bedroom and Jose sat in the dark of the living room. It seemed as if we'd never be in the light again.

Chapter 16

The room was filled with the Saturday morning regulars. Most of the members were chatting, with the bright-eyed looks of those who had enjoyed a full night's sleep. A few hid behind coffee cups filled with fresh brew. I wished that I could sit with my sunglasses on to hide the gray circles under my eyes, but that would be against any norm for this group. We were supposed to look into each other's eyes, if not souls. I concentrated on the shades hanging on the wall that listed the Twelve Steps and the Twelve Traditions.

"Daisy." Greg slipped into the empty chair beside me. I immediately regretted coming to the meeting.

The Promise, *We will not regret the past nor wish to shut the door on it*, came to mind. What happened between us couldn't be erased. It had to become part of my experience, strength, and hope.

"Mind if I sit here?" he asked. Clear-eyed and gorgeous as usual. Not a care in the world. At least, not as far I could tell from where I sat.

"If you name it, it's your seat," I said.

"You know what I mean. I know that you've been trying to avoid me. Unless your cell is on the fritz, you've ignored all of my reach-outs. Not good for my ego."

I laughed. "You're right. There's a lot going on and, well, I—"

"Yeah, yeah, I know," he said. "Too much going on to see that the sun is shining? That there are about thirty people here who share your sobriety? That I'm trying to connect with you because I really like you?"

"I wasn't ready for that one."

"Maybe how we started out was unorthodox," he began, but the chair had begun reading the Preamble.

The rest of the meeting was predictable, just as I wanted it to be. Another member read from How It Works. Just hearing the words in the quiet room reminded me that indeed the sun was shining. Although we were in the church basement, light filtered through the small arch-shaped windows.

The speaker was a woman about my age who was celebrating ninety days of sobriety. She told her tale, so different from mine, but so much the same. I listened to her qualification. Her story bore that same emptiness about a life of isolation.

"Except for my evening trysts with Stoli, I had no relationships," she said. "I'd become such a loser. One night in college I went to a party. I argued with my friends when they suggested I cool it with the beer keg. I walked a couple of miles back to my dorm at three in the morning on a dirt road. All I was concerned about the next day was that my pedicure had been ruined."

The laughter in the room erupted, and my shoulders loosened. I identified so deeply with the absurdity of my life while drinking and the danger that I'd easily ignored. Today I could laugh with the others. As long as I kept going to meetings, I would never have to depend on spirits for my spirit.

At the end of the meeting we held hands and said the Serenity Prayer. As I turned to leave, Greg stopped me.

"H-e-l-l-o. You forgot me?" His smile was engaging.

Lame struck. "Not really. I wasn't sure you still wanted to chat."

"Let's have brunch," he suggested. "This time it's my treat. And, no, we don't have to go to my place if that would make you uncomfortable."

I paused before I heard myself say, "Brunch would be nice."

We sauntered along Sixth Avenue from St. Augustine's Church. The quiet avenue, with its huge overhanging trees, was a delight compared to the bustle on Seventh Avenue, where strollers vied with people standing in the middle of the street with their elbows sticking out as they compared stories about the neighborhood food co-op. I didn't need to walk around an obstacle course. I needed tranquility.

"Where would you like to go?" Greg asked.

"Surprise me," I said. "Wait. Never mind about that. Let's go to Purity. It'll be a nice walk, and I'm in the mood for a huge stack of buttermilk pancakes."

"Purity it is." We continued on Sixth until we reached Seventh Street and made our way up the block.

"We're at my job," I said. Windsor Medical Center sprawled over more surface area almost daily. Fortunately, I didn't come across any of my co-workers. I'd almost forgotten I was on vacation. I relaxed knowing Sophia wouldn't be anywhere around. Anything she had to take care of on a Saturday would be done by phone.

We were seated in the diner, and the server gave us a nod and told us he'd be right back with our menus.

"I thought that you were taking karate lessons on Saturday mornings." The statement jolted me. I'd be testing for my yellow belt on the following afternoon, and I hadn't done much to prepare.

"This afternoon," I said. "I have the kids."

"That's right," Greg said. "It's your teaching day."

"If you can call it that," I said. "You must have a better memory than me. Did we talk about this?"

"How else would I know?" he asked.

We received our menus and browsed through them, although my mouth was already watering thinking about a stack of pancakes. The big question was, did I want them with sausage or bacon?

"What are you having?" Greg didn't miss a beat.

"The buttermilk pancakes with bacon."

"Sounds good. I'll have sausage. Okay with you if we share?"

I nodded. It was easy with Greg. Too easy.

As usual, the restaurant was lively. It hurt sitting there watching everyone enjoying themselves in what seemed to be deep conversation, and I wasn't sure why. I slipped into a sudden funk. We finished our meal silently. I couldn't pretend to be happy when I was feeling so low.

"Would you mind terribly if we just paid the check and I went home?" I asked. "I know, I'm a real pill."

"No problem." Greg pulled his wallet out of the pocket of his thin leather jacket. He placed a few bills down on the table.

"Here, let me pay for mine," I said.

Greg stopped me. "No, this is my treat. I'm glad that you ate something. You don't look so happy."

"Nothing, unfortunately, comes between me and a meal." I pushed my chair back, readying to leave.

"Daisy, wait," he said. "I want you to know that I'm here for you whenever you want to talk. Take it as slowly as you need to. I want a true friendship with you."

"But you don't even really know me."

"That might be true, but it doesn't mean that we can't get to know each other. Like I said earlier, life happens. I'm around. You're around. Friendship. I can respect your vibe."

"I like that. Respect a vibe. I can respect your vibe too."

He extended his hand toward me. "Shake on the friendship?" he asked.

I took his hand and we shook. My eyes met his. Although we'd been intimate, his hand seemed unfamiliar to me.

"So, I'll see you tomorrow?" he asked.

"I don't think so. I'm testing for my yellow belt. Now I'm totally confused!"

"Sensei asked me to be on the panel to observe his students' testing tomorrow."

"That's crazy," I said. "I had no idea you were in martial arts too! Why didn't you say anything? How are you connected?"

"I'm a second-degree black belt. I met Sensei at another dojo years ago. We studied together, actually. Teens at the teen club. He had a couple of years on me." Greg laughed as he gazed into the distance. "I think it was the PTA that had this guy come in who did more talking than teaching, but it was a great start for us. Kept us out of trouble. Red said there's you and a couple of women who are moving toward their black belts. And a guy who's testing for his brown belt."

I sat back deflated. "Jake."

"Yes, that's the name." Greg stood up. "I guess you need time to work out the last kinks before your test."

"But, wait, you've been friends with Sensei all along?"

Greg hesitated. "No, we met up recently at a tournament."

"This is really coincidental," I said.

"I prefer to call it serendipitous."

"Is it ethical for you to test me when you know so much about me?" I asked. "A little too much."

"No worries. I'm there to look at technique. It has nothing to do with anything else. You won't be thinking about me; you'll be focused on your test.

I groaned inwardly. He was right. I had to think about that test. I tightened my abs. Next would be my fortitude.

A soft rap at the door brought me back to the present. Spending the afternoon with the children had been sweet. Hearing them call me *Miss Daisy* was even sweeter. The last two hours of kicks, punches, and blocks in my apartment had turned into a deep meditation. I reluctantly got up to open the door.

"Hey," Jose said, "I wondered if you were home. I heard some noise earlier, and then it got really quiet up here."

"Come in," I said. "I was meditating. I'm having my yellow-belt test tomorrow, and I figured the least I could do was to practice. What time is it? I lost all track of time."

"It's almost eight," he said. "I got a call today. Something I was totally not expecting."

"Sit down, tell me all about it." I gave him the once-over. He was wearing white again. I was wearing gray.

Jose remained standing. "I heard from Rubio's mother. She's coming up here."

"Are you kidding? Why would she do that?"

"That's exactly what I asked her. She said that she wanted to accompany his body down to Colombia."

"How's that for you?" I asked. My monkey brain was back in action and began to create a million little stories. So much for meditation.

"I'm not sure. She wants to stay with me for the few days that she'll be up here to see which of Rubio's belongings she'll want to bring back to Colombia."

"Are you serious? What gives her the right to do that? He was up here for years. This is his home."

"I agree. Believe me, I thought about all of that. But she needs to find her peace too."

"You're too good," I said. "I don't know how you can be so obliging. I don't think I could be."

"If I remember correctly, you were pretty cool with Lou's mother and aunt when he died."

"That was a totally different story." I shuddered to think about that time. It was always popping up and would most likely continue to do so for the rest of my life.

Jose paced the floor. "Maybe I should tell her to stay at an Airbnb or something. It might be better for both of us."

"For God's sake, Jose, please sit down," I said. "You're making me nervous."

"Sorry," Jose said, as he chewed on one of his cuticles.

"Stop that! Aren't you the King of the Mani-cure?"

Jose gave a soft laugh. "At one time I was a lot of things. I can't vouch for today."

"You have a one-bedroom," I reminded him. "That's a good excuse."

"Not really. Rubio was using that second room for his studio. He had a futon in there. If she doesn't want to sleep in there, then she can stay elsewhere."

"Can I ask you something?"

"Is it related to this? I don't really have room in my head for anything else." Jose shifted uncomfortably.

"What about Rubio's artwork?" I asked. "What are you planning to do with it? He's got some beautiful pieces."

"Believe me, I thought of that," he said. "As far as I know, she may want all of it."

"How can you avoid that from happening?" I asked. "I mean, isn't all of his property yours?"

"You have way too many questions, Daisy. I'm speaking with a contact that one of the lawyers at my company referred me to. And to answer your next question, I took him into my confidence about our relationship."

"That still makes my blood boil," I said. "Having to hide the fact that you two were a couple."

"Please, let's not get into that again, okay? Really, I can't."

I held my hand up. "Sorry. I'll stop."

We sat gazing into space for a few minutes. The evening light had darkened, and I hadn't put any lights on. The light emanating from the streetlamp was sufficient. Rubio's paintings. The gallery. Everything was a crapshoot at this point. Then I remembered. *The gallery in Manhattan!*

"Jose, did you know that Rubio had some paintings for sale in SoHo?"

"What are you talking about?" he asked. "How do you know this?"

"I forgot to tell you. I went to a meeting to sort of check out Rubio's steps and met his sponsee, Ryan. He told me that Rubio had paintings in a gallery called the Moratorium, or something like that."

"Miguel's Moratorium? Are you serious? How could you forget to tell me that?"

"Come on, you know things have been messy," I said. "I'm telling you now. Doesn't that count for something?"

A mix of emotions cascaded visibly over Jose. "Did you see his work there?"

"No, I didn't go there. Or to the White something." I winced.

"The White Buffalo? My God! He wanted to have his paintings there so badly. That's all he talked about for so long."

"His dream came true, then, didn't it?"

"Yes," he said.

"You don't sound thrilled by that."

"How could his dream come true and he not share it with me?" he asked. "There's so much I don't know, isn't there?"

"Let's go to the galleries tomorrow," I said.

"He didn't want me to know they were there," he said. "Why would I go there now?"

"Let's just go, Jose," I said. "We'll meet after my testing at the dojo. I'll come back for you."

The pain in Jose's eyes was unbearable. I wished that I had answers for him. I wished that I could comfort him. I sat in silence with him until he was ready to leave. We'd both spend the night alone and take our chances.

Chapter 17

My gear bag landed with a soft thud at the bottom of the staircase. I followed it down one step at a time and bent to pick it up where it landed in front of Jose's door. My eyes lifted and met with his as he stepped out of his apartment.

"What's with throwing luggage down the stairs, Daisy? Is this what you do when you think no one's around?" Jose took my bag from me and continued down to the second floor with it. He stopped in front of the main entry door and handed it to me when I reached him.

"Thanks. I didn't mean to bother you," I said. "Where are you going, anyway? I thought we were going to meet later. If I finish at the dojo early enough, we might be able to make it to both galleries."

"Today's your testing. I'm going with you. I wouldn't let you go to that by yourself. It's important."

"God, you are sweet, and I love you for that," I said. "Did I ever tell you that my parents missed my kindergarten end-of-school recital, and I've never been the same since?"

"Yeah, that's why I'm going." He laughed. "You must have told me that story a gazillion times."

I nudged him in the ribs. "Don't you know that I'm scarred for life because of that?"

"Yeah, sure, whatever," he said. "The real reason I'm going is that I thought it would be good to get out. Focus on you rather than me. I know you like that a lot better than the other way around."

"You're incorrigible."

We walked down to Fifth Avenue and made our way to the dojo. The morning was a bit chilly after a string of warm days.

"I think it might rain," I said. "Look at that sky."

"No, it'll clear up," he said. "I'm sure."

"How do you know? Did your psychic sensibilities give you that information?"

"I checked the weather app before we left," he said. "No umbrella-carrying if I can help it."

"I'm glad to hear you sounding, I don't know, lighter. And I do appreciate your coming with me. You don't have to, but you are. I didn't tell you that there's this guy, Greg, from AA, who is going to be there. He's a black belt. It's like worlds colliding for me. I mean, we're not dating, and Rod is so important to me, but—"

"Daisy, stop!" Jose said. "I'm pleading with you. I might have to go home after all unless you stop to take a breath."

"I was just sharing my feelings," I said. "I'm anxious."

"Maybe now is a good time for you to be chill. You know, reflect on the test that you're about to take. Take a moment to envision that yellow belt around your waist."

"I have been meditating, you know. I just hope that I've been practicing the *katas* enough. What if they make me spar? I—"

"Shh! Daisy!"

We walked the rest of the way in silence. Jose was right. I immediately began to feel calmer. The sun peeked through the clouds, and I instinctively felt that everything was going to be all right. I took a couple of deep breaths, and the wet spring air filled me with hope and a tinge of joy. I was ready to try for that yellow belt.

The entrance to the dojo was buzzing with parents giving last-minute instructions to their children as they tied their *obis*. Most of the children also wore white belts. A couple of yellow- and green-belted children dotted the sea of white. They would be tested first, Sensei told me, after I'd introduced him to Jose. Sensei stood near the door welcoming his students. I was relieved to see that Greg wasn't there.

I walked down the steps to the dressing room. Suddenly, I was face to face with Greg, and Jake was coming up right behind him.

"Sorry, Daisy, hold on a sec." Greg gallantly stepped back down the stairs to allow me to pass. It would have been a tight squeeze.

"Hey, you two know each other?" Jake seemed genuinely surprised.

"We have mutual friends," Greg volunteered.

"Nice. It's a small world," Jake said. "See you upstairs, Daisy."

I entered the dressing room, which was filled with the women who were changing into their uniforms. This time I smiled at a couple of them as I prepared to change into my *gi*. They smiled back and spoke words of encouragement to one other, me included. I did the same. Maybe things would be different if I acted differently.

The dojo was filled with excited children. The pressure was high. Parents stood around as if the children were vying for the Olympics. Three kids had completed their *katas*, forms that were at their levels. They were expected to spar with each other, and only one little boy, Troy, looked as though he were about to burst into tears. He stopped quickly enough and finished his match. He joined the rest of the children and accepted his green belt from Sensei.

The adults were next. I identified with Troy and was about to burst into a fit of nervous tears. My anxiety was getting the best of me. Instead of crying, I warmed up as the children filed out of the room, with the obligatory bow at the door before exiting.

As we lightly stretched, a few of the women gave each other fist bumps. Encouragement. I found myself doing it too. A woman who sported a black belt entered the dojo. I'd never seen her before. Greg emerged behind her. I closed my eyes to ground myself again. When I opened them, Jake was standing next to me.

"Good luck, Daisy," he said. "I'm testing too. For my brown belt. Wish me luck."

"You know I wish you luck, Jake," I answered. "Just don't break a leg!"

We smiled at each other. The twinkle in his eye reminded me of the night that I'd accidently punched him in the nose. We could be friends, as he'd said. My world was opening up and so different from how I'd ever imagined it would be. I almost hugged myself as I practiced walking through *Gekisai Dai Ichi*, my level of *kata*.

We were called up to the front of the room with the other white-belted students, and we bowed before our judges, as they, in turn, returned the bow. The first *kata* we were directed to do was *Gekisai Dai Ichi*, just as I thought it would be. An inner knowing engulfed me as I went through each step, and I sailed through it. I'd practiced regularly before the tragic events, and my body's memory came through. There was no stumbling or hesitation, and the form was over quickly. My fears were put to rest.

Next, we were asked to don our safety equipment. I put my mouth guard in after I was tucked into the padded gear. One of the ladies, Jeri, was placed across from me. She had on a green belt. A stab of fear cut through my stomach. I again remembered to breathe and center. I was ready. And even if I wasn't, I knew that Sensei wouldn't let any harm come to me.

We went through a couple of rounds of *kumite*. Jeri punched me right away in my solar plexus. I moved to block myself more adequately. It hurt. Maybe I wouldn't win the match, but I wasn't going to allow myself to go down. She must have heard my thought, because the next thing I knew, I was on the floor. She caught me under my knee with her strong leg and swiftly swept me down. The wood was hard as I plopped down on it. We grappled for long moments. I pulled her down over me and wouldn't let go of her. She was immobilized by me as we remained virtually locked in an embrace.

"Okay, you two, enough," Sensei called. "*Yame!*"

Jeri and I stood up and bowed to each other. The match was over.

We sat over to the side as several other matches and various *katas* were performed. I heaved a sigh of relief. Whatever the outcome, I had suited up and shown up. This was important to me, and I hadn't realized how much until today.

At the end of the testing, we were instructed to form parallel lines. Sensei walked the length of the room, with Greg next to him holding various colored belts. Sensei congratulated each person as he gave out the belts. We'd all passed.

This time I allowed a tear to roll down my cheek as I held my cherished yellow belt. When I'd entered the dojo for the very first time, I'd bought my *gi* and *obi*. Today, I'd earned my *obi*. I pulled off my white one and replaced it with my reward. It was mine, and I was ecstatic.

After we had each received our belts, we bowed to each other, to the judges, and then to the dojo. We filed out of the room. Laughter filled the air. Tensions were gone. We congratulated each other, hugged, and patted each other's backs. Our joy filled the air.

I'd just spotted Greg smiling at another student, when Jake came over and hugged me.

"We did it, Daisy!" he crowed. "Congrats. Well done!"

"Congrats to you too!" I matched his glee. "This is better than I ever expected. You must be so proud! A brown belt. Wow!"

"I can't lie, I am," he said. "Do you want to go out for lunch? A little celebration?"

"I'd love to, but I can't," I said. "I wish I could, but I promised my friend that we would go into the city. There's something important we have to do today."

"Rain check?" he asked.

"Absolutely," I said.

"Great," Jake said. "Anyway, this was a great morning, and we are now officially promoted."

We quickly hugged, and as we released each other, I noticed that Greg had been observing the whole interaction. I excused myself and went downstairs to change my clothes. The ladies were in varying stages of dress, but everyone stopped to hug me and offer their congratulations. I did the same for them. I relished the time and felt a part of something that I didn't often experience.

After I had showered and dressed, I returned upstairs. Sensei stood with Jose and Greg. The dojo had emptied out quickly.

"Thanks, Sensei," I said. "I'm so happy!"

"You deserve the promotion, Daisy," Sensei said. "Don't lose focus. You seem to have a knack for this."

"Maybe I do have a knack, but it's more like I practiced!"

He laughed. "Excuse me! You're so right. But you do have promise. Karate may be the way of the empty hand, but it also helps to empty yourself of everything that's not needed. What do you say, Greg?"

"I'm not sure if I told you that Daisy and I know each other on the outside. Daisy knows that I try to enjoy what's in front of me. The beautiful sky, the beautiful day, a beautiful girl. That's my segue into asking you out for lunch. How about it? We can celebrate."

"Sorry, I'm booked," I said. "Jose and I have a date. We'll talk soon."

"This time when I call you, please answer!"

Greg's impish grin was sweet, but mixing my relationships in karate with my personal life could be a ticklish situation.

I smiled, tucking my arm into Jose's, and we began our way back to the house.

"So why didn't you tell me that you were so popular," he said. "If I knew, I wouldn't have made plans with you for this afternoon."

"Forget about that, okay?" I begged. "Let's just be on our way. It's still early. We can eat something after we've decided what we're going to do about Rubio's pieces."

"Great. Let's go."

The rhythm of the El was lulling. The earlier threat of rain had completely disappeared. A few puffy clouds lingered against a backdrop of azure blue sky. Beautiful.

"I feel like I'm crashing right now." I leaned my head against Jose's shoulder.

"I would imagine that the high of this morning's promotion would have this effect. Last-minute training and expectations can do a number on a person."

I roused myself. "What about you? What are your expectations about going into the city?"

Jose gazed through the window as the buildings slipped by in a whir. The world around us had turned into an impressionistic portrait.

"Not sure. I don't know which paintings he gave to the gallery," he said. "He did so much without me."

I nodded and nestled close to my friend. I knew there were no words that could make him feel better. This time Jose leaned his head against mine. I'd done the right thing.

We got off at Prince Street and climbed the steps up to the bustling street. That old saying, *the city never sleeps*, was true. The only time it was empty was during a commercial or movie shoot. In those cases, large trucks hiding actors and equipment were kept out of the camera's view. There was a certain artificiality to the city that I hadn't noticed before. The beautiful people roaming the streets and frequenting the galleries and shops were all wearing casual expensive clothing. Many carried latte-filled paper cups. I was suddenly feeling oppressed by the atmosphere.

Jose woke me from my reverie. "I'm not feeling very happy right now. This is depressing. Where are the regular people? It's like a movie set."

I laughed. We often shared the same thoughts. I was glad we still had that connection. We walked a few blocks, and there in front of us was Miguel's Moratorium.

Jose seemed to steel himself at the gallery entry. "Let me do the talking, okay?"

"Yeah, sure."

The gallery was cavernous. A red-headed greeter handed us a brochure with a map of the current artists and their entries. Rubio's photo was one of the last of the images. It was a kick to the gut.

"You okay?" I asked. Jose's face held no emotion. It had become a mask, like one of the medieval masks that filled the wall to my left. I could have used an armored suit before seeing that picture of Rubio.

"I'm all right," he said. "I've got to get used to stuff like this. Nothing should take me by surprise anymore."

We walked through the gallery. Medieval regalia shared space with some futuristic type of pottery that made no sense at all to me. The next room we meandered into held a grouping of portraits of somber faces that was entitled, *Friends*.

"That artist must have been a friend of Munch's," I said. "Don't you think?"

"To each his own."

"Sorry. I didn't realize that you didn't want to talk."

"God, Daisy, no. I'm sorry. Yeah, I see what you mean. I'm just a tad uneasy right now."

We proceeded into a vast array of rooms, each organically leading into another. Whoever owned the gallery was quite wealthy. The rental fee had to be enormous. It dawned on me that I was always thinking about money.

"There." Jose pointed his chin to the back wall. There were Rubio's portraits; his *Moonlit Eyes* series. A chill went through me. I had tried to get a sneak peek when he had been working on the portraits of people in varying degrees of conversation or meditations, as he called them, with the moon. They were stunning. The urge to cry caught in my throat, but I held it in and breathed deeply of the magic displayed on canvas.

"Oh Jose."

"Yeah, exactly." We held each other's hands as we stood before Rubio's art.

"They've all been sold," Jose said.

Bright red stickers showed the dates they'd been purchased. All had been sold on the morning after his death.

"How could this be?" I asked. "I wonder who bought them."

"Let's see if we can find out."

Jose strode over to the greeter. "Excuse me. I'd like some information on one of the artists and his paintings."

"Sir, did you receive one of our brochures when you came in?" The redhead was about to hand him another, but he stopped her.

"Yes, thank you. I'd like more information. Who can I speak to?"

"Unfortunately, our curator is not available today. I can give you a card, and you can call on Wednesday."

"Wednesday? But it's only Sunday."

"I apologize, sir, but we are closed on Mondays and Tuesdays."

Jose breathed deeply. "Are you sure that he or she isn't available now?" His right temple began to visibly throb, and the energy around him appeared to change. I felt that I had to intervene before he lost his temper.

"May I help you?" A gentleman in his forties came forward from behind the desk. His salt-and-pepper goatee didn't match his shaggy brown hair. It had to be a toupee. The well-cut suit he wore did not hide his pudgy figure.

"I'm Mr. Cusumano," he said. "How may I be of service?"

"I was asking for the art curator," Jose explained.

"Excuse me." The head of flaming curls disappeared into a group of tourists wearing tee-shirts and white sneakers.

"I am he." Mr. Cusumano bent slightly at the waist. "How can I help you?"

"The Mauricio Rubio exhibit." Jose led us back to the wall of portraits.

"Exquisite, aren't they? They are quite popular. These have been sold, of course, but there are many who are interested in his work. He's a fairly new artist. How are you acquainted with his work?"

"I know him personally," Jose countered.

"I see." The curator's eyelids shifted downward. "Then I'm sure you've heard."

"Heard?" Jose asked.

"My understanding is that the artist was a victim of his own hand."

Chapter 18

All motion in the gallery seemed to cease. I searched my friend's face for a reaction and saw none.

"Really." Jose appeared nonplussed. "I hadn't heard that at all."

"I'm not here to gossip, but he was such a wonderful new artist at the cusp of an illustrious career. Imagine, found floating in the Gowanus Canal. Of all places!"

I was uncertain whether the curator's arrogant tone would survive the moment. Jose kept his cool, though.

"Actually, I knew Mr. Rubio quite well," Jose said. "If you choose to tell his story, please keep it authentic. Mauricio Rubio was murdered. And he wasn't found floating in the Gowanus Canal. Got that?"

Mr. Cusumano's countenance abruptly changed. "I didn't intend any offense, my dear gentleman. What is it that you wanted to know when you asked my assistant for help?"

"Who bought the portraits?"

"I can't share that information. It's privileged."

"Did the same person buy the four portraits?"

He thought it over a moment. "I guess there's no harm in saying yes. That is really all I can share with you, sir."

Suddenly, Jose was steering me out of the gallery. "Let's

go," he whispered in my ear. "We're not getting anywhere with this pompous puss."

We reemerged into the natural sunlight, which was a far cry from the almost trance-inducing lighting in the gallery. It was no wonder people paid thousands for the artwork in there.

"Is that why you're a child of Obatalá?" I asked. "You were able to keep your head in there."

"I don't know about that," Jose said. "But I do know that it's important to keep your *ori* cool. There's no need to react like a hothead just because someone acts like an ass. In theory, anyway."

"So infuriating," I said. "I wonder why he wouldn't share the names."

"He's probably obligated to protect his clients."

"Whatever." I looked up the block. "I'm getting hungry. We didn't eat anything after the promotions this morning."

"There's a diner across the street," he said. "Lunch on me?"

"Sure. I'd love a burger."

New York is known for its diner experience, and the menus are virtually the same wherever one lands. Somehow many of the restaurants managed to maintain the high rents. I assumed that many owners still had family businesses in which the original owners had bought buildings.

"Daisy! Daisy!" Jose attempted to get my attention. "I hate when you go off into la-la land."

"I'm here. Sorry." We entered the diner. It must have been redone in the last few years, but there were still built-in booths near the windows. The host asked if we wanted to sit at a table by the kitchen. The simultaneous shakes of both our heads gave him the message. Booth only.

Once we were seated, we perused the menus intently. The cheeseburger was tempting, but so was the chicken wrap. Sweet potato fries as a side. No, I had to have a cheeseburger. That was one of my favorite diner dishes.

As we waited for our lunch, I summoned up the gumption. "What next? We're at a standstill."

"We've got to think this through. There's always an opening, as hard as it might be to find. We'll get there. Rubio is depending on us."

"You're right," I said. "You know that I spoke to the security guard down at Red Hook? I don't remember if I told you anything about that."

"Everything's a blur," he said. "Did you get anything from him?"

"*She* said she'd seen Rubio getting on the ferry frequently," I said. "I followed what I thought could be his trail and found a meeting downtown in the city. Exchange Views."

"He told me that he attended that one when he had business in Manhattan."

"I met his sponsee there. Ryan. He was pretty upset about the whole thing."

"Aren't we all?" Jose sipped his iced tea, which had just been served.

"I'm not really sure now if that was the right trail," I said. "Going to a meeting is not anything out of the ordinary."

"Murder is, though."

"That's what I mean. Maybe the fact that he went to the meeting didn't have anything to do with his death. We're just finding out more about his daily activities. Meetings. Shopping his art. What else did he spend a lot of time on?"

"Painting."

"That's a given," I said. "All four of his paintings were sold on the day after his death. It's such a morbid coincidence. What do you think?"

"Would the murderers really go ahead and purchase the paintings the next day? That would make for an awfully big finger pointing at them."

"True. I'm not sure, though, that whoever did this was really careful."

The server came with our plates. Looking at Jose's tomato soup, I was sorry I hadn't ordered a bowl too. I dug into my burger, which was dripping with juices. I had made the right decision when it came to choosing my meal.

"You don't think they were careful?" he asked. "The police don't have any clues yet. I think the murderers are a lot more careful than you give them credit for."

I chewed the delicious burger and swallowed. "They are dangerous, though. Poor Marge could have been hurt badly. It's fortunate that she'll be home in just a few days."

"Don't get off track, Daisy," he said. "We're trying to figure out a pattern in Rubio's steps and where he might have gotten off this path."

"I hate to bring this up, but don't you think that if he was using again that might have been a strong factor? Maybe he owed someone money. There was the robbery at the gallery and Charley's death, and a few days later, he was gone."

"That all seems simple, but it's too obvious," he said. "Blame the junkie, right? That's, of course, if he was actually using again. We don't know that."

My hand flew to my mouth.

Jose continued, "Not you. The cops. That's probably why there's no movement on the case. What about that guy who was stalking the house? The police were supposed to be watching him, and he's suddenly off the face of the earth after two suited guys came and picked him up. It's crazy. None of it makes sense. The police aren't doing their job."

"Is that what you think?" I asked, squirming in my seat. Those cops included Rod and Liz.

"I can read you," Jose said. "You think I'm including your ex-boyfriend and his partner. Well, I am."

"To be fair, Rod isn't my ex-boyfriend. He's my almost boyfriend that didn't happen, and he isn't even on the case. Sam Harris is the one to blame if we're going to blame anyone. In any event, I'm not sure that we should be blaming anyone. Focus. Let's not be negative. That's what we need to do. Steps, remember?"

Jose nodded. "Okay, so if we're looking at Steps, think of it this way: we're at Steps One and Two. Everything is unmanageable and insane."

"Yes, that's right," I said. "This is a great way of looking at it."

"Did we finish the first two Steps, though? I'm not sure if I've reached Step Three yet."

"Giving it over to someone or something that knows more than us? Is it that simple? I'm not too sure about that."

"Well, it's not perfect, but it's a framework. Think of it as a guide for us. That's all. We've figured out that we don't know anything, right? So what do we have to do? Give it over to someone or something that knows more than us."

"That would be the police, though, wouldn't it?"

"Maybe." Jose shrugged as he gazed out the large window. "Step Two is coming to believe that a power greater than ourselves could restore us to sanity. I don't know if I believe that in this case."

"But if we are in Step Three, have we taken our wills back yet?"

"Hmm. You've got a point. I'm not about to make the police my higher power, though."

"I don't plan to do that either," I said. "But we do have to remember that they know something."

"What do you mean? Do you think that they're holding out on us?"

"I wouldn't say that." I hesitated.

"You sounded sure just then when you said they know something."

"That's just it," I said. "Of course I don't know for sure, but I have this feeling that they do."

"Why would they hold back information?"

"Maybe they want to trip us up," I said. "Like maybe we're involved."

"Daisy, stop now," Jose said. "We're involved in Rubio's murder? Really, how could you say that?"

"I didn't mean it like that. What I meant was that maybe they think there's a connection between you two. Other than being partners. It could be that they think you'll lead them to the murderer."

"Oh, that makes me feel really comfortable, all right." Jose threw his hands up. "That idea just seems too rickety. It doesn't hold up. Unless the murderer is someone both Rubio and I know. That's too eerie even for me. I really don't want to have to look over my shoulder all the time. It's a lot more comforting to think it was a mistake. A botched robbery. Like Charley Sprague."

"Okay," I said. "What about Charley Sprague? Let's say it wasn't a robbery gone bad. Why would he be someone's target? Do you know anything about him?"

"I know that he got on Rubio's nerves a lot."

"How so?"

"Rubio said he would turn up late or be there at odd hours in the morning. He wasn't someone that you could count on. He had no routine. Curators, at least when things are being set up, need to be available. He had a cell phone but never answered it."

"Do you think he was trying to elude someone?" I speculated. "Maybe he knew he was being targeted."

"This is all hypothetical," Jose said. "But what? Should he have gotten a bodyguard?"

"Okay, maybe you're right. Why don't we go talk to Sam Harris? What do we have to lose?"

"I'm not exactly thrilled with the way he handled it when Rubio was shot in the arm," Jose said. "Rubio should have received some sort of protection. Don't you think?"

"I'm so sorry to have to say this, but, remember, he left the hospital against medical advice."

"So, it was Rubio's fault? Is that what you're implying?"

I sat back in my chair, dejected. "No, that's not what I meant. You know better than that."

We sat quietly as we finished up our meals. A line had begun to form. The waiter placed the bill on our table.

"Can't a person think around here without being asked to leave in a not-so-subtle manner?" I asked.

"It's Sunday," Jose replied. "It's an all-day-brunch affair. Where should we head next?"

"Aren't we going to the White Buffalo?"

"I'm not up to that at all. I don't know how many other surprises I could handle today."

"Do you want to go to Exchange Views?" I asked. "Maybe we'll see Rubio's sponsee there."

"I don't think there are meetings there on the weekend."

"I'm not sure. Let's look it up online." I fished out my phone and saw I had messages from both Rod and Greg. I needed a breather.

"No, don't look it up," he said. "I'm not in the mood for a meeting."

"That's exactly when you need one."

"Daisy, please." Jose's voice was low and level. "I don't really need you telling me what to do in terms of my meetings. Going to that meeting was your idea, not mine."

"Okay, okay," I said. "How about going to the wharf? Do you want to do that?"

"I'm not up for that either. Let's just go home."

"I thought you were gung-ho to get some information. That's why we're here, isn't it?"

"Look, Daisy, just because we helped with that case at Windsor Medical Center doesn't mean we're detectives. I don't want to go out on a wild goose chase. Rubio isn't here anymore, and I need to grieve. By getting involved in trying to find his murderer, I end up putting a hold on that process."

"Why didn't you tell me that before? I wouldn't have pressured you to come out here today."

"I think it just occurred to me," he said. "It wasn't anything about what you did."

I nodded my head. We paid the bill and walked out to the street. I suddenly felt panicky when I saw the throngs of people walking the artsy neighborhood.

"Should we go home?" I asked.

"Yeah. I'll give Detective Harris a call. See if anything's going on."

"You look so disheartened," I said. "This is tough."

"Hold up a minute." Jose put his hand out to stop me from crossing the street as we headed toward the train station.

He pulled his phone out of his back pocket and said hello. The next few minutes were spent with him nodding an occasional yes to whoever was on the other end of the communication line.

"That was Detective Harris." Jose slipped the phone into his pocket. "That dude must have ESP. Or maybe it's you. You mentioned that he may have information for us. Voilà! He called because he wants to come over to talk about a few pieces of evidence they found. He'll meet us at the house at about five. Do you mind being there?"

"Of course I don't mind," I said. "You never have to ask."

As we rode the subway train back home, I felt as sad as Jose looked. He was right. Just because we had helped solve the Campbell case didn't make us detectives. I wanted to believe that I could be of help for Rubio, but, more especially, for Jose.

The train stopped and four men got on with conga drums and began playing. The beat reminded me of the *tambor*. I had gone to that drumming before Jose had gotten initiated in the religion. That memory triggered another of the night I was in Puerto Rico at the water's edge. I realized then that wherever we were or whatever we did, we were under the protection of the Orishas. The music was very moving, and I dropped a couple of dollars into the bucket one of the men held out before they got off the train.

"Have you heard anything about Hector?" Jose asked. "Do you know if he's going to stay in Florida or if he's coming up soon?"

"I haven't heard a thing," I said. "If *Padrino* isn't able to present me with my Warriors, can Ana give them to me instead? She was my *ayubona* when I received my beads. She's my second in command. I should have thought to ask her when I was there last."

"Forget it," he said. "It has to be a man."

I didn't even bother answering. The patriarchy of the religion was one of the main things that was so difficult for me to tolerate. But as I thought further about it, I realized that most religions are male-oriented. We women had come a long way, but there was so much more to be done. I sighed and settled back in my seat. There was no reason for me to stress out. Things would happen the way they were meant to happen. I wasn't going to push for anything.

Chapter 19

Half a block from the brownstone I saw Detective Harris leaning against the over-a-century-old wrought-iron railing seemingly deep in thought. We'd had more officers at the brownstone than Park Slope ever saw in the sixties during the times before the gentry arrived according to the lore. We were probably considered riffraff by the neighborhood elite. I thought briefly of Marge, who'd lived there most of her life, and her parents, who had owned the beautiful building before her. She was due to be discharged from the rehab center before long and would soon be back in her space. Just as she deserved.

Detective Harris lifted his head and nodded at us as we neared him.

"No more signs of your stalker?" he asked.

"No," I said. "We haven't seen him since the night we thought he was being escorted off the block by you guys."

"You've gotten the locks changed I hope?" he asked.

"It had occurred to us," I said, "and then we promptly forgot."

"We wouldn't want anyone to have the ability to enter again. Say they'd found a stray key . . ."

I thought back to my bathroom items having been moved the night that Marge had been at the mercy of the intruders.

Sam Harris was right. The perpetrators could easily come back if they'd found a key. The paranoia began creeping up in me again.

"We'd better go inside," I said. "I have to feed Ms. G."

"I thought you had some news for me, Detective." I was surprised to hear Jose's icy tone.

"I do, my good man," Harris replied. "Let's go inside and talk."

We entered through Marge's first-floor door. The cool, dark interior was a far cry from her usual bright, cheery environment. Other than Marge, the one thing that I missed was the smell of baking coming from the kitchen. It was like being in a different house. A stranger's house. The warmth to it was gone in only a few short days. Marge and Ruffian needed to come home.

We went up to my apartment and the three of us automatically went into the kitchen. I filled the kettle with water as they sat at the table. I placed it on the stove and offered them cups of tea. Detective Harris politely declined, while Jose agreed with a quick nod of his head.

"I won't belabor this, Jose, but someone went deep and hard into Rubio's belongings. The bag we found at the train station was his drafting portfolio. Empty. I'm thinking that whoever found it set fire to it in order to get rid of the evidence."

"I thought that a homeless man had set fire to it," Jose said.

"We did too," Harris said. "The man, James Moran, was sleeping under a tarp. There was some garbage around him. He just happened to be there, and we questioned him. He was somewhat out of it, but he swears he heard someone going through the bag. That's unfortunate, but the good thing is that the person going through the bag probably didn't even realize that Mr. Moran was underneath there."

"Wait a minute," I said. "That can't be right. I heard on the news on Friday that there were papers in the bag. It's Sunday night. Why did it take you so long to tell us this?"

"That, Daisy, was not true," Harris said. "The reporters often spice up news or talk to bystanders who don't have accurate information. That, I can tell you, was embellished. For whose sake, I don't know. I'm only going to share facts with you. I hope you can trust that."

"I trust that." Jose didn't appear pleased but, rather, resigned with the report.

"Someone went through my apartment more thoroughly than we originally thought the night of Marge's ordeal," I said. "Some of my things were out of place."

"Did you touch anything after you noticed it?" he asked.

"I'm kind of obsessive. Yes. I put everything back in its place."

"Hmm, that's not the best thing to do when you think someone's gone through your place. I can still have the apartment covered for fingerprints. Your set is on everything anyway. A stranger's set will be easy to lift if they're there at all."

"They did take fingerprints," I said. "Didn't you know?"

Jose caught my eye. His earlier point was well taken.

"I'll follow up on this," Harris assured us. "Do you have that little map you made that night for us?"

My body flushed with heat. That crude drawing was more embarrassing than calling the police twelve times in one day. But, then again, Harris's embarrassment had to top mine. Not knowing what his men were doing in a murder case didn't make for good teamwork. I opened the kitchen everything-drawer. I'd dropped it in there after showing it to Liz. I'd felt ridiculous having done a psychic reveal, or so I thought at the time.

"Thanks. I'd like to take this with me, if you don't mind," Harris said.

"Do you think it might be important after all?" I asked.

"Could be. I wouldn't want any details to get lost. There might be something to this; otherwise, why would you have drawn it up?"

"Would you mind if I quickly scan it before you leave with it?" I asked. "It might jog something for me."

"Sure, go ahead," he said. "No rush. Do you have a scanner here, or will you be going outside to a print shop?"

"Detective!" I shook my head and smiled, then produced my phone and scanned the sheet within a couple of seconds.

"It's hard to keep up with technology," he admitted. "We're also living in the Dark Ages at the precinct."

Jose grimaced. That was the last thing he needed to hear. There was technology that could find Rubio's murderer on double time, but that was on television. The real world didn't take DNA samples on routine inspection—or so I gathered based on the lack of expert techies on the team.

"Can you tell me what it means for the case that Rubio's bag was retrieved?" Jose asked.

"Well, for one thing, it means that the criminals are close by. They're still in the neighborhood. The bag was found at the local station. They were even willing to set a fire that was risky as well. Detective Rodriguez is browsing through the station videocam recordings to see if it captured images of the murderer."

I sighed deeply. "That's good to hear, but I thought he wasn't on the case."

"He's helping out," the detective said. "That's all. Liz is also following up on some leads."

We sat quietly for a few minutes, all of us staring into space, thinking our private thoughts.

Harris broke the stillness by asking me pointedly, "Were you able to get pictures of the person who was sitting outside the building?"

I inwardly flinched. "I haven't had the opportunity."

Harris was thoughtful. "There's a good chance that guy will be back. I suggest that you and Jose continue staying together for a few days."

I snuck a glance at Jose. He was still in his own little world, that was certain, and Rubio took up a lot of room in that world. Jose and I had already separated, and I hoped that he wouldn't wake up from his short musing to tell Harris that.

"Yes, sure," I said. "We'll stay in one of the apartments. Most likely mine."

"Do you have a time stamp for Ms. Talbot's rehab discharge yet?" Harris was on a roll. I wondered whether a spark from the train station fire had lit his flame.

"Not yet," I said. I'd been blaming the police for not moving fast enough, and here I was not concentrating on my own actions. I hadn't called Marge.

"No worries," he said. "I just think it would be safer for her to stay away from here as long as possible. I'm hoping you can persuade her that it might be safer for her to stay with a family member temporarily."

"She does have a sister," I said. "But Marge can be as stubborn as they come."

I thought back to her recuperating after she'd fractured her hip. I wanted her to come straight home, but he was right. It might be too dangerous for her to do that.

"One other thing," Detective Harris said. "Daisy, can you take some time again to come down to the station? I'm sorry that it didn't work out the last time. I got tied up that morning. I should have called you. We have some photos for you to review. We'd like you to let us know if you recognize the stalker."

"I can do that," I said. "I have some time off from work."

"Great," he said. "It shouldn't take too long."

"Should I come down too?" Jose asked. "I got a pretty good look at the guy too."

"I was just about to ask you that," the detective said.

"We'll be there," Jose said. "Nine o'clock?"

"Don't forget to have your camera ready tonight," the detective reminded me.

"I won't," I said. "See you tomorrow."

We saw Detective Harris to the door and retired for the night. Jose slept on the couch, while I tossed and turned in bed. I was wired. I got up and smudged with sage and cedar that burned in the abalone shell. The aroma immediately helped in clearing my head, and I decided to draw a tarot card. It might shed some light on what seemed to be continuing obstructions in tracking down Rubio's murderer.

I closed my eyes and took a deck from the basket. The *Graciella La Gitana Oracle*. I smudged them with the still burning sage and shuffled them a few times. I closed my eyes. Centered. I fanned the cards out on my writing table. I pulled. The Wind.

The image of a young barefoot woman, whose eyes were covered by her hair blowing in the wind, appeared before me. She had a smile on her face. A tiny white dog pranced playfully by her side as it watched a red shawl take flight away from the woman.

I knew this card. Today it told me that I had to trust. Close my eyes and trust in forces that were more powerful than me. I needed to trust that I was protected by them and to do so joyfully and lovingly.

Step Three, Believing in a Power Greater Than Myself, had largely been a theoretical practice. I needed to embody it in my soul. I wanted to do that but had placed conditions on taking the step of giving over to my Higher Power. I would be shown the way.

I still had so much to learn. I thought of how I'd start after looking at the photos in the morning. Or after my next meeting. After I practiced some karate techniques. After. After. After. I was beginning to get the message. Surrendering to a Higher Power wasn't predicated on the situations in my life. It had to be now.

Chapter 20

The precinct stood in front of us in its 1960s glory. The orange brick was the backdrop for a wide set of concrete steps. Over to the side of the building, a ramp had been added to accommodate wheelchairs. The street was lined with blue and white cruisers. Several unmarked cars were also parked against the curb. There were quite a few gray ones like Rod's, so I had no idea whether Rod was already inside.

"We can take a walk around the block to give you time to prepare yourself," I said. "We've been here a little too often."

"I'm okay," Jose said. "I'm almost used to it. I'm not so sure about you, though. Do you need to take a minute."

I turned around and there was Rod emerging from a dark blue sedan. He'd changed cars. Yet another thing I didn't know about him. *Reel yourself in, Daisy*, I told myself.

A few strides, and he was next to us, shaking Jose's hand. I jammed mine into my pockets. I wasn't ready for that.

He got the hint and nodded at me. "I spoke with Harris. You guys ready?"

"Yes, let's go in," Jose said.

The two of us waited inside while Rod settled into his office. The building was bustling with people. It had seemed much quieter on the outside. Crime never took a day off. As I sat on the bench, I thought about how important it was that I get to a meeting after I finished at the precinct. I'd ask Jose to come with me. He seemed to be attending fewer and fewer meetings. He should have been doing the exact opposite during such a stressful time.

I crossed my legs, and the right one began to shake.

"Stop that." Jose put his hand on my knee. "It's not that bad, is it? Are you sure you're okay with coming here?"

"Sorry. I didn't realize that I was so nervous," I said. "We're a pair of I-don't-know-whats. I don't want to make you anxious too."

He scoffed. "You can't make me any more tense than I already am. I heard from Beatriz."

"Beatriz?" I asked. "Now I'm totally confused in addition to being nervous."

"Rubio's mom. She called when I went to my place this morning. She's coming this afternoon with his sister, Valentina. The plane is landing at JFK at two. I told her to get a cab, and I'd be home to welcome them."

"That's kind of fast, isn't it? Doesn't it take longer to arrange getting here from Colombia than that?"

Rod peeped out from his office and called us in. We walked over, but I stayed near the door. I didn't want to risk standing too close to him.

Rod's look of concern told me that he cared deeply. Behind him, Liz Munroe sat tapping her manicured nails against the old wooden desk. She seemed to be scanning the sky.

"Let me ask you something, Daisy. Do you mind?" she asked.

"Go ahead. I'll try to remember everything this time."

Munroe placed her hands behind her head and slunk down in her seat a bit. "I've been wondering. Does the name Juan Echevarria mean anything to you?"

I knew him well and didn't want to talk about him in this room.

"Take your time," she said. "There's no need to rush through the identification process. We want you to be sure."

As she spoke, she pulled open a folder that sat on her desk. Suddenly I had a feeling they were going to play good cop/bad cop. She took out a couple of photos and shoved them toward me. Black-and-white shots of someone I'd known very well.

"Why are you showing these to me?" I asked. "What does he have to do with Rubio?"

"Or Marge? Or you?" she asked. "He could mean something."

Jose picked up the photos. "Who is this?"

Munroe answered before I had a chance to open my mouth.

"Juan Echevarria. Aka Lefty. Aka Johnny Esquire."

"Aka Juan Escobar," I said. "I know him, but only through Lou. Luis Galván. My ex."

"Daisy!" Jose rubbed at his temples. "Are you kidding me? How is your ex involved in this?"

"He can't be," I countered. "He's dead."

"When was the last time you saw Mr. Echevarria?" Rod asked.

"Before Lou died." My voice squeaked. It was Jose who couldn't tell a lie. It wasn't me. "It's more than a few years now."

"Did you ever hear from him after Mr. Galván's death?"

I skirted around that question. "Are you saying you think that I'm a suspect or mixed up in Rubio's murder? If you are, that's way out of line. The last I'd heard, Echevarria was in jail."

"You're correct. He had a few petty crimes that added up to about a year, city time. He was released about six months ago."

"But Daisy wasn't living in the brownstone when Lou died," Jose said.

I was totally unprepared for this. "He's right, I was still at the last apartment I'd lived in."

"We have the reports of Lou's death," Liz said. "We're not going through that with you."

My body sagged against the desk in relief. "Thank you," I said gratefully.

"But we do need you to look at a lineup."

"What? Oh no," I said. "I can't do that! Are you going to arrest him for murdering Rubio?"

"Not right now. We need evidence for that. What we would like to arrest him for is stalking you if you can identify him."

I knew that if Juan Echevarria was in the lineup, I'd have no trouble spotting him in a second. He had that stupid beauty mark over his left eyebrow that he thought made him so good-looking. The photos they'd shown me were a bit grainy, but I could see it clearly. I also saw it clearly from my window.

"Okay, but are you sure he won't know that it's me? He can't see me through the mirror, can he? And you'll wait for me to leave the precinct before releasing him?"

I'd watched plenty of *Law & Order* reruns, and I wasn't about to get caught out in a corridor or something.

"If you ID him, he won't be released. We'll hold him."

"I didn't expect this!" I wailed between my teeth. "It might not be him, either!"

"Daisy, why so nervous?" Rod asked. "Is there something we should know?"

I exhaled. "It's just that seeing him brings back a time I thought I was free and clear of, that's all."

"You won't have to make face-to-face contact with him today," Liz said.

"Not today." I almost laughed. "But I will have to face him in court eventually."

"Will you try to ID him?" Liz asked. "It's your choice."

"Okay, just give me a minute." I pulled out the small vial of hand disinfectant and rubbed my hands. I continued for a few moments until Jose put his hands on mine.

"Turning into a wreck isn't going to help any of us," he said. "You don't have to do anything you don't want to or can't do."

I blinked back my tears. "I'm sorry. I do want to help find Rubio's murderer. This is just awful. I never anticipated having to go back to a courtroom with any sort of connection to Lou."

I looked up in time to see Liz exchange a glance with Rod. Here I'd been holding the secrets of my past close to my chest, and these two had aired them as though they were hanging sheets on a line to dry.

"Are you guys going to tell me how this came up?" I asked. "How suddenly my past is up front and present?"

"Daisy, we need to do our job in finding Rubio's murderer," Rod said. "We don't want to leave any possible openings unexplored. Just let us know if you're ready to go in. No pressure."

"I'll do it if you think it's going to help," I said. "Jose, will you come with me?"

"Is it all right?" Jose directed his question to Munroe and Rod.

"Sure," Rod said. "We'll be with you too."

I stood in front of the lineup and held my breath. I looked at each one of the men slowly and carefully. I was finally able to exhale.

"I don't know any of these men."

"You're sure, Daisy?" Detective Munroe stood close to me.

I nodded. "I've never seen any of them."

"No worries," she said. "We'll find the person who's been sitting outside your apartment and find the link to the murders."

"How can you be so sure that there is a link?" I asked. "Aren't you just assuming there's a connection?"

"We're looking at all angles, but you're right," she said. "In the end, we may find out that it was all coincidental."

We stood there in the dark room as the men filed out. Jose touched my arm.

"Listen, I've got to get back. Rubio's family should be landing at the airport any time now. I want to be home for them when their cab arrives."

"Sure, I understand," I said. "I'd like to go home with you as long as there's nothing more for me to do here."

Rod and Munroe nodded their heads in unison. We started out into the anteroom when Rod caught up with us.

"Daisy, I'm spending the night at your apartment tonight." I was surprised at his statement of fact but also felt an instant feeling of relief.

"Okay," I said. "That's fine with me."

"Good," he said. "See you later."

As Jose and I walked out onto the sunny street, I was struck by how cool the morning was. I hadn't noticed when we'd entered the precinct building. I shuddered. The sun could fool me into thinking everything was all right, but inside I felt like I was entering a dark tunnel. I hated thinking of Lou and all the memories that threatened to flood me. I needed an escape.

"Hey, let's stop at that bakery!" I said. "Across the street."

"Good idea," Jose said. "We can pick up some rolls or cakes. I should have something at home for Rubio's family."

The old-fashioned bakery had an array of muffins, cupcakes, and rolls on display on the counter. The cash register reminded me of the ones I had seen growing up. I picked out a few corn muffins, and Jose chose the black-and-white cookies, anisette biscotti, and colorful seven-layer ones. I bit into a black-and-white cookie and savored the rich taste of chocolate before we left for home with our bounty.

As soon as we arrived, I threw myself into cleaning my apartment. I found dust where there wasn't any. I scrubbed the bathroom until the old tiles shone. The kitchen appliances sparkled. The apartment was finally cleaned to my standards, and yet I was still jittery. Cleaning usually helped relieve me of anxiety. I was glad that the black smudges left by the police when they came to lift the fingerprints were now gone. *Who had entered my personal space?* There was a lot that I didn't know, and I didn't want to go down that road. Instead, I put on my leggings and began doing stretches to music. If I wanted to keep that yellow belt, I needed to practice my stances and *katas*.

The music was on high volume. The sweat poured down my forehead. A booming knock at the door cut through my concentration. I turned the music down and opened the door. Jose stood there.

"Oh hi," I said. "I didn't expect you to come back up so soon."

"Daisy, it's after four. Rubio's mom and sis are here. I'm inviting you over for an early dinner."

"Are you sure you want me there? I mean, this is personal, isn't it?"

"Well, I really don't want it to be." His forehead wrinkled as he gazed down at me. "At least not right away. Come on down, after you've showered."

"But I thought I'd wait for Rod."

"Please, Daisy, I need you there," he begged. "She's a handful. And so is her daughter. I don't know what to do with them."

"Okay, but first I need to finish my workout."

"Just come down as soon as you can," he said. "I'll see you later."

Jose backed out of the apartment, and I turned the music back up. I needed to work my weak side kick. It might come in handy. Everyone in the brownstone could be at risk.

Chapter 21

"Daisy, I'd like to introduce you to Beatriz." Jose's voice was strained.

I dredged up my old Spanish knowledge. "*Mucho gusto.*"

"*Encantada.*" Beatriz engaged me with her limp hand. She didn't appear enchanted to meet me at all. The wad of tissues in her other hand was proof that she was having a terrible time. Her blond hair was mussed, and her gray roots stood out in the light-drenched room. Beatriz's nostrils were reddened and her eyelids bright pink. She was the vivid portrait of a mother who had traveled to pick up her deceased son's body.

"Valentina," Jose said.

Rubio's sister emerged from the bedroom. Valentina was slight, and her dark blond hair was pushed behind her ears. I couldn't help but notice that both women had perfect complexions. While Beatriz wore makeup, Valentina's dewy complexion appeared as though she'd never applied blush or foundation onto her skin.

"*Hola,*" she said. Valentina proceeded to speak in a husky accented English. "My brother told us about you."

"I'm glad to meet you," I said. "I'm sorry it's under these circumstances."

"Would you like one of these?" she asked — the perfect hostess in her brother's home.

Valentina pointed at a couple of bottles of Sapporo's Space Barley. It hadn't occurred to me that there would be alcohol at Jose's. I had never seen any in the apartment before today.

"Rubio," I began, and then stopped. What was I going to say? That we never drank together? That he was sober when he was murdered?

"Rubio what?" his sister asked. "Mau is gone, and no one has found his murderer yet. They say that Colombia is terrible, but look at this America!"

Beatriz burst into another fit of tears at that statement. No wonder Jose had implored me to stay for dinner. Tears and booze were not the best combination, although they'd seemed like the perfect couple to me for years.

Jose handed Beatriz a new pack of tissues and put his arm around her.

"Where am I to sleep?" Valentina demanded. I could see that they were both going to be needy, albeit in different ways.

"There's the pull-out here." He pointed to the living room sofa. "There's a futon in Rubio's studio. You two can decide where you'll sleep, but those are the choices."

"Not the bedroom?" Valentina asked. "Your bed is king, no? It looks very comfortable."

"I'm sorry. I'm sure we have different schedules, and I'll need to get to the bathroom and my closet early in the mornings. I wouldn't want to wake you."

Valentina shrugged as she picked up one of the bottles and flopped down on the couch. The long swig told me she was no amateur. I was reminded of myself drinking alcohol before I was eighteen years old, scoffing at anyone who suggested I at least wait until I was twenty-one. I hoped she wasn't headed for a path similar to mine.

"Mind if I get some water?" I asked as I made my way to the kitchen.

Jose ignored me. He was still sitting with his arm around Beatriz's shuddering shoulders.

A few minutes later they were still in the same position. "How about we go out for dinner instead of staying here?" I asked. After a good meal, I hoped they wouldn't be so emotional.

"The ladies wanted delivery. I ordered from Bedawi. It should be here in about twenty minutes."

"Oh." I was taken aback. "And me?"

"I hope you don't mind. I ordered the chicken platter for you. And a small order of hummus."

"Sounds about right," I said. "I always order the same thing."

"Where is my brother's artwork?" Valentina asked. Her eyes were glazed as they scanned the walls.

"Some pieces are in his studio." Jose's voice had a hardened edge to it.

"And the rest?" Valentina may have asked the question, but Beatriz's sharp look proved she wanted to know the answer too.

"Some were recently sold at a gallery in Manhattan." He stopped, and I knew it was a discussion that he didn't want to have.

Eventually, the bell rang. Jose extricated himself and went to meet the delivery person on the second landing. I stood near the door as the hall light went on. It was so rare for the lights to be off. The whole house was usually glowing. Ms. G must have felt the same because she was suddenly rubbing against my ankles.

"Please! Take her away!" Beatriz sneezed several times in succession.

"Jose," I called. "I'm going to feed Ms. G. Give me a few minutes."

I picked up the cat gently and brought her to my apartment. "Don't let that old meanie bother you," I whispered in her furry ear.

After I'd filled her bowl with dry morsels, I texted Angela. *We're having dinner with two people who are drinking beer. I'm not going to drink, but I will text you again as soon as the evening is over.* Bookending events with a sober contact had saved me from getting sloshed more than a few times. I didn't feel like drinking, but Rubio's family was triggering. Feelings were my downfall. Drinking to hide my feelings was my default. Ms. G's purrs told me she was satiated. I needed to eat too.

I returned to the apartment as they had begun emptying the contents of the cardboard boxes onto plates. The aroma was delightful, and I was happy to dig into my dinner. Three of us ate while Valentina sullenly drank from her bottle, alternating with picking the label off.

"Try the baba ghanoush, Valentina," I suggested. "It's very good."

"I'd rather not." She sat with her feet on the chair.

"Nina, *respeta!*" Beatriz turned to us. "I'm sorry. Valentina has not been herself since we received the terrible news. She loved her brother very much."

Valentina's brown eyes flashed. "Valentina is sitting right here. Valentina is neither a child nor a puppet, so Beatriz doesn't have to speak for Valentina."

Jose and I locked eyes across the table. Dinner was going to be a challenge. I didn't want to think of what the next few days would hold.

Beatriz opened a couple of fresh new bottles of brew. They both drank their way through those as I concentrated on my basmati rice and grilled chicken. A few minutes later, Beatriz began to cry again. The beer had set into her blood.

"I must tell you a few things," she said. "I think it's for everyone's good."

"*Ay, Mamá*," Valentina said. "It might be good for you, but please remember that not everyone is you."

Valentina had a point. But having been at the mercy of beer, I knew that we'd have to hear it all anyway. It wouldn't matter what anyone else wanted, she'd take the floor. I sat back in my chair and waited. I could leave anytime I wanted to, I reminded myself, but I was here to support Jose.

Through her sobs, Beatriz began to speak. "It's my fault, you know. I killed my baby."

Jose was about to stand up, but I put my hand out to stop him. I shook my head slightly. He sat back as he murmured something about me needing Al-Anon.

"You must understand! If I hadn't turned my back on him, he would have still been in Colombia with me. He would have married—"

"*Mamá*, get ahold of yourself." Valentina stood up. "Even you know better than that. Mau was never going to marry a woman. I don't care how many candles you burned for his *poor sinful soul*, as you called it. He was who he was, and we are who we are. No one needs you to start castigating yourself in public. Save that for your bedroom or your confessional."

The sparks were flying. I expected Beatriz to don a black kerchief. Her martyrdom was deep and, yet, suspiciously transparent. Jose's skin tone became pallid. He'd warned me about her, and she'd proven him to be perfect in his appraisal of her. What I hadn't been prepared for was Valentina's antagonism toward her mother even if it was warranted.

"It was also your father's fault, Nina! Never forget that."

Valentina's eyes looked up to the heavens. "I will not enter into this conversation. Jose, would you mind if I go lie down on your bed for a while? I have some calls to make."

"You can go into Rubio's studio and make those calls," he suggested.

"I would prefer your room. It's so empty and cold in Mau's room." Valentina flounced out of the living room and headed to Jose's room. I noticed she was dressed casually, in pants and a sweater, but the fabric and texture of her outfit spelled m-o-n-e-y.

"It's important that you hear me out," Beatriz started over again. "It is Mauricio's fault too. He was unable to separate business and family."

"Look, Beatriz, I know that you mean well, but I'm not really certain that I need to or want to hear this. I hope you understand."

"Jose, *mi amor*, you must listen!" she said.

Jose. *Amor.* We'd entered the realm of the ridiculous now.

"You see, the only reason my son was destined to marry Rita was that his father thought it would be good for business. Two of Colombia's most prominent families pooling their resources would have been fortuitous."

"Fortuitous for whom?" Jose asked quietly. The vein at his temple was visibly throbbing. He was at his boiling point, and the conversation had just begun.

"For all of us. Maybe not you, but then you would have never met my son."

"We became friends in high school, and you had already sealed his betrothal at birth. My God, Beatriz."

"That is our way," she said. "You may never understand it, but it is our custom."

"You're right," Jose agreed. "I will never understand this. No matter how many times you try to drill it into my head. In fact, every time we get together you bring up this same topic. What you don't understand is that I really don't want to have this discussion again."

I interrupted. "Can we stop? We can talk about this another day when feelings aren't so flammable."

They both shot dagger eyes at me indicating clearly they wanted me to butt out.

"You never talk about how he insisted on coming to America to live with his aunt when he was barely a teenager. Why not? Let's talk about that. You never want to!"

"I still say it would have been good for my Mau to have married Rita." Beatriz sobbed. "If he had, he might be alive today."

"What you're saying is that he's dead because he was with me."

"You're mixing up what I'm saying!" she insisted. "He would have been comfortable. He would never have had to work and sell his paintings for a living. Never have had to sink so low."

Jose shook his head pityingly. "When you talk like this, it proves you knew nothing about *your son*. Rubio took great pride in his work. He loved selling his paintings. It was a dream come true for him."

"Mau had no relationship with his father, but he was heir to the family company. It's all so complicated. Someone must have taken my son as revenge!"

Beatriz's speech had begun to slur, though I hadn't seen her drink anything but the beer. Either she was a lightweight or she'd been spicing up the beer with something else. Whichever it was, her words were hurtful to hear.

"Revenge? On whom, Beatriz? Rubio? Me? For being who we are? Because we're gay men? We don't believe in this crap. Sorry, Beatriz. I don't think it's a good idea for you to be here after all. There are plenty of hotels in the area."

Valentina walked out of the bedroom. "Give her a couple of minutes. She'll be snoring, and you won't have to continue listening to any more of my mother's rantings."

Just as she said this, Beatriz's mouth became slack. She placed her head on the table.

We all simultaneously walked over to the couch and threw the cushions to the side of it. We pulled out the bed, and Valentina put the sheets and blankets on that Jose had thoughtfully brought out earlier. We helped Beatriz onto the mattress. She was dead weight. There was no way to change her into her nightwear. She'd be sleeping in her clothes tonight.

"Well, that was a quick dinner," I observed.

"That's what you call quick?" Jose responded. "I thought it would never end. Good way to lose your appetite. I'm going to put the food away."

"No, wait, I haven't eaten yet," Valentina said. "I don't usually bother until I know she's finished."

It was still early. I had no idea if Beatriz would wake up again that evening, but I wasn't in the mood to find out.

"Mind if I go back upstairs?" I asked. "You know how it is. Rod is coming tonight, remember?"

"Yeah, sure. I'll see you in the morning. Call me if anything, okay?"

"Wait!" Valentina perked up. "Can I stay at your place?"

"I don't really have the room. It's best if you stay here tonight. Your mother might need you."

"No, she won't wake up until noon," Valentina said. "I can sleep on your sofa, no?"

"No, I'm expecting someone tonight."

"Oh." She furrowed her brows. "Is it your boyfriend?"

"It's just not going to work out," I said. "I don't have enough room."

I turned to Jose. "What's the plan for tomorrow?"

"We'll be arranging for Rubio to be transported to Colombia."

"Just so you know, that was my mother's idea," Valentina offered. "I told her that his life was up here and that she should leave it alone. But no, all she can think of is what her backwards friends would think if she let him rest up here."

"What does your father want to do? I haven't heard from him."

"My father?" Valentina gave a short laugh. "That's a subject for another day. I'm going to bed."

We watched Valentina's back as she went into Rubio's studio. While she was shorter than him, her slim build and wavy hair favored Rubio. There was no doubt they were siblings. Another painful thing for us to deal with.

Chapter 22

I closed the door behind me. My apartment was dim, but the stray illuminating shafts from the streetlamps lit the room in random patterns. I decided not to turn on any lights. It was calming not to have anyone with me asking for things or taking up all the air in the room. I began thinking about Rubio again.

Why was he at the waterfront that night? Who had done this terrible thing to him? We'd received valuable information from previous *misas,* but to do a séance to summon someone so newly crossed over wasn't how it was done. He would have to have been gone for at least a year. This played in my mind because I knew he'd tried to contact me and give me information with the crude map I'd drawn. If only Jose had gone down to the waterfront with me, maybe we would have received some messages together.

I remembered the brochures that I had stuffed into my bag at the gallery. I pulled them out and dropped them on the coffee table. Maybe there was something to his work being displayed at such an enclave for well-known artists. He'd arrived. But only briefly before his life was snuffed out.

I lit a tall glass-encased white candle and placed it on my altar. There was no need for me to do anything more but sit and close my eyes. If any messages were to come through, this is how it would be done. The *boveda* glasses were still filled although I hadn't refreshed my altar during the week. The water had bubbled in a few of the glasses, and I knew that indicated there was spiritual presence in the room. I said a few prayers of thanks and then for Jose, who was going through a terrible time. I also remembered to say a prayer for myself. I didn't have to wait to do Step Eleven—prayer and meditation were there for me always.

Keeping my eyes half closed, I easily entered the meditation zone. I tried not to tell myself it was because I was so tired. Images began flickering in my mind's eye just as the flame of the candlewick danced and changed in proportion and intensity. There was Rod and his child. It changed to a vision of the small boy who'd contacted me during the *misa* I'd attended a year earlier. A moment later, Rod's figure was no longer in the picture. The boy stood there with his hand extended out to me. He then reached up and grabbed the hands of two adults standing on either side of him. My parents. This was my brother—the one who had been killed as a child. The little one looked at me and mouthed the words, *Go home.* I saw myself kneeling, wearing an old-fashioned lace mantilla. I prayed. He was no longer holding the hands of my mother and father. A bouquet of daisies appeared in his little hands. He gave me the daisies and smiled. The next thing I knew, he'd disappeared.

There were so many places I could go with this meditation. I lit a small lamp and found the journal I wrote in and began an entry. This was a meditation I'd have to sit with for a while. I felt something shift inside of me. Love was a major message here. I'd been given love; not unconflicted, but love, yes.

The doorbell rang, and I hid my journal under the couch. There were some things that I'd never stop doing no matter how old I got. I was still so paranoid. Afraid that my feelings would be found out by someone that I shouldn't trust. After such a beautiful meditation, moved to tears, and I was still shielding myself. Vulnerability wasn't something I handled well.

The bell sounded again. I went downstairs. Rod stood there hesitantly on the landing. I opened the door for him, and he entered the vestibule.

"What's with the Rolie Bag?" I asked. "Moving in?"

"Just want to be prepared, that's all."

"Give me a second," I said. "There's so much mail on the floor here. The postman must have come by while we were having dinner."

I bent down and gathered the mail. There were the usual bills and what looked like greeting card envelopes addressed to Jose. Those had to be sympathy cards. I glanced at them casually and noticed that one was from Ryan Jones. I turned the envelope over and saw that his return address was on Wolcott Street.

"Of course!" I said. I handed the envelope over to Rod.

"Of course what?" he asked. "What are you showing me?"

Suddenly I had a case of the guilts. I couldn't tell him that Ryan was Rubio's sponsee. That would be breaking his anonymity, a cardinal sin of the program.

"This was a friend of Rubio's," I said. "I guess that might be why he spent so much time at the waterfront."

"A friend? I thought he went down there for the art galleries. Or art supply stores. We combed the place. He may have traveled on the ferry. I'm sure he had friends in lots of places."

"But that's where he was killed," I said. "The location is important, isn't it?"

"Think about it, Daisy."

"Don't be so condescending, Rod."

"I'm not trying to patronize you," he said. "All I said was think about what you're saying. Location is important, I agree with you. But Rubio traveled to a lot of different places."

"It was your tone, basically," I said. "There was something in it that I didn't appreciate. That's all."

"I'm sorry. I didn't mean to offend you. Let's look at a map. That much I think we should do. See how close that street is to where he was found."

I nodded. Rod was here for two minutes, and already we'd begun to quibble. Gathering up the rest of the mail, I realized that the envelope belonged to Jose. I took a photo of the address with my phone. We could look it up once we entered my apartment.

On the way upstairs I separated Jose's mail and placed it on the tiny antique table that they'd placed near their front door. Their. It would always be *theirs* or *them*. Would it ever be *his*? There were plenty of envelopes that were addressed to Rubio too.

"What's wrong, Daisy?" Rod asked. "Something just happened here."

"It occurred to me that it will probably be a long time before Rubio stops receiving mail. That's going to be hard for Jose."

"For you too." Rod's expression was soft as he gazed down at me.

"Yeah." I couldn't think of what else to say. I also couldn't think of what else to feel. This would have been the perfect moment for Rod to wrap me in his arms, but that was out of the question at this point. Had he ruined it, or had I?

He abruptly changed course and tilted his head toward *their* door. "How did it go with the family?"

I placed my forefinger on my lips and then pointed upstairs.

Once inside my apartment, I began to relax. "I'll put water on for tea," I said.

Rod turned around to scout out a place to sit. I realized that I'd left some clothing on the couch and other items, like my makeup bag and hairbrush, on various surfaces around the room.

"Oops, sorry," I said. "The place is a mess."

"I've seen other messes a lot worse than this one."

"I bet you have. Being an officer, I guess you get to see the worst of places in the most dangerous situations."

"Yeah," he said.

"Is that all you can say? *Yeah*? I'm trying to make conversation here."

"You don't have to," he responded.

"I know I don't have to. I want to." I shrugged. "I'm doing the best I can here. We need to move forward, and I don't want us to get stuck. I want to be your friend."

This time, Rod turned away from me. "My friend?"

"Yes, your friend. I care about you. That hasn't changed."

"Maybe we need to steer clear about you-and-me talk today," he said. "I don't know if I'm ready for it."

"Okay," I said. "I have to say that it will be hard, but we can try. If I ask you when you expect your daughter to arrive, would that be talking about us?"

"Good point," he said. "Everything we discuss would be about us, ultimately, won't it?"

"Yeah," I said. The tea kettle whistled. I dropped one of my sweaters on the makeshift pile I'd started and went into the kitchen to turn off the stove.

"Chamomile okay?" I yelled out to him.

"That would be fine," he said, standing right behind me.

I jumped. Rod had followed me into the room. "Whoa, you scared me!"

"Sorry. I'll do better," he said. "Things are so up in the air."

"Let's sit here." I poured the steaming water into the mugs.

"Have any honey?" he asked. "I've started using honey instead of sugar. Tastes nice. Mild."

"I do have honey, and that sounds like a great idea."

I watched Rod as he poured the gooey substance into his cup.

"I like this," I said.

"Me too," he said. "All of it. Sitting with you in this kitchen is something I enjoyed the first day I was here. I hope I can come back after this is all over."

I didn't know how to answer that one. I hoped that too, but it seemed next to impossible given the circumstances.

This time I changed the subject. "You wanted to know how it went with Rubio's mom, didn't you?"

"Yes. Safer topic, you'd say?" He laughed, and I saw that twinkle that had me practically swooning when I'd first met him.

"They're basically a regular family," I said, "with all their complexities. The mother was really into her cups." I briefly thought about the Queen of Cups card in my tarot deck. I'd never thought of this aspect of that card. She usually represented patience and an air of abundant intuitive knowledge.

"Hey, where'd you go?" Rod asked.

"You know that I like to work with the tarot, right?"

"Yes, of course. And you like tea, cookies, and, um, wait, wait. Dancing."

"You do have a good memory," I said. "Especially dancing. Except these days I feel like I have two left feet. Anyway, I was going to say that there's a definite air of mystery to his mother."

"How so?"

"She was drinking. A lot."

"That signals mystery?" he asked. "I don't get the connection."

"When you put it that way, I don't either. But there is something she didn't talk about. Her husband. Rubio's father."

"I hate to say this, but you're all over the place, Daisy," Rod observed. "First it's tarot, then it's his father."

"The tarot, then. We'll stay with that for a minute. There are so many ways to look at a card." I stopped to purposely inhale slowly and then exhale. It never hurt to take a moment to ground myself.

"I'm thinking of the Queen of Cups as Rubio's mom. Her name is Beatriz, by the way. Anyway, the image of this card is the Queen gazing at a lovely cup. The cup is closed and there's a question mark on it. There's a body of water behind her that is probably a lake. Water is the element of the Great Mother. Get it? The cup holds the water, symbolic of emotions, clearly meant to depict Beatriz. Second, she needs to watch out that the lake, or emotions, don't overwhelm her. She just lost her son. It must be awful for her."

"Okay, so she's basically drowning in her emotions—"

"And she isn't seeing clearly at all. She's just sort of staring into the distance. Not in a meditative way, but more like in an out-of-it way."

"But isn't that normal, Daisy?" Rod looked concerned. "Like you said, she just lost her son."

"She needs to be careful," I said. "Drinking or being stuck in your cups while you're in that kind of pain doesn't allow you to process at all. The emotion is stuck under there. Imagine a deep well. Not easy to get to the water unless you make it a point to get that bucket in there and hoist it up one bucketful at a time."

"I'm impressed," he said. "Have you ever thought of becoming a therapist?"

I stole a glance at him. He was serious; there was no indication that he was making fun of me. These types of conversations were one of the reasons I had become so interested in Rod. He listened to me, and we enjoyed sharing conversation.

"Therapist, me? Interesting thought. It's really information that's just coming to me from thinking about the card."

"Why not become a card therapist?"

"*I* should probably go to therapy first." I laughed. "I haven't done readings for anyone but me. I'm still pretty much a beginner."

"Why don't you do a reading for me?" he said. "Or for us. Can't you pull a card for us?"

"I'm not sure I want to do that." I admitted. "What if it's bad news?"

"Look, you've already said you don't want to see me personally anymore. How much more bad news could there be? Come on, just for fun. We're stuck here with each other tonight, remember? It'll give us something to do. Where are your cards?"

"I'll get them, even though I'm not sure it's the right thing to do."

Rod grinned. "Okay. I'll look at the card, and if it looks bad, I'll turn it over and you'll never know. I promise."

Rod did have a funny way of looking at things. He was encouraging. What was wrong with me? I was pulling a card; I wasn't refusing an engagement ring. *Keep it simple*.

I went into my room and fished a deck out of my basket with my eyes closed. I was going to keep this really fair. I opened my eyes. It was a regular playing card deck. I'd heard that some seers used these types in their readings. I'd never used them, except for a game of Solitaire during my loneliest evenings. I brought them into the kitchen.

"Look at these," I said. "Playing cards. Want to play a game of poker instead?"

"Do you read these?" he asked. "I didn't know you could."

"I've heard it can be done, but this is a first for me."

"Let's do it," he said. Rod leaned back in his chair. "This will be fun. First time I've ever been read for, except that *misa* we attended."

"All right, I give up. Let's do this!"

I pulled the cards out of the box. They were still in manufacturer order. I shuffled them several times and spread them out in a fan-like structure.

"One card, okay?" I asked.

"Sure," he said. Then he laughed. "That's a good start."

"Be serious," I said. "Concentrate. On us."

I allowed my hand to do the drawing of the card from the spread. Intuition reigned. From our heads to our hands.

Thoughts to action.

I turned it over. The eight of diamonds. I took a deep breath and allowed myself to look at the card with soft eyes.

"Ready?" I asked.

"Ready," he replied.

"The eight of diamonds. First of all, the eight is the number of the Goddess and infinity. That's what I know about the number; others might tell you something different. The diamonds represent the beauty and purity that is a rock that comes from deep within the earth. Everyone wants one, but they are very expensive. That's if you want a quality one, correct?"

"I guess. Sounds about right to me."

"Look at the way the diamonds appear on the card. Almost like slits that we can look through—like windows in a prison fortress. A thick façade. If we can look out of ourselves, we can envision the future. If we look at it from a different perspective, the image almost looks like a child's paper cut-outs. The snowflake kind. Remember those, Rod?"

"Yeah, sure. I used to make those too. I guess all kids do in kindergarten or first grade. I remember being afraid to make a mistake. One wrong cut, and you'd have a wonky snowflake. Some kids always made perfect ones. I wasn't one of those kids. I doubt my mother saved my snowflakes."

"I can relate, believe me," I said. "Now we have the symbols and need to break this down into a reading."

"Not *a* reading," Rod interjected. "*Our* reading."

"*Our* reading." I smiled. "I hope I'm not making this up because it's what I want to see. It clearly shows that we must go deep to pick the perfect diamond. But a diamond isn't found in the earth as we see at the jewelers. The diamond cutter works on it to unearth it from its rock after the miner retrieves it from the earth. Many hands go into the process. There has to be trust that no one is going to steal it, first off. Second, the diamond cutter must be practiced in order to reveal the beauty out of a substance so hard yet so divine. Third, there could be a flaw, and that means the person who eventually buys it will accept that fact about the diamond. Most outsiders would never know about the flaw. The most a common eye would see is a pretty, shining gem, but the true owners would know what they have accepted, even if it's not perfect."

This was talking to me about my relationship with Rod. It was uncanny. He grabbed my hand.

I continued to read the card. "As I said, number eight is symbolic of the Goddess and infinity. I would say that She blesses this, for all times."

"The Goddess? I'm not really sure what you mean by the Goddess."

I sighed. "I hope you can stay with me on this, Rod. I'd never thought about it for most of my life, but I'm learning things now."

"I'm open to hearing what you have to say, but I need more explanation. I don't really get it."

"What I mean is that the Goddess has many aspects and faces to Her. Different cultures and traditions see Her as a different persona, if that's how we can describe it, but it's still the Goddess. Sort of like God, Allah. Well, you get it."

"Can you give me an example of the Goddess, though?"

"The Great Mother, Gaia, Isis—she's Egyptian—Yemayá from the Lucumí tradition, or Lemonja in Brazil. If you don't mind, I'd say that for you, you grew up with Mother Mary. She's the Great Feminine. They're all different images of the Goddess. See what I mean?"

"I do now. So that means we're blessed by Mother Mary and all those other Goddesses."

"Yes, that's how I read this." I smiled and leaned back against the chair. "So that's it." I shuffled the cards and put them back in the cardboard box.

"Wait," he said. "Don't put them away. Let's do more readings. Maybe I have a question or two."

A heavy feeling came over me. I didn't want to look any deeper into this crystal ball.

"I'd rather not." I sighed. "I hope you don't mind. I took a chance doing this one. Readings are so personal, and I don't think that I'm the right person to do this for you. If you really want a reading, you can see someone else. Maybe Ana would read for you."

"Yeah, okay," he said.

"Don't look so glum." I fidgeted with the deck. "What we did just now is so important to me. I don't do readings for other people. I'm just a novice myself here."

"You sounded pretty sure of yourself. Professional."

"When I do the cards, I can step away from my own thoughts in a certain kind of way, but I don't want to take any more chances. We haven't been on steady ground for a while."

"Yeah." This time it was Rod's turn to sigh. "While I'm not glad that we have a stalker out there who might have actually been in this house, I'm really feeling good about being here with you."

"I guess me too." I nodded. "More tea?"

Rod drained the last of the liquid in his mug. "No, I'm good. Thanks. I want to set up this video camera I brought with me. This way it'll be ready just in case the guy shows up."

"It's getting late," I said. "I'll put a pillow and some bed linen on the couch for you." I didn't give Rod full eye contact. I didn't want him to know how much I desired him.

Chapter 23

The sound of something tumbling across the floor woke me up. I peered through one eye to see Ms. G playing with a small object. The moonlight streamed in through the bay window in my sanctuary.

The item rolled under the dresser, and Ms. G couldn't reach it. Her scraping against the floor would keep me up all night. I got out of bed and put on my robe. The house was always chilly during the night, even during the hottest summer days. I bent down and felt under the dresser to retrieve whatever it was. I hadn't even remembered that she'd brought any of her cat toys into my apartment.

I drew close and finally found it. It was small and round. I enclosed it in my hand and pulled it out. It was a ring. I tucked it into my hand and sat on the bed. Ms. G purred as she pushed her compact little body against my shins, clearly coveting her prize.

I turned on the lamp and opened my palm again to reveal a man's gold school ring.

"Rod!" I called out. A second later, Rod was at my door in his shorts rubbing the sleep from his eyes.

"Look at this," I said, determined to keep my focus. "It's a ring."

He took it from my hands and looked at it closely.

"And?" he asked. "I don't understand."

"Ms. G found it here. I woke up to her playing with it. It's not mine. I've never seen it before. Oh Rod. This proves that someone has been in my apartment. In my bedroom!"

Rod nodded solemnly, and asked, "Are you sure that it doesn't belong to Jose or Rubio?"

"I've never seen either of them wear a ring like this. I'm certain of it."

"I don't want to pry into your personal life, but is it possible that someone else left it here?"

I knew the answer to that question without taking a pause to think it through.

"I'm positive." I blushed. "There hasn't been anyone here."

"Okay," he said. "Sorry about that, but it's important to eliminate the possibilities."

"I get it," I said. "No problem."

"Are you okay? Finding this in your room can be disturbing."

"No, I'm not okay," I said. "You're right. It's one thing to think someone has been here, but to have the evidence makes it all worse somehow."

"This proves that we didn't search with a fine-tooth comb when we were here the night that Marge was almost abducted."

"I'm glad that you're here, Rod." I leaned into him. I couldn't help myself.

"Me too," he said.

We held each other close, like we used to do not so long ago. I loved his scent and the feeling of his arms around me. He buried his face in my hair. I had missed this terribly.

"What's next?" I asked.

"That's up to you."

"Can the ring wait until morning?"

"The ring can wait until morning."

I released myself from his hug and took him by the hand. We crossed the room over to my bed. Ms. G had perched herself smack in the middle of it. I pushed her off, and we took her place on the warm spot she'd left for us.

The morning light streamed through the windows, and I took the opportunity to fully gaze at Rod's face. He was gorgeous, with his brown skin and dark hair. I'd been attracted to him the moment I'd seen him at Windsor Medical Center. We had been so careful staying away from a night like last night because I hadn't wanted to move too fast during my first year of sobriety. Now, I was in my second year. What was time? *Time takes time* is all I could think of.

"Hey." He opened his eyes and swept me in his arms again.

A rush of love and tenderness flowed through me. "Hey yourself."

Being so fully loved during the early day's hour was new for me, and I sank into it. All the distractions of a future were put on hold as we learned new and deeply pleasurable things about each other.

We remained together until the sound of the phone's alarm prodded me into fully awakening. As he turned to stop the insistent beeping, a tattoo on his back was revealed and in full view. A snake snarled out of the one empty eye socket of a skull. The other eye was profoundly malevolent. A flag with lettering sat right below it, but he turned back to me before I could read it.

"Time to get up, Daisy," he said.

"I'm staying here with you forever." I laughed. We remained quietly together for a few more minutes.

The coffee pot turned on automatically. The sound of the bubbling brew in the kitchen was a comforting one. Soon the apartment would be filled with the aroma of the *Uppity West Side* coffee I'd bought from my friend who worked in the ER and made gourmet treats on his days off. For this moment in time, life was good, and I wished it would stay like this forever.

"You should get up and shower first, Daisy." I woke up to Rod kissing my face. A half hour had gone by since the alarm had sounded.

I nestled closely in his arm. "Are you sure? You can if you want. I'm off today."

"Let's not argue, okay?"

"No, no arguing." I melted inside at the gentle love in his voice. "I'll go first."

"No, I'll go first."

"I'll get there before you."

We got up simultaneously and entered the shower. Whatever the rest of the day brought to us, we were going to start it as we wanted. Together.

We sat across from each other at the kitchen table. The oatmeal steamed in the bowls we'd set before us. The coffee was perfect.

"What's with that tattoo?" I asked. "It pretty much takes up your whole back."

"Work wounds," Rod said.

"Seriously, that's a mean one. I don't know if the snake or the skull or the eyes ..."

"Like I said, it's a work wound. Sometimes when you're undercover you do things that you wouldn't usually do in civilian life."

"I guess I shouldn't go any deeper on that?" I asked. "Or can I?"

"Let's leave this tidbit for another day, if you don't mind."

I sipped my coffee. "Sure, I can respect that. But let's change the subject before I start asking any more questions about it."

"There's no video," Rod said. "You realize that?"

"I do. I'm kind of glad about that. You could use it against me later if you wanted."

"Very funny," he said. "While I don't have any regrets, and believe me when I say that, I do know if there was someone outside the apartment last night, I totally missed them."

"I'm grateful that Ms. G did her job and found the ring, though. At least the night wasn't a total loss."

"I would never describe it as a total loss. Not even a little one."

"No, not even a little one." I stretched. "What's the plan for today? Will you take the ring downtown, or should I?"

"I will. It's interesting that the name of the school isn't fully inscribed on the ring. It's just initials. *TM*. It could have come from anywhere. Now that I think of it, I do regret that we didn't do a more thorough search of the house that night."

"No regrets allowed!" I said. "The main concern we had was Marge. You guys made sure to have the ambulance come out for her immediately."

Rod shrugged off my comment. "That's what we're supposed to do, Daisy."

I nodded. "I should go visit her today. I feel guilty that I haven't been showing up."

"I'm sure she'll be glad to see you," he said. "Send her my regards."

"Yeah, sure." I felt distracted and decided to address the reason for it. "Do you remember that the officers kept coming out that night? I didn't even want to call you anymore when I realized that someone had been looking through the bathroom. It's only because I'm weird about that type of thing that I even knew that my stuff had been moved."

"And your weirdness came in handy," Rod said. "You'd make a good detective."

"I'd only be good if all the evidence was in my room," I said. "But thanks for the vote of confidence."

"Didn't you mention that you thought someone had been in Jose and Rubio's apartment earlier?"

"Yes, I did. You remember that I said their apartment had been a mess the day he was in there. Rubio had papers all over the place. I had to move them just so I could sit down."

We remained quiet for a moment until Rod broke the silence.

"Can I come back tonight?"

"Yes," I said. "I hope that you do. Not only because of the stalker, but because I want you here with me again."

"Shouldn't we talk about that?" Rod was somber.

"Why don't we hold off," I suggested. "Let's just stay where we are for now."

"You mean on our own private cloud?" he asked.

"Yes, on our own private delicious fluffy cloud!" I exclaimed. "What could be better than that?"

He looked pensive but didn't pursue the topic, and I wanted to bask in my feelings.

"How about some corn muffins I brought home yesterday? This oatmeal isn't going to last long. I promise you will love these."

"I can never say no to a corn muffin," he said.

I took my favorite skillet out of the cupboard and butter out of the refrigerator. As the butter melted on the hot pan, I halved the muffins and placed them on the sizzling surface.

While the muffins browned, Rod took over the placement of the dishes and utensils. He also took a jar of plum jelly out of the fridge.

We sat at the table, savoring our breakfast. "I'd almost forgotten about this jelly," I said. "I got it for Christmas and always forget to open it. I'm glad you noticed it. It's delicious."

"Like our private cloud delicious?"

"Yes, exactly like that."

We sat enjoying our breakfast and our time together.

There were only a few crumbs left when I pushed my plate away and read the label on the jelly jar. "This jelly is yum-worthy. It's made in France. Maybe I need to go to Paris to buy a few more jars."

"Correction. Maybe *we* need to go to Paris."

"Wouldn't that be something? France. It never occurred to me before."

"It's an idea, isn't it?" Rod's expression clouded over for a moment. "So, what's on today's agenda for you?"

"First I'll check in with Marge and then with Jose. I hope that he survived last night. The mother was totally out of it. We had to put her to bed."

"Drunk?"

"Yes, drunk."

"That must have been hard for you," he said.

"Right now, I'd say that it was sad. I'm glad I'm not doing that anymore. It's hard to see her bury her feelings. The way she and her daughter communicate is tough to witness. I can't say that I'm the poster girl for good vibes with my own mother, though. We have similar issues. Lots for me to think about, but, like I said earlier, it's *cloud* day for me."

Rod waited a beat before responding. "Sure, Daisy. You have to do what's right for you."

My phone buzzed on the table. Letty. Rod pointed to the bedroom and mouthed the words *getting dressed*.

I answered the call. "Letty, hey! How are you guys?"

Her voice sounded muffled. "Things are as all right as can be. What can I say? Hector is going to be discharged from the hospital today. He still has a few drains and things that need to be watched. The nurses showed my sister what she needs to do to keep everything in working order."

"That's great news," I said. "Tell *Padrino* that I'm thrilled he's on the mend."

"Daisy, Hector let my sister and her husband pray over him and talk to him. My brother-in-law stayed in his room for a couple of hours. Hector wouldn't have allowed that in the past. He used to say he would always give our sister respect about her choices from a distance and that she needed to do the same and not condemn his choices. Now I feel like they're trying to convert him, and he's fine with it.

"Maybe he's in a dark night of the soul," I said. "You know, like a spiritual crisis. He'll be himself again. Sometimes things like this happen when you see your life flash in front of you. Prayers are prayers, Letty." I hoped I believed that myself.

"It's so good to talk to you. I wanted to call you before, but I feel like I've been in a time warp here. I haven't been able to take the smallest actions. Something's not right. We think it's time to get back home. Hector's healing, and he's staying with Marisol. I don't even know what to say."

"I'm sorry it's been so hard to manage," I said. "And I haven't been there for you—"

"Please don't worry about that. There really isn't anything you could do. You've had your hands full up there with Jose. I still haven't had time to process what happened to Rubio. Is there any movement on finding who did this?"

"Not really," I admitted. "There have been bits of information here and there. Someone bought all his artwork the day after he was found. I'm not sure if that really means anything. It could just be a macabre market. People think that it will be worth more for a resell eventually."

"Yes, I get that," she said. "Look, I have to go. The baby is cranky and bothering Jorgito, who's been such a little angel. I have no idea why I dragged the two of them here. Eva would gladly have taken care of them. I can't wait to get back up there. It feels as though I've been held under one big spell."

"Well, whoever cast this one used a large net. It seems we've all been in a spiritual battle. I'm so glad that *Padrino* is getting better. I don't know what we're going to do about Jose. I think once the murderer is found, he's going to crash."

"I think we'll all be dealing with this later," Letty said. "Everything's happened so fast that none of us has had time to absorb it all."

"There's more I want to talk to you about, but we'll do it when you guys are back home," I said. "But, wait. You haven't said a word about Mike. Did he come back up to New York?"

"No, he's still here and holding up all right. That's because Hector isn't his brother. I hate to sound so cynical about it. I just don't feel like he's gotten it. Mike is paying a lot of lip service, but that's where it ends. I've been taking care of the kids and trying to deal with going to the hospital every day. Oh, I forgot to ask about Marge. Is she okay?"

"I'm going to reach out to her today. I think she should be ready for discharge from the rehab. You know her, she never complains about what she's going through. I feel so guilty about not being there for her. We've all needed some kind of help."

"Can I make a suggestion, Daisy?"

Letty sounded so caring that tears came to my eyes. This was happening all too much lately.

"Of course," I said. "You know that I'm always open to your suggestions."

"Ha." She laughed. "Maybe today you are. It's not always the case. You've got to admit that."

"Yes, you have me there," I said. "What's your advice?"

"Take care of yourself before you take care of anyone else. Make sure you have enough of you to go around. It's so easy to be there for others, but we drop the ball when it comes to self-care. You know exactly what I mean."

"You shouldn't worry about me," I said. "I'm not going to pick up a drink, if that's what you're afraid is going to happen. I promise to take care of me first."

Just as we finished our conversation, Rod appeared from the bedroom dressed for the day.

"I'm off to the station," he said. "I'll bring the ring and see if we can find out anything about it. Of course, it doesn't help that we've put our own fingerprints on it."

"And cat saliva," I said. "Don't forget that. Some paw prints too."

"I doubt we'll find anything, but you never know. At least maybe we'll get some info about the markings."

"I hope so. I also hope that if someone was in my apartment it was the night that Marge was assaulted and not some other time. Otherwise, I don't think it's safe for me to stay here. Know what I mean?"

"Have you thought about staying at my place?"

"What?" I almost shrieked. "No!"

"It wouldn't be the worst thing for you to do. At least until we get the perps."

"It wouldn't feel right for me to leave Jose alone in the house here. I don't think I can do that, Rod."

"It's just a suggestion," he said. "Think about it."

"Sure." I nodded. We kissed, and he left the apartment.

Just like in my meetings, the word *suggestion* meant that if you wanted help, you should take the suggestion. No one forced anyone to do anything they didn't want to do. I needed to take an action, and I wasn't sure which to take. As I watched Rod leave, Letty's advice was still ringing in my ear. My plan had been to run downstairs to see how Jose was doing with his exhausting mother and sister-in-law. I thought about what I could do for myself that would strengthen me for what could end up being an ordeal.

My *kata* forms. I went into the living room and pushed the ottoman away from the couch. That left me plenty of room to stretch and focus on *Gekisai Dai Ichi*. The last thing I wanted was to be demoted back to white-belt status. I spent the next half hour repeating the form as if my life depended on it. Sensei Red Norman had made it a point to tell us that one day our lives might depend on the *bunkai*, the hidden meanings, of the form. I had no idea what he meant, but if I practiced enough, maybe I would understand one day.

I was in the middle of a drenching sweat-fest when my phone lit up where I'd dropped it on the ottoman. Greg. I ignored it. I had to stay away from him. He was a nice guy, attractive, and really seemed to like me. The problem was that I had used him as a drug to keep my feelings hidden. That was dangerous for me. First, I'd be engaging in the behaviors that went with my drinking, and the next thing I knew it would be a shot of tequila chased by a beer or a neat scotch or iced vodka. *Stop the thinking. Engage in an action.* I finished up the form, did a few stretches, and went into the bathroom for a shower. Rod had left his towel hanging on the bar. I held it against me.

Not long afterward, I sat at the dining room table with Rubio's family. Beatriz was bleary-eyed and dozing into her huge coffee mug. Valentina made no eye contact as she poked her fingers into a large unbuttered roll. Jose sat dressed in a business suit, finishing up a cup of espresso.

"You're not going into the office, are you?" I blurted out.

"Are you always down here like this?" Valentina interrupted. "Or is this a special occasion?"

"*¡No empiezas, Nina!*" Beatriz implored. "It's too early!"

Valentina shrugged, and Jose had the grace to give me a guilty look.

"I need to take care of a few things there, Daisy," he said. "The ladies want to go to the waterfront to see where Rubio was found. Do you think you could take some time to go with them?"

I flinched. This was the last thing I wanted to do this day.

"I want to visit with Marge today," I said. "Maybe we can all go to Red Hook together when you come back from the office."

"I have meetings scheduled all afternoon," he said. "There are clients waiting for plans."

"Can't you get out of those meetings?" I asked. "It would be better for us to go as a group."

"If you don't want to go, just say so, okay?" Valentina said. "You sound like a married couple. We can go ourselves. Just give us the address, and we'll take a car service."

I heard the strong tone of hurt that was beneath her bravado.

"I'll go with you," I said. "How long will it take you to get ready? I'll call a car to take us there."

Beatriz pushed the hair out of her face. "Can we leave about two? I need to wake up."

I looked at my phone. It was eleven o'clock. I needed a meeting, and I'd have time for the *Midday* meeting. I'd visit Marge later that day or at another time.

"I'll meet you both downstairs at two o'clock," I said.

I left Jose's apartment and went upstairs to get my jacket. I'd have to breathe the day through. I was sure it wasn't going to be an easy one.

Chapter 24

The noon meeting consisted of the usual crowd. Mothers pushed enormous carriages down into the basement of the church. One even came down the accessible ramp with a double stroller. Men who hadn't seen a razor in a year or two chatted over coffee. People who looked too old to be in college and too young to be retired sat across from each other sharing their latest bits of news. There would be a business meeting today. I had enough with my own personal business than to be involved with those, despite Angela urging me to take a service commitment.

I poured a cup of coffee from the bottomless aluminum urn and went to find a seat. It had to be situated somewhere not too close to the front or to the back. I didn't want to get lost in the group. Someone jostled my arm, and my coffee spilled over the top of the Styrofoam cup.

"Oh, I'm sorry." Ryan stood in front of me. "I didn't mean to do that. I'm so clumsy."

Ryan leaned over the table and picked up a wad of napkins. He started to wipe my hand, but after taking a look at my face, he simply handed them to me.

"Really. Forgive me, okay?" he said.

Ryan seemed so young, with his blushing freckled face. My heart softened.

"No worries," I said. "Where are you sitting?"

"Right at the front," he said. "I'm qualifying today, so I'm glad to see a familiar face here. I'm used to going to the Manhattan meetings. The chairperson invited me from my home group."

"Oh, that's great," I said. "I'll look for a seat. Maybe we can chat after the meeting."

"Sure," he said. "I'll find you on the way out."

The chair of the meeting read the Preamble and How It Works. He introduced Ryan, and I was fascinated by his qualification. Growing up in New England in a closed but very addicted environment was only relieved for a short time when he went away to college. After graduation, he returned home. Sans employment or anything to give him structure, he soon began a quick downward spiral after a few years of dabbling with alcohol and opioids. His move to New York City almost proved deadly, but, fortunately, he ended up in detox and a long-term rehab program. The twenty minutes of his story flew by, and when he had finished, many members eagerly raised their hands to share. As with me, his story of an upbringing with an alcoholic mother and a father who wasn't around for other reasons must have resonated with them. I didn't feel like sharing and decided to soak up the group's experience, strength, and hope.

When the meeting was over, Ryan signaled me to meet him at the door. We walked outside toward the corner, where we were caught off guard by a gust of wind. Something flew into my eye and stung me. I searched for a napkin to dab at my eye as it began to tear. In a flash, Ryan handed me another wad of napkins, and I managed to remove the culprit.

"Thanks," I said a few minutes later. "That really hurt."

"I guess you'd better go home and take care of it," he suggested. "I just wanted to know how Jose was doing. I sent him a card. I hope he's all right."

"He's managing." I thought of him all suited up and ready for work. We all coped differently.

"What about you?" Ryan was so caring.

"Me too," I said. "But it has been hard."

"Have they any leads as to who did it?"

"Well, a few threads here and there, but nothing that will lead to an arrest anytime soon."

"They say that after forty-eight hours it gets really hard to figure out who did it. The trail gets cold. It's been way over that amount of time."

I was taken aback by the comment. "I watch *48 Hours* too. I also watch the news and see that some murders are not solved until years later."

"Do you watch *Cold Case* too?" Ryan had that eager childlike look on his face.

I needed to cut this short. "I have to get going," I said.

Ryan gave me a stiff side hug, and I walked away, still pressing the napkin to my eye.

As I neared my building, I realized that I hadn't asked him how he was doing. The conversation had taken a strange turn. I didn't have to think about Ryan, though. I needed to check my eye and wash my face. I had about a half hour before Beatriz and Valentina would be outside waiting for me.

By the time we arrived at the docks, I'd found out that Beatriz and Rubio's father, Mauricio, Sr., had divorced when Rubio had come to the United States. Mauricio, Sr., had been involved in a business that neither Beatriz nor Valentina fully described. He spent a good deal of time in California. I also learned that Valentina had applied for a United States school visa. Her dream was to attend New York University in the undergraduate Film and Television Program, and she'd been accepted. As she spoke about herself, I could hear the pride and excitement in her voice that was a far cry from the sullen teen I'd met.

The day was mild. The steel-hued waters weren't as choppy as the last time I'd been to the area. I was glad for Rubio's family that the environment seemed much more peaceful. Stores were open, and a few people strolled on the wharf enjoying the atmosphere.

Valentina's face appeared pale. She stood back from the place I'd led them to — the spot where her brother's body had been found. The black and yellow caution tape had been removed. There was nothing there to indicate what had occurred.

"I wish I'd brought some flowers or a candle for him," Valentina said. "There's nothing that shows his life was taken here. There's also nothing here to show that my brother even existed."

"Of course he existed, Nina!" Although Beatriz sounded angry, her face revealed deep anguish. "We will bring him home and have a beautiful place for him to rest. This was not his home."

"It was, *Mamá*," Valentina contradicted. "As much as you want to believe what you do, Rubio had made this his home. You might as well drop your fantasy about him."

I had the urge to run from the pair, but instead I walked closer to the rocks. They needed time to process this trauma as a family. I didn't relish getting caught up in their conflict and kept at a safe distance from them.

I moved over and stood in front of a stained glass establishment and watched the river water flow while also keeping an eye on them. The two were talking and seemed to take turns crying. A man with iron gray hair, wearing eyeglasses, whom I took to be the store owner, came outside.

He quickly fled back inside when he saw what was happening. I found myself moving toward the store.

The old-fashioned bell chimed as I entered the business. It seemed a cross between a factory and a museum. The room was filled with stained glass creations. I put my hands in my pockets out of fear that I would break something. A few beautifully colorful pieces were displayed on the walls. There were several that were leaning against crates, ready to be packed for shipping. This was a thriving business. No wonder he didn't want it tarnished with crime.

A middle-aged man came out from a back room. He wiped his hands on a towel. I was almost a hundred percent certain he wasn't the man I thought was the owner. This one was reed thin and had reddish hair. He wore a dark blue cap.

"May I help you?" he asked.

I cleared my throat. "Hi. I want to speak to the owner. Is that you?"

"He's not here," he said. "I'm the manager. My name is Phil. Is there something I can do for you?"

"Oh. I thought that I'd seen the owner come to the door just a few minutes ago."

"You must be mistaken." Phil's eyes were level with mine. "He's not here. I can show you what we have, or we can help design a piece that you have in mind. Are you interested in custom-made?"

I was stymied. I had just seen someone else, and I wasn't ready to let this go.

"I'll look around and let you know if I see something that might fit in my window."

"Ah, a hanging stained glass piece for your window. Those are quite popular. Let me show you what we have in stock. You can come back here."

I felt uneasy following him to the back, but the mother and daughter duo were still right outside, and I was certain they'd seen me walk into the storefront.

We entered the showroom. The place was vast. Countless stained glass creations were festooned against the walls. Many of them had "Sold" signs on them.

"Tell me if anything here interests you. We can make it to order. Any details, such as a particular image or certain colors, could be worked into whatever design you choose. It can be personalized any way you want."

The vision of a piece with a daisy on it filled my mind.

"Thank you. Sounds great," I said. "I'll just look at these for ideas."

Instead of looking at the window hangings, I scanned the room for something I wasn't exactly sure of. To the side of an automatic garage-like door were several packed shipments ready for delivery. They were of various sizes. A few were much larger than the ones that were hanging inside. I reached out to touch one, and it moved easily. The label was addressed to Miguel's Moratorium.

"Hey, what are you doing?" Phil asked. "Please don't touch those."

"Sorry about that," I said. "I just wanted to see how heavy they were. I don't know if my windows or walls could hold these. I live in a very old house."

"You must live in one of those brownstones," he said. "We do a lot of business in those. Most of them are renovated, but whatever type of house you live in, we install the mounting, and we do the hanging. You wouldn't have to concern yourself with that aspect."

I was intrigued by the packages at the door. They looked ready to ship. Something told me they were important. I wanted to see what was inside the brown paper wrappings.

"Is it possible for me to come back with my husband this afternoon so he can look at these with me?" I asked. "I do like the idea of this large-sized one, and it would be great if he could see it. We have this huge bay window, and it might be a perfect fit there."

"These are going out tomorrow afternoon. Come in before that. We open at ten. Just make sure that your husband takes measurements. This room is huge, and a person can be fooled by size in here. Remind him about measuring twice for accuracy."

That man-speak made me recoil inside, but I gave him a sweet smile. I couldn't be too mad because I was the one who'd brought up the husband bit. I could measure just as well as my made-up spouse.

"I'll be sure to remind him," I said. "Do you have a card that I can take with me just in case we can't come back?"

"Sure," he said with a nod.

We retraced our steps to the front of the store. I noticed a couple of doors leading to other rooms on the way out. One had a plaque on it stating, "Office." Phil ushered me toward the exit when I hesitated for a split second.

"Did you give me your name?" Phil asked as we shook hands at the entrance.

"Daisy."

"And your husband's?" he asked. "Just in case he calls."

I hesitated. I wasn't sure whether I'd come back with Rod or Jose.

"Oh look. Those are my friends waiting for me," I said. "I've got to get back. We'll be sure to be here before tomorrow afternoon." I hurried out of the store.

Beatriz and Valentina were standing at the water's edge. Fortunately, there was a rail there. It seemed as though Beatriz was either going to faint or go right over. Tears streamed down her pale face.

"I'm so sorry," I said. "I hadn't realized—"

"*Basta*," she said. "I needed this time here."

I didn't know how to respond. Beatriz was different. She was present.

"I can feel him," she said. "He's here."

The day suddenly took on a dimension of clarity. Maybe it was the sun or river flowing. I couldn't be sure. There was a hum I hadn't been aware of before. Suddenly, I felt him too.

Valentina joined closely with her mother and remained quiet. There were similarities in their build, in their complexions, but mostly in the way they carried their grief.

"My husband had a very hard time accepting Rubio for who he was," Beatriz said. "He expected him to follow in his footsteps. He never allowed him to fully express his art. He should have been proud."

A second later, Beatriz added, "I was the same way with him. I could not accept him for who he was."

The two continued to stand with their faces turned to the breeze, which had become balmy.

"I have to find a bouquet of flowers to offer to the water," Beatriz said. "I must leave a gift for *Oxum*."

Oxum was Oshún, of course, the Orisha of the rivers, all things sweet, and Rubio's fierce Mother in the tradition. It surprised me to hear her mention Oshún, although I knew that Rubio had been crowned a child of Oshún during his infancy. There were no outside signs that his family practiced the religion. Neither wore beads nor white clothing. I had a lot to learn. Most people didn't wear their religion or spirituality on the outside; it was an inside job.

"Let's take a short walk around here, and maybe we'll find a florist," I suggested.

We walked along the wharf. There were many buildings that had been converted to shops, and it became a maze. Once we moved farther into the labyrinth-like area, I was afraid we wouldn't find our way back.

"There, look!" Valentina pointed to a woman selling flowers and fruit from a cart.

They both bought bouquets of sunflowers, and I picked out an assortment of colorful wildflowers. There were a few daisies sprinkled in it for Rubio. I wanted him to remember me.

Valentina led us back, and we wove our way to the site. We stood at the edge of the dock, and I prayed silently while Beatriz prayed aloud in words that I couldn't understand but found hypnotic. I found myself being drawn closer to the water's edge. The water gleamed and shone in response to Beatriz's prayers. She separated the flowers in her bouquet and threw in each bloom individually. Valentina also prayed and did the same. I prayed quietly and followed suit. Afterward, the two held hands, and I was moved when Valentina reached out to include me. We stood together and watched as the flowers moved into the waters. Tears flowed silently down my cheeks, as well as his mother's and sister's. I couldn't help but think we'd become the maiden, the matron, and the crone in our trio of mourning.

"I'll never forgive myself for not accepting his choices," Beatriz lamented.

"*Mamá*, I'm sure Mau would forgive you," Valentina responded. "That was one of *his ways*."

The change in their interaction was astounding. I couldn't believe that these were the same two bickering women I'd come to know.

We kept walking and eventually came to a location with benches that was off to the side of a lively part of the wharf. There was a restaurant nearby. There was also the water taxi station near the dock. I remembered taking the ferry alone searching for clues. That had turned out to be a dead end. Then I remembered meeting Ryan at Exchange Views and his telling me that Rubio had artwork in a couple of galleries in SoHo. So much had happened these past few days, and we were no closer to finding Rubio's murderer. I buried my face in my hands.

"Daisy, are you all right?" Valentina put her hand on my arm.

"Yes," I said. "I am. Thank you, Valentina."

"What did you know about Rubio?" she asked. "What did he like doing here in the States?"

Beatriz's eyes flashed. "You knew your brother! Why are you asking a total stranger about my son?"

"*Mamá*, you know about a boy that came here to study. Neither of us truly knew the man he had become."

Beatriz did not fight back. She merely sat there impassively.

I realized they were waiting for me to describe a man who was an enigma. There wasn't an adequate way to describe him. Rubio was very quiet and kept to himself. He'd been like that all the time that I knew him. I always attributed it to him being an artist. The truth is, I had also attributed his isolation to his history of addiction. I didn't know how to say that part without hurting their feelings. I hesitated. A vision of him sitting alone in the Seventh Avenue Donut Shop filled my consciousness.

"Please, Daisy," Valentina encouraged. "It would be so helpful if you could tell us what you know about Rubio. I miss him so much."

"I miss him too, Valentina," I said. "It's shocking to me how someone could do this to such a gentle person. Rubio kept to himself. His love was in his painting. Rubio could spend hours in his studio."

I thought about his love for Jose and how the two beamed when they entered my apartment hand in hand for my first-year-anniversary celebration. Those two had been made for each other.

"Rubio had a lot of love in him. He was a passionate artist and person. He loved deeply."

One of the program Promises came true for me at that moment. We were promised that *we will intuitively know how to handle situations which used to baffle us*. That Rubio loved was the most important thing for me to share.

It seemed as if that's all they needed to hear. They both settled back onto the bench. We watched the river flow easily as boats navigated the waters. I wanted to be like the river. It seemed much easier than being a woman who was mourning one of her dearest friends.

Chapter 25

During the cab ride back, Beatriz and Valentina resumed their bickering. I still felt raw from being back at the site where Rubio had been killed and didn't want to be hostage to their passionate arguments.

"I'm going to my place, and you two can have some alone time," I said. "This afternoon was pretty emotional for me. I mean, for all of us. Are you two okay with this?"

I wanted to bite my tongue. I hadn't meant to add the last thing I'd said to them. If they weren't okay with it, I'd be their audience for the rest of the day.

"Thanks, Daisy," Valentina said. "I appreciate the time you took to take us there."

"Of course," I answered. "I can't even imagine what this ordeal is like for the both of you."

The cab let us out in front of the brownstone, whose windows looked like sleepy eyes. Everything was quiet.

"Oh, can you do me a favor?" I asked. "When Jose gets in, can you ask him to contact me?"

"Sure," Valentina said. We all started to go up the steps.

I turned to Beatriz and watched as the glassy veneer overtook her features. She didn't need alcohol to disconnect. She had a built-in detacher. The two entered the third-floor apartment, and I continued up to my fourth-floor refuge. I fed Ms. G and curled up on the couch.

I stealthily picked through the packages that filled the warehouse. None of them were labeled with addresses. The smell of the wooden crates was strong and permeated the structure. The room changed before me, and I found myself standing in a barn. The woody smell mixed with the immense piles of straw that filled the room. The packages were gone. I searched frantically through the straw. *Where were the packages?*

"Daisy, are you in there?" There was a loud knocking at my door.

I pulled myself upright on the sofa. I stood up and opened the door to find Jose standing there.

"Are you okay?" he asked. "I've been banging on this door for a while now."

I stifled a yawn. "Yeah, thanks for waking me. I must have gone into some sort of nightmare, although I don't even remember what it was about. What time is it?"

"It's six," Jose said. "I just got in, and Valentina told me that you wanted to talk to me."

"Yes, that's right," I said. "We went to the wharf today. I'm not sure how much they told you about the visit."

"Nothing really. Beatriz was asleep in my bedroom, and Valentina was in Rubio's studio. She came out to give me the message, and then she went right back in."

"I'm glad she did. It was strange down there. I mean, I knew it wasn't going to feel right because of what happened to Rubio, but, in fact, that part went better than I expected. They both behaved. Beatriz prayed for him. We bought flowers and offered them to the river. I could feel him. The water changed. It was magical."

"I'm glad you experienced that." Jose was somber. I wondered what his experience was like. Having Rubio's difficult family here must have put a wedge into his own grief process.

"That part was good," I said. "I know how that must sound, but it was. The rest seemed kind of odd. When we got there, I noticed some man was watching us from the stained glass factory near where Rubio had been found. When I walked into the place, there was someone else there who told me his name was Phil. He acted like he was alone. He's the manager."

"Okay, so what does that mean?"

"Maybe nothing, but when I went inside, there were loads of packages ready to be delivered."

"Daisy, it's a factory, isn't it? Why wouldn't there be packages ready to be delivered? Seriously."

"Seriously this. Some of those packages weren't the heavy type. The stained glass creations weigh a ton. But these were lighter, like paintings, maybe. They were addressed to Miguel's Moratorium."

"And?" Jose wore his impatience visibly.

"And, well, I thought—" I stopped. "Never mind. I'm sorry to put you through this."

"No, I'm sorry," he said. "I'm here talking about packages in a stained glass factory while a stranger is sleeping in my bed. I should be downstairs meditating, cooking, waiting for Rubio to come in from the gallery."

I nodded. "But I can't help thinking about the shop. I bet they have some of Rubio's paintings in there ready to go to that gallery. It's just a hunch, but it's a strong one. I wanted us to go down there. They close at seven. I was hoping you wouldn't mind."

"We'd have to leave right now. It's getting late."

"I'll be ready in a second," I said. "But you'll have to pretend to be my husband."

Jose glanced at me over his shoulder as he left my apartment. "I'll get my jacket. I'll meet you in front of the house."

"They're still open, I think," I said. We'd exited the Uber and stood at the curb. A few of the establishments still had their lights on. It was a short distance to the stained glass factory, but it would still take us a few minutes to get there by foot.

"Someone is leaving," Jose said. "I hope they're not closing. This is a pain in the neck. I don't even know what we're going to do once we get in there. Are we really going to ask whether Rubio's paintings are being shipped?"

"Don't be silly," I said. I peered down the expanse at the figure quickly turning around the corner at the other end.

"What are you going to say?" he asked.

"I'll think of something," I said. "Wait a second. I'm sure that I know that person."

Jose's expression was clouded under the lit streetlamp. "I don't think I should be around here. It doesn't feel right. I'm sorry I came."

"I didn't mean for that to happen," I said.

"It's not your fault," he said. "How would you know?"

Jose turned around in a circle and then walked to the edge of the water. "So this is it. This is where Rubio took his last breath."

Jose's own breath became short. His trembling hands reached up to pull his collar open.

"I can't breathe," he gasped. "My heart feels like it's going to jump out of my chest."

I placed my hand on Jose's back. He wasn't kidding. He was having trouble taking deep breaths.

"It's a panic attack," I said. "I'm sure of it. Just try to breathe slowly. You'll be okay."

I fished around in my bag looking for anything that might

help. A brown paper bag was the treatment for this. I dug into my oversized tote and found only a few plastic grocery bags squished at the bottom.

As I twisted my hands in desperation, trying to think of a solution. He began to breathe more slowly.

"There's a bench down there at that end." I pointed to the area where I'd sat with Beatriz and Valentina that afternoon.

"What about the store?" he gasped. "They'll be closing."

"Don't worry about that right now," I said. "Let's take care of you first."

By the time we sat down, Jose's breathing was almost back to normal. He took a white handkerchief from his pocket and wiped the perspiration beads from his forehead.

"I'm humiliated," he said. "That's never happened before."

"No worries." I patted his back again. "It happens. You've been under a lot of stress. It was wrong of me to bring you back here without thinking it through."

"I feel numb now," Jose said quietly. "I want to feel, but I can't."

"We're all different," I said. "You feel what you feel."

We sat quietly together for a while. The storefront lights began to go off one by one. The wharf was vacant except for a couple jogging together.

"Everything seems so normal here, doesn't it?" he asked.

"On the outside, yes," I acknowledged, "but something isn't right. Rubio's death wasn't an accident or a case of mistaken identity. There's more to it. That robbery at the gallery was a precursor to his murder. They were looking for him. I'm sure of it. They didn't get him the first time, but then they did. We just need to find out who did it and why. Charley Sprague's death was not an accident."

"It seems like it's been a year since all this happened," he said. "What are we going to do about the packages you think are Rubio's canvases? The place is closed now. That person who left was probably their last customer for the night."

"We can come back tomorrow. We'll get here early. They open at ten."

Jose shook his head. "I have an important meeting tomorrow. I can't miss it. I feel like I'm treading water at work. They haven't said anything. I haven't said anything either, but I'm not as sharp as I usually am. I've been missing things. Nothing super important, but I'm not at the top of my game. They expected more when they hired me."

"I understand why you haven't said anything to them about what's going on, but maybe you're the one who has high expectations."

"No. It's a cruel world out there in finance. Everyone is pushing for profit."

"And it was the same for Rubio, wasn't it?"

"You really think it has something to do with the gallery?"

"Things just seemed lighter when he was only painting," I said. "When he began planning to buy the gallery, he seemed much more burdened."

"I'm still not sure why the decision was to lease the gallery and not buy the building."

"Come on, be reasonable," I said. "The buildings on Atlantic Avenue cost a fortune."

"He had it," Jose answered. "Rubio was loaded. His family is wealthy and then some. Rubio never had to worry about money. He was a full-time artist because he could be. He never flaunted his wealth, but it was there."

This was new territory. We'd never discussed their finances before.

"How is it that they're so rich?" I asked. "I mean, of course, if you don't mind my asking."

"It doesn't really matter now, does it?"

The lights from the lampposts competed with the stars. I gazed up at the sky. The wind was beginning to pick up, and I took a scarf out of my bag and tied it close around my neck.

"I'm just curious, I guess." I smiled at him, but he was concentrating on the shifting river waters.

"His father. The whole family comes from a line of producers."

"Producers? Really? Television or the movies?"

Jose laughed. "That would be nice, wouldn't it? Neither. Producers as in the cocaine industry."

"Oh." I was taken aback. "How come I didn't know this?"

"For one thing, Rubio wasn't proud of it. For another, he was tormented by his own issues. Imagine being from a family where you're the only one addicted to the merchandise your family sells. He tried to put it behind him."

"Well, I guess he was successful." I sighed. "Gosh, I've known you guys for such a long time and didn't know any of this."

"He already had a problem when he came up here to school. Then there was the gay-boy thing. His didn't occupy a popular family position as far as his father was concerned."

"So, can I ask, why didn't his father come with Beatriz and Valentina? Are his feelings that negative toward Rubio?"

"The answer to the second part of your question is a big *I don't know*. The first part is easier to answer. He's in for life."

"What? Jail? Are you kidding me? I thought he was in California."

"No, not jail. Maximum-security prison. In California. He was the head of one of those cartels. Crazy, isn't it? It's not something that Rubio was proud of, obviously."

"You're not kidding about crazy, are you? My God."

"Yeah," he said. "I know all of this, and I'm supposed to play dumb when Beatriz comes and acts so high and mighty."

"But where is the money coming from when he's in jail? Does the family get to keep the money when someone is found guilty of something like this? I don't get it."

"They were smart," he said. "Rubio's father had also built a strong, clean business that was kept in Beatriz's name."

"What is that business?" I asked. "It never came up when we spoke today."

"Pharmaceuticals and perfumes." Jose chuckled. "Don't ask."

"Don't ask? Of course I have to ask! Pharmaceuticals? Now, that's really crazy!"

"It's South America. I can't even begin to explain it, but Rubio's father got caught up when things were really hot down there."

"But aren't you talking about the eighties or nineties? That's a long time ago."

"You really don't want to know."

"I do!" I begged, "Come on. Don't hold out on me."

"It wasn't that long ago," he said. "Rubio was sent up here to school right before the legal issues were up front and center. The authorities had been observing the family for years. But remember that most of the authorities down there are in on everything. It's probably only because of a fissure within the ranks that someone sold out Rubio's father. Bad blood between brothers."

We sat side by side for a while. It was breezy, but the sound of the river had a calming effect. Many of the boats were moored for the night, and there was a peacefulness that was even more profound than my experience that afternoon.

"I thought that I knew everything about you guys," I said. "We've been friends for so long."

"True, but there are a lot of things I still don't know about you and Lou either."

My heart started to palpitate this time. "I really don't want to talk about that. Maybe I'll go for therapy or something, but it's not going to help me or you right now if I do."

"I love you, sis," Jose said. "I wouldn't want to push you."

I leaned my head on his shoulder. "I don't want to push you either. Just let me know if I'm doing that."

"I'll be the first," he said. "What are we going to do about tomorrow? I wish I could be here with you, but I can't."

"I'll figure something out," I said. "I'll see if I can get Rod out here."

"He spent the night, didn't he?"

I was glad he couldn't see me blushing with the night lighting. "Yes. He just wanted to keep an eye on things since that stalker hasn't been found yet."

"What about you two?" Jose asked. "Is that topic taboo?"

"No," I said. "It's a safe one. I'm almost afraid to say anything. I think we're on. Let's just say that we're definitely more on than off."

"That's great, Daisy," he said. "Don't let love get away just because the details don't fit with what you think life should be."

"I know that's how you feel about it," I said. "My thoughts haven't changed much since the last time we talked about this."

"Grab on to love while it's there," he said. "Things may turn out better than you think they will."

"Should I say thanks?" I asked. "Now I'm more confused than ever."

"Remember to take it one day at a time," he said. "That may sound cliché, but that's how we do it."

"Do you know how much I appreciate you?"

"The feeling is mutual," he said. "You're my closest friend."

"It's funny that maybe we weren't able to find out more at the shop, but this was good. Minus the panic attack. I'm glad we had these few moments to be ourselves again."

"It's the river." Jose looked pointedly at it. "Oshún. My Mother. She wanted us here. She heals."

We continued to sit quietly for a while, and when the wind became fiercer, we left for home.

Chapter 26

Rod stood in the kitchen whipping up a perfect dinner of pancakes and turkey bacon. I pretended to be his sous chef while he combined the ingredients. The evening meal had become breakfast.

"The whole point is to enjoy comfort food without going into today's gory details."

"How is it that you don't gain an ounce?" I asked.

"Haven't you heard the saying, 'You can eat everything, just not all of it'?"

I abruptly changed the subject. "I need you to pretend you're my husband."

He was about to flip over a pancake, and the spatula stopped in midair.

"In the morning," I tried to explain, without saying too much.

"Hello?" Rod expertly finished his pancake maneuver and turned the flame on low.

"I want to go back to where Rubio was murdered. There's a distinct vibe at the stained glass factory. There's something about that place. I was there today. Twice."

He interrupted me. "What do you think is going on there? They seemed all right when we questioned them. They didn't know about Rubio until they opened that morning."

"They have these packages that they are going to deliver."

"And? Isn't that why they're in business? They want to sell stained glass." Rod tried to chuck me under the chin. "Aren't you the cutest!"

I stopped him with a high block. "Don't you dare," I warned. "That's so sexist. I can't believe that you just did that."

He chuckled. "Got me, didn't you? My mother always says, 'Don't play with your hands, Davey.'"

"She's right," I agreed. "But it's your fault. You started it with that *you're the cutest* routine."

"The thing is, I meant it," he said, while attempting to nuzzle my neck. "You are the cutest! But your point about the packages; tell me more."

I relaxed a bit. "Something, my gut, tells me that they're selling Rubio's paintings. One was addressed to Miguel's Moratorium. I know you're going to say it's a coincidence. I don't think it is. What are the chances that Rubio was murdered right in front of the place, and the next day his paintings are all sold, and then I see a package at the factory addressed to the gallery that sold them?"

"Whoa! You're going way too fast there," he said. "Back up. Start over again. I'm listening."

We sat down to eat our evening breakfast spread, and I told him all the details. I started with my outing with Jose on the Sunday after my karate promotion leading to this evening. I added how Jose's panic attack meant we ended up not entering the stained glass factory after all.

As we were clearing the table, Rod grabbed on to my hand. "I'd like to act like your husband in the morning, but I've been there already. I did some questioning there with Munroe."

"You hadn't told me that," I said. "I thought you weren't going to be active on the case."

"Well, I'm not," he admitted. "Sometimes we do things a little differently to see what kind of information we can come up with."

"Did you get any information?" I asked.

"Well, Harris did ask specific questions, as you'd expect, but then Munroe and I went there to see what we could come up with. We didn't exactly tell them we were on the force."

"No, don't tell me, you acted as though you were her husband that day? Tell me I'm making this up."

"Though it may not look like it to you, we've been doing everything we can to solve this case. What better foil than to have a gentrified couple come in to canvass the place."

"You don't look like anyone gentrifying anything," I said.

"I'll ignore that. We got in and asked questions, and no one was the wiser. We can have someone else go with you tomorrow. Did you ask Jose yet?"

"Yes, but he can't," I said. "He has a work meeting, and he had that panic attack. Not a good idea. I don't know if I should be telling you this, I don't want to break a confidence, but they don't know he's gay at his job."

"And?" Rod was matter-of-fact. "It's against the law for them to ask any questions or make decisions because of his personal life."

"I know that, but he's feeling very shaky at work." I piled the dishes in the sink and turned on the hot water. "Let's go sit inside while these soak."

"Sure. Just keep the lights off in the living room," he said. "If anyone is out there tonight, I don't want them knowing that we can see them."

"Just concentrate on the reason you're here tonight," I said. "No card readings or anything."

"Hey, I forgot to tell you about the ring Ms. G found," Rod said. "We were able to decipher where it's from. By the way, do you have anything sweet? I've gotten spoiled with the cookies that you and Marge always have on hand."

"Stop. Concentrate!" I said. "I just said that we can't get distracted like last night."

"Just a cookie," Rod insisted. "I need something sweet."

"Sweeter than maple syrup?" I asked. "You're a case. They're on that shelf."

I pointed to the shelf on the far wall. He brought me the tin filled with cookies. I took one out and led him into the living room by holding it under his nose.

"Did you get fingerprints?" I asked. "Were you able to identify them?"

"That I can't answer, but I can say where the ring is from."

"Go ahead. Don't stop on my account."

He took a big bite out of the cookie before answering. "Thomas More."

"Where is that?" I asked. "Don't make me ask you for details. Just give them to me already!"

"It's in New Hampshire. It's a four-year college. Liberal Arts."

"But you couldn't figure out who it belongs to?" I grabbed at a cookie. A little emotional eating wouldn't hurt.

"I was going to ask you about that," he said. "Is it possible it belongs to a friend of yours? Someone who might have visited you in the past? They might have left it on the nightstand and forgot it was there? Maybe it got swept under the bed?"

I counted to ten and then breathed for another ten seconds before responding. "I've never seen that ring before, Rod. I know that for a fact. I told you that before."

"Okay, okay!" he said. "I had to ask. It's what I do. This is a big house. It's possible it's been here for a while. It's also possible it belonged to the person who was in here that night. The one who put Marge in the shed."

"Marge. Right." I hadn't gone to see her after all. My shame was overwhelming.

"Marge what?" Rod asked. "Where'd you go?"

"I was just thinking about the shed, the hospital, and rehab,"

I said. "The fact is that Marge could have been killed too. This could be a case of attempted murder."

"Right now, it's an assault and a possible attempted kidnapping. We've got our eyes on this too."

Rod walked over to the window. "Daisy, come slowly. I want you to look and tell me if you know that guy and that woman who are standing across the street."

I sidled up next to him. "That's the neighborhood *tecata*. I shouldn't call her that. She's sweet, but she's always high. The guy, I don't know, but he's definitely not the same one who was out there before."

"False alarm, then," he said. "We should keep an eye on them. People will do anything for money. Let's just sit here."

"Okay, sounds good to me."

We sat in the dark. Ms. G came in, purring loudly. She was ready for bed. I was too but was also determined to stay up with Rod.

I woke with a start to a knock on the door.

"Why'd you let me fall asleep?" I asked. "I wanted to watch with you."

"I didn't want to wake you," he said. "You were snoring. I'll get it. It's probably Jose."

Rod opened the door. Valentina stood in the frame. I introduced the two.

She entered the room. "Do you live here too?" she asked Rod.

"No, Valentina," I interjected. "But the real question is, what are you doing here at this time of night."

"I couldn't sleep," she said. "I slept when I got home, and now I'm wide awake. Can you call me *Nina*? No one calls me *Valentina*, except for my mother — at least most of the time."

"Nina," I said. "It's late. You really should be getting back downstairs."

"Wait a minute," Rod said. "Why can't Nina go with you

tomorrow? That way, you won't be alone, and I'll feel better about your going there."

"Go where?" she asked as she slumped on the couch. "You're not going to invite *Mamá* too, are you? She's under my skin enough already."

"What do you say, Daisy?" he asked. "Think it'll work out?"

"I don't have much choice, do I? Since you already played hubby to Liz the other day."

"Really! Tell me more!" Nina sat there as though she were about to watch a movie and just needed a bucket of popcorn.

"No!" Rod and I said in unison.

"My goodness, you people are so high-strung here in the U.S."

I spent the next few minutes telling her my plan to return to the stained glass shop. She said yes immediately. Nina was eager to help in any way she could to find her brother's murderer.

"For some reason I thought you'd oversleep." My greeting to Nina was not exactly cordial. I did manage to hide my relief that Beatriz hadn't shown up. I gave myself a plus for that.

Nina responded to my thoughts. "*Mamá* was up early. I made sure that she stayed inside. I read the weather forecast to her, and she gladly went back to bed."

"Jose went out and didn't come back home last night," she said. "It's so strange. Does he do that often? Is something wrong? Were he and my brother having problems in their relationship?"

We walked down to Fifth Avenue. The sky was gray and drizzly. I rolled her questions around in my mind before responding. They were fair ones.

"If you want to know about your brother and Jose, I think it would be best for you to discuss it with Jose. It's not my place to speculate. The truth is, I don't really have the answers that you're looking for, Nina."

That seemed to satisfy her, and she turned her attention to the small shops on the avenue.

"Why didn't you tell me there's a spa here, Daisy?" she asked. "I could use a massage."

"We can make an appointment for you later on today."

I could probably do with a full-body massage myself. This kid was teaching me something about self-care.

"Marge told me that this spa used to be a fish market," I said, "before the neighborhood became all trendy. It was supposedly famous enough that people from Queens and Staten Island came here to buy their fish."

"Marge? I don't know who that is."

"Marge owns our house," I explained. "She's more than a landlady, though. She's been a best friend to all of us. Hey, how would you like to visit with her? She's in a rehab facility right now."

"Aren't those places smelly?"

"Not really," I said. Again, my case of remorse where Marge was concerned began to grow. I hadn't really been attentive to her since the situation at the house. This adulting was really kicking my butt.

"I'm going there this afternoon. If you'd like to come, just let me know."

"I don't think so," Nina said. "I'm going to see about that massage. I hope they do deep tissue. I love deep tissue!"

I raised my hand when I saw a cab coming, and it pulled up right in front of us. The number of cabs I'd taken to the waterfront was mounting. My sponsor had suggested I stop taking Ubers all the time because they turned out to be one of my biggest expenses. I already owed so much on my credit card. This was a temporary situation, I reminded myself, or at least I hoped so.

We settled in, and I watched as Nina bounced around, looking at all the boutiques we passed before the cab turned toward Gowanus. The city became grayer and grittier as we headed west below the overpass. The gray of the sky matched the streets. The traffic going toward the Brooklyn Bridge was practically gridlocked. A few pedestrians wove their way through the stalled cars against the red lights. I closed my eyes. I hadn't come up with a plan yet.

"Daisy, are you sleeping?" Nina's voice was in my ear. "We're here."

I groaned inwardly. We had reached our destination, and I paid the driver. Next time I'd bring cash so I wouldn't have to look at the transaction on the bank app. Dollar bills would take care of it, and I could let the memory fade.

"What's wrong?" Nina asked again. It was much easier going out with Jose, who had gotten used to me.

"Nothing. I'm here." I tried to sound reassuring but felt like I was coming up all ways of short. What had I planned to do now that I was here?

"Let's just walk around a bit before we go inside," Nina suggested. "I don't know if it was too wise for me to come back so quickly. I said goodbye to Rubio yesterday. I shouldn't have come back. It's not good to look backwards."

"I've heard that it's okay to look back but not dwell," I said.

Nina mused for a moment. "I never thought of it that way."

"If you don't mind, let's not walk around," I suggested. "We won't stay long. I promise. I just want to look around inside. They're expecting me. It shouldn't be awkward."

"Awkward for who?" Nina had a quizzical expression on her face. "Come on."

The storefront for the stained glass factory was dark. They were still closed. It was about nine forty-five, and they didn't open until ten. We'd arrived early.

"Let's go around the back," I recommended.

"The back?" Nina wore the expression I'd come to know as an indication there might be a full whine coming on. Maybe I should have come by myself, but that wouldn't have been the safest or most prudent thing to do.

"Come on, or, better yet, stay here," I instructed. "If I'm not back in five minutes, send the dogs in for me."

"The dogs?" Nina sounded confused. "What dogs?"

"I'll be right back," I promised. "You'll see."

I hoisted my bag over my shoulder and pulled my scarf closer around my neck. Immediately I thought to take the scarf off and place it into my bag. I didn't want to be strangled by anyone. Not that there were any people around as far as I could tell.

Venturing farther into the rear of the warehouse, the back entrances came into view. A silver pickup truck loaded with large parcels was parked against the back of the door. Phil stood next it. An assistant, dressed in a fluorescent green vest, was leaning against the truck making a phone call or texting someone. He spotted me just as I was about to back up.

"Hey, can I help you?" he asked.

"Ryan?" I was flabbergasted. "What are you doing here?"

"Daisy? I work here." He lifted his arms to display his vest. On the front of it was a badge that read, "Red Hook Stained Glass. Ryan."

Phil looked at me. "You were here yesterday," he said. "Bring your husband?"

"Uh, no," I said.

Ryan looked puzzled but didn't say anything. Just at that moment, Nina came around the back.

"This your daughter?" Phil asked. He came over with his hand extended to me.

"No way," Nina said.

My mind went blank as I shook Phil's hand. Fortunately, I'd learned that I didn't have to fill up spaces with words. Someone was bound to say something.

Ryan came forward. He stuck his phone into his pocket. "We're about to open in a few minutes."

"We were planning to pick out a piece for my apartment," I explained.

"Sure," he said. "Give us a few. Okay with you?"

I nodded and hoped that Nina would keep quiet. A poorly thought-out plan would have been better than no plan at all. What had I been thinking, and what was Ryan doing here?

A few minutes later we were all inside the warehouse. I was describing to Phil the image of a daisy surrounded by bees in shades of yellows with oranges and greens. I told him that some brown would be okay too. Before we'd sat at the desk, I noticed that the office was open.

"I can give you an estimate of the price if you give me a few minutes. I'll work it out based on the dimensions and the specifications. Okay with you?"

"Yes," I said. "Can I browse around a bit while you do that?"

"Just be careful." His voice was sterner than I expected it would be.

"Sure." I smiled. "Nina, come look around with me for a few minutes while Phil is figuring out a few details."

Nina rolled her eyes, and I had the distinct feeling I'd crossed over to the enemy campsite. I wasn't even her mother. I wondered how her mother felt when she did that. *Not much*, my gut told me.

We sauntered over to the back of the warehouse. The packages to Miguel's Moratorium were no longer there.

"Damn!" I whispered. "If only I'd thought to look more closely yesterday."

"You couldn't," Nina said. "That's why we're here now."

I sighed deeply. "You're right. But I was hoping that we'd find something."

"I'm not really sure what you're looking for. You haven't said a thing to me. But, if you don't tell me now, we're never going to find anything. That man doesn't look too happy."

I glanced at Phil who was going over the numbers with a grim look on his face.

"I'm not sure, that's the thing," I said. "Just see if you see anything."

Nina raised her eyebrows. "Oh yes. Why didn't I think of that?"

We separated, and she went over to a section of stained glass door panels. I immediately veered toward the office. The door was still ajar, and I decided to peek. Inside the room was an old-fashioned large metal desk. The kind I was used to seeing in *Cagney & Lacey* reruns. Behind the desk was a safe that took up most of the area between two windows that had iron bars across them.

There they were! The packages that were addressed to Miguel's Moratorium. I stepped into the office and tried to move one, and I was sure that it had to be a canvas. It was heavy but didn't have the weight of a stained glass item. Those were immovable. There were several other similar packages that were all wrapped and ready for shipping. This was my chance to explore!

Chapter 27

"May I help you?" a gravelly voice boomed.

I looked up and saw the same man from yesterday who had stepped outside. He was wiry and had a shock of iron gray hair. The lines on his face told a tale of the paths that he must have taken. The eyes behind the steel rimmed frames he wore told me to beware. There wasn't a hint of a welcome in his demeanor.

"There's a sign on that door that says, 'Office.' Most people read that as 'Private.'"

"Oh sorry! Phil was just putting together an estimate on a piece I'm interested in, and I asked if I could look around."

Phil walked into the room. "She's right, Cal. My fault." He turned to me. "Your estimate is ready, ma'am. Let's go outside, and I can give it to you."

Phil took me by the elbow and escorted me out of the room. I wanted to shrug him off, but I held back. Something told me to go along with him. We returned to his desk in the main room, and he gestured toward the chair. I sat down.

"This is it." He placed the estimate in front of me. *Thirty-five hundred dollars.*

I made a quick calculation in my head. If I went ahead with this, I'd be in hock. I already owed so much on my credit cards. I wanted to shake myself. I hadn't planned on buying anything. I had to remind myself that this was only a ruse to get back in and search for clues.

"I'd like to order it," I heard myself saying.

Phil leaned back in his chair. "Great. We need a deposit of at least twenty-five percent so our artist can begin working on it."

"Oh. I was under the impression that you were the one who made them."

"No." He cleared his throat. "Not me. The woman who makes them usually comes in later in the day."

"Really? I'd love to meet the artist. Maybe I could even watch her as she makes it. Of course, if that's all right with her and you."

"Meet her?" Phil leaned over and took out a printed schedule. "She's here a few afternoons a week. She does come in Friday mornings to give classes."

"That sounds great," I said. "I'll make it a point to come in on one of those days."

"I hope you don't need this by a certain date."

"Anytime is fine. No rush. I'd still like to meet her. Get to know her energy."

"Oh. Are you one of *those* people?"

"Yes, I guess you can say that," I said. "What's her name?"

"Ruth Arnold."

"And you're sure it's okay for me to watch? I mean, she is an artist. Some of them don't like to be interrupted while they work."

"Nah, she's a talker," he said. "How would you like to pay, ma'am?"

I pulled out my credit card and handed it to him. Phil deftly charged the twenty-five percent. I signed the receipt and decided I'd have enough sleuthing for the day.

Once outside, I realized that I had forgotten all about Nina. Just as I began retracing my steps, I heard her voice. She was leaning against the wharf railing. Ryan was standing next to her. A cold chill went through me.

"Ready?" I called to her.

Nina took a few minutes to say goodbye to her new friend before sauntering over to me.

I waved to him, about to leave, but changed my mind. "One minute," I said. "I'll be right back."

"I'm coming with you." For a split second, Nina reminded me of Cal, the owner of the stained glass store. Everyone had an attitude.

"Hey, Ryan," I said. "Haven't seen you in a while."

"Yeah, I haven't been around."

The last thing I meant was for him to let Nina know that we knew each other from meetings. I didn't want her to know that I was in the program.

"You two know each other? From where?"

This was it. I'd never break his anonymity and held my breath waiting until I heard him respond.

"We have mutual friends," he said. "Like I was just telling you, I knew Rubio."

"Yes, that's right," she said. "Ryan says that Brooklyn is a small place."

A wave of relief swept over me. "I didn't know that you worked here, Ryan. I thought you were a bike messenger."

"I guess I never got the chance to tell you that Rubio got me a job here."

"Rubio?"

"Yeah, remember I told you about Miguel's Moratorium? And the White Buffalo? He sold some of his work there. Our shop also ships paintings and large items that aren't easily mailed out."

Ryan pointed to the sign above the door. "Red Hook Stained Glass." Then he pointed to the window from which hung a large red and yellow sign stating, "Shipping For Oversized Items."

"I think the owner added this to keep the greenbacks coming in," he said. "You can't wait on people to decide they need stained glass. It's expensive. But I do have to say, there is a market in Park Slope. It's a thing."

It was a thing, and I'd fallen right into it.

"Had Rubio arranged for you to get this job?"

"Yeah, right before, well, you know." He glanced over at Nina.

"It's okay," Nina said. "I like to hear everything about my brother."

"We talked about the bike messenger job. It's kind of dangerous. Not too many people know that. People walk out right in front of you and expect you to stop with heavy loads on your back. Or it's the trucks. But, man, those cabs! Well, anyway, he thought this would be a safer way for me to get a steady paycheck."

"Wow, I had no idea," I said. "Leave it to Rubio. He was so quiet. I never knew what was brewing in his head."

"Yeah." Ryan nodded.

We hung out together for a few more minutes. Ryan gave Nina his phone number. I knew that she was almost a grown-up, but, still, I felt responsible for her. I called for an Uber, and we settled in the back seat as we rode home.

The hum of the car was soothing. I thought of Ryan who had a good reason to be at the shop. Rubio must have used the shipping services to send out his completed canvases. The owner was so elusive, yet he made sure to surface whenever I got close to him. All of my questions were overridden by the stained glass piece I had commissioned. I'd have to figure out how I was going to pay for it.

As the Uber neared the brownstone, the driver began sputtering swear words. I nudged Nina with my elbow, and she glanced up from her phone. A green and white ambulette was parked in front of the house. White-haired Marge was sitting next to it. A uniformed attendant pushed her tiny form in a wheelchair.

Our driver parked behind the ambulette. I jumped out of the Uber immediately, thankful for the app that had already paid him. Nina followed from the passenger side.

"Thank you. I can go in on my own," Marge said as soon as they reached the black iron gate. She wore an arm immobilizer, just as Rubio had, which made me shudder.

The attendant looked at me sheepishly. "Are you her family?"

"Yes, I am," I said. I looked down at Marge. "Why didn't you tell us you'd be back today?"

Nina had an incredulous look on her face as she stepped in first to open the gate. This was their first meeting, and I had no idea what she expected. Ruffian walked solidly by the wheelchair. Marge sat in her carriage like a diminutive queen.

"Well, I knew you were busy!" Marge said. "Is this a new guest?"

Nina looked at me but addressed her question to Marge. "How did you know I was here?"

"Not only did I know you were here, but I suspect you dowsed yourself with a mix of patchouli and something I can't put my finger on. Smells wonderful, I must say, after the odors I had to endure in the hospital. Let's not talk about the rehab!"

The attendant attempted to interrupt, but Marge and Nina had gotten on a roll.

"You are exactly right!" Nina cooed. "You are amazing."

"When I lost my eyesight, I was blessed with the most extraordinary sense of smell and, well—that's for another time."

I was shocked to see an almost palpable bond created between Marge and Nina so quickly.

"Thank you. You can leave," I told the attendant. "We've got her from here."

"The wheelchair." He pointed at Marge's carriage. "It belongs to the company."

"I'll just get up, and you can take it right back from where it came."

Marge stood up with the help of the attendant and Nina, who held her under her unaffected arm.

"I don't have the key," Marge said rather unceremoniously. "I didn't exactly leave under normal circumstances. Do the honors, Daisy."

I did as she requested, and a few minutes later Marge was back in her home. We hadn't had time to suggest to her that she go visit with her sister until this nasty affair had blown over. In fact, I'd practically ignored her the whole time she was away.

"No worries about not contacting me, dear," she said.

Marge's knack for saying what I had in my mind was always a surprise. She was sharp.

"No hard feelings. I was taken care of a little too well. I didn't need the rehab, but they insisted. Aging is not for the faint of heart. What I do need is someone to go shopping for a few necessities. Daisy, dear? This could be your opportunity to make up for ignoring me."

Marge laughed and Nina joined in. I hadn't taken my jacket off yet and happily agreed. Doing some grocery shopping for Marge would allow me to make amends. Marge quickly reeled off a list of items she needed. She took charge as I'd hoped she would when she returned. The first floor already exuded the warmth it had been missing.

"I'll be happy to go to the store for the small stuff," I said. "Then we'll just order on the internet for delivery of any heavier items you may need."

I left for the store, determined that when I got back we'd talk about her being alone in the apartment. Convincing Marge that staying with her sister was a good idea would be a hard sell.

Chapter 28

Supermarkets weren't for me. A shopper's brash *excuse me*, while she simultaneously pushed into my hips with her cart, had me wonder whether this behavior only took place in Park Slope or whether it happened everywhere. I was almost sure that it didn't in Los Sures but, then again, I never shopped when I lived there. Or maybe I just didn't remember. I must have had to shop to eat even while practically living in a blackout.

I took a deep breath and browsed through my phone for any viable piece of news that would keep my mind off standing in line surrounded by self-righteous shoppers. There was a new karate class on the dojo schedule. Sensei had mentioned that it would be a good idea to offer a women's self-defense class. It seemed like a great idea a month ago, but now I couldn't fathom how I would add that into my personal schedule. I was concerned about Marge.

I dialed Jose and he answered on the first ring. "We might have to help Marge all over again. She's home."

"Daisy, I can't, I have my hands full," he said. "I have to be home this evening. I have some work that I need to complete before tomorrow's meeting. More importantly, if I don't get into my bed tonight before Beatriz, I'll be sleeping on the floor. This is so not working out."

Jose kept talking. "Did she ask you to stay with her tonight? She didn't even let you know that she was coming home. You just happened to get there when she did. Maybe she made other arrangements. You know Marge."

"I hope so," I said. "It didn't occur to me that she'd make plans."

"You're the one who works in a hospital," he said. "You should know that they do that sort of thing."

"I'm keeping my fingers crossed." There was a beep, and I looked at my phone. Letty was trying to get through.

"I've got to go. I'll talk to you later." I switched calls.

"Daisy, we're back!" Letty squealed into the phone. "Hector's doing much better, and he's going to recuperate at Marisol's house. They'll send a physical therapist there to help him regain his strength. I can get back to my life again."

I was relieved to hear Letty speak her truth. She didn't have any problem admitting that, while she cared about her family, her own life was important too. I'd learned hard lessons from my mother that I should never say or even think something like that to myself. My parents made me crazy, but it was time to connect with them again. I missed my dad.

"Daisy? Are you there? Can you hear me?"

"Sorry. I got distracted," I said. "I can't wait to see you guys! It's been wild up here. I'm so glad you're back. Maybe you can meet Rubio's family."

"We've got so much to do getting the kids ready for school. Since Nati is still a toddler, she probably only missed coloring, but Jorgito probably has lots of make-up work to do. Oh, by the way, he doesn't want to be called *Jorgito* anymore. He goes by *Jorge* now."

"Oh no. Are you serious?" I asked. "What happened to you guys in Florida? I can't stand it."

"Jorgito wanting to be called *Jorge* is nothing. Wait until I tell you about Hector. It's soul-killing. Anyway, I've got to run;

the doorbell is ringing. They're delivering our groceries. Thank God for the app. I ordered during the cab ride from the airport. Talk to you later."

I pressed the red circle on my phone and moved one cart up. I'd be there for a while. A kid with a snotty nose peered at me from his shopping cart seat and started to wail. I turned around and pretended I didn't see him or hear his mother momsplain about what bacteria would do if he didn't stop wiping his hands on his face. I couldn't take another minute. *Milk, Bread. Stay task oriented. You've got this.*

"Here, I'll take those." A hefty blond woman lifted the packages out of my arms. I followed her into Marge's apartment, closing the door behind me.

Marge sat in her kitchen. "You guys were wonderful when I fractured my hip. I hope I don't hurt your feelings, but I hired Edith to help me. I should have done this the last time. She'll stay with me as long as I need, at least until I can do things on my own again. Anyway, I'm not getting any younger, and that nest egg of mine could use some cracking open."

"I'm so relieved, Marge," I admitted. "Having someone here with you is great planning."

"I remember what happened that night," she said. "A little too well. I don't want to be alone down here for even a minute. They've got to find those criminals."

"I guess we haven't really talked about that night," I said.

"We might not have, but the police did," she said. "They asked me everything under the sun."

"Were you able to give them anything?" I asked.

"Well, the woman with him was the scariest! She kept asking me if we had a key to the basement. I kept telling her there's a sub-basement, but there's nothing there but the furnace and a few storage boxes. I don't think they could understand that I can't function with a lot of clutter."

"A woman?" I was incredulous. "I had no idea! All along I imagined, well, I don't know what! This really changes things."

"I'm surprised Detective Harris didn't say anything about it to you."

I sat at the large butcher block island that was for chopping but mostly used as a table. Ruffian was in his usual spot near the door. It was almost like old times. If only Jose would walk in, then we'd be ourselves again. I could pretend that Rubio was at the studio and that Nina wasn't tickling the ivories in the parlor upstairs. I might even pretend that Edith wasn't in the pantry taking an inventory.

"Daisy? You're still there, aren't you?" Marge asked. "You're so quiet."

A twinge went through my heart. She seemed so vulnerable.

"No, Harris didn't say anything," I said. "He hasn't really been around. They had someone watching the house. Rod stayed a couple of nights. But as to anyone saying anything about a woman, no, nothing."

"They must have their reasons." Marge shook her cookie tin. "Empty. Someone will have to bake soon."

"I bet it's me!" I blurted out.

"What, dear?" she asked. "Do you want to bake?"

"No, Marge, don't you get it?" I sobbed. "Why wouldn't they tell me that a woman was involved? I've done everything I could to find the man, and it was a woman who was here! They probably think I had something to do with the whole thing."

"Stop yourself there," Marge demanded. "That's an impossibility. You wouldn't have done something like that. They don't suspect you. I'm sure they just want to see how things unfold."

"I don't know about that." My paranoia sirens were flaring at full force.

"I do. I don't suspect you, Daisy. That's the most important part of this whole thing. I trust you. I trust you as much as I trust the boys."

We held hands for a few moments until Nina came down the stairs, holding on to Ms. G.

"Am I interrupting?" she asked.

"Come, dear, sit down," Marge said. "Tell us about yourself."

The I-don't-care demeanor I'd come to know dissipated in Marge's presence. Nina was a chameleon. Before I knew it, Nina had told her life story, beginning and ending with her desire to attend NYU. I couldn't figure out whether she was merely charming or a grand manipulator. Possibly both. I recognized that type of character. I had lived that way myself for so many years.

"We should have dinner together," Marge suddenly declared. "Tonight."

Over her shoulder, I spotted the home attendant glaring.

"Ma'am, how about you settle in for a few days before making plans?" Edith suggested. "You must build up your stamina. Remember the instructions that the physical therapist gave you?"

"Being with my friends is what I need." Marge took control of the situation.

"We must stock up on groceries too," Edith said. "The larder is empty."

"That's true enough," Marge agreed. "But we'll certainly be ready by tomorrow, won't we, Edith?"

"Yes, ma'am." Edith began to scour the stove, and I had the distinct feeling that we were being dismissed.

"I am rather tired," Marge said. "I suddenly feel like a nap would be in order. Where is my kitty? Have you seen her?"

Nina spoke up. "She just went back upstairs. I'll bring her down. Where is your bedroom?"

"I'm on the second floor next to the parlor," Marge explained.

"I'll wait for my little one there."

"I'm going upstairs, Marge," I said. "Please have Edith come and get me if you need anything."

I lit a candle. Focus and clarity were all I craved. There'd been so many people in and out of the house, and it needed a good smudging. I lit sage and the pungent smoke wafted across the apartment. My shoulders relaxed, and the tension I'd been carrying automatically began to release. A lavender bath would be luxurious.

As I prepared the bath, my phone began vibrating where I'd placed it on the sink. It was Greg, and I had to answer. I couldn't hide from him forever.

"Hey, Greg, how are you?"

His voice sounded cooler than I'd remembered. Maybe I'd been too harsh with him after all.

"Hey, Daisy, glad you answered," he said. "Just wondering whether you'd like to get some ramen. There's a new restaurant on Seventh. Deeper into South Slope. What say?"

I hesitated. Rod would be over later, but some hot soup sounded good, and I had to learn how to build friendships.

"Sure, why not? I'm about to take a bath. A long one. I'll meet you there at about six-thirty. Does that work for you?"

"That's my girl," he said. "Perfect."

"See you soon," I said. "Just text me the link to the restaurant so I can find it."

As I hung up, I had a nagging feeling at the base of my neck. I wasn't trusting my instincts. I'd never learned to trust the nice ones. I always seemed to gravitate toward the losers like me. It was possible that Greg was a loser because he pursued me.

I sunk deeply into the hot water. The steam rose, and I closed my eyes. *En las nubes.* That's what my mother called it when she felt like she was either in a trance or daydreaming. I always thought that those times were when she was in a drunken stupor. I'd misunderstood. Now I understood what she meant by that phrase. That's exactly what a lavender bath did for me: suspended me in the clouds. My intuition told me that I had to be vigilant. Someone was after us. Marge had managed to avoid disaster twice. Maybe I should stay home after all. At the end of my bath, I wasn't any more focused as I'd hoped to be, but I was calmer and cleaner.

I glanced over at the clock. It was six already. It wouldn't be right to cancel Greg at the last minute. I grabbed my thick yellow towel off the rack and dried myself. I'd go anyway. I picked out a black pair of pants and a matching pullover sweater. New York black was always in fashion.

We arrived simultaneously. Greg was just putting his phone into his pocket. I stood aside while he opened the door to the ramen shop. It was warm and wonderful. The low lights shone over a couple who sat entangling their fingers and a large family with children who were sharing about their day—loudly.

Greg and I were guided to a table facing the window. We wouldn't be facing each other, and somehow that was comforting to me.

"So, it's been a couple of days since I've seen the sun set on you. How are you?"

"Poetic, aren't you?" I said. "I'm still trying to wrap my head around my friend's murder."

Greg nodded. "I guess you would be. About the dojo thing. I don't want you to think that I was holding out on you. I was as surprised as you."

"Hadn't we discussed it?" I asked. "That I'd be there?"

"I don't think so." Greg waved the waiter over and asked for the menus.

We perused the selections and Greg quickly put his menu down next to his glass of water.

"I'm going to have the beef ramen. It's always good and it's got that just-right level of spicy. You can always dip into my soup."

"I'll have the beef too. That's always a good choice, wherever I go."

Greg ordered for both of us and then asked the waiter, "What do you have on tap?"

"Beer?" I interrupted. "I thought you weren't drinking."

"Yes, of course," he said. "I'll have some tea. Daisy?"

I nodded and tried to cover up my bewilderment by looking out the window. Every time I thought I knew him, I was proven wrong.

"I don't know what I was thinking," he said. "You know what they say; old habits die hard."

"How long have you been in the program, Greg?" I asked.

"Why are you asking, because I had a slip-up by ordering a beer? Are you one of those *Big Book* thumpers?" He laughed.

"That laugh made your question just a wee bit less snarky."

"Hey, no harm done."

"No harm done?" I asked. "What does that mean? I don't get it." This conversation was getting more unwieldy by the minute.

"I'm kidding. It's like when someone tells you something about yourself, and you say 'you're welcome!' Get it?"

"Not really," I said. "But do tell. What about the program? How long have you been in it?"

"Oh, I've been around for a few years."

"A few years?" I repeated. "That's vague."

"I feel like I'm getting the third degree, woman!" He laughed again. "I've been in and out for a while. I like to keep things light and loose, like I've told you before."

I didn't say anything and looked around for the server. *Where was my soup?*

"All right. I'll come clean." Greg's eyes glowed. He was like a child. "I've got a couple of months under my belt with a couple of years coming around."

"Oh, I don't know what made me think differently," I said. "I guess that's how it is for some of us."

"Yeah, glad you understand," he said.

The server brought the tea and I watched as he poured the amber liquid into the tiny cups. The couple at the table near us seemed to be getting ready to leave, and the woman dropped her phone. Greg swooped over to pick it up and handed it to her. He was a gentleman; why was I having such a hard time around him? *It's probably me*, I thought to myself.

The server carried in large bowls of soup on a tray. He adroitly placed them down in front of us. I decided to try again with Greg. Building a friendship took more than one or two tries.

"We have the program and the karate in common," I said. "How do you figure that? It's such a coincidence, isn't it?"

"Coincidence? I would say it's synchronicity. You know that our meeting was meant to be. I haven't forgotten our afternoon, Daisy. I hope you're okay with it. I was and still am."

Rod came to mind when he said that. I had made a firm decision to stay away from Greg and, yet, here I was.

"I thought we could be friends, Greg. Is that something you could do? I mean, the way we started out and all. A little too fast I have to say."

"Why don't we see how nature goes, Daisy?" he said. "I don't want to limit my, our, options."

"Sure," I said. There was no point in arguing. Friendship was apparently not on Greg's agenda.

"Tell me, how is it going since your friend passed?" he asked. "I haven't seen you at the dojo. I've also been to meetings and haven't seen you there either."

"I'm doing okay. We're still trying to find out how it happened."

"Aren't you into that religion? Can't you find out who murdered your friend by killing a chicken or something?"

I shivered at his words. "Where did that come from? Really! Anyway, how did you know about my religion?" I rarely ever wore my beads or wore white.

"I saw you with your friend at the dojo, remember? He was wearing white. I put two and two together."

"True, but that's my friend, not me," I said. I sipped at the soup. It was piping hot.

"Anyway, let's talk about us," Greg said. "Want to go to a movie after this?"

"I have some friends who are staying at the house. I don't want to be away too long. It's not right, as the host, to do that."

"You're hosting?" He looked perplexed.

"Yes," I said. "Why wouldn't I be hosting?"

"Most hosts don't go out for dinner when they have guests over."

My gut told me not to explain that they were Rubio's family. They and Jose deserved some privacy.

"They had something to do tonight."

Greg laughed. "You know me, *live and let live*. When you're free again, give me a call. I'd like to see more of you. Take that any way you want."

Visions of that afternoon in his apartment entered my mind. This wasn't really something that I wanted to revisit.

"As I said before, I'd like to be your friend," I said. "But things are complicated for me right now, and I'd rather not add another one right now. If you'd like to see more of me, maybe we should stick to meetings."

"That's interesting," he said. "Me, a complication? That's the first time I've been described that way. Lighten up, babe."

I proceeded to eat my soup silently. Greg was someone I wouldn't hang out with again.

"Safe territory, that's what we need to talk about," he said.

"I know, the dojo. I was surprised to see you there. How long have you been training?"

"Not long at all," I said. "You saw me testing for my yellow belt. I'm a newbie."

"Gotta start somewhere. Most people start when they're kids. Like me. That's why I'm a second degree. What made you start later in life? Not that you're old or anything."

"Or anything," I repeated. "I had passed the dojo a few times. It just seemed interesting. I wanted to work out, but I'm not a gym person. Too much perspiration on the machines."

"All right," he said, and we both chuckled. It was obvious that we were both visualizing the same thing: people who didn't wipe the benches or handles down after drenching them with their sweat.

"How did you get all the way to having an advanced black belt if you were drinking all along? How were you able to manage that?"

"It's a myth that all alkies are complete failures. You know that. Many of us do some great things while we're still drinking. Maybe that's why I'm still on the fence. I haven't reached my bottom. One or two, maybe, but, well, you know how that is."

"I have to admit, I don't. When I stopped it was because I didn't know what my future would hold if I didn't stop. I knew what my life was already. It sucked!"

"You're funny," he said.

"Funny? I'd say I'm truthful," I answered. "Or at least I try to be."

We sat eating, and after a while he pushed his bowl away and leaned back. The server immediately strode over.

"Would you like anything else?" the waiter asked.

"Yeah, you can take this," he said. "But I do think I'd like that beer after all. Do you have those ginger ones? Alcohol free."

I concentrated on my soup. There was no reason to get upset about a ginger beer. But this was just another example of things not feeling right around Greg. Why upset the balance? I couldn't drink a ginger beer, or a non-alcoholic one either. I'd be off to the races if I did. Everybody had their own brand of sobriety. I needed to get off my pedestal. But just hearing the word *beer* gave me a craving sensation in my mouth.

Greg winked at me as he gulped down the ginger beer.

"This stuff reminds me of growing up," he said. "Common in the Caribbean. We'd drink it pretending we were our aunts and uncles. One time I was imitating my Uncle Cliff, and I pretended to pass out. I fell flat on the back of my head. Knocked me senseless."

I remembered pretending to be my mother. Yelling at my father. The memory of him pulling me aside and talking to me gently about how that hurt him was still painful. I had been so ashamed but not enough to not turn into my mother just a few short years later. The Promises told me, *We will not regret the past nor wish to shut the door on it.* But I still did.

"You look so serious, girl. That was a funny story I just shared."

"Yeah, I'm not at the part yet where I'm over things."

"Gotcha." He nodded his gorgeous head slowly. "Let's not go on an archaeological dig."

This guy was a bundle of contradictions. Contradictions and complications. My life was made up of them.

"I don't understand," I admitted. "Why? Because of not being able to get over things or just not wanting to do the work?"

"Both, maybe," he said. "I really do like a beer every once in a while. The problem is only when that beer turns into a six-pack. Like they say, one is too many, and a thousand aren't enough. But that doesn't happen too often."

Greg's tone made me think he was romancing a beer more than romancing me. This guy was a human red alert.

"I should be heading out," I said. "This place was a great choice. Thank you. I appreciate this evening."

"Should I take that as a firm good night?" he asked.

"Yes. I'd better get home."

"I'll walk you over," he said. "Just let me pay the check first."

I checked out my MTA app. "The bus will be here in three minutes. The stop is across the street. Thanks, Greg."

"You're a tough sell," he observed. "I hope I didn't offend you in any way."

"No, of course not," I said. Rod would be reaching the house at any minute.

"OK, well, seriously, call me. I'd love to get together with you again."

When he said that, his hazel eyes bore into mine, and I couldn't resist looking at him.

"Maybe I'll call you for another soup." The words slipped from my mouth. He did have a certain power. My old self seemed to respond to him.

"Great," he said. "I'll be waiting for that call."

"I'd better run," I said. "I've got one minute to get across the street." I picked up my jacket and bag and quickly left the restaurant. The bus was heading toward the corner, and I made it just in time. On the bus, I realized that I would get too close to a drink if I kept seeing Greg. It would be devastating.

Just as I entered the brownstone, my phone vibrated. Rod.

"Hey!" I was glad to hear his voice. "Are you on your way?" I felt immediately deflated when he said he couldn't make it.

"I'm disappointed," I said. "I looked forward to your coming over."

The acuity of my sadness told me that I wanted to be with him for more than safety. I cared about him. Maybe even loved him.

I thought of calling Angela, my sponsor. When I picked up the phone, it began ringing. It was Letty.

Chapter 29

We sat across from each other at the kitchen island holding hands. The steam from the mugs of lemon tea traced the air. It had been a while since we'd been together. Letty looked as graceful as always with her long dark braid trailing down her back. Her face was pale and drawn, though. It showed the misery she had gone through in Florida. If she had been to the beach, I couldn't see it on her.

"It's so good to be here, Letty," I said. "I probably shouldn't say this, but I feel guilty being here and not seeing Jorgito. Nati too, of course."

Letty laughed and then became solemn. "Forget the guilt. They were exhausted, and even though they complained about going to bed, they both fell asleep the minute their heads hit their pillows. The last couple of weeks have been stressful to say the least. Jorge kept begging to see his Uncle Hector. Mike and I spoke about it, and we decided that he probably should. It was tough, though. It was the first time he'd seen anyone so beat up. Jorge is just a little kid, so it was an experience."

I sipped my tea. "Do you think that's why he wants to be called *Jorge*? His way of adulting?"

"I didn't think of that, but you may be right," she said. "Lots of things are changing, Daisy."

My default feeling of fear reared its head. "How so? Are you and Mike okay?"

Their past separation had taken a toll on Jorgito. It had taken a toll on all of us. At the time I felt like we had all separated, even if it wasn't so. When they reunited, I probably felt the happiest of all.

"I'm glad the kids are in bed for the night," Letty said. "I always appreciate the quiet of this hour."

"Okay, now you're stalling, you haven't answered my question," I said. "What's going on? You're scaring me."

"It's about Hector," she said. "I think he's planning to leave the religion."

"What?" I asked. "Why?"

"My sister really got to him. She blamed the accident on his spiritual practices. She even went so far as to say that he wasn't in a relationship because of it. Just anything you can think of to stoke that fire."

"What did he say to that?"

"He listened to her," Letty said. "At first he told her that his beliefs weren't her business, but then he started to take her statements to heart. We were kind of at her mercy being there."

"Hector is in a susceptible state and questioning his life and what's next," I said. "I wouldn't worry."

Letty nodded thoughtfully, obviously trying to make sense of it all.

"That said, how does it work?" I asked. "Can you just walk away? What does he do with all of his Santos?"

"I don't really know," Letty admitted. "Maybe I shouldn't have mentioned it again. It's not really my business, but I wanted you to know just in case. That's one of the reasons we came back so fast. I mean, yes, Mike wanted to get back to work, but Marisol was driving me crazy."

I went into the living room and paced. The fireplace was unlit, but I felt like I could spark a fire in it with the current of electricity flowing through me.

Letty followed me into the living room with the cups of lemon tea and placed them on the coffee table.

"What am I going to do?" I fretted. "I'm supposed to be receiving my Warriors. We were all ready!"

"Maybe the accident happened for a reason," Letty placated.

I shook my head. "I waited years for a spiritual direction. I thought this was it. Do you think maybe I'm not on the right path?"

"No, that's not what I'm saying." Letty sipped some of the tea. "Sometimes things happen for a reason. Oh, I don't know! I have no idea."

"*It happened for a reason*. That's what everybody says when things go wrong. That's not enough anymore. I can't just say things I don't believe. Maybe someone has it out for me. But who?"

"Drink your tea and calm down," she said. "No one has anything out for you."

I drank the tea as she advised, but it didn't have the quick calming effect a Tequila shot would have had on me.

"Daisy, this is about Hector and his faith."

"Well, what about Rubio and Jose?" I countered. As I said it, I knew that I sounded foolish.

"That is a tragedy where Rubio is concerned. It's painful because we're all connected. Especially Jose. I'm just grateful that Hector wasn't killed too."

My face flushed. I was relieved that she didn't add a sentence about it not being all about me. My embarrassment overrode my narcissism.

"I'm sorry about my reaction," I said. "I'm just so disappointed. I care about Hector; you know that."

Letty patted me on my knee. "I know. Don't worry. I understand."

"I don't even understand it all." I sat on the couch and placed one of the plush cushions on my lap. "What do I do now?"

"Just be," Letty said.

"Easy for you to say," I said. "You've lived in this family all of your life and never moved forward, other than receiving beads. It's not like you're missing anything."

"You sound just like the fourteen-year-old I once knew, Daisy," she said. "Time to grow up, isn't it?"

The front door opened and was closed quietly. Mike was home. The sounds of him placing his coat on one of the hooks attached to the pier mirror in the foyer made me a little nervous. He'd never said anything rude to me, but I'd spilled one glass of red wine too many in front of him.

"Daisy, how are you?" Mike came into the living room. "I bet you two couldn't wait to get together."

"The first thing I did when we got home was call Daisy," Letty said. "You're right. I couldn't wait."

I went over to him and gave him a kiss on the cheek. "I'm glad to see you too" I said. "I'm hanging in there."

Mike went into the kitchen and returned holding a cognac. "My God. Rubio. Such a good person. How's Jose taking it?"

"Hard. We're just trying to find out who did this and then maybe we can have some closure. It's hard to concentrate on the grief part. The detectives are still nowhere close to an arrest."

"Maybe I'll be a pair of fresh eyes when I'm in tomorrow."

"Oh, you weren't at work today!" I exclaimed. Somehow, I thought he and Rod would have been talking about the case.

"I went up to help my mom out. She's not getting any younger. We have someone coming in every day, but I'm in charge. You know, being the oldest. It was good to see her."

"How's Mom doing?" Letty asked.

"All right," Mike responded. "Insisted on cooking for me. I'm stuffed. I hope you didn't wait for me to eat."

"I ate with the kids," she said. "We'll have that much more for leftovers tomorrow. Those will come in handy since I'll be back at work."

"I'm turning in," Mike said. "Well, it was nice to see you."

"I hadn't realized the time," I said. "I'll be on my way."

"Don't you dare," Letty said. "We haven't caught up yet. Please stay."

"Are you sure?" I asked. "It is getting late."

Letty curled her feet under her and settled back into the cushions. "The kids are upstairs. Mike is home. The dishes are done. I'm enjoying this visit. Sit down. You're not going anywhere."

"I get anxious when Mike is here."

"No need," Letty said. "There's nothing there. He always has something on his mind. It's not you. It took our separation before I really understood that. Being a detective has its stress. Enough about Mike. Let's talk about you. Something's up, isn't it?"

"Am I that obvious?"

"No, it's just that I know you. It's also that we couldn't really talk when I was in Florida. I know I rushed you off the phone a couple of times. I'm sorry about that."

"Don't worry about it," I said. "You had your hands full. You're right, though. Stuff has been happening."

"First I'm going to put the kettle back on for another cup of tea."

I leaned back into the sofa with my eyes closed listening to the sound of the water filling the kettle. Letty was back in a couple of seconds and nestled back into the cushions. A sense of gratitude washed over me. My girl was back.

"Tell me," she said. "I want the details."

"I ended up in bed with Greg. Rod is married. He has a kid. Oh, and I got my yellow belt."

"Come again? Rod is married?" Letty shook her head in disbelief. "And you're still standing? And who is this Greg person?"

"Some guy I met in the rooms. He's in AA too. I know, I shouldn't have gotten involved. It just sort of happened. It's not serious, but we had dinner earlier tonight."

"I can't leave you for a minute!" Letty said. "Daisy! I thought you were totally in love with Rod."

"Did I tell you that?" I asked. "I thought that I was falling in love. Then all this happened. Rubio and Charley Sprague were both murdered. Then I'm sitting there listening to Rod tell me that he has a wife in Chicago and that his mother has his three-year-old and wants him to raise her. Maybe it didn't happen all in that order."

"Wow!" Letty exclaimed. "I wonder if Mike knows that about him. Sometimes Mike says absolutely nothing at all to me about what's going on. Stuff that I think is important."

"Rod and I were intimate," I blurted out. "I know! No judgment, please."

"That's the sanest thing I've heard you say tonight."

Tears started falling down my cheeks. "I feel like a mess. While I may not have taken a drink, I feel awfully hungover."

"It's just regular life stuff, Daisy." Letty placed her hand gently on my arm. "It's not because of your drinking problem."

"But look at you," I said. "You've been married almost forever. I'm stuck. I feel like I never grew up."

"Do us both a favor and don't compare," she said. "Remember, I've had my share of troubles too."

Compare and despair. That was a famous saying in the rooms. She was right about that, but I was still a mess.

The kettle whistled, and Letty went into the kitchen. She was back in a few minutes with steaming mugs.

"This time it's chamomile. I don't know about you, but I could use just a bit more calm."

We sipped our teas, and I did relax a bit. Unloading all my news to Letty had been a good thing. I hadn't realized how much I had been holding on to until then.

"Oh, and congratulations on your yellow belt," she said. "I know that's important to you."

"Is it really?" I asked aloud, although I knew I was the only one who could answer that question.

"I think that you're way too hard on yourself," she said. "Life has to go on. Rubio being gone has really changed things. Tell me about Jose."

"Lord, you don't even want to know!" I said. "Rubio's mom and sister are here. They came to pick up his body so they can bring it back to Colombia. The mother is totally out there. His sister, I haven't put my finger on. It's like she has a million personalities. One minute she's so defensive, usually around her mother, and then she's a princess around Marge."

"I didn't even think to ask about Marge."

"She was almost kidnapped. Someone broke into the house, and we found her in the back shed. She's back home now and seems to be okay. Thankfully, she hired someone to take care of her. Twenty-four hours a day. Otherwise, I wouldn't be here tonight. I feel so guilty about her. I've practically ignored her."

"Remember that you're her friend," Letty said. "She's not expecting you to be her nurse."

"I know," I said. "But I still feel guilty."

"You feel guilty about a lot of things."

"You're right about that," I said. "I'm probably tired. It's getting late."

"Aren't you still on vacation?" she asked.

"Yes, but it's been a wicked day."

"Come back next week," Letty suggested. "We'll have a real dinner. Like the first time you and Rod were here. It'll be fun. I'll ask Mike about his schedule and call you."

"Sounds good," I admitted. "Real good."

We hugged and I left her house. I checked the MTA app and saw that the B63 would be there in a few minutes. If I hurried, I'd make it down to Fifth on time. It was the cheapest and easiest way to get home. I walked down to the avenue and made it just in time for the bus that was swinging in toward the curb.

Chapter 30

The brownstone was quiet as I entered the second-floor entrance. I climbed the stairs to my fourth-floor apartment. I craved being alone for a while. Popcorn and an old movie would be the only two things that I would entertain tonight.

Nestled on my couch in my fluffy white robe, I turned the television on and searched for *To Have and Have Not*. A Bogie-Bacall movie would take me out of the day. I put the movie on pause as I went to the kitchen to prepare a big bowl of my favorite snack. A few minutes later I sat down to watch the movie. I knew it practically word for word. I sat engrossed when suddenly Ms. G jumped onto my lap. I'd gotten into the habit of leaving my front door slightly open so she could come and go as she pleased. Being almost alone was so much nicer than being truly alone.

My mind wandered as I petted the little fur ball. I remembered how I imagined I was Bacall to Rod's Bogie when I first met him. The way he dressed fit in perfectly with my love of old movies. My mistake was that he wasn't a film figure. He was real and brought all those real things that I didn't want to deal with.

My eyes were just closing when I heard a noise coming from my bedroom. Ms. G jumped off my lap and landed squarely on the floor. I stood up quietly and made my way toward the sound. I had been in my bedroom already, and I knew no one was in there. But the hairs on my arms stood at attention.

I was right. There was no one in my bedroom. I walked back to the living room and stood behind the window shutters and saw him. Standing right across the street, looking up at my window, was the one person I wished would disappear. The camera was within reach, but I had no intention of snapping a picture.

To make matters worse, there was Beatriz being held up on either side by Jose and Nina on the outside stoop. Jose looked up and spotted me just as I was about to back away. I waved to indicate I'd go down to open the door.

"Perfect timing!" He sounded relieved as I swung the door wide to let them through. "You just made my life a little easier."

I waited as they climbed the stairs gingerly. While my day had been long, I realized that it hadn't been as long as Jose's. They were adept at getting her into the apartment. Nina quickly took her mother's jacket and shoes off, and Beatriz was snoring before her head hit the pillow.

"You guys have got this," I said. "I'm going back upstairs."

Jose walked back out into the hallway with me.

"Taking them out for dinner turned into a fiasco," he said.

"Sounds awful," I commiserated. "I want to hear all about your evening. But you must be bushed. I am too. How 'bout we spend some time together tomorrow?"

"Tomorrow doesn't work for me," he admitted. "I have a full day at work, and I'm sure I'll have to stay late. I was wondering if you could spend some time with them. Nina likes Marge. Maybe you can all do something together. They'll be leaving on Friday."

"Marge had invited us all to have dinner," I said. "Her aide wasn't too keen on it since Marge just returned home. Edith is not the warm and cuddly type. But, yes, I'll take charge of them. You can count on me."

We hugged quickly and then parted.

After turning the television off, I went into my bedroom. Ms. G had somehow burrowed herself under my heavy comforter. Her tiny black-and-white head peeped out. I got in next to her and yawned. We were out for the night.

Ms. G purred loudly in my ear. It was morning already, and she was ready for breakfast. I was famished too. My stomach howled. I remembered my soup-and-popcorn evening.

I heard the doorbell as I brushed my teeth. The clock in the bathroom told me it was later than I thought. Eleven o'clock.

"Hold on, I'm coming!" I ran down the stairs to open the door. Rod's silhouette filled the glass-paneled door.

"Hey, you're here early," I said. "Well, not really so early, but kind of."

He laughed. "You sound like you again."

Rod was right. I felt better than I had in a very long time. Nothing had changed, but my feelings had. I'd be sure to get to a meeting later in the day. I wanted to keep on the upswing.

I laughed too. "I guess you're right. I had an amazing night's sleep. You're in time for bacon and eggs."

"I had my breakfast about four hours ago. How about an early lunch?"

I nodded. "Sounds perfect. I just have to jump into some clothes, and I'll get it started."

"Have you thought of not jumping into clothes and getting things started?"

I stopped short when he said that. Greg popped into my mind.

Rod gave a low whistle. "Did I say something wrong?"

"No, forget it. Let's eat breakfast, I mean lunch. I'm starved."

As I put the coffee on, I took a deep breath. I relished the fact that he'd come to see me. I did care for him. Deeply.

"Do you want me to make the toast while you're doing that?" he asked.

"Sure, you can be my sous chef." I quickly put the bacon in the microwave and covered it with a paper towel.

"I'm not going to get GMOs by you doing that, am I?" he asked.

"GMOs?" I asked. "In the paper towel?"

"I guess not," he said. "I read this article, though. It's crazy what GMOs have done and will continue to do if we take them into our systems."

"I don't know too much about that," I said. "You do know that nitrates aren't the best to put into your body either."

"You're right," he said. "I'll just close my eyes when I eat."

The browned bread popped out of the toaster, and together we prepared BLTs sans the lettuce. We worked in coordination and finished together. We could be a team.

We sat down at the Formica table that I'd bought soon after renting the apartment. It made me happy to just sit at it.

"So, what's going on?" I asked. "I'm surprised to see you here. I thought you'd be working."

"There are a couple of things I need to tell you."

"Glad I'm sitting down," I said. "It's got to be serious if you're here to break the news."

"Sam Harris made an arrest last night."

"Oh. I don't know if I'm ready for this after all," I said. "Rubio's murderer?"

"Actually, no." Rod's voice was steady. "We know who was in your apartment, Daisy."

My belly felt as if I were in an elevator dropping several floors. "Is it someone I know?"

"Yes. Are you ready?"

"No, but go ahead anyway."

"Ryan Jones," he said. "Rubio's friend."

I was dumbfounded. "Rubio's sponsee? Here?"

The coffee maker beeped, and I jumped. Everything suddenly felt fuzzy.

"How did you find out that it was Ryan? Are you sure?"

"It was easy enough to find him through the ring," Rod said. "We made some phone calls to New Hampshire. Thomas More College. We got a listing of the people who graduated that year. Ryan was on that list."

"But what does that mean?" I asked. "Are you telling me he's involved with Rubio's death? What about Jose? Does he know?"

"Sam is talking to Jose."

"But did Ryan kill Rubio? That's what I want to know!"

Again, everything was surreal. Rubio was Ryan's sponsor. I heard him share at meetings. He liked Nina. Nina liked him.

"He's not talking, Daisy. So far we don't have any evidence that ties him to the murder. That was done very cleanly. Give us time, though. I promise you we'll find out who did this. Now that we have Ryan, we'll have other answers very soon."

"Did he tell you why he'd been in here?" I asked. "Does this mean that he's the one who did that to Marge? How could he?"

"Like I said, he's been quiet. Not saying much about anything. I wish I could shake it out of him. I suggest you stay in the moment, please."

I took Rod's hand. It felt safe and secure. I wanted to hang on forever.

"He was so nice to me. In the meantime, he'd been in my apartment. He went through my things."

"Come on," he said, "let's go sit in the living room."

We walked in together and settled on the couch. A pigeon flew to the window and hit lightly against the pane as it settled on the windowsill.

"What's the other thing, Rod?" I asked. "You said you were here to tell me two things."

"It's my daughter," he said. "She'll be here in a week."

"Can we talk about this some other time?" I asked. "I don't think I'm ready for this too."

"It's important to us," he said. "I want to be sure that you're prepared for it."

"Me? What about you? Are you prepared? Isn't this going to put a dent into your work schedule?"

"My mom is coming too," he said.

"Are you serious?" I asked. "I thought you said she couldn't take care of her anymore."

"Just for a transition period. They're very close."

I shook my head. "So not only is your daughter coming, but your mother is too. Wow."

His tone was gentle. "I care about you, and I want you to know everything about me."

Suddenly the bacon felt very heavy in my stomach.

"I don't feel well." I got up and hurried to the bathroom. I always had a sick stomach. My nerves were attached to it.

"That bad?" he called through the bathroom door. "I didn't think you'd be affected like this."

I didn't even bother to answer. I sat on the tub and took a few deep breaths. I wet a washcloth with cool water and dabbed it on my forehead and the base of my neck. *You're being silly. You're being selfish.* Now my own thoughts were attacking me. I had to be better than this, but I wasn't. I didn't want to share him with his daughter. I wanted him all to myself.

"Go home," I said. "I need some time alone."

"We have to talk this through," he said. "I'll be out here when you come out."

I sat there for a few more minutes until the nausea subsided. He was right. There had to be movement. We could go forward, or I could decide that I didn't want to move at all.

I opened the door and walked past him into the living room. I sat on the couch.

"Okay, talk," I said. "I don't know what you're going to say, since we've already had this conversation. But I'm listening."

"I wish I had answers," he said. "I wish that I could tell you exactly how it's going to work. The truth is, I don't know. I'm scared too. I've never taken care of her without her mother or my mother there."

"You're supposed to convince me that it's going to be great. That I'm going to love the way it turns out. Why aren't you doing that?"

"I'm not a miracle worker. I have my own feelings about this. You're not listening to me. It's going to be hard. I never thought I'd be raising a daughter on my own."

I moved close to him and put my head on his shoulder. He placed his arm around me. The only thing I could hope for in a relationship was being honest, open, and willing. That was something I'd learned in program. Those were concepts I aimed for but sometimes still fell short. Another thought popped into my mind. *One day at a time.* I didn't have to commit for the rest of my life. I only needed to commit for today.

I turned my face up toward his and kissed him. "I can't make any promises," I said, "but I'm willing to see how this goes for us. It's all question marks to me."

Rod sighed deeply. "All I ask is that if something doesn't feel right to you or if you're, I don't know, anything, promise you'll tell me."

"Sometimes I'm not even sure of what I'm feeling," I said. "But once I do, you'll be the first to know. The same for you. If there's anything you feel an off vibe on, let me know."

"Yes, that's a promise."

We sat on the couch together savoring the promises we were able to make to each other. It seemed like forever since we'd spent this type of quiet time together without looking into the future, and it felt so good. Being in the moment was such a sweet thing.

"Daisy?" He softly said my name.

"Hmmm?"

"I was just wondering. Are you going to continue taking those karate lessons?"

I nestled more deeply into his arms. "I think so. Why?"

"It just seems like a good idea," he said. "Maybe it's my skewed perspective, but the world can be a dangerous place."

"What's this all about?" I asked. "That was a jump from what we were talking about, don't you think?"

"Not really," he said. "It's just that I was thinking of how I met you. You were kind of involved in the Campbell case—"

I interrupted him. "Kind of? No, if I remember correctly, Jose and I solved that case."

"We were right with you the whole way, if you remember correctly."

"Okay," I acknowledged him. "I get that."

"And now this thing with Rubio," he said. "I guess what I'm saying is that you need to be able to take care of yourself."

"Are you saying you care?" I asked flippantly.

"What I'm saying is that I love you."

My heart skipped a beat. "Me too."

"You too what?" he asked.

"I love you."

We continued sitting together on the couch. The playground sounds of the children at recess across the street wafted over to us. The pigeon cooed on the sill. Ms. G jumped onto the couch next to us. For just a few sweet minutes, I allowed myself to relax in our private world before getting up.

"Would you like some more coffee?" I asked. "I could use a refill."

"Sure, that would be great," he said.

I went into the kitchen and picked up the pot. There was only enough coffee for a half cup. "I'm making more," I said. "Just hang out for a little while."

"Sounds like the perfect thing to do," he called out from the living room.

I bustled in the kitchen for a few minutes and returned to
him as soon as the dark liquid began brewing.

"I'll go back in as soon as the alert sounds."

"What are these?" Rod sat there looking through the
brochures that I'd picked up at Miguel's Moratorium.

"These show the artwork at the gallery where Rubio had
some of his paintings for sale."

"Had you ever seen his paintings?" He continued to glance
through the brochure nonchalantly.

"Yes, but he was private," I said. "I went to one of his shows
a long time ago."

"I didn't know," he said. "You two go back a ways."

"Yeah," I said. I hoped that he wouldn't ask me questions
about that night. I'd ended up making a fool of myself.

"You look like you're having a hard time thinking about it."
Rod asked. "I'm sure it's painful to think about the good times
with Rubio."

"Yeah," I said. "He was a great artist. You can't really tell
from these tiny photos."

I pointed to the pieces of art displayed in the brochure. "The
vibrancy of the colors he chose always surprised me. Yeah, it's
terrible that he's gone. And his work too."

Rod scanned the brochure. "When you went to the gallery
with Jose recently, were any of these still on sale?"

"No. As I said, they had all been sold the day after Rubio's
death. The curator said that happens sometimes. So macabre."

"I don't get that," Rod observed. "The *next day*? He's
murdered, and the next day all his paintings are sold? Was that
the only gallery he had his work in?"

"No," I said. "The other place is called the White Buffalo Art
Gallery. We never ended up going there. It was too much for
us after being at Miguel's Moratorium. The people there were
kind of condescending. That was the afternoon of my yellow-
belt test. We just came back here."

"I'd like to pass by the White Buffalo." Rod began looking through the phone for the address. "Feel like taking a ride?"

"I'd love to," I said. The idea of hanging out with Beatriz and Valentina all day wasn't very appealing. I hated to disappoint Jose but texted him before I chickened out.

"This isn't official, Daisy," he said. "Remember that."

"I know. If it were official, you wouldn't invite me," I said. "But can you put on the siren for me? I've never been in a police car before."

"It's my car and, no, no siren."

The coffee maker alarm beeped three times. "Oh! I forgot the coffee. We have time for another cup, don't we?"

"Only if we can sit here together," he said. "Just like this. It's nice, Daisy, real nice. I really don't ever want to get up again."

I laughed. "I'll get the coffee, and we can sit here as long as we want to. I like this too. A lot."

Sitting with his arm around me, drinking the hot coffee, was so reassuring, and loving. We had turned a corner. The apprehension of what I would find was still there, but my heart felt at peace, and I always looked forward to a little excitement.

Chapter 31

We stood outside the White Buffalo Art Gallery. The street, as in most of New York City, was filled with tourists. This gallery, half the size of Miguel's Moratorium, seemed much less pretentious. We walked in to see that one of Rubio's pieces took up much of the front wall. I was stunned to see it. There was a red "Sold" sticker under it.

I went over to the anemic-looking woman sitting behind the desk. "Hi, I'm interested in this piece."

"Oh, you have a good eye," she said while extending her hand to me. "My name is Stacey Pugh. And you are?"

"Daisy Muñiz," I said. I shook her hand briefly but firmly. I'd learned just the right amount of grasp.

"Nice to meet you, Ms. Muñiz." She pushed her blunt cut behind her ears. "Unfortunately, this piece is not for sale, as you can see. I may have a couple of smaller ones for sale. Would you be interested in looking at those?"

"Definitely. The artist does have a certain way with color."

We walked over to the front wall, where Rod stood in front of the painting.

"Ms. Pugh, please meet David Rodriguez." I introduced them. "Ms. Pugh tells me that she does have a few smaller pieces that we might be interested in looking at."

"Wait here a moment," Ms. Pugh instructed. "I'll be right back."

"I cannot believe they have more of his work!" I said. "What a great idea to come here today, Rod."

We waited for several long minutes. A flustered Ms. Pugh finally emerged from a back room.

"I'm so sorry." She apologized profusely. "I was mistaken. There are no more of his paintings for sale. I was so certain, but the pieces we do have are all waiting for delivery to the purchaser. They've all been sold."

"Really? My goodness. I was very taken with this one. I'm so disappointed."

"It's okay, Daisy," Rod interjected. "I'm sure we'll find something like it."

"No. This one is perfect for my décor," I said as petulantly as I could muster. "Please, allow me to take a look at Mr. Rubio's other paintings."

"I'm not permitted to show you a piece that's being prepared for shipping," Ms. Pugh said.

"Please? I just want to see if I should look for any of this artist's other pieces."

"That isn't possible," she said.

"Well, then I'd like to contact him for a custom-made piece. His work would be divine over my mantel."

"I should tell you. The artist is recently deceased."

"I see." I swallowed hard. "I had no idea. Please, may we have a look at his other pieces?"

"I think I can make an exception this one time."

"David, come along, please, hon?" I grabbed Rod's hand, and we followed behind Ms. Pugh.

Walking into the open door, I had to hold on to a sneeze. The room was small and jammed with paintings, sculptures, and other media. The footage of the room was sorely lacking. It had to be that way, I realized. The majority of the building's footprint was taken up by the gallery, where the throng of customers gathered to peruse the art.

"Here they are." Ms. Pugh pointed to a couple of canvases that leaned against each other alongside a wall. These were smaller than the ones in the gallery area. Rod and I simultaneously reached out to them.

"Darling, we're both so eager!" I exclaimed, batting my eyelashes at him. "You can do the honors!"

"Remember that these are sold already," Ms. Pugh warned. "Please be careful."

"Excuse me, though," Rod said. "There aren't any "For Sale" signs on these."

"One moment." Ms. Pugh poked her head into a tiny office next to the storage room. "Excuse me, sir," she said. "Are we certain that the Rubio paintings have been sold? I have a couple here who are interested in them."

"No one should be back here. You know that. Please see them out."

Both Rod and I looked at each other when we heard the response. There was no mistaking the gravelly timber.

"That's Cal, the owner of the stained glass factory."

"I'm sorry, sir," Ms. Pugh said. She reentered the room. "We'll have to finish our discussion outside. I'm sure we have other pieces that might fit your needs."

The gallery manager took hold of my elbow and steered me out. I turned around and saw Rod about to enter the adjacent office. Cal had reentered the inner sanctum before either of us had a chance to say anything.

"Excuse me, sir, you too," Ms. Pugh stammered. "You'll have to leave too."

Rod followed us out. We stopped in front of Rubio's painting in the main space.

"Why did you tell us that the paintings inside were sold?" Rod asked. "There aren't any stickers on them."

"If you notice, the "Sold" tags are under the paintings on the wall here. See? We wouldn't want any of the paintings damaged. Many of them are quite valuable."

"What are the prices for these paintings?" he probed. "Everything else has a price on it."

"We take the prices off once an item is sold," she countered. "Look around. You can see for yourself."

"Thank you," he said. "We'll do that. But first, I want to echo my wife's interest in buying Mr. Rubio's work. What can I do to ensure my wife's happiness, Ms. Pugh?"

My belly flip-flopped. He sounded so convincing, even to me. I had a glittering flash of my future. Beach wedding. Honeymoon in Bali. It immediately dissipated when the screams of a toddler kicking her father with her tiny legs broke into my reverie.

I was back in reality just in time to hear Ms. Pugh assure Rod that she would contact him if any more of Rubio's works were to come in, although she warned that it was unlikely. She handed her card to me, and I took it graciously. I was tired of playacting, and I had more questions than when we started out that day.

We stepped outside into the cool afternoon, and I sensed a change in the atmosphere. It seemed like everything had dimmed, and the wind blew harder than ever.

"What was that all about?" I asked. "Were they for sale or not?"

"Not even that, Daisy," Rod said. "Didn't the stained glass guy recognize us? He just turned around and acted like he'd never seen us before. I wanted to say something, but he was gone in a flash. Maybe it's because we were together. It's possible that the fact that he'd met us at different times made it hard for him to connect the dots. Some people are like that."

"No, I don't think so," I said. "He had a good look at me when I was waiting for Phil to give me an estimate on the piece I had ordered."

"A piece?" he asked. "It couldn't have been Rubio's."

"No, a stained glass piece."

"What? I don't get it."

"I kind of got carried away. The work there was really beautifully done. Maybe we can go down there and check on its progress. I told them that I'd go back to meet the artist. What time is it?"

"What are you talking about? Sometimes I just don't follow you."

I shrugged. "I went to investigate, and the next thing I knew, I had ordered a stained glass piece. I put a down payment on it."

"You want to go now?" he asked. "It's five o'clock."

"You're right," I said. "I promised Marge that we'd have dinner with her. We should head home."

"We? Us? You mean me?"

"No, but she wouldn't mind if you came over too. That would be nice. She likes you, Rod."

"Daisy, she barely knows me."

"But she has met you before, and she was grateful that you guys came out and saved her. You don't really have an excuse."

"Just you?" he asked. "Who else is going to be there?"

"Can you stop being a detective for just one evening?" I asked. "You guys have already arrested Ryan. That's going to be good news for Beatriz and Nina, and, I hope, Jose. He might have to work late. I'm sort of in charge of Rubio's family."

"Wait. All of you guys are going to be there?"

"And Edith."

"Who's Edith?"

"Marge's home attendant."

Rod shook his head and looked up to the heavens. "You are kidding me, aren't you?"

I stood in front of him boldly. "No, I'm not kidding. Marge is like a grandma to me. You know that. Jose is like a brother. They're my family."

"I know, and you still live at home with them."

"Ha, very funny," I said. "Just be glad that you won't be meeting my biological family. *That* would be a fun evening."

"Maybe I would like to meet them."

I blushed. "You would want to meet them?"

"Yes," he said. "Why wouldn't I? You'll be meeting my mother before you know it."

"And your daughter," I said. The realities were coming in waves.

"Okay, you've got a deal," he said. "I'll meet your adopted family tonight, but you have to promise that I'll meet your biological family soon too. No holding back. When I'm in, I'm in."

I nodded. Why wasn't love simple? Why was it like eating at a fancy restaurant and needing to learn to use extra forks and spoons? Here I was thinking of his daughter and mother as accoutrements, yet I couldn't imagine what he'd think of my mother. Not a pleasant thought.

"Sure, once things are more settled, I'll call them," I said. "I'm not sure about dinner, but at least a cup of coffee. It might be better to start with a short visit."

I spotted a hot dog stand. "I'm getting hungry," I said. "We should probably go home. We can talk in the car. Otherwise, I'm going to buy one of those hot dogs!"

"No, you won't," he said. "Do you know how many germs are in those carts? Let's just get in the car. I'll have you home soon enough."

"But they smell so good," I said. I took a side glance at Rod and decided not to pursue a hot dog. He was willing to go to Marge's for dinner and to meet my parents. That was enough for today.

"We could always go to the factory tomorrow," he offered. "It's not a coincidence that the manager was in both places. There's something to that, and we just need to find out exactly what it is."

My phone started buzzing. Jake. It felt odd, but I wanted Rod to know that I had male friends. Not everyone was a love interest. That was in my past life, and I needed to let it go.

Rod pulled out of the parking space and headed into the busy traffic.

"Hey, Jake, what's going on?" I asked. "Haven't seen you in a while."

I put him on speaker. Having Rod hear the phone call, helped me to deal with my guilt of the past more easily.

"Hey, Daisy," Jake said. "Just wondering if you're coming to the dojo on Saturday. Sensei is going out of town and wants to know if we can take over for a couple of classes. You know, teach the kiddies."

I looked over at Rod, who shrugged. *Why was I checking in with him?* I always did that sort of thing in relationships.

"Sure. Can it be for the afternoon?" I asked. "Just in case I have something to do in the morning."

"That works great for me. I'm busy in the afternoon and was hoping for the morning class. He said it's okay to keep the dojo closed Sunday, and he'll be back by Tuesday. If you don't mind, I'll drop the extra dojo key over tonight. Just give me your address. I'll head over in a couple of hours."

I gave him my address and was about to click the phone off, when an unfamiliar number appeared.

"I'm not taking this call," I said. "It's probably spam."

"Ignoring those calls is the best thing that you can do," Rod said. "Now, let's get to Marge's before I eat your hand."

Rod pretended to nibble my fingers, and I settled into the seat of the car. I was preparing for a wild ride with him and looked forward to it. I did wish the siren was on.

Chapter 32

The three of us sat in Marge's backyard. The evening was surprisingly warm, and the lights overhanging the garden made for a magical place. It felt right that Jose had made it after all.

"Can you believe it?" I asked. "How did she manage that?"

"*Hija de Oshún y Ellegua,*" Jose said. "They want Nina here is all I can say. Otherwise, it wouldn't happen no matter what she did."

"I totally didn't think about that aspect of it," I admitted. "In my mind, we create our own lives."

"We're not alone in anything we do, whether it be making choices or decisions. At the end of the day, it's more than our say-so."

Rod tilted his head toward me. "I told Daisy that my mother believed in the religion when I was little. That was a long time ago."

"What about you?" Jose asked. "Do you?"

"I don't know," he said. "With the things that I've seen in my job, I find it hard to believe that a God would allow certain things to happen."

"I've had my own doubts," Jose said. "I can't say that I'm okay with what's happened because, of course, I'm not. That said, I do believe that everything happens for a reason."

I listened. He sounded like Letty, with a reason-for-everything philosophy. Never in my life had I heard men talk about spirituality so casually. This was new for me, and I wanted to savor it. I also began thinking about my beliefs and what I wanted.

"My mother would say, 'Life is a trip,'" Rod said. Then he laughed. "I'm Mr. Thoughtful tonight. It has to be all the food I ate."

"How did we get on to talking about life like this?" I asked.

"You were trying to figure out how Nina managed to score a bedroom here when she returns for school."

"That's right!" I exclaimed. "I don't think I would have had the nerve to ask."

"And look," Jose said. "Somehow you've managed to rent a whole apartment here in this old brownstone.

"Oh stop," I said. "This entire experience is out of this world for me. Do you know when Nina's planning to return?"

"She mentioned that she's been accepted for the fall semester. Beatriz is pretty upset about it. I heard her tell Nina that she lost her son in the States, and she doesn't want to lose her daughter too."

"It must be awful for her," Rod observed. "I wouldn't want to be in her shoes."

We sat quietly for a few minutes, each of us lost in our respective thoughts. Eventually the spell was broken when the bell rang. I went to the front of the house to find Jake waiting there.

"You made it," I said. "Would you like to come in for a drink? A soda or lemonade? We're just hanging out in the garden."

"No, but thank you. Maybe I'll take you up on that another time." He smiled. "We've missed you at the dojo. It's a big commitment, but you're up to it, Daisy. Come back."

"I haven't left, Jake," I said. "Why would you say that?"

"I'm sure you've been going through a lot since, you know, your friend passed. Karate-Do can strengthen you. Don't forget that. Anyway, here's the key. I'll be on my way. You can always call me if you need to. Remember that the lock sticks sometimes. Just rattle the knob a bit and then turn it a couple of times to the left. It'll open. You should be okay with it."

"I'm sure I will be," I said. "Thanks for the key and your words. You're right. I haven't been motivated to take classes. Plus, we've had my friend's family up from South America. They're leaving tomorrow. I'm sure my schedule will be back to normal soon."

Jake left, and I watched after him before turning back to go inside. He was right. I hadn't been making as many classes as before Rubio's death. My schedule would never go back to normal. I'd have to create a new normal.

I returned to our impromptu garden after-party, and Jose stretched and yawned.

"Marge and Nina really hit it off," he observed. "Maybe they know each other from a past life. Nina was probably her mother. Did you see her cater to Marge tonight? Making sure that everything was perfect for her and that she was comfortable?"

I laughed. "I thought Edith would have a heart attack.

"I would have thought that Beatriz would be even more perturbed," Jose said. "The two of them have such a peculiar relationship. One minute they're fighting, and the next they're ignoring each other."

"Like many mothers and daughters."

"Or sons and fathers and sons and mothers." Jose stretched again and crossed his arms. "At least they're spending time together, even if they're not talking. You haven't seen my family around, have you?"

"We're here," I said. I extended my arm and placed my hand on his.

"You guys have been here," Jose said, "and I'm grateful. It's been hard for me to talk about the fact that it was Ryan who had broken into the house. He was Rubio's sponsee."

"I know," I said. "I didn't want to bring it up until you were ready."

"Imagine. Here Rubio is trying to give back to the program, and what does this dude do? He breaks into the house. Are you sure that he isn't the one who took Rubio's life, Rod?"

"We don't have any evidence yet to prove that he did," Rod said. "The good thing is that with the ring, we have proof he was in the house. That, at the very least, keeps him in jail."

"His lawyers weren't able to get bail set for him?"

"They tried," Rod explained. "Because the case is probably linked to Rubio's death, the prosecutor offered that as a good reason why he should stay behind bars. They pushed that he could be a danger in the streets."

"I'm glad that the judge was sympathetic," Jose said.

"Me too," I said. "I wonder if Ryan was the one who tied Marge up. Marge told me that a woman was here that night. Who could that have been? There are so many loose ends. I can't help but think about how one minute your apartment was a mess and then it was tidy. I wonder if Ryan had something to do with that too."

Jose shrugged. "I can't even begin to figure that one out."

Rod spoke up. "I wish I had more for you, but I can't do much. My hands are tied. Fortunately, Ms. G found the ring. That made all the difference. Sam is working on this, though."

"We know that," I said. "But the longer the murderer isn't found, the colder the trail gets. I saw that on *48 Hours*. It's been way longer than forty-eight hours now."

"That's a TV show, Daisy," Rod said. "There may be some truth in it, but it's the show's draw. They entitle it like that to keep you at the edge of your seat."

"They do, with that ticking clock. It's been eight hours, now it's been twelve hours—"

"Now it's been a week," Jose said.

"Oh, Jose, I'm sorry, I didn't mean that. You know, Ryan brought up *48 Hours*. I thought he was being insensitive, and here I am repeating it."

Jose stood up. "Well, guys, I'm going upstairs. Hopefully, the ladies have gone to sleep. And not in my bed. Thanks for sitting out here with me. I couldn't face another evening of crazy. I'm kind of glad they'll be leaving tomorrow. Did you say your goodbyes?"

"Right before they went up to finish packing," I said. "I thought that Nina might be hurting. She seemed to hit it off with Ryan. He's such a user."

"You spoke to her about it?" Rod interjected. "I wonder what her take on him was?"

"She's a kid," I said. "She just thought he was cute. Probably something to get her mind off her brother as well. They only had a few minutes together at the stained glass factory."

Rod stood up too. "Well, I'm off. I'll connect with you in the morning, Daisy. Let's go back to the factory. Maybe the artist will add something more than we already know."

"Okay," I said. I hesitated before adding, "Are you sure you don't want to stay tonight?"

"I've got some midnight laundry to do," he said. "I'll be here bright and early."

"Good night, you guys," I said. "I'll stay out here just a little bit longer."

I watched as they walked through the door and then closed my eyes. I couldn't allow myself to be afraid of bad guys — or any guys.

"Daisy?" Nina's voice woke me a few minutes later. "I saw you from the window. Is it okay for me to sit here with you for a few minutes? I want to ask you something."

I rubbed my eyes. "Yes, of course. What's going on? What time is it?"

"About midnight."

The vivid image of Rod putting his underwear into a washing machine entered my mind.

"Oh, I must have been dreaming." I yawned. "Sit down."

"It's something that Ryan said. Now that I know he was arrested, his words seem to repeat in my head. I thought he didn't know any better when he first said them. Some people are intrusive without realizing it."

"What did he say?" I sat upright, fully awake now.

"He asked me if Rubio had a strong box, like a safe. Or if he had a safe deposit box at the bank to keep his important papers in. I said that I didn't know, and that Jose handled all of Rubio's business. Strange, but maybe he thought he might be in Rubio's will. Maybe he knew about Rubio's finances and hoped he included him. Well, that crossed my mind."

"I don't know why he'd think that," I said. "Theirs wasn't that kind of relationship. Did he ask anything else that wasn't any of his business?"

"Not really." Nina flushed. "Well, yes. He wanted to know if he could see me again. I told him that maybe when I came back for school we could get together."

I felt a surge of compassion for the young woman. "I'm sorry that it turned out like that. I'm as surprised as you are that he asked you those questions within five minutes of meeting you. It still doesn't mean that he did anything to your brother. It's possible Ryan's just an opportunist."

"That's the story of my life." She sniffled. "Because of the money, everyone wants to ask me out. It's never me just for me. My mother reminds me of that all the time."

"You'll see. One day Mr. Right will come your way, and you'll know."

"Or Ms. Right," she said.

"Or Ms. Right," I repeated. "There's someone out there for you. You'll know when it's the right person."

"We were here only a few days, but you really helped us. I know it wasn't easy. I'm glad that Rubio had you for a friend."

I was stunned. My heart broke into a million pieces.

"Can I give you a hug, Daisy?" This was the first that I'd seen of Nina's shy aspect.

"Of course." I gathered her in my arms and embraced her warmly. Rubio had gifted us with Nina, and I hadn't realized that until now.

"They left for Colombia this morning. It must be terrible for Jose. Rubio's body went with them. He said that Rubio is in his heart when I tried to process it with him."

Rod and I sat over morning coffee, quietly processing the events of the last few days.

"Ryan was looking for papers," I said. "I know that for sure now. He blatantly asked Nina where Rubio kept his business papers."

"I guess he felt he had nothing to lose by asking her. So brazen," Rod said.

"Daisy, look, at this." He handed his cell phone to me. "The stained glass artist gives classes on Friday mornings. You want to head over? If she'll talk to you, we won't have to wait until the evening. I'm not sure I should be there. If the owner is there, he'll get suspicious. Up to it?"

A shiver went through me. "I think you should be close by just in case anything happens. Phil, the manager, told me about the classes, but I don't really trust those people. It's all heading too close to home. The paintings, Ryan, and Cal, who I think of as the Marlboro Man. Way too close."

"I had no intention of letting you go there alone. I'll be there the entire time you are, just not in the stained glass class. Not exactly in my repertoire."

"Anything can be in your repertoire," I said. "By the way, I have that karate class to teach tomorrow afternoon. The kiddies."

"Yeah, I remembered that, but for right now, are you ready to go?" he asked. "The class starts at eleven. You probably have to register or something."

"Give me a minute," I said. "I'm almost ready."

A short time later we were out the door. The house was quiet again. Beatriz and Nina had left for the airport early. Jose was at work. Marge and Edith had gone to the physical therapist's office for an assessment.

"Make sure you lock that securely," Rod said. "It has a different kind of ambiance with everyone out."

"Now that Marge is back there is a strong spiritual presence. She was a well-known Spiritist back in her day when her partner was still alive. The energy is just right for that here."

Rod nodded and held the gate open for me. I looked back and saw Ms. G sitting inside the parlor window licking her paw.

"Ms. G will watch the house for us. She's not going to let anyone in this time."

Rod laughed. "And how do you know that?"

"She just told me."

Rod took a glance at the cat and then me but didn't say a word. We continued to the car. I called and said I'd be in for this morning's class. Me, in a stained glass art class.

Chapter 33

"You're Daisy! Of course! You look exactly as I imagined you would. Come in! I'm so glad that you've decided to take a class. We can take care of the paperwork afterward."

The artist was everything I'd envisioned too. Her straight light brown hair leaned in on her cheeks in a razor-cut fashion. The headband she wore did nothing to keep it off her face. As though from another time, she wore an artist's smock. Underneath it peeked a long floral number, and her shoes were red Mary Janes. Around her neck hung a beaded Christmas necklace with a pair of lavender readers that dipped into one of her smock pockets. Eccentric. She was a kitschier version of my boss, Sophia.

Sitting across from me at the worktable were three other women. I hadn't had time to feel out of place because she immediately introduced us. They each smiled and welcomed me.

"Hannah, Morgan, and Lorraine! I'd like you to meet Daisy. This is the perfect opportunity for me to show you how a commissioned piece is completed, not only according to the buyer's specifications but also to the *elán* of the intended party! This is going to be so much fun."

"This is my very first class," I said. "I don't know if I can be trusted with the materials yet."

I was here because of Rubio, but maybe I could learn how to make stained glass marvels like the ones that surrounded me.

Ruth Arnold was thorough. Not only did she teach as she went along in a measured manner, she also asked me questions about my favorite colors and happily noted that I'd chosen to have a panel made that was the image of my name.

"Ladies, this is a testament to us valuing ourselves," she said. "How many of us would allow ourselves the opportunity to have a piece made that symbolizes ourselves?"

I snuck a glance at the three ladies across from me. Their names wouldn't be so easy to immortalize in a physical form. Lorraine caught my eye and smiled.

"A daisy does symbolize wonderful things," she said. Her warm smile reached her eyes.

"Do tell us something about that, Lorraine," Ms. Arnold encouraged.

"I do know that daisies are the Goddess Freya's most beloved flowers," Lorraine said. "She's the Goddess of love and fertility. Think new beginnings and motherhood."

Hannah chimed in. "Lorraine is our expert when it comes to the Goddess tradition. Freya is a Norse Goddess. I know a bit more about the Celtic Goddesses."

"We don't want to scare you off, Daisy," Morgan said. "This is a stained glass workshop. You're in the right place to learn, as we are. We do tend to talk about our Goddesses, though. There aren't many places that we feel free enough to do so."

"We hope you feel comfortable enough to come back. You'll learn a little about stained glass in the bargain!" Lorraine had a deep throaty laugh.

"You ladies do come on a bit strong," Ruth said. "My priority, of course, is the artwork, but we do want to continue our circle of women's knowledge here."

I was taken aback. I'd come here for one thing and something entirely different began to take shape.

"I work full time," I said. "I don't know if I can come back. I'm on vacation for a couple of weeks."

"After class, while you complete some paperwork, we can talk about the schedule. In the meantime, let's talk about margins."

The two-hour class passed pleasantly. Our lives were different. I was sure about that. The connection was that we were women in search of grounding ourselves in spiritual lives. I almost laughed out loud. Who would have figured that in attending a workshop I'd find myself with women that were more like me than different?

"Bye, ladies, see you next week!" Ruth waved to them from the door. She turned to me as the last car drove off. "Now let's get you signed in."

We set out to fill in the blanks. The usual: name, address, email address, and phone number. At the end of the process, she looked at me squarely.

"There's something here that you're looking for, isn't there? I don't think it's about learning the names of the Goddesses either."

I gaped at her. I had the same feeling that I did when Ana gave me a spiritual reading. This woman was more connected than I'd realized. I decided to be fully honest with her. I had nothing to lose.

"You're right," I said. "I do want the panel I ordered, and I absolutely adored the class and the women's honesty. The reason I came was to find out anything I could about the selling or shipping or anything about the paintings that my friend Rubio made. He's an artist. I don't know if you know about him. He's dead."

"He was found right outside. I'm sorry about what happened to your friend." Ruth's demeanor was calm. She seemed focused and not surprised at what I'd said.

"We're going crazy trying to find out more information," I said. "Anything. Can you help? Anything you could share would be invaluable."

"I've had my studio here for many years," she said. "I wouldn't want my ability to have this space jeopardized. I hope you understand that."

"I do, believe me," I said. "I wouldn't want anything like that to happen."

"The owners here have a penchant for business. You might have noticed that. It's a stained glass factory. It's a shipping company. A business."

She looked at me meaningfully. "I don't know if you understand that. The owners turn a profit. My holding classes here is totally unnecessary to their operation."

"Can you tell me what type of business other than the stained glass and shipping goes on here?"

Ruth Arnold's laughter was like sharp tinkling glass. The curious person I'd met turned into a bird right before my eyes. A small wren that transformed into a grackle.

"Listen to your thoughts, and you will understand what I'm talking about. Don't underestimate yourself."

I had no idea what she was talking about.

"Stop gawking," she said. "You know exactly what I mean. Look at the image in your mind as I speak."

The crude map that I had drawn in ink showed itself to me in a vision. Just like that. As plain as the mole on her forehead.

"That's it," she said.

"How do you know what I'm thinking of?" I was bewildered.

"How would I know what you're thinking? I can't read your thoughts. Your eyes told me that you had focused on the image that would answer your question. Go with that. Talk it over with your boyfriend. He'll know what it's about."

"My boyfriend?"

"Yes. He's sitting right in your aura. He's on this side, and he is leaning heavily on you."

"How do you mean *he's leaning on me*?" This was getting

wackier by the minute.

"He depends on you! What else would I be talking about? I have to get ready for my next class." She thrust a postcard into my hands. "Take this."

"The women are meeting a week from Saturday at my house. We'll be gathering for a women's circle. There will be a few other women there who don't attend this class. You're invited. I hope you can make it."

I looked at the postcard. Depicted on it was the image of a crow against a white full moon and an indigo sky. The address was in the North Slope, only a few blocks from our brownstone. I had a flash of inner recognition, but the glimpse was gone before I could get an actual look at it.

"I'll do my best to make it there," I said. "Should I bring anything?"

"We love sweets. No need to call beforehand. Just show up. We'll be there. We meet once a month. You'll fit in perfectly."

Ruth, the stained glass/goddess teacher, began straightening up her worktable, and I was dismissed.

We again sat next to each other in Rod's car. It had started out as another balmy day, but a sudden breeze began blowing whirlwinds of dust and litter around.

"This is like a mini-cyclone," I said. "Was it like this while I was inside?"

"I think it's you," Rod said. "It only started when you came out of there. How did the class go?"

"The teacher, her name is Ruth, is really good. I don't think I learned anything about stained glass making, at least not yet. I might in the future if I'm able to continue taking classes."

One quick glance at Rod reminded me why I'd taken the class to begin with.

"Sorry, no, I didn't find anything out that would help in terms of finding Rubio's murderer. But she did invite me to her house for a women's group next weekend."

"Just like that?" he asked. "To her house? She invited you the very first day that you met her? What for?"

"I just told you," I said. "It's a women's group that she holds. I think she said it's once a month."

"What is it, a book club?"

"No, it's a Goddess group."

"A Goddess group?" he asked. "I don't exactly know what that means, but are you going?"

"Maybe. It seemed awfully interesting. The women weren't arrogant like I thought they'd be. They were nice. I don't really have any women friends."

"Letty would be hurt if she heard you say that," he said.

"Oh, Rod." I shook my head. "She's my best friend. But you know how that is. She's busy with Jorgito and Nati. And Mike. He's another big kid."

"She said that?" Rod looked surprised. "Maybe he just wants a little TLC after being on the job all day."

"No, she didn't say that. I did. It just seems like he takes up a lot of air when he comes home. She didn't complain. I guess I did. We go back a long time."

"I get it," Rod said. "You have a little bit of jealousy going on there."

"Let's just say people change, and so does life. I don't blame her. She's totally absorbed in her family and job. That's a lot of responsibility. I think I will go to the women's group. Just to check it out. It felt nice to be invited."

"Just be careful."

"No worries, I will. She lives right around me. I'm sure it'll be safe. The worst that could happen is that she serves tofu and celery as a snack."

I laughed and Rod joined in as we headed back to my apartment.

The bedroom was lit by the moon's rays. The bluish light was cast down upon Rod's form sitting at the side of the bed. Ms. G sat on the window seat, gazing out into the night.

Rod looked down at me. "I want you to be happy. I want you to eventually say that you've made the best choice that you possibly could."

I opened my arms, inviting him back to bed. "Where are you going?" I asked. "I was happy until you got up."

"Are you sure you want me to stay?" he asked as he settled back under the comforter. "I thought I should go home. That that's what you would want."

"No, you should have asked me, silly," I said. "Stay. We need to stay together as much as we can."

"That sounds so ominous." Rod tightened his embrace. "Nothing's going to happen."

"It never occurred to me that something would happen to Rubio. I'm sure Jose never thought it would either."

"Let's not think like this. We shouldn't spend our time looking at the bad things right now. It's *our* time. Let's keep it positive. Okay?"

I nodded and found comfort in his embrace. He was right. I could easily go down the rabbit hole, and it wasn't fair to bring him along with me. *Treasure what you have.* The words resounded in my head as if someone else had just said them.

"I think I'm hearing voices." I laughed.

"Well, tell them to be quiet," he said, and began kissing my neck.

The rest of the evening was delicious. The thought or the voice was right. I would treasure what I had for as long as I had it.

Rod nudged me. "Daisy, wake up. You're not going to believe this."

"Hmmm?" I could barely open my eyes. "What time is it?"

"About one in the morning. It's your stalker friend. He's back outside."

I immediately jumped out of bed and grabbed my robe. "Oh God. I thought he was gone. And he's not my friend!"

Rod hurriedly put his clothes and shoes on. "I'm going out to have a little chat with him."

"No. What if something happens to you? Please stay. It's safer in here."

"Nothing's going to happen to me," he said. "I'm carrying."

My insides felt like they were caving in. Now I knew how Letty felt when Mike went to work. I must have been living in a bubble. The danger hadn't seemed so close before tonight. I felt nearer to a panic attack than I had in years. I watched as he went out the door, and then I dove back into bed.

A few seconds later, I emerged. It was always a choice between love and fear. I didn't want to stay stuck in fear. I got up and threw on a pair of jeans and a tee shirt. When I got to the bottom of the stairs, Rod reentered the brownstone.

"He left when he saw me. He just high-tailed it up the block. At least he knows that someone is watching him now, and I'm not going to let up. I did go across the street and picked this up."

Rod opened his palm and showed me a vape wrapped in a handkerchief. "These are easy enough to get anywhere. I'm wondering if we could get some prints from this. My ex used to tell me that I was too compulsive with my *hankies,* as she called them. Glad I never got out of the habit of having one in my pocket at all times."

"I'm glad too. I hope that we find something this time. I feel like we've been going on a wild goose chase. Like doing the same thing over and over again, expecting different results."

We were back in bed. The thought of the stalker gnawed at me.

"Do you really think there's a connection between the guy out there and Rubio?"

"We'll only know when we catch him and he talks," Rod said. "If he does."

"I need a meeting," I said. "My head is buzzing trying to make sense of everything."

"I may need one too if I'm going to be hanging out with you," he said. "Don't you think?"

"No, but yes. I mean, you could go to an open meeting to see what goes on there. You could also go to Al-Anon. That's for friends and family of alcoholics. What I am, you know. Hey, I'm talking to you! Your eyes are closing. That's not right."

Rod yawned. "I'm exhausted, Daisy. I'll go to a meeting with you tomorrow. I promise. Let's just go to sleep now."

I listened as his breath became regular and his light snore filled the room. Ms. G jumped into bed with us. She kneaded the comforter near Rod's feet. The serenity in the room filled my heart. But my thoughts were on the well-known stalker. I didn't want to keep secrets from Rod but had no options. Eventually, Rod's breathing lulled me to sleep.

Chapter 34

The speaker droned on and on with a too detailed drunk-a-log, and I snuck a peek at Rod, who sat to the right of me. Because it was an open meeting, anyone could attend. I was embarrassed and afraid he'd lose all respect for me once he saw who I truly was. It was mid-morning, and the basement had a lot of empty seats.

I closed my eyes and had almost willed myself out of the room, when I heard the chairperson make the usual announcements. He passed the basket, and most of us threw in a dollar or two as a donation. The chair then announced a five-minute break before the meeting would resume for people to share.

"How are you doing?" Rod leaned down toward me. "Are you okay?"

"Yes, I'm good," I said. "I guess I'm more worried about how you're feeling than me."

"I think they have Co-Dependents Anonymous meetings for that," a familiar voice said.

I turned around to see Greg sitting in the row behind us. I wanted to crawl under my chair. This guy seemed to turn up everywhere I was, but I didn't want to let him know that affected me so adversely.

"Hi, there. Have you two met yet?" I asked. "Greg, I'd like you to meet David."

The two shook hands. Neither of them mentioned the fact that Greg had butted in with his stupid comment. I followed suit and ignored it too. Having the two of them meet was a bit too much for me.

"Daisy, where've you been, girl?" Greg asked. "I haven't seen you here lately."

"I'm hardly ever at this particular meeting," I said.

"I've been to the dojo too," he said. "Can't say that I've seen you there either."

"True. Family obligations. I'm back at both, though. See, I'm here now."

"Glad to see you." Greg flashed that smile that I'd almost fallen for. I grabbed Rod's hand and gave it a quick squeeze.

"I'm going to get a cup of coffee," I said. "Come with me. Maybe I can introduce you to a couple of my other friends. You don't mind, Greg, do you? You know how it is when you're a newcomer."

"I didn't realize that you were a newcomer, champ." Greg was smooth.

Rod got up without a sound. I took one of my keys off the ring and placed it on his seat after placing the ring on mine. Even though the room wasn't spilling out with people, I wanted to keep our seats together.

"*David?*" Rod spoke under his breath. "Who's the dude?"

I was mortified. "I know him from meetings."

"I figured as much. Is it usual for people to jump into other people's conversations around here?"

"Actually, yes," I said. "I never thought about it that way. Some of us are a bit clumsy with social interactions. There's no juice to lubricate the situation."

"Don't talk dirty to me in a public place, okay?"

We laughed and the tension dissipated. We got coffee, and

I didn't see anyone else I knew in this unfamiliar room. The chairperson was already calling for the meeting to come back to order. I noticed that Greg had left. He'd come in quietly and left the same way. I swore inwardly that I wouldn't entertain even a friendship with him. He'd left me with a bad feeling, and I wasn't going to allow myself to get further involved on any level with him.

After the meeting I reminded Rod that I would be teaching the Saturday afternoon kiddie class.

"Do you want me to go with you?" he asked. "Just to hang out. I can watch you teach."

"Thanks," I said, "but, I'm sure that you have something else you could be doing on your day off."

"I was planning to buy a bed for my daughter, but I've got plenty of time to do both."

I wasn't prepared for that statement. "Oh. Of course. Do you want me to go with you? After class? I can help you pick one out."

"No, I'll be ordering it online. My mother sent me the ordering information. Would you like to come over after you're done?"

"To your place?" I asked. "This would a first. Up until now you've always been to my place."

"I know that," he said. "Come over. It's about time you visited me."

"I'd like that," I said.

"Me too." He smiled. "I'm on St. Marks Avenue. Off Flatbush."

"How come I didn't know that? How did we start off so fast? Here I am thinking about commitments, and I didn't even know your address."

"It's my fault. I don't know what I was thinking. Here I want you to accept my daughter, and I've never had you over for dinner. I think we need to start all over again. What do you say?"

"I say I love that idea," I said. "Can we go back to the Mexican restaurant we went to on our first date?"

"You've got it," Rod said. "We can start off again, but in a different way?"

"Yes, that would be perfect," I said. "You have to admit, though, that we have a pretty good beginning, don't you think?"

"I do. I'm glad that you said that." Rod smiled at me again.

I nodded. "After class, I'd like to go home to shower and change, and then I'll take a cab to your place. Let's say we meet about six?"

"Sure," Rod said. "I'm excited. To sweep and dust too. I'm kidding. But just so you know, it's one of those long rambling apartments. The dust from Flatbush covers everything if it's not kept up. I have someone come in every couple of weeks."

"You have a room for your daughter?" I asked.

"There's one of those rooms off to the side of the living room. It's mostly been filled with boxes."

"Still? You've been in New York for a while."

"It's hard for me to commit."

We both laughed. "Okay, I'll be on my way. But first you'll have to tell me what you thought about this morning's meeting."

Rod fished into his pocket and pulled his phone out. He spoke for a moment and then looked at me somberly. "It's Sam Harris. Ryan is ready to talk. Twenty-four hours there, and he's gotten a bit antsy. I have to head over. Six. I'll be waiting for you."

"Wait," I said. "Are you sure that I shouldn't go with you or call Jose? Tell him to go to the precinct?"

"We're nowhere near there yet. If anything comes up, I'll reach out to you. Sometimes these guys just waste our time. They get out of their cells, and then they clam up when they're put to the test."

"Be careful," I said. "I'm eager for any news, so text me if there's anything important. Otherwise, I'll see you later."

We hugged and separated. I looked forward to the kiddies. Maybe I could be a power of example for them. *You are who you practice to be.*

The Saturday afternoon clouds were dark and ominous. We were in for a downpour. I inserted the key into the dojo door. Jake was right. The lock stuck. Right or left? I jimmied it a bit and finally got inside. I changed into my *gi* before the parents toted in their children, and I made sure to warm up before the door opened again. Once done, I sat at the desk at the entryway waiting for them. Before I knew it, I'd be standing in front of a bunch of kicking tots who never missed a shin.

The door swung open and the first of ten tykes came inside. "Hi, Miss Daisy!"

The children were a mix of sweetness, clumsiness, and runny noses. Proof spring was here could be seen in the tiny red noses that lined the entrance room. I'd heard that once one got sick, the others did too.

"You guys are prompt!" I said. "Go down and get dressed. If you need help with your *obis,* bring them upstairs. I don't want Mom or Dad fixing them for you. We'll do them together up here in class."

I'd already taken charge when it came to the parents. A couple of them looked at me askance.

"Are you sure, Ms. Muñiz?" Mrs. Smith-Bowman asked. "Sensei Norman always lets us do that for the kids."

"I'm sure," I said. "Maybe you can help them practice at home. It's great as a technique to learn patience. They'll be proud of themselves when they can tie them on their own."

The looks of skepticism went into the dressing rooms along with the children.

About fifteen minutes later, the youngsters were lined up in varying degrees of undress in the dojo. They bowed to me, each other, and to the far end of the room to show respect.

"Who here knows how to tie their *obi* correctly?"

A few tiny hands shot up in the air.

"Great! I'd like whoever has their hands up in the air to turn to their closest buddy next to them who doesn't. Excellent! Now, help each other out."

The children busied themselves. There were a few extra kids who didn't have anyone to help, so I went over to them. Another fifteen minutes, and we were ready to begin class.

I had them all face the mirror. We bowed again, and I led them through a drill of front kicks and then front punches. I knew most of them enjoyed the grappling exercises. When it seemed they couldn't lift their little legs again, I had them form into pairs for the scrappy type of fighting.

I had to stifle my laughter. The kids were adorable. I had missed them, and I was glad that Jake had called me to take over the class.

The ninety minutes were over in a flash. We were all flushed, perspired, and smiling as we ended the class sitting in *seiza*. I marveled at how the little ones sat so easily in the position with their eyes closed. I kept mine opened and gazed onto their radiant faces.

"Okay, guys," I said a few minutes later. "Open your eyes. You all did great today. Especially the part where you helped each other with your *obis*. Practice tomorrow, and then you can surprise Sensei when he returns next week. Be careful and remember that the fighting stance is the running stance. There's no shame in either when it comes to defending yourself. See you next week."

One by one they lined up again to bow to me as their teacher and then to the dojo. Each child ran or skipped out into the entryway, where their parents were waiting for them. I waved to each one as they left the dojo.

The afternoon made me take pause. My trepidation at Rod's daughter coming to New York was disproportionate to any reality. I loved children and needed to explore why I was so terrified of that little one. Therapy had to be the place to sort through my thoughts and feelings. I had to make a move in that direction too.

Chapter 35

I pushed the front door closed and went downstairs into the girls' dressing room to change. The floor was strewn with leg and arm pads. I'd have to place them back in the bins outside in the hallway. There were a couple of teeth protectors on the floor. I stuffed them into my equipment bag. The kids would have to drop down and give me ten push-ups for being so sloppy. I chuckled to myself, knowing that having them do push-ups a week later would be useless.

The boys' dressing room was no different. I carried the stray equipment to the door. I'd come back for them after I dressed. I heard a sound in the entry. One of the little ones had probably forgotten a sock or *obi*. I listened and heard the front door slam shut. Whoever it was must have quickly found what they'd come looking for.

I reentered the girls' dressing room and pulled off my cotton *gi*. I dried my skin with the towel I'd stashed in my gym bag. I pulled my clothes on. In a few minutes I'd be home, getting ready for my evening with Rod. My body hummed in anticipation. I'd finally get to see his place and together we'd surpass another level of intimacy.

I flicked off the light switch in the girls' dressing room and pushed my equipment bag into the entryway with my foot. On automatic, I went into the boys' room and placed all the equipment back in the bins. The afternoon was taking longer than I'd planned. I was about to walk out, but when I passed the desk, I saw that a couple of the parents had dropped checks on the desk. Perhaps some of the grandparents paid for the children's classes. Most people I knew used phone apps to pay bills. I had forgotten to keep track of the numbers at the dojo. It was getting a bit dark in the room, and I turned the desk lamp on. I wrote the entries in Sensei's account book and placed the checks in the metal box he kept in the top drawer of the desk.

The bathroom door slowly slid open.

"Hello?" I called out. "Who's there? We're closed."

"Hey, Daisy."

Greg sidled his way out of the bathroom. He grinned at me. A chill went down my spine.

"What are you doing here?" I asked. "How long have you been in there?"

The thought that he might have been watching me change flitted through my mind. I had to get a grip. He had probably just ducked in to use the bathroom.

"I thought you might be here today," Greg said. "I was hoping to connect. After seeing you at the meeting, I couldn't wait to talk to you again."

He came closer to me, and I could smell the alcohol on his breath. I hoped he was an easy drunk.

"You should have called me," I said.

"I have called. A few times," he said. "You never pick up."

"You called me? When?" I got up and walked around the desk. My intuition was on high alert.

"I called you a few times," he repeated. "You never answer."

"I have answered, Greg," I said. "We even had soup the other day."

"Then I see you with someone else. What does he have going on that I don't? I don't understand it. You sweet on him? Because he's your people?"

"Don't go down that road, Greg. That has nothing to do with it. I've been dating him for a while. It has nothing to do with you."

"It has everything to do with me," he said. "I want to be with you, Daisy."

Greg leaned closer to me. I could practically taste the Bacardi on his lips.

"Sit down," he demanded. "I need to ask you some questions."

I sat down and looked around the desk for some type of weapon I could use to clonk him over the head with if he got out of hand. A logbook, the almost empty metal box, and a couple of pens were the only weapons I had within reach. My phone was jammed into my bag. There was no way I could get to it easily.

"What are you looking for?" he asked. "Something to defend yourself?" He laughed. "I'm a second-degree Dan. Remember that."

"What do you want, Greg? How can I help you?" Using a crisp professional tone might wake him up from his madness.

"Think. Carefully. Did you find any papers in your friend's apartment?"

"My friend? What are you talking about?"

"You know who I mean. Rubio."

"Why are you asking me this?" Beads of perspiration began forming on my forehead and my armpits suddenly felt soggy.

"Just tell me," Greg said. "It's better for you, and especially me, if you just let me know if you found any important papers in your friend's house."

"Papers?" I shook my head. "No. Nothing."

"Maps, Daisy, maps."

The image of the crude map I'd drawn came to mind, but that couldn't be what he meant.

"I don't know what you're talking about," I said. "David is

waiting for me. I really have to go. Next time you want to talk, give me a call." I began to rise out of my chair.

Greg slammed the desk with his palm. "Sit down, I said!"

I wasn't as scared as he'd hoped. I was sick of men telling me what to do.

"I can't help it if you're three sheets to the wind. You know that I'd never talk to you when you've been drinking. I can call a friend for you if you'd like. Remember, men with the men and women with the women."

"Shut up, Daisy," he said. "This isn't about program. It's about you coming clean. Tell me about the papers you found in Rubio's house."

"I already told you that I have no idea what you're referring to, Greg."

"I'm going to give it to you straight. Unless you give me those maps and papers, there are some people who are going to be very unhappy. And it won't be just your friend you'll be grieving over."

"Are you threatening me?" I was dumbfounded. "I have no idea about any maps or paperwork, so just get out. Now!"

I stood up and came face to face with him. The smell of rum was bearable, but the reek of his body wasn't. Surprisingly, the stench of fear permeated him. I tried to step around him to get out of the dojo.

Greg kept in step with me. I tried to dodge past him again.

"I came here to talk to you," he said. "You'll leave when I say you can."

"I have a dinner date." I tried to keep my voice level. "They're waiting for me. You should leave. Sensei doesn't want anyone here without his permission."

This time Greg grabbed my arm. I'd missed the first step of avoiding a grab and the second of blocking it. I had to think calmly.

"I'm not going to plead with you, Greg. You've had too much to drink. Don't do something that you will regret. Let go of me."

Greg's grip on my arm became tighter. "You know what I'm talking about. If we have to sit here all night, I'm okay with that. Sensei is nowhere around. No one comes to the dojo on a Saturday evening. Now tell me, where are the papers?"

"Let me go," I demanded.

Instead, he intensified his hold on me. Instinctively, I dropped down to the ground, and Greg swayed over me but didn't fall with me as I'd hoped he would. He continued to hold me until I bit his ankle as hard as I could. Greg yelped, and I dug harder with my teeth. My free hand brushed against my pocket. My keys were in it. Greg began pulling me back up. I grabbed the keys and dug them into the top of his hand. This time he let go, and I ran to the door.

But the door wouldn't budge. Greg held on to the waist of my pants, and I struggled to stay upright. The doorknob was stuck. I rattled and twisted it until it was finally open. Greg let go of me, and I fell out the door onto the sidewalk. My right shoulder slammed against the hard concrete.

A hand pulled me up. It was Rod.

"Greg!" I sputtered. "He's in there."

Behind Rod were Detectives Munroe and Harris. Sam Harris moved quickly despite his bulk. Liz Munroe had become a gazelle. They ran toward the dojo calling out for Greg to come out.

I ducked low behind a parked car and waited. I rubbed my shoulder and watched as the three of them separated. Rod ran into the dojo, Liz sprinted down the side alley, and Harris went around the block. A couple of blue-and-whites careened down the street and screeched to a halt in front of the dojo.

A few minutes later, Rod emerged from the dojo, leading a cuffed Greg outside. I came from around the car.

"I didn't kill your friend!" Greg spat at me. "I didn't do anything!"

A few passersby had taken up their phones and were

videotaping the whole thing. I shrank back. I didn't want anyone to know that I was involved in any of this.

Rod covered the top of Greg's head with his hand as he helped him into one of the awaiting police cars. A uniformed officer took over for Rod and began reading Greg his Miranda rights.

"Are you okay?" Rod asked me.

"Yes," I said. "Does this mean that Greg killed Rubio?"

"Hold on, Daisy, we're not arresting him for the murder. We don't know if he killed Rubio. Ryan gave us enough to know that they were both involved in some dealings with Rubio, but there aren't any confessions yet. Be patient."

I shook my head. "He was drunk."

"They'll test his blood alcohol level," he said. "Are you okay?"

"My shoulder. I fell right on it." I moved my arm around. "I think it's all right."

"You'd better get an x-ray and make sure nothing's broken," Rod said. "Did he touch you?"

I lifted my blouse sleeve. The markings of his fingers were deep red against my skin.

"I want you down at the precinct too, after the x-ray." Rod said. "We'll write out a report and have some pictures taken. I'll take you to the ER."

"I just remembered that I bit his leg!" I wrinkled my nose.

"You should have a tetanus shot," he said. "Let's go."

"Wait. I have to lock the door." I still had the keys in my hand. "Sensei will be upset if anything is missing."

"Don't worry about that. We're taking some prints and doing an investigation first. Give me the keys, and I'll make sure they close it up before they bring any evidence down to the precinct."

I handed him the ring of keys. "I used them to defend myself. I jammed them into his hand."

"We'll need those too, then." Rod looked around. "Hey,

Marty, get a locksmith up to padlock the door when you guys are done in there."

"A locksmith?" The fresh-faced officer seemed incredulous. "Are you serious?"

"It won't take that long. A friend of ours owns this place."

Rod turned his back to the policeman. "Let's get in the car. The quicker we get you checked out, the better."

I stood there for a moment. I needed to get my bearings. "Wait, Rod. How did you know he was in there with me?"

"We didn't know. Ryan had let us in on their little tête-à-tête, and we went to his place to look for him. Liz suggested that we come looking for you after I told her about the interaction at the meeting."

"So now she knows that I'm in recovery, too? You told her about the meeting? How could you?"

"I'm sorry," he said. "I understand your concern about anonymity, but Liz is my partner. I trust her with my life. If I can't talk to her, I can't talk to anybody."

Liz Munroe strode over to us. "That was quick, Rod," she said. "How are you. Daisy?"

"I'm okay," I said. I didn't want to see any pitying or disgusted looks from her.

Rod interjected. "She's not okay. Check out her arm."

"We need to get photos of this," she said. "But first you should go to the ER to get it checked out."

"We're on our way," Rod said. "She hurt her shoulder when the door opened. Fell right on it."

"It got pretty physical in there, I'm guessing," Liz said.

"He's a second-degree black belt." I laughed weakly. "I just received my yellow belt. It's probably good he was soused."

"I guess your karate skills came in handy," she said. "I've toyed around with the idea of taking classes myself."

"It was a street-fighting skill I used. Sensei stressed that self-defense tactics were priority."

Liz laughed. "Then I don't need any lessons. I grew up with four brothers. I've grappled my way through life. I'm going downtown with Harris. I'll meet you two down there."

Looking at her expertly cut and styled blond hair and never-peeling manicure it was hard to picture her tussling with brothers. She probably had a good story to tell.

Rod and I got into his car. He turned on the ignition but didn't pull out.

"Are you sure you're all right?" he asked. "Want me to call an ambulance?"

"No, I'm really okay," I said. Tears began streaming down my face. "It's just that, oh, I don't know what."

"Daisy, give yourself a break. You've just been through something horrendous with Greg."

"Yes, but it's more than that." I bawled. "It's Rubio. I wish we could have done something sooner. Like, before all this happened.

My sobs were coming on full force. Rod caressed my head, and I leaned on his shoulder. He kissed my eyebrow.

"I thought you weren't coming back from Chicago." I took a deep breath. I hadn't realized that I was still holding on to that. "Everybody left me. Rubio. Hector."

"I'm here, Daisy," he said. "I'm not going anywhere."

During the next few minutes, I allowed myself to feel my feelings, and the tears seemed like they'd never end, but I knew that there was more to be done.

"My shoulder is killing me," I said. "Ready?"

"Ready to go," Rod said. He pulled out on to the avenue, and we made our way to Windsor Medical Center.

Chapter 36

We sat in Jose's apartment, knee-deep in the search for the paperwork or maps that Greg had demanded from me.

"I'm done," I said. I sat back on my heels and pushed a large illustration pad away from me.

"If your shoulder is hurting, you could put a warm compress on it," Jose said.

"It's not really that," I said. "I don't think we're going to find anything."

"How can you give up? I think we're finally on the right track. Both Ryan and Greg said that Rubio had paperwork that needed to get back to the rightful owners."

"Not rightful owners but murderers," I said. "I can't believe it's here."

"Go do something for yourself. Eat, drink," Jose said. "We'll keep looking."

"I'm not really giving up; it's just that I'm frustrated," I said. "The snack idea is a good one, though."

I went into the kitchen and found the makings for one of my favorites, peanut butter and jelly sandwiches.

"Who else wants a PB&J?" I asked.

"Not me," Rod said as he flipped through one of the oversized art books that were in the built-ins. "Greg said blueprints. Ryan said important papers. I hope that they didn't send us on a wild goose chase."

"I still can't believe that those two creeps set him up," I said. "What they did is totally against the code of AA. Not that there is a code that says you can't be an ass."

"You told me before that being in the program is about not drinking," he said. "It's not going to change anyone's personality or motives."

Jose looked up. "If that were the case, none of us would stay in the program. Many of us do find useful lives. Being sober is more than not getting soused at a club and puking your guts out."

"Or hugging the porcelain throne." I had to laugh despite the seriousness of what we were doing. "That was one of the first things I didn't miss anymore when I got sober."

"For me it was my mother locking the door so I wouldn't come in at night."

"My mother did that, and I hadn't even had a drink!" Rod laughed. "Those were the days."

I finished my sandwich and helped to sift through the books and papers that had accumulated over years of the two living in the apartment.

"Maybe we'll get a message or something," I said. "Like the night that I saw the map and drew it. I swear I could feel Rubio that night. I wish he'd come through right now."

"Me too." Jose was wistful. "I wish he were here every day, in the flesh."

"The last time I was here he'd had the surgery and didn't want me near him. I wish I could have done more for him."

"You and me both," Jose said. "When things weren't going well, he tended to withdraw, while I just buried myself in my work."

"You did what you had to," I said.

"I probably should have gone to meetings instead. I still feel terrible. Maybe we can get to one tonight. Want to go together? Like we used to."

My heart was about to burst. "Yes, let's do that. Like we used to."

I retraced that last afternoon I saw Rubio in the apartment. "I came in, even though he stood by the door. He really didn't want me in here. I remember thinking what a mess this place was. No offense, Jose. He had all these papers splayed out on the coffee table and couch. They were large. I had to move them just so that I could sit."

"Large?" Jose thought for a moment and then stood up. He went over to the desk and pulled out an artist's large portfolio case that was stashed behind it. It had been completely obscured by the desk. He placed it on the floor and opened it. It was filled with illustrations that Rubio had started with the intention of completing them on canvas.

Jose took them out of the portfolio and spread them across the floor and coffee table.

"Oh, Jose, I can feel him," I said. "It's like, when you opened this, he arrived with them."

Jose nodded. "He's here."

We remained quiet for a moment taking in Rubio's energy. My heart again swelled with the love that filled the room.

"Ready?" Jose asked. "Let's do this."

We began going through the pages that filled the portfolio and placed each aside, carefully looking at them. After a while, Rod lifted one piece toward the sunlight that shone through the window.

"This is really beautiful," he said. He shook his head.

"Take it, Rod," Jose said. "I'm glad to see that Rubio's work still moves people."

Rod stood up and gave Jose a quick embrace. Rubio was able to create new friendships through his artwork even though he wasn't physically here. The energy in the room shifted. The sunlight came in with a certain slant.

"That one," Jose said. "It's that one."

He went over to one of the pieces and picked it up. He looked at it and then turned it over. He touched the corner and separated a second page that was adhered to it.

"This is it." Jose unstuck a sheet that had blue writing on it. A list of sorts. Names and phone numbers were jotted down in someone's handwriting.

"There's more," he said. "Keep looking."

We continued to look through the sheets, and Rod picked a second one that had another piece affixed to it.

"A list of art galleries."

We scoured the pages. "Is Miguel's Moratorium on the list?" I asked.

"That one isn't but the White Buffalo is," Jose said.

We continued to sort through the illustrations. Rod picked one up, his face ashen. "Daisy, look."

He pulled two sheets apart. A blueprint. A map.

"What is it?"

"Some sort of industrial-looking building," Jose said. "This has to be a blueprint of the property that Rubio was looking at."

"We need to bring these to Harris," Rod said. "They're going to want the entire portfolio. Will that be all right with you? You'll get it back as soon as possible."

"Sure. Anything that will help."

Jose lovingly gathered the illustrations and replaced them into the portfolio with the other two sheets. He handed the portfolio to Rod.

"Take care of these, okay?"

"You'll have them back in your possession," Rod said, "where they belong, soon enough.

Jose and I tagged along with Rod down to the precinct. We couldn't help ourselves. I made myself as comfortable as

I could on the wooden chair. Jose and Rod stood next to Sam
Harris as he shed light on the circumstances. He'd had several
conversations with Ryan and Greg, both of whom were still in
custody.

"This is amazing," I said. "So the statement *being in the
wrong place at the wrong time* was true in Rubio's case."

Sam cleared his throat. "I can give you a rundown, if you
like."

"I think they're entitled to every detail," Rod said. "It's a
hard story. But we already know the ending, don't we?"

Jose nodded. "Nothing's going to bring Rubio back. It's
important to know why it all happened, even if it's senseless."

"It basically starts with Greg and Ryan as opportunists.
Especially Greg. He has a long rap sheet for misdemeanors,
steering, and other petty-type crimes. They meet Rubio in the
rooms. He's a nice guy, and he takes them out for coffee, lunch,
a few times. In talking, they find out that he's looking to buy a
gallery."

"But he was leasing from the Montoyas, wasn't he?"

"Yes, but he didn't want to be involved with them much
longer," Sam said. "They had a history. I don't know if you're
aware of this, but he relapsed when he first started working
with them."

"I knew that," Jose said. "It was short-lived."

"Rubio cleaned himself up quickly, I understand," Sam
said. "He was working with Ryan, as a sponsor. He shared a
lot with Ryan."

"Yeah, the sponsor-sponsee relationship is like that," I said.

"Ryan knew that he was looking for a gallery, and Greg
is always in some mix. They get him an appointment to see a
warehouse down in the Red Hook area. The realtors also had
their hands in a few pots. They showed copies of the blueprints
of the warehouse to Rubio. They apparently placed them on
a work surface that had the missing papers on it. I'm sure

that Rubio just inadvertently picked them all up together and placed them in his portfolio case. He probably just figured that would be a good place to store them. He'd take the blueprints home to look over again. He'd voiced his interest in buying the property."

"That must have been what he was doing the last morning I saw him in your apartment," I said. "Listening to all of this must be so difficult for you, Jose."

Jose nodded. "Yes, but like I said, I prefer to know than never know why or how this all happened."

Sam continued. "They did everything they could to get the blueprints back."

"Were they the ones who injured Marge? I know Ryan was in my apartment, but I still can't believe that he would do that to her."

"We're still sifting through all of this," Sam said. "Greg and Ryan were certainly not in charge of the operation. They probably thought they'd get a few bucks. I'm certain there's a lot more to it. We'll give you information as we receive it. But for now, I can only suggest that you remain patient."

Chapter 37

Rod and I were back in my living room. Jose had asked for some time alone to get his head together and promised he'd connect with us later in the day. My nerves were on fire, and I paced the length of floor.

"Daisy, for the hundredth time, can't you just sit down? You're making me anxious."

"You might be used to this sort of thing, but I'm not," I said. "There's got to be something we can do. It's not fair to Jose that he gets only a little piece of the puzzle. He must really be going through it."

"You're going to burn yourself out."

"I'm not a candle," I said. "It's important for him. And his family. How are we going to break the news to Nina that Ryan was involved in her brother's murder?"

"Nina already knows something," Rod said. "She was still here when he was arrested for breaking into your apartment."

"Ugh, don't remind me." I sat down next to him at the edge of the couch. My right knee bobbed up and down. "There's got to be something we can do."

"I'm technically not on this case, remember?"

"Yeah, I know." I thought the information through. "But I have an idea."

"Do you want to get something to eat?" Rod asked. "Because that would make a lot of sense."

"I can't eat when I get anxious," I said. "I thought you already knew that about me."

Rod shook his head. "I think this is going to be a long evening."

"It doesn't have to be," I said. "Let's go art hunting."

"I'm not exactly sure what you're suggesting," he said. "I think we should just stay here and order delivery. How about Chinese? We can get sesame chicken. Maybe an order of ribs."

"No. Let's go to Miguel's Moratorium. Just to see what they have on their walls. See if that uptight art curator is there. I'm sure he knows something. He had Rubio's art for sale. I'm sure he'll help us."

"He wasn't very helpful before, was he?"

"No, he wasn't," I admitted. "But I haven't turned the Daisy charm on him yet."

"I don't like the idea, but okay, I'll go with you. Just do yourself a favor and don't buy anything else. You've already ordered a stained glass piece. Next thing I know you'll be ordering a Renoir."

I threw a sofa cushion at him. "Don't be funny. I'm sure they don't sell Renoirs there. It might be SoHo, but it's not that fancy."

"Seriously, I don't think that this is a good idea."

"So blame me if it turns out to be a bad one," I said. "I'll take total responsibility for what happens. I just want to see if they're still selling Rubio's art. That's all. I promise."

The third time that Rod toured the area of the block for a parking space, he pulled up at a hydrant a few stores away from the gallery.

"There is no parking," he said. "There will be no parking. There's never any parking. So, don't expect any."

"Don't be such a pessimist," I said. "Can't you put one of those benevolent cards in the window so you don't get a ticket?"

"No, I'm not going to put a PBA card in the windshield," he said. "I'm going to wait for you right here in the car. You go in and just take a quick look to see if any of Rubio's artwork is there, and then we go home. Weren't you guys going to a meeting or something?"

"You are so not funny," I said. "If a space opens up, just come in behind me. We drove all the way out here. How can we just go back home without taking advantage of the afternoon?"

"Look at those clouds," he said. "There's probably going to be another rainstorm."

"Come on, please," I pleaded. "If you can park, do it. I'm going to take my time in there. I'd like to see the other artists' works too. I think I'm starting to appreciate art more than ever. I could get something for my bedroom. Especially since no one will be sneaking through there now that Ryan's in jail."

"I'll be there, won't I?"

"Yes, but you won't be a creep like him," I said. "At least I hope not."

Rod's expression turned serious. "I don't think it's a good idea for me to go in there with you. Just in case. I have a feeling."

"*You* have a feeling, and you're still going to let me go in alone?" I opened the car door. "Give me fifteen minutes. If I'm not out at that point, come in like gangbusters!"

"If I find parking, that is," Rod said. "Kidding! I'll be watching you from out here. Everything will be all right."

"I'll be cautious," I said. "The art curator is a bit arrogant, but that's nothing I can't handle."

As I walked to the gallery, I gathered my denim jacket closer to me. It was cool and a couple of raindrops splattered on my face. But Rubio's spirit was with me. I knew this within every fiber of my being.

The doorbell jangled as I entered the gallery. The paintings on the wall were different than the ones that had been there less than a week before. The first room was dedicated to "Autumnal Summer." The art was by Nashua Levitt. The second room contained pottery and a few sculptures. The room behind it had a sign that took up the entire door opening. "Under Renovation." I couldn't remember what this room had previously held, but I knew for sure that it wasn't Rubio's work.

There were a few glazed pottery pieces that seemed perfect for gifts. I picked one up that I eye-marked for Marge. It would be lovely on her piano. I turned it over. I gaped at the price. I carefully replaced it on the stand and continued to saunter through the gallery.

None of Rubio's paintings were on the walls. I gazed up at one painting by Nashua Levitt. Gorgeous. The leaves were golden and blended beautifully with the stark blue of the sky. Somehow the artist managed to convey both seasons, as promised in the series title.

"Good afternoon, ma'am. This piece is one of the last that the artist finished while in France. He's traveled extensively."

"Yes, I was admiring it," I said. "It's delightful."

The curator turned to face me fully. His toupee sat atop his head as before, and his left eyebrow lifted in surprise. "We've met, haven't we?"

"I was here recently, yes."

"Ah, yes, now I remember you," he said. "You were interested in the art of Mauricio Rubio."

"You must have hundreds of people coming through that door," I said. "I'm flattered that you remember me. But, yes, I was here, and you said that his pieces had already sold. You're right. I am still interested in buying something for my home."

"Hmmm," he said. "I might be able to help you. It seems that one of the buyers is no longer interested in the painting. It's very possible that you would like the piece. Indeed."

"Indeed," I said. "How can I go about seeing this painting, Mr. eh, excuse me, I don't remember your name."

"Mr. Cusumano." He extended his hand to me. "Your name also escapes me. Please excuse me."

"Ms. Muñiz." We shook hands, and he ushered me to his office. I hoped that Rod was watching me as he'd promised.

"I have it right here. It's an earlier work of his. I'm sure that you'll be very pleased with it."

"Oh, I can't wait to see it," I said. "Do you know who the subject is? Do you have any information on that?"

"No, I'm sorry, I don't. Here, let me unwrap it, and you can see for yourself. The quality of Mr. Rubio's work is outstanding. He will be sorely missed in the community."

Mr. Cusumano carefully unwrapped the painting. When he had removed the entire covering, he turned it to me. I gasped.

It was a portrait of Jose looking at me with soulful eyes. This was the figure of the man that I'd met in high school. Dark. Intense. He was dressed entirely in black. I wanted so much to reach out to him and hold him. Still under the effects of alcohol. The agony, yet the hope, in his face depicted vulnerability. I hadn't remembered him that way.

"This is an amazing portrait," I said. "Are you sure that you don't know who the subject is? I know that I already asked. But this is unreal. I feel as though I could touch him, and he'd be here in the flesh."

"I'm sure that the subject had a powerful connection with Mr. Rubio. But, no, I'm sorry, I don't know who this is."

"I'd like to purchase it," I said.

"But, ma'am, you have yet to see the price," he said. "Please sit down."

Mr. Cusumano took a writing pad from his desk and wrote a number on it. He pushed it across the desk to me.

"You must be mistaken," I said. There were two extra zeros at the end of the number.

He looked at it again. "No, that's the price, ma'am."

"I love the painting," I said. "But I'm sorry that you unwrapped it for me. There's no way I can afford it."

"Let me make a phone call and see what I can do for you."

Mr. Cusumano picked his cell phone up from his desk and made a call. "Pardon me for a moment," he said, as he turned around in his chair. His next words were unintelligible.

He looked over his shoulder at me. "Miss, what did you say your name was?" he asked.

"Daisy Muñiz."

Suddenly Mr. Cusumano swiveled his chair back around and sat across from me, pointing a snub-nosed pistol in my direction. His benign yet pleasant bearing had turned into a sinister expression.

"You should not have come back, Ms. Muñiz," he said. "I thought I'd dissuaded you."

My heart skipped a beat as I tried to come up with words.

"Cat got your tongue?" the curator scoffed. "Well, let me answer for you. There was no reason to return. This painting, as well as the others, have all been sold."

"As I said, I'm very interested in buying one of his paintings."

"Why don't you tell me what about Mr. Rubio's work that fascinates you. Did he tell you something? Something that you'd care to share with me?" He motioned with the gun for me to stand up.

I did as his gun directed me to do and automatically lifted my hands in the air. He came closer and frisked my body.

"You don't have to touch me there," I said. "I don't have any weapons on me."

"My dear, you could very well be wired."

"That might be true, but I'm not. I don't know who you think I am, but I'm only here to buy a painting."

"If that were the truth, as you call it, you would have jumped at the price I wrote down for you," Mr. Cusumano said. "That price is more than fair for the value of that painting."

I scanned the room looking for a way to escape, or at least to divert his attention. Rod wasn't around, and I needed to save myself.

"Are you sure that gun is loaded?" I heard myself ask.

Mr. Cusumano chuckled. "Would you like me to test it out on you?"

"No," I said. "Of course not." My brain was numb. Staring at a gun was not in my collection of life tales.

Mr. Cusumano attempted to navigate me into the corner. I saw a spindle of cord there. I was not going to be tied up and at his mercy. He began pushing me into the small space. Suddenly I heard the words I'd said a moment earlier to the curator. I may not have had a weapon on me, but, as I'd heard Sensei say countless times, *I have no weapon. I am a weapon.*

I said a quick Serenity Prayer, spun around, and did a lightning-fast sweep that toppled the curator. Luckily, he didn't have the balance that Greg did. He was on the ground in no time flat. Grappling! My favorite. Cusumano did his best to hold on to the gun but was unable to as I took a chunk of skin out of his thigh with the hardest pinch I'd ever mustered. He yowled, and I grabbed the gun as I pinned him down by sitting astride his bloated belly. I'd barely had time to point the pistol at him when the office door flew open.

Rod and two officers clad in blue came charging in. They immediately took over. Rod grabbed the gun and helped me up as one of the officers clicked the cuffs on Mr. Cusumano. The other quickly began reading him his rights.

"I did that all myself, you know!" I glowed inside. "I didn't let him take advantage of me. Even with my shoulder smarting like it is!" We sat next to each other in his car again.

"You did," Rod said. "I came in as fast as I could. I called back-up right away. I knew in my gut something wasn't right. I should never have let you go in there to begin with. I'd never be able to live with myself if something had happened to you."

"You could never have stopped me," I said. "Even if my decisions aren't the best ones, I always stick to them. I wouldn't have ever blamed you if something had happened to me."

Rod squeezed my hand and flicked the siren switch on. I finally got my wish. But it was bittersweet.

Chapter 38

The garden was filled with yellow daffodils and bright red tulips. The slightly oniony smell of the lavender alliums surprised my senses.

"It's so beautiful out here, Marge," I said. "I'm glad you trusted me with the bulbs last fall. It never occurred to me that the planting needed to be done then."

"The air smells so fresh," Marge said. "I hope you'll be just as excited about planting fragrant roses. It'll be time soon. I'm going to enjoy this old yard as often as I can this year."

"You'll need to ask Edith for permission, I think." Edith was stationed in the kitchen, sipping tea while she watched Marge through the window.

"This is going to take getting used to," Marge said. "I already have Ruffian here watching my every move."

"We're all adjusting," I said. "I think I may be able to start grieving Rubio now."

Rod and Jose walked in with a couple of large pizza pies and set them down on the table. The string of twinkling lights danced above us. Jingling chimes hung from the old magnolia tree. The men pulled up chairs and sat with us.

"Sam is looking for parking," Rod said. "He should be here soon. Some guy put his bike on a rack and was just about to pull out."

"I'm glad," Marge said. "I'm looking forward to having some closure here, and I think the only way we can do that is to know for certain what happened."

Jose excused himself to wash his hands, and, when he returned, he pulled the slices apart and handed one to each of us.

"Where did you buy this pie?" I asked. "The crust is perfect."

"I drove up to Smiley's on Ninth. It's the best pizza in Brooklyn."

"Save a couple for me," Sam called out as he emerged from the house. Ms. G looked down at us from the fourth-floor window ledge.

"Detective Harris, please tell us whatever it is that you know about the doings," Marge requested.

"As long as you call me *Sam*, I'll be happy to tell you whatever you'd like, ma'am."

"Sam," Marge said. Her throaty chuckle told me that she was feeling good.

"Of course, details will continue to come in, but so far both Ryan and Greg have corroborated the information," Sam explained. "Cusumano has been quieter, relying on his lawyer."

"As you already know, Rubio befriended, or sponsored, I'd guess you'd call it, both Ryan and Greg. They'd go out for coffee and meals, share tidbits about themselves, and they knew he was looking to buy an art gallery. Hell, Rubio had even gotten Ryan a job with the shipping and packing business in the area. That was a coincidence. Rubio had no idea that Ryan was already connected with that business. He must have thought he was doing him a big favor. Greg and Ryan played him from different angles."

"The stained glass place!" I blurted. "I knew it."

"Exactly, Daisy. As for Rubio, it seems he had ultimately decided not to renew the lease for the place on Atlantic Avenue with the Montoyas."

Jose shook his head. "He was always an artist. I wonder if he was still trying to prove to his father that he could be the businessman that he wanted him to be."

Sam cocked his head to the side. "Anything is possible when it comes to family. Rubio's work was still showing there, but it wouldn't be for long. Greg and Ryan set him up with a realty management company, Marlux Realty, and arranged for a meeting. That's where the realtors, Malloy and Rehnquist, come in. They met Rubio at the warehouse that was for sale in Red Hook. They'd gone over the blueprints with him. When they were done, Rubio didn't realize that he had picked up the list that showed the galleries that were going to be robbed. On top of that, he'd also mistakenly picked up a piece of stationery that had the names and phone numbers of the people who were involved."

"I don't understand why the information was on paper," I said. "Everyone uses computers these days."

"Cusumano is one of a generation that hasn't been that easily adaptable to the computer or the internet. When we picked up Malloy and Rehnquist, they both voiced their frustration and blame for Cusumano and Sprague."

"Mr. Sprague! So was that a robbery attempt at the Atlantic Gallery?" I asked. "Or did they go in specifically to kill Sprague and Rubio?"

"Thanks to Greg and Ryan, Malloy and Rehnquist knew that Rubio could be found at the gallery in the mornings," Sam said. "They went there looking for him. Charley Sprague wasn't involved, but he likely tried to intervene by hiding the fact that Rubio was upstairs. I can only guess that he didn't want Rubio harmed, but Sprague himself ended up murdered that morning."

"The art curator was the heist mastermind," Marge interrupted. "Were the Montoyas also involved?"

"Apparently not," Sam said. "Surprisingly so, I might add. They're not usually known as reputable people, but this time we haven't found any connections at all. If there's a thread, we'll find it, but, so far, no one has implicated them. They are powerful. It's possible the criminals who have been caught are being cautious by not naming them."

"Follow me on this one," Sam said. "Rubio's shot at the gallery. Our bet is that he'd been coming down to the first floor and got caught by a ricochet when Sprague was shot. I don't know that they purposely went to kill anyone. Too dirty. But they needed the missing data and tried contacting Rubio repeatedly. We were able to obtain his phone records. They called him incessantly. Then Rubio left the hospital.

"He goes to the stained glass place. As you well know, he had his paintings shipped from there. Cusumano dogged Malloy and Rehnquist into following Rubio. Apparently, Rubio figured out what was going on. He didn't want to be part of a business that was basically stealing art and selling the pieces for astronomical prices. He, in his naivete, thought they could make a clean exchange. His artwork for the papers. They pushed him into the car. They argued. Neither Malloy nor Rehnquist wanted to face Cusumano or Cal without the data again. The security guard, Peeples, was walking down the alley. Rubio tried to get out of the car and Malloy panicked and shot him. The next place Rubio is found is where they left him at the wharf."

"I met the security guard. She didn't say she saw him in the car. I don't understand."

Sam nodded. "Unfortunately, she was wearing headphones that cancel out all noise. She didn't hear anything. As far as she was concerned nothing was going on. It isn't unusual for cars to be in the area all times of the day and night."

"My God, how tragic," I said. "Was Cal the connection at the stained glass window shop? He acted so suspiciously, avoiding us at all costs."

"What about this Cusumano character?" Marge asked. "How did he become involved in such a terrible business? To think that he would point a gun at Daisy too. My goodness, has he absolutely no regard for life?"

Sam took a deep breath. "As an art curator, Cusumano had access to a rich source of connections. He could find out who was being shown, where they were being shown, and the worth of their work. The list of galleries that they compiled would have kept them busy for years. They were careful to time out their jobs, to postpone one if they thought any detail had been overlooked. The fact that Rubio inadvertently picked up the papers changed everything for that enterprise."

"But what about the Marlboro Man?" I asked. "How does he figure into all of this? He manages the shipping company, and he was at the White Buffalo Art Gallery."

Sam put a finger up. "Hold on. Any reason that you call Cal the Marlboro Man?"

"No." I slumped back in my seat. "It's just that his voice was gravelly. He sounds like he smoked one pack too many."

"Gotcha." Sam smiled. "Cal's business was very convenient for Cusumano. Cal has another shipping store at Fourteenth Street on the West Side of Manhattan. The meat-packing district. Now, it's a pretty chichi area."

I thought of the stained glass class I took. "What about Phil and Ruth? Are they on the level? Can I trust her?"

"They're actually married. She's had her business there for about twenty-five years," Sam said. "We couldn't find anything on either of them that would connect them."

"Basically, it means that Rubio talked about his desire for a gallery, and those two knuckleheads ruined everything."

"You can put it that way."

Marge was thoughtful. "Did you ever find out the identity of the woman who was there the night I was attacked?"

"Yes, we did," Sam said. "Francois Jordan. She's Gregory Pierre's girlfriend."

"That was the man who assaulted me." Marge shivered. "I could have easily been killed."

I felt myself flush deeply. The thought of my becoming intimate with Greg was appalling. This wasn't something that I would ever share with this group. I hope he won't say anything either. Maybe he should listen to his own words—*live and let live*—and leave me alone.

"You look upset, Daisy. Are you okay?" Rod asked.

"Yes. I'm just thinking this all through," I said. "It's so much to take in. Greg just insinuated himself into everything. AA, Rubio's life, and even the dojo. That he knew Sensei had to be another coincidence. It's such a small world."

"While Greg was dragging Marge into the shed, Ryan combed through the apartments and lost his ring in your room, Daisy. He was there more than once."

"Was there a connection with Rubio getting his art into the SoHo galleries and Greg? How did all of that happen?"

"As far we know, Rubio legitimately presented his portfolio to Cusumano, and his art was accepted for show at the galleries. Cusumano connected Rubio with Cal for shipping. Cusumano had Greg connect with Rubio any way he could. I'd have to say Greg is mostly a con and listened for whatever vulnerabilities that he could find in Rubio. Ryan is a desperate type of guy, trying to fit in wherever he could. He was genuinely sorry he lost his job at the stained glass shop."

"It's so sad that Rubio was trying to help those two out," I said. "It's actually scary."

"That's the work we're left with as we grieve," Jose said. "Finding the ability to trust again. AA has been our safe haven."

Marge straightened in her chair. "Can someone go inside and get me a warmer jacket? I'm suddenly feeling quite chilled."

"I'll get it," Jose offered. He went inside and returned quickly with Marge's lightly quilted silk jacket. "Will this be warm enough for you?"

"Yes, but I don't think it's the weather. I think it's one of my angels. It's been so long since I've experienced anything like this."

"Would you like a glass of water?" I asked. "I can run in and get it for you."

"No, dear," Marge said. "She's here to offer light and guidance, if you'll receive it."

Rod and Harris looked at each other and simultaneously nodded. Jose murmured a low *yes*, as did I.

Marge closed her eyes. "She'd like us to begin nine nights of prayer for Rubio and for Charley Sprague. The angel requests that you pray for their clarity and light. Will you do this?"

"Yes, I will, absolutely," I said. "For both."

Jose said, "I'll start tonight. Please thank your angel for us."

Rod looked uncertain. "I'm not really sure —"

"No worries," I said. "I can help you with this."

Sam cleared his throat again. "Would it be all right for me to ask my pastor to pray? I feel more comfortable doing that."

"Yes, indeed," Marge said, opening her eyes. "She's gone." Marge relaxed in her chair and drew her jacket closer to her body.

"Thanks for carrying the message, Marge," Jose said. "I don't know what we'd do without you. This situation was terrifying for you."

"I'm fine now, and that's what counts, dear," Marge said. "I am ready to go inside. Would one of you gesture to Edith to come out to give me a hand, please?"

Standing at the window, Edith had already anticipated Marge's need and was moving toward the back door.

Jose turned to me. "Did I thank you already, Daisy? I'm still choked up about that portrait. I had no idea that Rubio had painted it."

"You have thanked me, more than once," I said. "That portrait is awesome. I bet he was planning to surprise you with it. Probably for your birthday or something. How did they get that one, Sam? Wasn't it in Rubio's personal collection?"

"Many of Rubio's paintings were stored at the gallery on Atlantic. It was easy enough for Cusumano to get his hands on everything. Jose will receive all of the paintings that we can retrieve."

"My God, to think he would just help himself as if he owned them."

"I owe you one, Daisy," Jose said. "You too, Rod. I'm going to hang it right where it belongs, over the mantel in the living room. I can feel Rubio in those brushstrokes."

Rod and I smiled. We, too, could feel Rubio's presence.

Eventually, Sam Harris said his good nights and Jose went back to his apartment, leaving Rod and me outside, snuggled together in the cooling night air.

"I still have one more question," I said. "Why were Rubio's paintings all sold the day after his death?"

"They weren't actually sold," Rod said. "Cusumano was hoarding everything and probably planned to sell them later."

"That whole map thing was amazing," I said. "The one I drew that night was a blueprint to the murder scene. Rubio was trying to talk to me. He was pointing us in the direction of the blueprints. One day I'm going to be clear enough to get messages that I understand. Wouldn't it be great if we worked together? I could be a psychic investigator."

"I'm sure you could be." Rod chuckled. "In fact, you already are. So, can I stay here with you tonight?"

"Yes, I'd like that," I said. "It's a beautiful night. Let's enjoy every moment we can together. You do know that I have to go back to work soon."

"Your vacation is up just like that?"

"Yes. Hopefully, I'll be getting back to normal soon," I said. "If only Jose could too."

"That reminds me, what about Hector?" Rod asked. "Is he coming back to New York? It seems like months ago that I went to Chicago, and you were so excited about receiving your Warriors."

"That's not going to happen now," I said. "I wish it were. Hector is living with his sister, and, let me put it this way, rethinking his religious choices. Now isn't the time for me to make a decision."

"There have been such big changes in almost every aspect of your life," Rod observed.

"I'm sticking to meetings, though, and my job is there for me," I said. "You too, even if it's going to be different."

"Yes, it will be," Rod said. "But we're together in whatever life brings."

After a while, I said, "I keep thinking about the fact that every time something was going on that Rubio wanted to warn us about, it began to get windy, or breezy, or just cool. I couldn't figure it out, since Oshún is his guardian angel. I looked it up, and it seems that Oyá, who is a fierce warrior woman, is somehow connected to Oshún. Oyá is the Orisha of the cemeteries. Maybe she was helping. I will have to do more research on the connections."

"That's pretty cool," Rod said. "I love when you share those sorts of things with me."

"I'm glad." I leaned in closer to him. "Let's stay out here a little longer. We can watch the stars. Maybe we'll find a shooting star we can wish on together."

The park bench was facing the lake. I remembered the day I had cried my eyes out on the same bench just a couple of years earlier. Letty had listened and cared. Today was different. The swans glided along. A couple of turtles slipped off rocks into the green-tinged water. Rod walked toward me with his little girl. She was mostly hidden by a large floppy bear that she managed to hold with one arm. Her steps were tentative, and her hand was completely enclosed in Rod's hand. My heart lurched. This tiny child had evoked such terror in me. My head told me that my life would be changed forever.

When they reached the park bench, the tot murmured something that I couldn't hear. I smiled at her and leaned in closer to catch her words. She remained silent.

"Christy, I'd like you to meet Daisy. Daisy, meet Christy. Her full name is Christina Marie, but she prefers to be called *Christy*."

"Hi, Christy. I'm very happy to meet you."

Christy's long dark eyelashes covered her lowered eyes. "Me too."

"Would you like to sit next to me to watch the swans?" I asked. "There they are." I pointed at the graceful birds as they fished for their dinner.

Christy nodded, and Rod picked her up and sat her next to me. She whispered something in his ear, and he asked her if he could repeat it. Christy shook her head from side to side but took her free hand and placed it in mine.

"She likes you," he mouthed. "I do too."

I smiled and allowed the simultaneous quaking in my chest to meld with the warm feeling I also held.

"Christy is going to stay with us for a while, and then *Abuela* is going to come, and we can all go out to dinner. Is that okay with you, Daisy?"

I nodded. "Sounds like a great plan."

Rod put his arm across the top of the bench and squeezed my shoulder gently. "Thank you," he said. "This is a lot more than you bargained for, but we'll make it work somehow."

"I hope so," I said. "I can handle dinner, can you?"

We laughed together. Christy looked up at us and giggled.

☙

That night, I prayed as usual under the light of the moon. I wasn't sure of what I needed, only what I wanted. I wanted to not be so selfish and to accept the knowledge that others had a right to their experiences too. It had to be hard on Rod and his mom. I couldn't begin to fathom how much Christy understood. My thoughts couldn't even wrap around the child's mother and her needs and desires. I left it in the Goddess's wise ways as I finished my prayer.

The shutters were still open. I hated to be hypervigilant, but the last few weeks had been eye-opening. Fortunately, both Ryan and Greg were in jail, and the other men had been arrested and were awaiting trial. As I gazed at the moon, who smiled at me, I pulled the wooden shutters closed but not before I spotted the familiar face looking up at my window. I shut myself away from those intruding eyes. This was one piece of the puzzle of my life that hadn't fit into the gaping hole that had yet to be closed.

Do you think you may have a problem with alcohol?

Alcoholics Anonymous
www.aa.org

Inter-group Association of AA of New York, Inc.
www.nyintergroup.org

About the Author

Theresa Varela is an award-winning author whose novels encompass the realities of Latina/o experiences in the urban landscape. In addition to her novels, she has designed the *Graciella la Gitana Oracle* © deck for those who are searching for spiritual awareness and clarity to enrich their lives. Theresa holds a PhD from New York University and is a psychiatric nurse practitioner working with the mentally ill homeless population in New York City. Her author website is TheresaVarela.com. Theresa's other creative endeavors can be found at LatinaLibations.com.

Instagram
@TheresaVarelaAuthor and
@LatinaLibations
Twitter @Theresa_Varela